SAIL AWAY

"You're a beautiful woman, Sarah," Jake said, feeling the truth behind those words more than he wanted to. "Men will be intrigued by you wherever you go."

"Beautiful?" she scoffed, looking at him as if she thought him insane.

Did she not know what a striking picture she made, he wondered, with her sable hair blowing wild, her soft lips red and inviting, her eyes liquid silver that glittered even in the dark? Had no one ever told her how exceptional she really was?

As he puzzled over the thought, she gathered her skirts and, without another word, headed for the hatchway, her back straight and her head held high as she descended to the deck below. As she vanished from sight, Jake had to suppress the urge to follow her. An urge he had fought for the past eight days, ever since their encounter on that moonlit night. She had made it clear she wanted nothing to do with him; and to his ire, the more she avoided him, the more he was tempted to seek her out. Insane, he admitted.

BOOK YOUR PLACE ON OUR WEBSITE AND MAKE THE READING CONNECTION!

We've created a customized website just for our very special readers, where you can get the inside scoop on everything that's going on with Zebra, Pinnacle and Kensington books.

When you come online, you'll have the exciting opportunity to:

- View covers of upcoming books
- Read sample chapters
- Learn about our future publishing schedule (listed by publication month *and author*)
- Find out when your favorite authors will be visiting a city near you
- Search for and order backlist books from our online catalog
- Check out author bios and background information
- Send e-mail to your favorite authors
- Meet the Kensington staff online
- Join us in weekly chats with authors, readers and other guests
- Get writing guidelines
- AND MUCH MORE!

Visit our website at
http://www.kensingtonbooks.com

SHADOW OF THE SUN

Tammy Hilz

ZEBRA BOOKS
Kensington Publishing Corp.
http://www.kensingtonbooks.com

ZEBRA BOOKS are published by

Kensington Publishing Corp.
850 Third Avenue
New York, NY 10022

All Kensington titles, imprints and distributed lines are available at special quantity discounts for bulk purchases for sales promotion, premiums, fund-raising, educational or institutional use.

Special book excerpts or customized printings can also be created to fit specific needs. For details, write or phone the office of the Kensington Special Sales Manager: Kensington Publishing Corp., 850 Third Avenue, New York, NY 10022. Attn. Special Sales Department. Phone: 1-800-221-2647.

Zebra and the Z logo Reg. U.S. Pat. & TM Off.

First Printing: January 2004
10 9 8 7 6 5 4 3 2 1

Printed in the United States of America

Thank heaven for Lunch on Thursday!
Victoria Chancellor, Rebecca Russell, Jane Graves,
Barbara Harrison, and Karen Leabo,
I couldn't survive without you!

Chapter 1

London, England
June 1798

"'Tis a thing of beauty, is it not, Sarah?" Roger Pendergrass murmured softly from his bed. "Absolute perfection. Who knew something so exquisite could lead to ruin."

Blood-red velvet curtains partially draped his tester bed, blocking him from view, and though Sarah hadn't seen him in two years, she recognized his voice. She should, she thought with an unwanted twist of her heart. He was, after all, her father.

"You've outdone yourself, as usual, Roger," she said, his name awkward on her lips, but no more so than "father" would have been. She couldn't remember exactly when she'd begun to call him by his given name. Five years ago, ten? She only knew the change had occurred when she realized he wasn't a father by choice, but by mistake.

With her features so controlled her cheeks felt carved from stone, Sarah Pendergrass considered the object of Roger's admiration. A woman's cape rested on top of an ivory table. But even she knew it was no ordinary cape. Made from hundreds of one-inch golden squares, each was inscribed with hieroglyphics and held together by tiny gold rings. The elaborate garment was unusually small, only long enough to wrap around her shoulders and cover her upper arms. Faint light from a nearby candle spilled over the piece, turning the metal to molten gold. The relic shimmered with unseen heat, pulsed with the illusion of life. Emerald-cut black onyx and lapis lazuli lined the collar, the colors so rich her fingers clenched with the impulsive need to paint.

For a moment, she considered asking permission to bring her canvas and oils, already imagining herself recreating the spectacular piece with her meager talent. But she dismissed the hasty idea, not wanting to ask Roger for anything.

However, her gaze lingered on the cape. It *was* beautiful, but then all the artifacts her father chose to add to his Egyptian collection were exquisite. The belongings of pharaohs who had been dead these four thousand years filled every corner of the estate. She searched for something to say, even as she wondered why she should bother, or why she stood rooted to the polished oak floor like a servant awaiting her master's next command.

The cloying sweet scent of age and decay—a scent she would always associate with her father's treasures—had soaked into the paneling and hearth, into the very air she breathed. The curtains had been closed against the night, shutting out the sound and smell of summer rain. She could throw open the paned windows, but nothing would dispel the musty odors. They were as much a part of this house as the stone and mortar.

The chamber was foreboding and claustrophobic—a mirror of her emotions. She wanted to turn around and march from the room, but she didn't, and the reason she stayed only increased her ire. It was the same reason she'd immediately changed her schedule after receiving Roger's missive. After two years of not hearing one word from her father, she couldn't ignore her irritating and childish need to see him.

"What is it you want?" *And please don't let it be that you want to gloat about your latest expedition with Jacob Mitchell.* She couldn't stomach another declaration involving that revolting man.

Concealed by shadows, Roger growled with annoyance. "Aren't you the least bit curious about what I've found?"

"It's another artifact you've stolen to add to your obsession." *Artifacts that are far more valuable than any daughter could ever hope to be,* she thought, wishing she could say the words out loud, but knowing they would fall on deaf ears.

"This is no ordinary discovery, girl! This . . ." He leaned forward, pointing a trembling hand toward the golden cape and giving Sarah her first glimpse of him. "This is *death,*" he hissed through thin, cracked lips. "Death that I've discovered!"

She sucked in a breath, not knowing which to respond to first, his ashen face and sunken eyes or his outrageous statement. Her father had always been lean with wiry strength. Not much taller than her five foot, four inches, he'd possessed the energy of a mongrel pup, happily sniffing out one new treasure after another.

To see him pale and ill unnerved her. She took a step forward, but caught herself, knowing better than to make the mistake of showing her concern. She'd only be rejected, and she'd suffered enough of that from her father over the years to shy away from it now. But she'd never seen him so frail, his tanned skin marred by deep creases. His dressing gown hung on his bony frame and was so wrinkled she thought he might have slept in it for days. Nothing about him was as she remembered. Except for his eyes, she amended. So like her own—a fact which annoyed her—they were still the hard, gray granite she saw in her dreams.

To escape the force of his gaze, she crossed to the table and studied the artifact. *He believes this is death? What kind of game is he playing with me?* "The cape looks heavy enough to make a person stagger under its weight, but I doubt it will kill you."

"A cape!" He moved as if he intended to leap from the bed, but a hacking cough seized him, forcing him to collapse against his pillows. His face red and glowing with sweat, and his breathing labored, he told her, "'Tis a corselet, girl. Are you so ignorant you don't even know what you're looking at?"

"How could I?" she asked tightly, feeling a tremor run though her limbs. "After Mother died, you sent me to boarding school." And that's where she'd stayed until three years ago when she'd rented her own townhouse in London proper with the monthly stipend Roger gave her. She had her art studies and her small circle of friends who didn't care that she'd created a scandal when she'd rented her own home. She could have lived at Whitehurst Manor with him but, scandal or not, she hadn't wanted to and, more importantly, he hadn't asked her.

"I wasn't allowed to be a part of your life in Egypt," she continued, all the while knowing she shouldn't, but the words were flowing from her mouth and she didn't feel particularly inclined to stop them.

"Of course you weren't. I put you where you belonged so you could learn whatever it is young women are supposed to learn. A lot of good it did you. I've received reports, you know. You've rejected two marriage proposals in the past eight months."

"I have as much desire to marry as I had to live sequestered at school."

"'Tis unseemly," he complained, swiping his graying brown hair off his forehead with a trembling hand. "You need a man to take care of you."

You mean, I need a man who can take me off your hands. The old resentments crept out from behind the walls Sarah had worked so hard to hide them behind. He could have asked her about her life, her friends and interests, but Roger Pendergrass, Viscount of Whitehurst, renowned archaeologist, didn't have time to speak to his daughter. To give him credit, though, he did have one of his servants recount her activities to him on a regular basis. As always, her father's caring overwhelmed her.

Her heart thudded heavily against her chest. She needed to leave, stop the old wounds from opening completely. She'd ask him the required questions about his newest discovery, then she'd return to the life she had carefully built. A life where she was independent, reliant on no one except herself.

"You mentioned a corselet. Just what is that?" she asked with feigned interest.

"By definition, 'tis a garment worn around the waist and hips," he said, his eyes taking on the familiar glint she remembered. "This one, however, is unlike any I've ever heard of. Made of solid gold instead of cotton or silk. It belonged to Queen Tiy, wife of Ramses the Third."

"It's lovely. Thank you for showing it to me. May I leave now? I canceled my lesson with my art teacher in order to come here." She headed for the door, fighting the urge to gather up her cambric skirt and run back to her small house across the city.

"You would come all this way for nothing?" he challenged.

She stopped, faced him. "You're right. If I hurry, I can reach the gallery before it closes. There's a new painting by Joseph Turner I would like to see. He has remarkable—"

"Why are you afraid?" Roger asked, his voice so brittle she imagined that was how his last breath would sound.

She shivered. "I'm not afraid of anything."

"Are you sure?" he taunted. "Don't you want to know about the queen?"

"Not particularly," she said evenly, refusing to be affected by his mockery or his weakened state. It wasn't any of her business, *he* wasn't any of her business; he had gone to great lengths to make it so. Gathering her cloak and umbrella, she opened the chamber door.

"Sarah, don't leave."

She didn't stop.

"Queen Tiy is the reason I'm dying!"

She froze, slowly turning to face the shriveled man lying beneath the velvet covers. "Excuse me?"

"I'm dying."

"What kind of nonsense is this? You don't look well, but you're not dying."

"Bring the corselet to me."

She glanced from her father to the artifact. Could he really be so ill? A chill lifted the hairs on her arms.

"Go on, touch it," he urged, his voice a soft dare. "Pick it up. I can see in your eyes that you want to know what it feels like."

She almost told him he was wrong. She didn't care about touching the corselet, but she did want to paint it, sketch the symbols imbedded in each golden square, try to reproduce the energy radiating from the row of gems. The artifact was complex, yet simple, tempting her to commit the unique piece to paper. It irritated her that she felt such a strong compulsion. Her father had pieces far more magnificent crowding his home, yet she couldn't remember any of them capturing her attention so completely.

She stamped down on her desire to find a pencil and sheet of paper by asking, "You want me to hold something that you believe will kill me?"

"Not you. I'm the one who took it. I'm the one Queen Tiy has cursed."

She wanted to laugh at the absurdity, but the resignation in his voice stopped her. Setting her umbrella and cloak on a chair, she picked up the corselet and carried it to the bed, the gold links clinking a soft musical chime.

The weight pulled at her arms, but it wasn't as cumbersome as she'd thought it would be. She laid it on the bedcovers and took a step back.

"Sit down."

She glanced longingly at the door, but her curiosity got the better of her, so she sat in the chair beside the bed.

"If I had known," Roger whispered. He passed his hand over the artifact, but he didn't touch it. "I would have left her alone."

Sarah lit another candle on his nightstand so she could see his face clearly, only to be stunned by the depth of fear in his eyes. "Roger, what is it?"

"She was a minor queen, but she had ambition enough to rival Cleopatra. Queen Tiy wanted her son Pentewere to become pharaoh, but knew Ramses the Third intended to choose another. So this cunning, beguiling woman plotted to kill her husband." He pointed to the columns of hieroglyphics. "This, this is the record of her crime."

"I still don't understand why you think this can kill—"

He raised one hand, silencing her. "The queen placed a curse on her tomb, promising retribution on anyone who dared disturb her."

"A . . . a . . . don't be ridiculous." Sarah pushed up from her seat to stare at her father. "This is a piece of gold. Valuable, but nothing more."

Roger's mouth thinned in a stubborn line. "You know nothing."

"I know you're ill and need to see a doctor." She started for the door. "I'll send—"

"You'll send no one," he ordered. "Sit down and listen to what I have to say!" He doubled over in a coughing fit.

Fisting her hands to keep from reaching out to help him, she returned to her seat, hoping her acquiescence would calm him down. After several tense moments of watching him catch his breath, he finally continued.

"Queen Tiy had been cunning, but Ramses discovered

her plot. He brought her to trial, along with her son Pentewere, and forty of the pharaoh's most trusted officials, his Chief of the Harem Chamber and Inspectors among them, men he had absolute trust in. It was a dangerous time, and though the conspiracy ran deep throughout the palace, all fingers pointed toward the queen. Her accomplices blamed her in an attempt to save themselves. Not that it helped them," he added with an amused grunt. "Thirty-eight were sentenced to commit suicide before the entire court. A ghastly practice, but very effective.

"Queen Tiy was the last to be tried. You can imagine her terror, watching as her son and friends were forced to take their own lives, knowing she was to be next."

Sarah's artist's eye could too easily imagine the scene Roger was describing. An ambitious woman who'd had everything, a pharaoh for a husband, a precious son, wealth, only to stand alone and face her own downfall and death.

Roger continued as if in a trance, "She also knew she would be denied the most sacred aspect of Egyptian religion—mummification and the right to journey into the afterlife. But as I said," Roger smiled with bitterness, "my queen was cunning. She accepted her fate, but she swore she would curse those who denied her the right of mummification, vowing that they would suffer, Ramses most of all. Ramses refused her. Then the unbelievable happened. During her trial, the pharaoh suddenly died."

"A coincidence, surely," Sarah insisted.

"Was it?" Roger asked, chuckling, the sound scratchy and raw. "After she took her own life and was buried in a common grave, a peculiar thing happened. Several of the judges and officers who had governed her trial were brought to trial themselves and found guilty of conspiring with the queen. They were condemned to have their ears and noses amputated. One judge committed suicide rather than bear the humiliation. The surviving council members feared their misfortune was a result of the queen's curse. To save themselves, they agreed to have Queen Tiy mummified and buried in the Valley of the Queens, where I found her."

"The story about her plot to assassinate Ramses might be true," Sarah said, "but the rest, well, it's an exaggeration to frighten people. The queen did *not* place a curse on you."

"Blast it, girl, don't you see? For nearly three thousand years her tomb remained undisturbed. I was a healthy man when I robbed it! Look at me now! Her curse is destroying me."

She stared at her father, not recognizing the wild madness in his eyes, the sweat streaming down his temples. He shook with anger and fear, frightening her in turn.

"Well . . . well," she stammered, searching for a way to appease him. "If you're certain there's a curse, then there must be a way to remove it."

He grabbed her wrist with surprising strength, drawing her to him. "Yes, yes! That is why I asked you here. You must take Queen Tiy back to Egypt."

Sarah gaped at him. "Excuse me?"

"Return her to her tomb, then seal it so no one will ever disturb her again."

"Are you mad?" She jerked free. "You want me to go to Egypt?"

"'Tis the only way I'll be free of her curse."

She backed away, shaking her head. "I've never been outside of England. I know nothing of Egypt."

He pulled an envelope, stamped with his seal, from beneath his pillow and handed it to her. "I've written down everything you need to know. Her mummy, coffin, and the rest of her artifacts are in the carriage house. I've hired two men to accompany you, and have arranged passage on a ship leaving tomorrow afternoon. You must be on it."

"No, no, this is insane." Her mind was spinning so fast she couldn't think. "You expect me to travel by ship, then . . . then into the desert where heaven only knows what dangers I'd have to face. No, I won't do it!"

"You can't travel under your real name," he continued as if she hadn't spoken. "I've registered you as Lady Sarah Elston."

"My mother's name?"

"Everything is set. There's nothing for you to worry about."

"Nothing? Napoleon's in Egypt," she said, her voice becoming shrill as his request sank in. "He wants control of their ports. I read it in the *London Gazette*."

"Gossip from idiots who want reform." He waved a hand in dismissal.

"It's more than gossip. You would be sending me right into his path."

"I promise you, Napoleon is not a threat. The Royal Navy has the Mediterranean and Egypt well protected."

"You can't know that."

"I wouldn't send you if I didn't believe you would be safe."

She searched his face for some sort of compassion, a trace of concern, but his lined face was set, determined. She asked, "Why have you asked me at all? Why not your protégé, the illustrious Jacob Mitchell?"

A flush darkened Roger's face. "Jake refused me."

"I find that hard to believe. He worships you like a father, the way you adore him like a son." She held her breath, foolishly hoping Roger would say something to deny her claim. Yet once again he confirmed what she'd known for most of her life.

"Yes, yes, yes, Jake is a gifted young man. I couldn't have asked for any better. Up until now I thought he'd do anything for me. But he's changed. He promised the queen's collection to the British Museum. Without my permission, mind you! Misplaced loyalties, that's what it is. He says that if he doesn't keep his word to the museum, his reputation will be ruined."

Sarah didn't know what to say. Her last glimpse of Jake had been seven years ago. He'd been with her father in the library, his dark eyes alive as he studied a diagram of a tomb. She'd watched from the safety of an alcove, invisible to both men. In his rich, easy voice that seemed to roll inside her, Jake had made plans with her father to retrieve their new treasure.

She'd wanted to approach him that day, talk to him, find out why her father seemed so enthralled. But she'd stayed hidden, knowing that while thoughts of Jake Mitchell tortured her mind, he didn't know she even existed. Since her father rarely allowed her to come home, she and Jake had never officially met. But she'd known who the rakishly handsome man was; she would have recognized him anywhere. He was her father's pride and joy.

He was the son he never had.

Sarah shook thoughts of the past away. She couldn't say where Jake's loyalties might lie after all these years, and as far as she was concerned he had the reputation of a snake. But seeing Roger's reaction, she assumed he viewed his protégé's promise to the museum as treason. A turn of events she wouldn't have expected.

"Does Jake believe in the curse?" she asked.

"He's blind to everything except his career. He won't listen to reason."

"Perhaps he's right." It irritated her to side with the horrible man, but really, a curse . . .

"He betrayed me, Sarah. Me! The man who saved him from the ditches and gave him the life he craved. Yet when I needed him the most, Jake chose to save his reputation over saving me!"

Just like you chose to love Jake over loving me.

The part of her heart that had hardened against her

father years ago gave a satisfied tug. After her mother's death, when Sarah had been ten, Roger's involvement with her had been minimal, but when he met the seventeen-year-old Jake two years later on a dig in Egypt and took him under his wing, her abandonment had been complete.

But now her father needed her. *Her.* It was obvious that he was too ill to return the artifacts himself. She could think of a dozen reasons why she should refuse him. She wanted to; it's what he deserved. But one indisputable fact kept her from walking away. Good or bad, he was her father, the only family she had in the entire world. If he truly was in danger of dying, and even if he wasn't, but suffering from irrational fear, could she abandon him? She wanted to say yes, she could turn her back on him the way he had to her. She had every reason to leave him wallowing in his fear.

But Jake has failed him.

If she succeeded in returning Queen Tiy to Egypt, her father might realize his devotion to Jake had been misplaced, and that even daughters were worthy of love. *But to travel to Egypt.* Her stomach muscles clenched with unease. Sailing by ship, then crossing a desert, possibly facing cobras or robber barons. She prided herself on her independence, but this was asking too much. But if she refused, she would lose the opportunity to outshine the rogue who had taken her place in her father's life. The temptation to accept the outrageous request tugged at her, tempted her. But it was insane. How could she hope to succeed?

She couldn't, could she? She'd likely end up dead, and all for nothing.

Roger reached out and caught her hand, surprising her. "Promise you'll do this for me, daughter."

Sarah didn't know which made her back stiffen more, that he'd touched her for the second time that day, or that for the first time in her twenty-four years he'd called her *daughter*.

She lifted the corselet from the bed and felt the weight as if it were pulling her into an abyss. Meeting her father's feverish gaze, she said, "I'll go."

"I tell you, Gavin, she's the most fascinating woman I've ever seen." Jacob Mitchell reined his mount to a halt on the cobbled drive before Whitehurst Manor. "She's as beautiful as she is mysterious, a combination I can't resist."

"So you've said," Gavin DeFoe mused dryly. "At least a hundred times now. But considering her reputation, I wouldn't become too attached to her. I've met women like her before, and they're not to be trusted."

"You say that as if you don't trust women of *any* kind," Jake said, then wished he hadn't when a dangerous emotion flickered behind Gavin's dark eyes, then vanished.

"I don't."

"Well, you might change your mind when you meet this one." Dismounting, Jake tossed his reins to the stable boy. Taking his notebook filled with his research from the saddlebag, he joined Gavin on the steps leading to the paneled front door. When Gavin joined him, Jake realized that though they were the same age, they made quite the odd pair. Gavin, the fifth Earl of Blackwell, looked as formidable as an Egyptian god. His eyes were cool and unbending, closed off to the rest of the world. Not for the first time Jake thought Gavin should be clothed in gold and clasping a scepter in his hand instead of a riding crop. Today he wore tan wool pants, a chocolate brown coat over a high-collared silk shirt. Even at this ungodly hour of the morning, his cravat was perfectly tied. All very noble, all very proper, and, Jake suspected, all very deceiving.

Aside from the rumors he'd heard involving Gavin's

dead wife, Jake knew little about the earl. But he had a feeling there was a harsh side to the man that wasn't altogether noble. Not that Jake cared. It was Gavin's thirst for antiquities and his ability to finance expeditions that interested him.

Jake hadn't bothered to change his travel-worn pants, cotton shirt and dusty Hessian boots. Another man might have tried to impress the earl by dressing for the part, but Jake had no intention of wasting his time. He knew where his talents lay, and they weren't in his ability to choose his wardrobe.

"Everything will change because of her." He rang the bell and wanted to curse when the door didn't immediately open. "Discoveries we can't begin to imagine are within our reach."

"You've already convinced me, Jake. That's why I've agreed to fund your next trip to Egypt. If Queen Tiy reveals the information you think she will, I want to be part of it."

"I've already translated the hieroglyphics on her corselet."

"The assassination attempt on Ramses?"

"Yes, but there's an inscription on the back of the garment that I've yet to decipher. It's written in a style of hieroglyphics I've never seen before." He rang the bell again, quelling the urge to barge in when he heard faint footsteps in the hall beyond.

"Have you made any progress?" Gavin clasped his hands behind his back, looking calm, in control.

"Some." *But not nearly enough.* The muscles lining Jake's back tensed. He needed to see the corselet, hold it in his hands, reassure himself that it was real and not some practical joke his mind had played on him. "I have a theory as to its meaning, but when Roger became ill only days after discovering the tomb, he didn't want to let the corselet out of his sight." Holding up his notebook, he said, "That's why I made a relief."

"Is Lord Whitehurst still insisting you return the queen to her tomb?"

"Not just return her, but make sure no one ever finds her again. Heaven only knows what he means by that. I've never seen him so stubborn, or so superstitious. But don't worry. He'll see reason."

At that moment Peels opened the front door. The short, sharp-boned butler ran Whitehurst with an iron fist. No one made a move without Peels knowing about it first. If Peels lost his position with Roger, Jake didn't doubt the man would make an excellent jailer at Newgate Prison.

"We're here to see Lord Whitehurst." Jake took a step forward, only to halt when Peels refused him entrance.

"My lord isn't in at present, Mr. Mitchell. Perhaps you could call back later."

"He's left Whitehurst so early?" Jake glanced at the rain-laden clouds, gauging it to be barely past seven in the morning. "Lord Whitehurst must be feeling better then."

"No, sir. He's gone to the country. Fresh air and such. Doctor's orders."

He frowned. Roger's health had slowly declined on the trip home, but once they'd reached London, his symptoms had eased. Or so Jake had thought. Had he been wrong? "Lord Pendergass left without telling me?"

Peels's stoic expression didn't change, and Jake knew he'd receive no further information. Not that it mattered. Perhaps it was best if Roger rested instead of worrying, while Jake readied the artifacts for exhibition. There was still a great deal of work to be done—including deciphering the corselet's secret message. Queen Tiy's mummy had to be examined, the four canopic jars containing her internal organs had already been tagged, but not drawn in detail for his personal records. The same went for the jewels he'd found in several black sepulchral boxes. The miniature alabaster statues depicting her daily life had to be reassembled and arranged so even a layman could appreciate the Egyptian's belief in eternal life. So much to be done, and he couldn't wait to begin.

"Very well. I'll take Lord Blackwell to the carriage house." He started down the steps, only to pause when he felt the butler's gaze on his back. "Is something wrong, Peels?"

The heavy oak door closed with a thud.

After the lock clicked into place, the earl murmured, "I take it we're not welcome to return."

"I suppose not." Dismissing the butler from his mind, Jake said, "Come along. What we came to see is around back."

Jake barely kept himself from running. He'd worked tirelessly since he and Roger had returned from Egypt six days ago. He would have worked all through last night if not for his meeting with the curators at the British Museum. They hadn't bothered to hide their distrust, a fact that had him gritting his teeth. He'd seen the questions in their eyes, especially since he'd withheld the details of his discovery, including Queen Tiy's name. Perhaps he was being overly cautious, but he refused to let anything jeopardize his latest find.

But he knew they'd wanted to ask if *he* had really made this discovery or had he taken advantage of someone else's research as he had before.

He clenched his hands at the memory, then reminded himself that the museum's head curator was a victim, just as Jake was, of lies and treachery. He shouldn't have expected a different response. This was England, after all. Nobility ruled above all else. Had they sided with a self-taught archaeologist whose bloodline was as common as the dirt he dug in, instead of Stuart Kilvington, the Marquis of Ashby, their social order would have collapsed.

Three years ago, while he'd been on a dig in the abandoned city of Abu Simbel, Jake discovered a temple devoted to the gods Amon and Re-Harakhty. Stuart, hungry for fame and fueled by the shallow need to outshine the younger archaeologist, had deemed them too common. Stuart had left Jake at the temple, boasting that he would find nothing but dust, while Stuart would find a tomb that would make him famous.

But Jake had sensed something special about the temple. Perhaps he'd been in awe of the carved battle scenes against the Hittites, or it might have been the utter stillness of the land. He didn't know, but he'd felt certain more than stone and ruined walls had been left behind.

And he'd been right. Two weeks of careful digging on his own, while the rest of his team worked another part of the city, had revealed a cache of silver urns and a golden crown, a uraeus, the cobra erect, his hood flared and his ruby eyes glittering with fire. The symbol of power reserved for pharaohs. Exhilarated with his find, Jake had worked tirelessly, certain he'd discover more.

One afternoon, while Jake worked inside the tomb, Stuart returned empty-handed and learned of the artifacts secured in a leather-bound chest in Jake's tent. He'd been furious; he had accused Jake of trying to steal the artifacts. Jake hadn't bothered to defend himself—he hadn't thought it necessary—until they'd returned to England. Stuart had brought his accusations before the curator, who had believed every lie that had fallen from the marquis's mouth.

Credit for discovering the artifacts had been stolen from him, and his reputation as a respected archaeologist had been reduced to thief. Jake could still feel the heat of his anger, like a fire burning along his skin. He'd warned Stuart that he wouldn't get away with his lies. But the marquis had only laughed, and then he'd delivered a threat of his own. One whisper in the right ear and Jake would spend the rest of his life rotting in prison.

Now the uraeus was displayed in the museum, a generous gift of Stuart Kilvington, Marquis of Ashby.

But last night Jake had convinced the curator that he had, in fact, found an important tomb. Within a month, the mark against his name would be wiped clean. Never again would anyone doubt his word. And never again would someone else claim one of his discoveries.

Smiling at the thought, he unlocked the carriage house door. Extra security wasn't needed. Whitehurst Manor was a fortress unto itself. An eight-foot-tall stone wall surrounded the one hundred acre estate, each section well manned to guard the treasure Roger had collected over the years.

Opening the door and entering the dark room, Jake felt his way down the wall and began throwing open the row of shutters to allow more light. He wanted Gavin to experience the full effect of the sun washing over Queen Tiy's gold coffin, warming it, bringing it to life. He recalled the overwhelming awe he'd felt the first time he'd really seen her. He'd been speechless, barely able to draw a breath. He felt that way still, just thinking about her and the secrets she might reveal.

"As I told you before, Gavin, I couldn't bring her outer stone sarcophagus to England. We didn't have the manpower or the right tools to lift it. I intend to retrieve it on my next trip to Egypt." Jake threw open another set of shutters. "I brought back what I could. Her gold coffin, which is incredible, and the mummy of course. The canopic jars and such."

He heard Gavin enter behind him. "All right, Jake. Where is she?"

"What do you mean?" Turning, he said, "She's right . . ." His heart lurched against his chest. "Where . . . what the bloody hell!"

Except for half a dozen bridles hanging from hooks along the walls, a wooden table, and a few empty buckets tossed in one corner, the room was empty. *Empty!* Blood roared in his ears; the floor pitched beneath his feet.

"She's gone," Jake whispered in disbelief, staring at the table where the queen's coffin should have been. "God help me. She's gone."

Chapter 2

"I'm going after him," Jake vowed, stuffing whatever clothes would fit into his satchel. "Roger has to be stopped."

"Are you sure Lord Whitehurst is the one who took the artifacts?" Gavin strolled into the room Jake had rented at the Thirsty Mule, a tavern in London's poor East End, not far from where Jake had worked as a mudlark when he'd been a boy.

Each day when the Thames River reached low tide, Jake would wade through the mud, cutting his bare feet on glass or shards of metal, scrounging for coal, rope, copper nails, anything of value that his father could sell. It was a memory he rarely revisited, not wanting to dwell on how his father had drunk and gamed away the precious coins he'd earned. His childhood had been difficult and dreary, but he didn't regret those years entirely. Searching for bits of treasure had given him his craving to find something more, something unforgettable. It had led him to Egypt.

"I'm certain it was Roger. Since he became ill he's talked of nothing except returning Queen Tiy to her tomb and sealing it permanently. The damned fool." Cold, angry sweat dampened Jake's skin as he added his book of vital notes to the bag. "If he succeeds he'll ruin everything we've worked to achieve during the past twelve years, and all because of a bloody superstition."

He still couldn't believe Roger had absconded with the queen, but the empty cottage and a thorough search of Roger's house—despite Peels's threats to summon the authorities with every step—had confirmed Jake's greatest fear. "I have to stop him. And when I do, I'm going to wring his blasted neck."

"How do you intend to pursue him?"

"There must be a ship leaving for that part of the world. There always is," Jake said. "I intend to be on one of them. No matter how many ships I have to travel on, I'm going to reach Egypt."

"Are you sure he's for Egypt? You told me before that we couldn't return until after the summer months."

"Suffocating heat and the flooding of the River Nile. There's little in the world more treacherous," Jake admitted. "But if Roger has gone to the trouble of stealing the queen, nothing will stop him."

"If that's the case, perhaps we'll find Pendergrass on one of the vessels in port."

"Perhaps, but I doubt it. Roger does nothing without a well thought-out plan. If I know him, he has hired a ship to take him directly to Rosetta."

Filtered light emphasized the thoughtful creases around Gavin's eyes as he glanced out the dirt-encrusted windowpanes. Jake didn't need to look to see the decrepit warehouses below where local fishermen gutted and cleaned their catch. The stench of rotting fish permeated the air, made worse when the breeze blew from the west. The odor of soured brine had long ago soaked into wood and hearth, into the straw mattress that served as Jake's bed. He'd hardly noticed the odors during the few days he'd been in London, so inured he was to life's unpleasant scents.

"I agree you should go after him," Gavin said. "But how will you manage it? Financially?"

Jake drew a breath through clenched teeth. He'd

never cared about money before, but now he wished he had a portion of Gavin's wealth. He'd considered asking the museum to fund his trip, but he'd immediately discarded the option. They still didn't trust him. If he told them his partner had disappeared with the queen, *had betrayed him . . .* it would mean death to his career. Which left him only one other option.

Crossing his arms over his chest, he gave the earl a measured look. "You agreed to finance my next expedition. I was hoping you could help me now."

Something dark flashed in Gavin's obsidian eyes, giving Jake the feeling he had just stepped into a trap. "And how would I be repaid?"

"I'll cut my percentage from our next expedition from one-third to one-quarter. That should compensate you."

"Provided you find anything."

His mood already dangerously black, Jake snapped his satchel shut when he really wanted to punch his fist through a wall. "If you wish to withdraw your support, do so now. I don't have time to reassure you that I know what I'm doing."

"Don't be so hasty, Jake. I'll cover the expenses to find your queen on one condition."

"You want my entire percentage, perhaps?"

"You can keep your percentage. I want to accompany you."

Jake shook his head. "Out of the question."

One corner of Gavin's mouth lifted with an arrogant grin. "Nothing is ever 'out of the question.'"

"I won't be responsible for your safety. This isn't a pleasure trip."

"I hadn't thought it would be. Nevertheless, I intend to go with you."

"For what possible reason?"

"My motive doesn't concern you."

Jake slammed his bag on the table and muttered a curse

about the wealthy and their pompous whims. "Egypt is a dangerous country. The Egyptians don't like foreigners and, where I'm going, there won't be anyone to cook you a fine meal or prepare your bath. Believe me," he continued, hoping to dissuade the earl by sending a scornful glance over his perfectly tailored clothes, "you don't want to be there."

"You can't deter me. If you want my money, you'll have to take me along."

"Bloody hell I will, Gavin. When I left there six weeks ago, I barely escaped without detection. Napoleon has already begun his invasion to oust the British."

"Yes, I know." Something hardened in Gavin's voice, giving the words more meaning than they deserved. "I've been giving Napoleon some thought. I know someone who can help us evade the French."

"I suppose you want to take an entire entourage?"

"Just one man."

Jake wanted to say no, the word thundered through his head. Gavin thought he was going on holiday, some great adventure to add excitement to his safe, comfortable world. He wanted to say no, God, he wanted to, but he couldn't. He needed Gavin's money. Trying to raise the funds elsewhere would only give Roger a greater lead.

"All right. But heed my warning, Gavin, I won't be responsible for your safety."

"Having a title doesn't make me completely inept, you know."

Jake scoffed and headed out the door. "I'll go to the docks and inquire after a ship sailing to Africa."

"I've already sent a man to secure passage for the three of us on whatever vessel is available."

Jake paused in the hallway and barely suppressed a rueful laugh. "Perhaps with your money and my knowledge of Egypt we'll find Roger before he ruins everything."

"We'll find him."

Jake recognized the confidence in Gavin's tone. He'd heard the same from Roger countless times before. It was something only the nobility possessed, a quality bestowed upon them at birth that made them believe nothing was beyond their reach. A trait reserved for those who had never had to fight just to survive.

He continued down the hall, every part of his being focused on the uncertain journey ahead. He would find Roger, then he would bring Queen Tiy back to England where she belonged. Feeling the blood pulse hot through his body, he swore nothing would stop him from claiming the credit for her discovery and repairing the damage done to his name and career.

Absolutely nothing.

Sarah pressed a perfumed handkerchief to her nose and closed her eyes, determined not to become ill. The rancid smells threatening to wrench her stomach weren't solely from the rotting fruit and vegetables that had been dumped and forgotten on the Thames pier, or the myriad of fish carts driven by the costermongers on their way to market. No, the odors that had her insides heaving to her throat was a product of the two men Roger had hired to accompany her to Egypt.

Standing on either side of her like immovable brick columns, with their arms crossed over their massive chests, her escorts wore identical scowls as a crew of men attempted to load the crate containing Queen Tiy's gold coffin onto the ship with a crane. Her escorts had tried to do the work themselves, but the captain of the *Phoenix* had ordered them to stand aside.

"They don't know what they're doin'," Eli Bebb complained on her right. Eli had a body as round as his bald head and, from what she'd witnessed, he moved like a slow-rolling boulder.

"Lord Pendergrass will 'ave our hides if we let anythin' 'appen tae 'is box." Thatcher Small growled the words, the sound reminding her of a huge black bear she'd once seen when gypsies had camped near her school. He even resembled a bear, she decided. Standing well over six feet tall, patches of curly black hair covered his head and the lower half of his rugged face. His arms were massive, his hands huge paws.

The men might be in desperate need of a bath, but they seemed to genuinely care about the task for which they'd been hired. She had to admit, all smells aside, their size and concern gave her some much-needed courage. From the moment she'd agreed to leave England, her confidence felt as vulnerable as a china cup teetering on a table's edge. With Eli and Thatcher to protect her and the artifacts, she just might succeed *and* return home with her life intact.

"That rope isna goin' tae hold, my lady," Eli told her, wincing when the hoist groaned under the strain of lifting the crate. The box packed with the queen's four canopic jars and the cedarwood box filled with small statues and jewelry were already on board, as was Sarah's trunk of clothes. The smaller crates loaded with the tools and gear she'd need once in Egypt were being hand-carried aboard by sailors now.

In the satchel she clutched in her hands, Sarah had the corselet. By not hiding it in one of the crates she knew she risked the possibility of someone seeing it, but the voyage to Egypt would be a long one, and since she had a private cabin, she intended to use the time to paint the golden belt.

Sarah held her breath as the six-foot-long crate rose high into the air, tilting from end to end like a child's see-saw as it hovered in that perilous space between the pier and the ship. If it fell now it would land in the Thames River. She shuddered at the possibility. She hadn't even left London and already she was in danger of failing her mission.

"What do you suggest we do?" she asked her guards.

The two men looked at each other over the top of her head and shrugged. Thatcher said simply, "The rope's goin' tae break."

"Not if I can help it." She couldn't just stand there; she had to do something. Insist the captain carry the crate aboard by hand, something, anything except what he was doing now.

She called out to the captain, but he didn't hear her above the din of people laughing and yelling and shouting curses, a roar of sound that only made her heart pound harder.

Holding her satchel close to her chest, she pushed her way through the milling crowd. "Captain Dunhill," she called. "I must have a word with you."

She reached his side and gripped his arm to gain his attention, but he was red-faced and bellowing at the workman who manned the hoist. "Captain, you're going to drop my crate. I think it would be best if we carried it instead."

Captain Dunhill shook off her hand and barked to the crewman waiting above them on deck. "Ready now. She's comin' yer way!"

The hoist abruptly pivoted closer to the ship, setting the crate rocking in the air. The men on board the *Phoenix* held out grappling hooks to snag the crate but it swung hard over their heads, out of reach, then back again above the dock. A five-hundred-pound pendulum that could crush a man's skull. People screamed and scattered out of its way.

"Captain Dunhill, I insist you lower my belongings before you drop them!"

"Stand aside, miss," he ordered.

At that moment, the hoist gave a rending moan. The

metal arm suddenly bent, dropping the crate several feet. There was a collective gasp from everyone but Sarah. She couldn't breathe. At any second Queen Tiy would tumble into the river, then sink to the muddy bottom where she would be impossible to retrieve. Sarah couldn't let that happen; she had to stop it. She looked about frantically for help. Dozens of people stood transfixed, watching the potential disaster with gleaming eyes, as if they were anticipating the moment her belongings splintered into a thousand pieces against the dock. To her despair, Eli and Thatcher were among the onlookers.

"Can't you do something?" she cried. She heard a metallic snap and spun around. One of the support beams on the hoist had broken in half. Sarah heard herself scream as the metal arm buckled to a ninety-degree angle. The crate jerked and flopped, coming within inches of striking the edge of the dock.

"No!" She ran forward, but something knocked her back into the crowd. She stumbled, going down hard on her knees. She grunted as her bag flew out of her hands.

"We need to balance the weight," someone shouted.

Pushing to her feet, she shoved past the people blocking her view. A man wearing tan trousers and a cream shirt grabbed the thick rope where it threaded through the hoist. He leaned back, gripping the coarse rigging with his bare hands, straining to keep the crate from dropping further.

He pulled and dug his feet into the wooden dock, struggling to tighten the slack. The muscles in his forearms bulged and flexed, his already tanned face darkened with the force of his effort.

He gritted his teeth and cursed. "Connor, steady it before it falls!"

Two men broke from the crowd. One, a huge man wearing pitch-black pants and shirt, pushed the base of the hoist toward shore, while the other man in a tailored coat caught the grappling hook a crewman from the deck above tossed down. As the crate swung past him, the gentleman succeeded in hooking the rope, but the force of the weight dragged him along as if he weighed no more than a child.

Sarah pressed her hands over her mouth, too horrified to even gasp. If they didn't stop the crate's momentum, both the crate and the man would be swept into the river.

Captain Dunhill leapt behind the first man fighting the hoist and gathered the tail end of the rope. Then another man joined them. Together they strained against the weight, sliding forward, losing precious ground, their boot heels leaving marks in the dock. The crate dropped dangerously close to the pier, but the man with the hook steadied the swaying. She watched breathlessly as Queen Tiy was lowered inch by inch, until finally, with a thwack that seemed to resound inside Sarah's chest, the box touched ground.

The crowd disbursed, grumbling with disappointment. Sarah couldn't move, certain her legs would collapse if she tried.

"I told ye the rope wouldn't hold," Eli said from beside her.

Sarah glared at him, then caught her breath. "My satchel. I dropped . . ."

He held it up and grinned like a fool. Taking it from him, she snapped, "Find some help and carry the crate on board."

Willing her pulse to return to normal, she approached the first man who had jumped to her aid. He had his head bent, studying his palms. Having lost his hat in his struggle, his sandy blond hair fell forward, partially hiding his face.

Reaching his side, she followed his gaze, then blurted, "Dear heavens." Angry red welts scored his hands. Drops of blood beaded his skin where the coarse rope had sliced him. "You're hurt."

"It's nothing," he said, a tinge of humor in his deep voice.

"I'm so sorry." Still gripping her handkerchief, she set her satchel down and wrapped the cloth around his hand, noting that beneath the wounds his palms were calloused and tough and marred with old scars. "These cuts will have to be cleaned. Do you have something I can bind your other hand with?"

"It's not necessary." Something in his voice caught her attention. Something familiar . . . Something . . . *No, it can't be.* She was just shaken and feeling distressed. And who wouldn't be considering what had just happened?

"I'll be fine," he said, tugging his hand from her grasp.

She felt something cold close around her lungs and squeeze, something dire and foreboding. She knew that voice, a combination of strength and mocking arrogance. It was a horrible, horrible sound, one she'd learned long ago to hate. Feeling a tremor of dread move down her spine, she willed herself to look up, even as she told herself not to. She didn't want to be proven right. Heaven help her, she didn't.

She raised her head regardless, and met the detestable dark blue gaze she'd never, *ever* wanted to see again. "Dear God."

Jacob Mitchell had found her.

The dock shifted beneath her feet. She swayed and her mind went numb.

"Steady." He gripped her arm, easily holding her upright. "You're not on the ship yet and already you've got sea legs."

The reality struck her as painfully as if he'd slapped her in the face. She pulled free, her gaze raking over him. He was different from the young man she remembered, but she'd know him anywhere. A night hardly passed that she didn't envision him before she fell asleep, hating him for taking her place at her father's side.

Jake's face was leaner than she remembered, stronger, his jaw a hard edge of flesh and bone. His chest was thicker, his shoulders wide, the combination creating a dangerous vision of manhood. She recognized the intensity in his eyes; she'd seen it before, a cold selfishness that drove him to pursue his own goals and others be damned.

At twenty-two, the last time she'd seen him, he'd been a rogue, a thrill seeker searching for adventure and fame. At twenty-nine Jake was all the more imposing. And a threat to the promise she'd made to her father.

She took several steps back, ready to turn and run. Her eyes widened when she saw her satchel with the corselet lying at his feet. She snatched it up, clutching it to her chest like a beggar grasping a stolen meal. He might be here to take Queen Tiy away from her, but she wouldn't make it easy for him. She would stop him. Somehow.

"I see you've worked your charms on the lady, Jake," the man wearing the tailored coat said, joining them. He executed a bow, his dark eyes distant and cool as he studied her face. "Gavin DeFoe, my lady. Earl of Blackwell."

Sarah stood frozen, hardly daring to breathe. Something was wrong. Jake wasn't shouting at her, accusing her of being a theif. In fact, as his gaze slid from her face, down her body and back up again, an amused light entered his eyes. Could it be that he hadn't tracked her down? Could she be so lucky? She almost laughed. He obviously didn't recognize her. She'd been a seventeen-year-old girl the last time she'd glimpsed him in her father's library. And he hadn't seen her at all.

Realizing the three men were watching her, apparently waiting for her to make a sensible response, she managed to find her voice. "I must thank you all for saving my cargo. My lord," she said to the earl, deciding it was safer to ignore Jake. "It's a pleasure to meet you."

She'd heard of the Earl of Blackwell—who in London hadn't? He had a notorious reputation as a ruthless businessman. But it was his personal life that kept mothers with marriageable daughters whispering about who the next Lady Blackwell would be. And wondering how long the poor lady would stay alive to hold the title.

"And this is Connor MacLeay," the earl said, indicating the red-headed, barrel-chested man who had single-handedly pushed the hoist away from the ship.

"My lady." He uttered the phrase with a Scottish lilt that was deeper and more melodious than any she'd heard before. She might have thought him charming if not for the fierce set of his jaw. He exuded tension, the dangerous kind that made her think of battles and blood and death.

Before she could even think of a response, the earl continued, "And you've already met Jacob Mitchell, the man who jumped to your rescue."

"Yes," she managed, nearly choking on the word. Moving away toward the gangplank, she said, "Thank you again. I wish I could repay you for your kindness, but," she glanced over her shoulder at the *Phoenix*, and was relieved to see Eli and Thatcher along with several crewmen struggling to carry the crate up the gangplank, "but I'm to set sail within the hour."

"As are we," Earl Blackwell said.

Her gaze flew to Jake, and she felt herself sway again. *Dear heaven above, this can't be happening!*

"You're . . . you're . . ." she couldn't even get the words out. "You're traveling on *this* ship?"

"I am," Jake said, wondering what he'd done to offend the woman. She was a tiny thing, the top of her head barely reaching his shoulders. The way she'd twisted her sable brown hair into a complicated knot at her nape made her cheekbones and jaw seem delicate and fine-boned, as if she'd break if someone handled her without care. And her skin—growing up no better than a mongrel pup in the alleyways of London's East End, then living in Egypt's crowded towns and forsaken deserts, Jake had rarely seen anything like her complexion. Honey and cream. But it was her eyes that stopped him.

Disbelief sparked like lightning in their smoky gray depth, making it clear she didn't care for the idea of sharing her ship with three strange men. Or perhaps it wasn't the three of them she objected to, but Jake. Her stunned expression seemed reserved solely for him.

He sighed when what he really wanted was to spit out a curse. This had been one bloody hell of a day. His queen had been stolen and he had to baby-sit Gavin and his bodyguard, Connor MacLeay, in order to get her back. Instead of minding his own business, he'd saved the woman's belongings, for which his hands now stung like fire. And her way of saying thank you was to become incensed that she might have to suffer his company. Well bloody hell. He wanted to get on board the *Phoenix*, nurse his cuts, and sail away from England.

The woman with her wide liquid eyes and trembling lips be damned.

"Now that the disaster has been averted and your cargo is safely on board," Jake said tightly, turning to leave, "you'll have to excuse me."

Gavin caught his arm, but his attention remained focused on the woman. "We've yet to learn your name, my lady."

"I . . . I'm Sarah . . ." She pressed her lips together for a second as if needing time to remember the rest, then she said, "Sarah Elston."

"Of the Devonshire Elstons?" Gavin asked.

She nodded hesitantly.

Jake glanced at his friend. For a brief moment he thought Gavin might be interested in the woman, but the suspicious glint in the earl's eyes told him otherwise. Then he recalled what Gavin had said that morning. He didn't trust women. Evidently, that included ladies in distress.

Gavin pried one of her hands from her satchel and bent to kiss the smooth skin above her knuckles. In a tone both cool and reserved, he said, "'Tis a pleasure to meet you, Lady Elston. I'm sure our trip to Egypt will be a pleasant one."

Blushing, she smiled at the earl. The effort softened her face and transformed her already lovely features. Her slender nose became more defined, her high cheekbones, elegant. Jake felt a tightening in his gut, and he had the bizarre urge to touch her as Gavin had. But her wary gaze quickly returned to him, quelling all thoughts of gallantry. He suspected that if he tried to kiss her hand, she'd use it to slap him off his feet.

Once Gavin released his propriety hold on her, silence fell over the group as she studied Jake. Both intrigued and irritated by her boldness, he endured her scrutiny. She tilted her rounded little chin as if she found him lacking and asked, "Are you traveling to Egypt on business or pleasure, Mr. Mitchell?"

"Business. And you, Lady Elston?"

"Pleasure." Contrary to her answer, her eyes narrowed like a cat's, ready to strike. Had he not known better, he'd think she blamed him for some misdeed. He considered questioning her to learn the reason for her animosity, but in truth, he didn't want to know. He had his own problems to deal with. He didn't intend to worry about Lady Elston's sudden, and unwarranted, dislike of him.

"Are you traveling alone?" Gavin asked.

"Of course not," she said, but didn't elaborate.

"Shall we board then?" Jake suggested, extending his arm to allow her to lead the way.

She nodded and strode past him without another word. To his ire he caught the scent of her skin, something fresh and sweet and as elusive as summer rain. When she smiled and accepted Gavin's arm to assist her up the gangplank, Jake gritted his teeth and followed the pair.

"I'm thinkin' she does no like ye, Jake-o," Connor said from behind him.

Jake glanced at the burly Scotsman, not surprised to find Connor's stern expression unchanged despite the humor underlining his words. He'd met the man barely two hours before, and still knew little about the Scot, except that he was an expert at tracking and subterfuge. He'd had to pry that paltry bit of information from Gavin. Connor's unexpected comment was the most he'd uttered since they'd met.

Still the man's assessment of Lady Sarah Elston was irritatingly on target. She did have an aversion to him. The question was, why? He grabbed up his satchel and hat where he'd dropped them when he'd leapt to her aid and started up the plank, scowling at the pair ahead of him. Gavin and Lady Elston made a perfect couple, the earl in his tailored suit coat and trousers. Sarah in an ice-blue wool gown embroidered with tiny silver flowers. The bodice laced up the front, revealing white ruffles of her chemise, a feminine touch that made her skin seem impossibly soft.

It shouldn't bother him that she preferred the earl to him, and dammit, it didn't, but he was curious to know what it was about him that offended her. Having lived most of his adult life in the deserts of Egypt, surrounded by workers and sand, the threat of cobras and the temperamental Nile, he'd kept little company with women, and even less with ladies. While he may not have Gavin's finesse, he liked to believe he wasn't completely without charm.

Jake swore under his breath. He didn't have time to worry about a strange woman and her even stranger behavior. His goal was to find Roger and retrieve Queen Tiy. Nothing would deter him. Not Gavin's or Connor's interference. Not Napoleon's army or the flooding waters of the Nile. Nothing would distract him from his goal. Especially not something like Lady Sarah Elston.

Chapter 3

Lamplight sputtered in the small cabin, throwing shadows and smoky light over the paneled walls and narrow bed. A blanket of coarse gray wool covered the thin straw mattress. Sarah hid the letter Roger had given her there, still not believing his final instructions concerning Queen Tiy. A combination desk and dresser had been nailed to the floor. Sarah took in the room she would occupy during her trip to Egypt with a sweeping glance and tried to think of this as an adventure, like one she'd often dreamed of having with her father.

But Roger wasn't here; she was all alone and this wasn't some grand adventure. It was a dangerous game.

Feeling the rising tilt of the sea, hearing the splash of waves against the hull, she knew with a rending twist of her stomach that there was no turning back. She was on her way to Egypt . . . with Jake nipping at her heels.

Sarah closed the tiny, porthole window to shut out the chilled night air, then pressed her ear to the door. For the fifth time in as many minutes she glanced at the wooden bolt to ensure it was in place. She didn't put it past Jake to barge into her room the way he'd barged into her life.

Hearing nothing in the companionway beyond, she opened her satchel, gently lifted the corselet and spread it on the bed. She held her breath, her heart racing against her chest.

The corselet glowed like polished ivory, sparkling with life and light. Each gold square seemed to blend with its mate until the garment appeared more like the cape she'd first thought it to be. She ran her palm over the smooth links as Roger had done, only she touched the soft gold, feeling the inscription on each square, marveling at the artist's ability to create a recording of the queen's life and death, a testament that would last for all time. Every artist dreamed of producing a work of art that would live forever. She felt that need inside her as well, like a hunger she couldn't fill.

Studying the corselet from every angle, Sarah told herself it was only another artifact, valuable and beautiful, but nothing more. Yet she knew that was a lie. There was something unique about the gold-linked wrap, something she couldn't verbalize. Which was why she wanted to paint it, bring to life the sensations the corselet stirred inside her.

She considered taking out her art supplies, but now wasn't the time. The captain had invited his guests to join him for dinner—Jake included. Her first impulse had been to decline, but this could be a valuable opportunity to learn what her adversary was up to.

A knock at her door sent her heart pounding against her chest. She snatched up the corselet, searched for a place to hide it.

"Who's there?" she asked, wincing when her voice quivered.

"'Tis us, my lady," came a hoarse whisper. She sighed, tempted to sink onto the bed with relief. Eli and Thatcher.

"We've come tae make sure ye're all settled in."

Placing the corselet in her dresser drawer, she unlocked the door and admitted her guards. "I'm glad you're here. There's something I need to discuss with you."

The two men squeezed into her cabin, and Sarah thought she might have to leave the room in order to close the door, but Thatcher pressed himself against one wall and Eli against the other.

"Pardon my say'n so, my lady," Eli said, "but I don't think we should be in 'ere."

"Shh, this will only take a minute," she whispered. "There is a man on board, someone who must not know who I am."

"'As he threatened ye?" this came from Thatcher, who clenched his beefy hands and puffed out his chest, taking up room they didn't have to spare.

"Not exactly. His name is Jake Mitchell. He . . ." she paused, not sure how much she should reveal to these men. "He wants to take my cargo."

Eli scratched his bald head. "But he 'elped ye save it."

"We should have been the ones to protect the crate. We messed up fine, we did," Thatcher said, looking at her as if he expected to be reprimanded.

"That doesn't matter now. Jake Mitchell only saved the cargo because he doesn't know who I am or what is in the crate. If he knew, he'd steal my belongings."

"Lord Pendergrass told us there might be a bloke after ye. Yer say'n this Mitchell fellow is the one?"

"Yes, so as long as we're on this ship, you'll call me Lady Elston. Can you remember that?"

"Course we can." Eli nodded to Thatcher. "We'll take turns guarding your crate, my lady. Don't you worry none. You can count on Eli Bebb and Thatcher Small."

"I knew I could." Smiling at the men, feeling somewhat relieved, she opened the door a crack and checked the companionway to make sure it was empty before allowing them to leave.

Once they were gone, she closed and locked the door again. *Sarah Elston.* If Eli and Thatcher could remember what to call her, then she had better not forget. When the earl had asked for her name she'd almost blurted out "Pendergrass." Only at the last second had she remembered Roger's instruction to use her mother's maiden name.

"I might be able to fool Jake with a false name, but I still have a dilemma," she murmured, taking the corselet from her dresser drawer. She fingered the cool surface of the lapis lazuli. "What am I going to do with you?"

She couldn't leave the corselet in her cabin for fear that someone—namely Jake—might find it. Nor could she hide it in Queen Tiy's crate. It was stored in the hold below, and she couldn't risk opening it. The crate was secured along with the rest of the cargo. If she tried to open it, and Jake happened upon her . . . no, it was better to leave it alone. Besides, she didn't want to let the corselet out of her sight, which left her only one alternative.

Before she could change her mind, she began to unlace the bodice of her gown. Pushing down her sleeves, she lifted the dress over her head, then laid it on the foot of her bed. Next she removed her petticoat, then her corset. With nothing on but her shift, she shivered as much from apprehension as she did from the cold.

She glanced at the door one last time to make sure that it was locked. Knowing it was now or never, she let her shift drop to the floor.

Her skin prickled against the chilly air, and her hands shook as she lifted the corselet, but before she could put it on, something caught her attention. She laid the belt on her bed so the inside faced up. Faint symbols had been etched into the squares. They were similar to the bold hieroglyphics on the other side that told of the queen's death, yet these were somehow different.

"Why didn't Roger tell me about these?" she whispered, frowning. She glanced at her paper and pencils, wishing more than ever that she had time to draw the strange pictures. Soon she vowed; soon she would study both sides of the corselet until she knew each symbol by heart.

Sighing with regret, she placed the belt around her waist and sucked in a breath as icy metal met flesh. She could have worn it over her shift, but for a reason she couldn't explain, she wanted Queen Tiy's corselet as close to her as possible. Quickly, she secured the hooks down the back.

When she finished, she ran her hands over her hips, feeling the gold warm to her touch. The weight settled around her, molding to her body like a second skin. She imagined how Queen Tiy might have felt four thousand years ago as she fastened the garment on one last time. Had the golden armor given her the courage to face the pharaoh she'd tried to kill? Perhaps the corselet had given her the strength to pick up a dagger and take her own life while an entire court looked on. Or had the corselet been added to her coffin after her death?

Realizing how absurd her thoughts were, she shook her head and snatched her shift off the floor. "I'm as bad as Roger. It's only a piece of jewelry for heaven's sake."

Already late for dinner, she wasted little time in dressing. Lacing her blue gown, she tucked loose strands of her hair into the braided knot at her nape. Touching her waist, feeling the corselet snug against her skin, she knew she looked the same as when she'd boarded the *Phoenix*, but she didn't feel the same. She felt determined, confident that she would succeed. Drawing a deep breath, she unlocked the door and left her cabin, certain she was ready to face whatever came next.

The ship bucked beneath her feet, knocking her into the wall. Sarah regained her balance and wondered if the sea had heard her vow and had decided to test her. Reaching the stairs, she climbed up one level, then continued down a passageway lit by oil whale lamps toward the captain's cabin. At the door she paused when she heard the sound of male voices. Jake was in there, his voice easily distinguishable from the others. A tremor shot through her limbs and her palms turned clammy. She felt dizzy suddenly, and knew it had nothing to do with the swaying vessel.

"No!" she whispered vehemently. "I will not let Jacob Mitchell frighten me." Squaring her shoulders, she opened the door and entered the cabin, only to come to an abrupt halt.

Every man in the cramped room stopped what they were doing to turn and face her. There were five of them, all tall and forceful and staring at her as if she'd arrived for their individual amusement. Since she'd spent most of her life in the company of women, she'd spent a considerable amount of her time and energy learning the valuable skills of snatching a good husband. She knew how to curtsey and drink tea, how to play the pianoforte and stitch a sampler. But boarding school had failed to teach her how to deal with a roomful of hard-edged men all by herself.

Feeling very much like a mouse stepping into the jaws of a wolf, she closed the door behind her and forced herself to smile. "I hope I haven't kept you waiting long."

"Lady Elston." Seated at the head of the table, Captain Dunhill pushed his round body out of his chair. His whiskered cheeks were pink and gleaming with sweat, but she couldn't tell if his condition was a result of spending a lifetime at sea or from the whiskey that filled his cup. "Ye are worth the wait. Allow me tae introduce ye tae your fellow passengers. This 'ere is Father Headington. He's decided to open a mission in Egypt. Believes the heathens are in need of saving."

"I'm sure we could all use a little saving, Captain," Sarah said.

Father Headington bowed slightly, his thin cheeks flushing. "I'm pleased to meet you, Lady Elston."

"And this is Jacob Mitchell," Captain Dunhill continued. "We've already met." Jake stood at the far corner of the room, like a hawk studying his prey, she decided, all sharp-eyed and ready to strike.

"Mr. Mitchell."

"Ah, that's right," Captain Dunhill exclaimed. "That damned crate! Ah, pardon my language, Lady Elston, but what in bloody blazes have ye got packed in there? The king's treasure? From the weight of it, it could be no less."

Sarah felt the color drain from her face. "No treasure. Just some . . . some furniture I'll need while I'm in Egypt."

At that moment a serving boy entered carrying a tray of steaming meat and vegetables, turning everyone's attention to their empty stomachs. Grateful for the reprieve, Sarah took a seat next to Father Headington, hoping she'd draw some much-needed strength from the holy man. She didn't think she could tolerate having to sit beside Jake. Gavin DeFoe sat at the end of the table next to her and their silent companion, Connor MacLeay, wearing his black clothes and blacker expression, took the chair next to the captain, which left the seat directly across from her for Jake.

It took Sarah only seconds to realize this arrangement was far worse than having him at her side. She couldn't move without feeling his attention on her. Granted, all the men were staring at her, but it was Jake's gaze she felt the most. His dark eyes moved over her hair and shoulders, then lower, the way a man's gaze seemed determined to do. She couldn't believe his brazenness. If it weren't for the other men in the room, she'd gladly put him in his place. As it was, she decided to wait until his roaming gaze made it back to her face, then silently convey her outrage.

But the moment those blue eyes lifted and met hers she felt a shivery heat brush over her skin, as if lightning had struck too close. The corner of his mouth curved, but it wasn't a smile. More like he knew a secret that he wanted to share.

Sarah rubbed her damp palms against her skirt and felt the corselet. Her heart began to pound in her chest and her breath was coming much too fast. She had to calm down. It infuriated her that he could unsettle her with a single look. It had to stop. The trip to Rosetta, Egypt, would take three weeks. If she didn't find some control, she'd never make it.

After taking a sip of red wine from her goblet, she turned to the earl. "Lord Blackwell, what type of business is taking you to Egypt?"

"Mr. Mitchell is an archaeologist. Some of his artifacts have been . . ." the earl hedged for a moment, ". . . diverted from their original destination. We're on our way to recover them."

Jake lifted his goblet, but he didn't drink. The muscles in his jaw flexed with sudden tension, and his eyes turned to chips of cold blue stones. What would happen if he learned the corselet was within arm's reach? Would his eyes stay cold and hard or would they burn with fury? Feeling empowered by her secret, she took another drink of wine to hide her smile.

"An archaeologist and the Earl of Blackwell united for a common cause. It sounds interesting." Sarah considered the Scotsman, almost as reluctant to attract his attention as she had been with Jake. There was something about Connor's blood-red hair and deep green eyes that warned her away. But she had to garner as much information as she could about her foes. "And what is your role in this mysterious task, Mr. MacLeay?"

"To see they come back alive."

Hearing the deadly edge in the Scotsman's voice, Sarah felt every part of her body go still. She knew Egypt was in turmoil, and even when it wasn't it was a dangerous place. But she hadn't thought it was *that* dangerous. Her father wouldn't have sent her if it really were so perilous. Or would he? If Jake and the earl needed a man like Connor to protect them, how would she fare with two simple-minded farmers?

"And what about you, Lady Elston?" Jake asked quietly. "A holiday in Egypt without companions seems rather foolish for a single woman."

"Eli and Thatcher are my companions."

Connor snorted and turned his attention to consuming his plate of food.

"I thought ladies never traveled without a personal maid," Jake said.

"You're right, Mr. Mitchell. It is unseemly," Sarah admitted. She had briefly considered bringing her maid, Ellen, but while she might be willing to risk her life to help her father, she hadn't been willing to risk the girl's. She couldn't admit that to everyone, so she said, "My maid took ill only a few days ago. Rather than wait, I decided to hire someone when I reach Rosetta."

"Jake's right," Gavin said. "With Napoleon's army swarming over Egypt, it's not safe for anyone from Great Britain."

"Yet you're going," she challenged.

"Unfortunately we have little choice," Jake said. "As soon as we find what we're looking for, we'll return to England."

Then you'll never return, Sarah wanted to tell him, because nothing was going to stop her from placing Queen Tiy inside her tomb. Then she'd follow Roger's instructions and blow up the entrance, ensuring that Jacob Mitchell would never, *ever,* lay his hands on the queen again.

An Isis moon hung on the horizon like a great metal disk, the Egyptian moon goddess guiding him home. Jake hadn't thought he'd be on a ship again so soon, and he'd never thought he'd feel so wary about returning to the desert land he loved.

Standing at the bow, watching the vessel's prow cut through rolling black water, he tried to envision Roger's ship ahead of him, concealed in the dark. His mentor had no more than a one-day head start. If the weather held, and Captain Dunhill raised every sail up the *Phoenix's* mast, they might land in Rosetta at the same time as Roger.

If only it were that easy. Considering his past, Jake didn't think he'd be so lucky.

Sighing, knowing he had no alternative except to be patient, he decided to return to the cabin he shared with Connor and continue his work on the relief he'd made of Queen Tiy's corselet. Thank God he'd made a copy. If he failed to catch up with Roger before he did something foolish, like destroy her tomb, his relief of the corselet would be the only proof that she existed.

He'd already deciphered the story about the end of her tragic life, and though he never tired of studying it, it was the mysterious scripture on the inside of the garment that had become his obsession. There was a mystery inside the strange verse, the riddle of the pyramids or the location of a great tomb, perhaps. Or something he couldn't begin to imagine. Whatever the inscription, he intended to discover its secret.

Turning away from the railing, he came to an abrupt halt when he saw a mystery of another kind standing beside the starboard rail. Lady Elston stared into the distance, the cool night breeze tugging her braided hair, the color so dark, it glistened like polished onyx. She wore a black cape that covered her from shoulders to shoes, concealing her feminine curves. Between the faint light from a nearby lantern and the moon's silver glow, she seemed ethereal, an illusion playing tricks with his mind.

He wondered if Queen Tiy had looked so regal standing on the deck of her felucca, sailing to her temple on Elephantine Island to pray to the goddess Hapi for a bountiful harvest. Jake found himself smiling at the comparison, but his smile quickly faded as reality took hold. Regardless that she held herself like a queen, Lady Elston wasn't one. She was a foolish aristocrat who had no idea of the danger she had put herself in.

Three days had passed since he'd last seen her. After their dinner the first night onboard ship, she'd stayed in her cabin, declining Captain Dunhill's invitation to dine with them. Jake suspected he'd somehow been behind the reason for her refusal, though he couldn't begin to understand why. Females and their peculiar behavior. He doubted he'd ever understand them. Which was why he preferred to devote his attention on the new woman in his life—regardless that she'd been dead for three thousand years.

Everything about Lady Elston, from the rigid set of her shoulders, to her grip on the railing, said to stay away, that she wanted to be alone. He wasn't sure if it was to assuage his ego or merely to appease his curiosity, but he found himself ignoring her silent rebuff and crossing to her.

"Good evening," he said, his voice barely louder than the wind. But it was loud enough for her to hear.

Gasping, she turned, taking a step in retreat. "What are you doing here?"

"Getting some fresh air. Same as you I imagine."

"Yes, well." She pressed her hand to her throat and drew a shaky breath. "I'd rather take my fresh air in private if you don't mind."

"Not at all." He rested one arm on the railing and settled in to watch her.

Her chin tilted and her eyes flashed like the points of a blade. "Must I be the one to leave, Mr. Mitchell?"

"Have I done something to offend you, Lady Elston?"

"Of course not," she said, folding her arms over her waist. "I don't know you well enough for you to offend me."

"Perhaps we could change that."

She sent him a scalding glare and turned to leave. "I'd rather not."

Jake caught her arm, surprising them both. She tensed beneath his touch, and though he knew he should let her go, he couldn't, not until he learned what it was about him that she disliked. He eased closer to her, but relaxed his grip, not wanting to frighten her anymore than he already had.

"Kindly remove your hand, Mr. Mitchell."

"I will as soon as you tell me why you're so set against me."

"If you don't release me this instant, I'll scream." She twisted her arm, trying to escape his hold.

Hearing the panic in her voice, he dropped his hand. "You didn't scream when Gavin touched you."

"Mr. Mitchell—"

"You're afraid of me. Why?"

"I'm not," she insisted, gripping the railing in a hold so tight, he could see her bleached-white knuckles in the near dark.

Jake knew she was lying. He scared her half to death. But why? He leaned against the railing and pretended to watch the ocean's swells. "Will you stay in Egypt long?"

A muscle pulsed in her jaw as silence circled around them. Finally, she asked, "If I answer your questions, will you promise to leave me alone?"

"If that's what you want."

She rolled her eyes in annoyance, making it clear that she wanted to be as far away from him as possible. "I'm an artist. I've always wanted to see the pyramids at Giza, paint them."

"You ran out of things to paint in England?"

She sighed in disgust. "I wouldn't expect you to understand."

"On the contrary," he said, sobering. "I understand completely. There's no place like Egypt in the entire world. It has a way of getting into your blood. England has a noble history, but we were living in caves when the great pharaohs were building monuments to their gods, using skills we can't even conceive of today."

Jake stopped, realizing she was watching him with a mixture of uncertainty and dread. An odd combination, but he thought he might be making progress. "Do you have family or friends in Rosetta?"

"No, I'm going to rent a house for a few months."

He arched a brow in disbelief.

"You disapprove?" she asked defensively.

"I didn't think English ladies would dare stroll through Hyde Park without an escort, much less travel to another country. You are aware that Napoleon—"

"Yes, I'm well aware that the French are trying to seize control of Egypt."

"Then you know that by even being on this ship you're putting your life in danger."

"What I choose to do or where I decide to go is no concern of yours, Mr. Mitchell."

She was right, of course. Her foolish plan to paint the pyramids wasn't any of his business. So why didn't he give her what she wanted and leave her alone? Jake studied her upturned face, noting her high cheekbones and slender nose. Her brows arched over eyes as silver as the full moon. Even with her defensive stance she seemed impossibly delicate, in need of someone to care for her. Why hadn't someone forbidden her from taking such a risky trip—like her husband?

Glancing at her hand, he noted she wore no ring. Still, didn't she have a brother or a father? An uncle to watch after her? Napoleon was famous for taking hostages, and if Sarah could afford a trip to Egypt, she would be a prime target for ransom.

Deciding to be the voice of reason, he said, "The pyramids aren't going anywhere. I think it would be best if you stayed on board the *Phoenix* when we reach Rosetta and return to England."

"I really don't care what you think, Mr. Mitchell."

"Jake. Once the fighting is over, then you can come back."

"Mr. Mitchell—"

"I'd prefer it if you'd call me Jake."

"I'll do no such thing."

"And I'll call you Sarah." He almost smiled when pure outrage fired her cheeks with color. He didn't know why he taunted her—it wasn't like him—but pulling reactions out of her was easier than scooping up a handful of desert sand.

"Of all the outrageous—"

"Having spent most of my life in Egypt, I've found that shedding all pretenses and titles help people become better acquainted." A dark strand of hair pulled free of her braid and flew against her cheek, looking like a saber cut slicing perfect skin. A sudden chill ran down his spine, reminding him of the dangers that lay ahead.

He brushed her hair away, touching her smooth face to reassure himself that the imaginary wound was nothing more than a trick of his mind. He purposefully grazed her cheek with the tips of his fingers. Soft. How could a woman be so soft? He would have touched her jaw, then her neck, and God only knew what else, but she stepped back and stared at his hand as if it were a cobra ready to strike.

"Mr. Mitchell," she said, her silver eyes darkening with unease. "I have no intention of getting to know you any better than I do at this moment. The only thing I want is for you to leave me alone."

Why are you afraid of me, Sarah? Instead of asking the troubling question, Jake fisted his hand to stop the tingling in his finger. He shouldn't have touched her. She was like cool satin, impossibly smooth, but even that didn't compare.

With one simple touch his suspicions had been proven right; Lady Sarah Elston was too fragile and well-bred, too *female* to travel to Egypt alone. He decided to add stubborn and naïve to her list of attributes. *And beautiful.* But beauty wasn't an asset for a single woman in Egypt. It would be her downfall.

Somehow he had to stop her.

The thought stunned him. *What am I doing?* He didn't have time to play nursemaid to an obstinate woman. Recovering Queen Tiy is what mattered, not Sarah Elston's safety.

But the niggling worry refused to leave him, and he knew better than to ignore his internal voice. It would be another two and a half weeks before they reached Rosetta. Perhaps he could use that time to talk some sense into her, convince her that she belonged at home.

"Mr. Mitchell—"

"Jake."

She briefly closed her eyes and huffed an exasperated breath. "Very well. Jake, you aren't going to leave me alone, are you?"

"Is that what you really want?"

She studied his face, slowly moving from one feature to the next, her gaze narrowing as if something unpleasant had just occurred to her. "Since you seem so determined to badger me, why don't you tell me about yourself. Lord Blackwell mentioned you were in pursuit of some artifacts."

"That's right."

"Let me guess. A chest full of jewels? A golden chariot?"

She took a step closer, bringing her soft woman-scent with her. "Whatever it is you've lost, I assume it's Egyptian."

"I didn't say I'd lost anything," he said, annoyed that she'd come so close to the truth.

"No, you didn't. You don't strike me as a man who would misplace his belongings. So what happened?"

"Let's just say my partner and I don't see eye to eye on where the antiquities we discovered should reside. I want the artifacts displayed in England, he wants them to remain in their tomb."

"Since you're on your way to Rosetta," she said with an amused smile, "I assume your partner has taken your discovery to Egypt without your permission."

"I'll get them back."

"You sound very sure of yourself. What if you fail?"

"I won't," he said, more forcefully than necessary.

The corner of her eyes slanted with feline shrewdness, making it clear she doubted he would succeed at all. "And how do you plan to retrieve your discovery?"

"By being at the tomb before my partner."

She stood up straighter and clasped the railing even tighter than before. "Perhaps your partner has a valid reason for wanting to return the artifacts."

"Becoming superstitious in his old age isn't reason enough to give up the discovery of a lifetime."

"So you would take the artifacts from him, even though your partner believes they should remain in their tomb? That's very selfish of you."

"If we leave them, someone else will come along later and claim them."

"Perhaps. But if it's so important to your friend that they remain in Egypt, perhaps you should let him have his way."

"This was *my* discovery!" he said, the anger he fought to control slipping free. "I won't let my partner's irrational fear ruin everything I've worked for."

"I see." Her expression chilled, and even in the pale light, he could see the color drain from her face. "Well then, Mr. . . . Jake, I wish you luck."

She turned abruptly, ending their conversation, and hurried toward the hatchway leading to her cabin. Jake watched her go, regretting his burst of anger. It wasn't like him to take out his frustrations on others.

Still, the woman had more emotions than the Nile had crocodiles. First she'd been angry, then righteous, then coy and now she was running. She was an enigma, he decided, one he would damn well avoid if he had any sense.

But she was also in danger. And that he couldn't ignore, even if she chose to. Somehow he had to gain her trust, convince her that she didn't belong in Egypt. *Gain her trust?* What were the odds?

So far in his archaeological career he'd had little luck receiving the glory for his Egyptian discoveries. It would seem he was having the same wretched luck with women.

Jake smiled with grim assurance as Sarah disappeared below deck, vowing it was time for his luck to change.

Chapter 4

Gleaming white sails crowded three imposing masts of sturdy brown oak. Fat with wind, they sent the *Phoenix* through the ocean's surf with the single-mindedness of a charging whale. The air blew warm and hard against Sarah's face, pulled at her braid and stole her breath. The skirt of her gown snapped like a flag behind her, fighting the gusts, threatening to throw her off balance.

She'd awoken before dawn to the sound of Captain Dunhill shouting orders to raise sails. When he'd announced that he wanted the ship running like a hen in a hailstorm, she hadn't been able to keep from smiling. After quickly dressing, she'd reached the main deck to learn from a passing sailor that during the night they'd left the North Atlantic, had navigated the Strait of Gibraltar and were now in the shimmering turquoise waters of the Mediterranean Sea.

Turning her face toward the rising sun that burned beneath a dome of cerulean blue sky, she welcomed the warm, dry heat, so unlike anything she'd ever known in London. She could almost believe this was a different sun under a different sky. Her skin felt alive, her muscles loose and languid. She was sailing to another continent, another world. If not for the constant pressure of the corselet around her hips, she would have forgotten the dangers that lay ahead and laughed until she cried. This was her first trip away from Great Britain, but she promised herself it would not be her last.

"A pleasant thought?"

The male voice shattered her private contemplation. She whirled around, a biting quip on the tip of her tongue for Jake Mitchell. Gavin DeFoe stood before her, not the glory-seeking rogue. Despite the rising temperature and rushing wind, the earl presented the ultimate picture of wealth and decorum. His dark hair was neatly combed, his perfectly tailored dun coat without a wrinkle. She couldn't say the same for her moss green dimity gown, which had suffered from her hurried packing. His black pants were tucked into knee-high boots that were so well polished she could see her reflection in the leather.

She couldn't deny that the earl was a handsome man, and looking at his aquiline nose and carved jaw, she could understand why women, young and old, needed to fan themselves whenever they caught a glimpse of him. If not for the wariness he didn't bother to hide in his obsidian eyes she might have required a fan herself. But for all his good looks and excellent manners he made her uneasy.

Still, she sighed in relief. Uneasy or not, at least he wasn't Jake Mitchell. "My lord."

"I didn't mean to startle you, and please call me Gavin," the earl said, his hooded gaze polite but far from warm. "Captain Dunhill asked me to speak with you. He believes you would be safer below."

"Safer from what? Am I in danger?"

"If you have to ask," Jake said from behind her. She turned in time to glimpse his arrogant, hip-rolling walk that was in harmony with the rocking ship. "Then you won't survive for long in Egypt."

"We aren't in Egypt yet, Mr. Mitchell." She touched her waist, startled. The corselet had suddenly grown warm, tingling her skin, vibrating as if it had come alive.

She shook her head, knowing the odd sensation was nothing more than a case of nerves.

Jake arched a brow, obviously aware that she'd reverted to his formal name. But calling him "Jake" in front of the earl seemed too personal, regardless that the earl had just invited to her do the same.

Arms crossed over his solid chest, Jake regarded her as if she were a child. "You're on a ship, sailing through foreign waters. That's dangerous enough."

"I'm aware of the risk of being at sea. Pirates, storms, shipwrecks, but with the exception of you being on board, I don't see anything that closely resembles a threat."

Jake had the nerve to smile at her insult. His whiskey blond hair fought the wind, brushing his shoulders, catching against his rough-shaven cheek. His sand-colored pants were well worn and his cream shirt was partially unbuttoned, exposing more tanned male chest than she'd seen in all twenty-four years of her life. Her mouth went dry. Compared to Gavin, Jake was a rogue, a scoundrel, a shabby, second-rate excuse for a man. She hated him, loathed everything he represented, and it infuriated her that she couldn't tell him so to his face.

There was another difference between the two men, one she was reluctant to admit. The passion, the thirst for living that burned in Jake's eyes didn't make her the least bit uneasy, it made her feel warm and jittery and in need of a *fan*.

Deciding to ignore Jake, she asked the earl, "Perhaps you could explain why I need to go below."

Taking her arm, Gavin led her away from the bow . . . and Jake . . . and toward the hatchway. "These are unsafe waters, Sarah. The captain is pushing his ship and his crew so we can pass through them as quickly as possible."

"I've stayed out of everyone's way," she insisted, feeling a wary tingle on the back of her neck and another, sharper, burst of heat from the corselet.

"What he means, Sarah," Jake said, bending close to whisper in her ear, "is that you're a distraction." And he should know, Jake thought. It took every ounce of his control to keep from jerking Gavin's hand away from her arm.

She faced him, her cheeks flushed from the wind, her heart-shaped mouth open in outrage. "A distraction? I am no such thing."

"No?" he said, stepping close so she had to crane her head back to hold his gaze. Only he stepped so close he could smell her clean scent, air and sunshine and sweet, sweet woman. "Look around you. Every man has one eye on you and the other on whatever task he's about. With their attention splintered, a man could lose his footing or miss a handhold. Have you ever seen a man fall from a three-story mast? It makes a bloody mess. If you continue to be stubborn, I'm sure that before long, you'll be able to see for yourself."

She took a step back, her hands clenching her waist as she studied the deck, the men scaling rope ladders, moving barrels of water and adjusting sails. Between tying knots and securing the rigging, the sailor's gazes repeatedly came back to her, some watching her with admiration, others with distrust.

The vibrant color drained from her cheeks. "I had no idea."

"You're a beautiful woman, Sarah," Jake said, feeling the truth behind those words more than he wanted to. "Men will be intrigued by you wherever you go."

"Beautiful?" she scoffed, looking at him as if she thought him insane.

Did she not know what a striking picture she made, he wondered, with her sable hair blowing wild, her soft lips red and inviting, her eyes liquid silver that glittered even in the dark? Had no one ever told her how exceptional she really was?

As he puzzled over the thought, she gathered her

skirts and, without another word, headed for the hatchway, her back anchor-straight and her head held high as she descended to the deck below. As she vanished from sight, Jake had to suppress the urge to follow her. An urge he had fought for the past eight days, ever since their encounter on that moonlit night. She had made it clear she wanted nothing to do with him, and to his ire, the more she avoided him, the more he was tempted to seek her out. Insane, he admitted.

"Well done, Jake," Gavin said, shaking his head. "And here I had tried the tactful approach. Next time I'll just scare her into returning to her cabin. Maybe throw her over my shoulder like a cave man."

"She needs to be frightened. If you knew what awaited us, you'd know she has no business being on this ship."

"She's none of your concern."

Wishing he could agree, Jake asked, "What kind of foolish woman would go to Egypt to paint the pyramids, now, when war is threatening?"

"Who knows what motivates a woman?" Gavin whispered in a tone that revealed a quiet anger, the kind of brewing rage a man buried deep inside his soul. Jake frowned at the earl, who was staring out to sea, and wondered once again about the earl's past. What had really happened to his wife? And hadn't he had a son? If so, where was he now? They were questions Jake wanted to ask, but sensed they wouldn't be welcomed . . . or answered.

"I think stupidity is motivating this particular woman." Jake frowned at the empty hatchway. "I intend to convince her that Egypt is the wrong place for a holiday."

"Your priority is to find Queen Tiy. Not to become distracted by a pretty face."

"Rest assured, nothing will interfere with my goal." Jake faced the white-capped sea, his gaze narrowing as he searched the glistening blue horizon for another ship. In a voice as unyielding as the walls of Karnak, he vowed, "Once we reach Egypt, Lady Elston will be on her own."

Because the only woman Jake cared about was somewhere ahead of him, waiting for him to find her. The one tucked safely in her cabin decks below didn't matter to him at all.

Two more days.

Sarah paced her small cabin. Three steps in one direction, three in the other. Two more days and she would arrive in Rosetta, Egypt, where the second part of her mission would begin. The second and scariest. Her stomach turned upside down. She'd reread her father's instructions so many times on how to hire a felucca that would sail her down the Nile she could recite them word for word. She even knew the directions to the Valley of the Queens, where many of the major queens of antiquity had been entombed, but reading the directions and actually carrying them out were two very different things, entirely.

But, scary or not, she was ready to escape her sweltering cabin. She had never dreamed such heat existed, fanning herself to dry the trickles of sweat dripping down her temples. The air was oppressive, suffocating, pushing against her clothes, making her gown too tight and confining. Her squeezed lungs resisted drawing in the hot, cloying air. And the corselet! She swore it was digging into her body, cutting through her bones. If only she could remove it, just for a few moments, but she didn't dare.

She only risked taking it off late at night. After all these days she still hadn't tired of studying the ancient relic, the strange symbols on the inside fueling her curiosity the most. She had studied every inch of the corselet, but she hadn't drawn it yet, afraid someone—*Jake*—would see the sketch. Perhaps she was being overly suspicious, but she'd rather be safe than sorry. Oh, but she would paint it soon. Just as soon as she was rid of Jake's infernal presence.

Sarah moved to the small porthole, hoping for a breeze, but barely a wisp made it through the window. If only she could leave her cabin, no, her *prison*. Since her last confrontation with Jake, she'd stayed confined to her room for all but a few hours.

The few times she'd ventured above deck for fresh air, she hadn't been able to enjoy herself for fear that she might cause a catastrophe. What if a man fell or cut himself or, God forbid, died, because she'd distract him? She couldn't bear to be the cause of someone suffering. Not that she believed Jake's assessment of her. *You're a beautiful woman, Sarah.*

"Ha! Obviously Jacob Mitchell is a liar as well as a rogue," she muttered, kicking her white muslin skirts out of the way so she could turn and retrace her steps. She lifted a strand of sweaty hair from her neck and tucked it back into its bun. Her a beauty? With mousy brown hair, strange gray eyes and an unremarkable face. "He was only trying to distract me."

And he's succeeded. Every time she stepped outside her cabin door, he appeared at her side, making her acutely aware of his size, his healthy male scent and jewel blue eyes. When he looked at her, she couldn't stop the quickening of her heartbeat or the jitteriness in her stomach. Anger, she told herself sternly, her reactions were a direct result of her anger. But it didn't end there. His presence made her painfully aware of the corselet, fastened tight around her waist.

Every time Jake came near, each of the gold squares began to warm, shooting tingles beneath her skin. She'd thought she'd imagined the bizarre sensation the first time she experienced it, but she didn't any longer. Some unnatural phenomenon caused the corselet to . . . to . . . heat up whenever she came into contact with Jake. Was it an unseen energy, she wondered, like opposing magnets? Or perhaps the artifact was cursed? She shook her head at the absurd idea. The only thing she knew for certain was that the phenomenon didn't arise because she felt any sort of guilt for deceiving him. No, something she couldn't explain was happening, an unknown element that gave her something else to worry about.

From the beginning, her situation had been perilous, but the strain of the past three weeks had begun to take its toll. The constant worry that she might slip and reveal her real name, or that Jake would learn what she had hidden in her crates or what she wore around her waist. If any of those things happened, he would take Queen Tiy from her and nothing she could do, short of killing him, she thought with a grimace, would stop him.

The possibility of failing her father the one time he'd asked for her help caused the muscles in her back to pinch. It wasn't only failing that worried her; Roger's fear of the curse was so great she didn't know how he would react. Would he eventually realize his imagination had caused his illness and recover? Or would he give up on life and waste away until he died?

She rubbed her chest to stop the pressure that was building around her heart. Roger might have been a miserable father, but he was all the family she had. She didn't want to lose him.

The *Phoenix* shuddered as Sarah turned to make another trip across her small room, throwing her off balance and knocking her against the wall. The floor tilted precariously beneath her feet, the wood groaning as the angle became more and more treacherous. She heard frantic shouts from above, but couldn't make out the words.

Were they capsizing? The sea had been rough, but no worse than they had experienced before. She pushed away from the wall and struggled to reach the door. If they were going to sink, she wasn't going down trapped inside her cabin.

She grasped the door handle just as the ship righted itself with a jerk, flinging her onto her narrow bed. The vessel's massive hull swayed, fighting the waves and gravity, the wooden strakes protesting the strain. The oil lamp swung wildly from the hook in the ceiling and her few belongings slid from the dresser to crash to the floor. Sarah scrambled from the bed, more determined than ever to reach the upper deck.

Grabbing hold of the door latch, she pulled it open. A gasp burst from her throat. Jake filled the doorway, his expression grim.

"Stay inside," he ordered.

"What's happening?"

"I don't have time to explain." He gripped her waist, forced her back a step. Sarah gasped and pushed his hands away, terrified he had felt the corselet beneath her gown.

"You'll be safe here," he told her, not indicating he'd noticed anything unusual.

Had she trusted him, she would have believed the strength behind his deep voice. She might have even turned around, sat on the bed to wait out whatever calamity had befallen the ship. But she didn't trust him. He was the enemy, the man she would best if it was the last thing she ever did. When he didn't demand to know why it felt as if she wore armor beneath her petticoat, she gripped the door and kept her ground.

"I'm not staying here," she announced, trying to move past him.

He straightened, and the pyramids of Giza couldn't have created a more effective barrier.

"Jake—"

"Do as I tell you, Sarah."

"You expect me to sit by when the ship could be in danger?"

"You going above deck will only make the situation worse."

She opened her mouth to argue, but blast it all, he was right. "If you expect me to stay here, then at least tell me what has happened. Are we sinking?"

"Not yet," he growled, the dire sound sending her panic up another notch. His blue eyes darkened with a dangerous gleam. "Have no doubt, Sarah, if we survive this, I'm going to tie you up and put you on the next ship back to England."

She ignored his threat. "Survive what?"

He ground his jaw and glared down at her as if whatever dilemma they faced were her fault. "Napoleon."

"The French general? He's here?"

"Not just the general, but what appears to be a good portion of his fleet. Anchored off the coast of Tripoli."

"How can you be certain it's him? The Royal Navy is supposed to be in the area. Perhaps you saw British ships."

His glare turned hot, as if she'd insulted him. "I'd bet Ramses' wealth that the British Navy has no idea the French have positioned themselves so close to Egypt. There's going to be a battle, sweetheart, and you've put yourself right in the middle of it."

She flushed at the endearment, regardless that Jake had made it sound like a curse. She glanced out her porthole, expecting to see enemy ships surrounding them, French flags waving, the gunports filled with cannon's ready to fire. As the *Phoenix* lifted on a wave, she saw a liquid blue sky capped with white, pillowy clouds. Riding down the swell, she glimpsed nothing but the same endless ocean she'd watched for days.

She arched a brow at him. "Are you sure you haven't over-reacted? Or perhaps you're trying to frighten me into giving up my holiday?"

"Woman, you are the most stubborn, irritating . . ." He swiped a hand though his sandy blond hair, pulling it away from his shoulders. "It's no wonder the men in your life let you take this foolish trip. They were probably relieved to be rid of you."

Despite his attempt to offend her, Jake hadn't put much heat behind the words. She obviously exasperated him, and that couldn't make her happier. "Let me pass."

"Like hell I will." He grabbed the door and so did she, willing to fight to the end before she allowed him to lock her inside.

A bell clamored topside. Jake froze, glanced at the ceiling. Grounding out a curse, he seized her by the waist. Sarah tried to twist free, but at that instant, the ship pitched leeward. She lost her balance, staggering back.

Jake's arm turned into a vise, cutting off her breath. "Hold on."

She grabbed his shoulders. He caught the doorjamb, stopping their fall. He held her snug against his chest, the heat of his body instantly soaking through her clothes. An unwelcome tingle skidded over her skin. She almost ordered him to release her, but if he did she'd fly across the room and crash into the wall. As the *Phoenix* gave a powerful shudder she looked out the porthole, and could tell they were turning hard and fast.

"What's happening?" she asked over the clamor of shouts, shifting cargo and the painful cacophony of the straining vessel.

"I assume we've been spotted and have decided to change course," he said, and unless she was hallucinating, the miserable man was smiling.

She stared at him, her mouth gaping. Was he enjoying this? She wanted to ask, but the words couldn't work past the knot of fear in her throat. She had enough to overcome, a heartless father, her own fear and ineptitude, a surly, wretched man she hated; she couldn't deal with the entire French Navy, too!

"Don't worry," Jake said, his voice softening, his arm cradling her as the ship righted itself. "We can outrun a few warships."

"How many are a few?"

"You have the prettiest eyes," he said, frowning as if the sudden admission annoyed him.

Her panic grew tenfold. Not only did Jake look like he had the insane idea of kissing her, but his fingers were splayed across her rib cage, moving lower, making her blood heat and tingle and the corselet burn against her skin.

"I have to see what's happening," she said, pushing against his chest.

"You shouldn't be here." His arm tightened into a crushing hold.

"So you've said before," she said, hating the breathless sound of her voice. "But it's really none of your business whether I go above deck or to Egypt. Now, I insist you release me."

"I wish I could."

"Let go."

His mouth closed over hers in a startling move. She tensed, overwhelmed by heat and soft lips, the scrape of his day's growth of beard. He shifted, slanting his mouth fully over hers, so her lips had no choice but to fall open. His tongue slipped inside, just long enough to fill her with his taste. Darkness and danger and rich, warm sin. The sensations left her dizzy and numb. Confused. A stunned part of her mind told her to fight, but she couldn't draw a breath, let alone push him away. She'd been kissed before, but those few times had been chaste, almost pure.

Boring.

Nothing like this.

A low growl rumbled from low inside his chest. The vibrations worked through her gown, into her blood, going deeper until she shook in response. His other hand came around her back, his fingers grazing the indention of her spine, moving up until he cupped her neck, holding her captive for the onslaught of his kiss. The ship rocked beneath her feet. She heard the splash of waves, the distinct snap of crisp white sails. But the sounds had little meaning as he stripped her resolve bare using nothing but the skill of his mouth, his strong hands, the overwhelming cloak of his body.

As quickly as he'd taken her, Jake pulled back, stopping the kiss, his breath a harsh rasp against her cheeks.

"Bloody hell," he ground out.

In one glance she took in his clenched jaw, the hard edge in his steel blue eyes, the angry tension that now radiated off his skin.

She jerked out of his hold, but she needn't have bothered. He released her so quickly, she thought he might have been struck by lightning.

Tilting her chin, her emotions close to riot proportions, she said, "For once I agree with you. Kissing me was a mistake. One you would be wise not to repeat."

The corner of his damp mouth curved in a rueful grin, the effect not coming close to reaching his eyes. "A mistake? I've made plenty of those, sweetheart, but kissing you wasn't one of them."

Blood rushed to her cheeks and a retort sprang to her lips, but the sound of heavy footsteps hurrying down the companionway stopped her from voicing it.

"There ye are," someone shouted.

Connor suddenly filled the hallway, his blood-red hair sweaty, his green eyes fierce. Bending at the waist to keep from banging his head on the ceiling, he said, "There be a chase, mon. Ye're needed topside. Captain Dunhill asked if we knew our way around a cannon. I told him aye."

"I'm right behind you," Jake said, though he didn't move when the giant Scotsman hurried up the ladder.

Jake heaved a breath, then looked at her, his gaze an intangible mixture of hot and cold, anger and lust. He glanced past her to the window. The muscles worked in his jaw and the light caught his eyes so they glowed with as much turmoil as they did excitement. *Excitement?*

It dawned on her then that he wasn't afraid of the coming battle. He enjoyed the chase, welcomed the thrill of danger. The same as her father. They both loved risking their lives, fighting sandstorms and cobras, desert robbers and ancient curses.

For Jake, kissing her had been just another game of hunt and seek and steal the prize. This time he had pursued a helpless woman instead of a tomb, she thought, clenching her hands, and had stolen a kiss instead of a mummy. He didn't care about her; she was just another token to claim. The resentments she'd harbored for a lifetime returned full force.

Well, she had a surprise in store for him. Resting her hands on her hip where prickling heat still radiated from the corselet, she welcomed the renewed strength pouring into her limbs. Standing straighter, she gathered her determination around her like a shield. Everything was a game to Jake. A mirthless smile threatened to cross her lips. He didn't know it yet, but there was one game he would never win.

Because the selfish, conniving Jacob Mitchell had already lost. He just didn't know it yet.

Chapter 5

"Someone should shoot me."

"I'll be glad tae," Connor offered with a wicked twist of his lips that might have been a smile. "After I sink one or two of those French frigates."

Scowling at the Scotsman, Jake picked up the pole with a sponge fixed to the end, dunked it into a pail of water and shoved it with all his strength down the throat of the cannon.

"Were ye want'n a bullet in the heart or perhaps just the leg?" Connor asked, adding wad and shot into the cannon's belly.

"In the head would suffice," Jake muttered, checking to make sure the iron barrel was clean.

Connor ran a thick finger along his jaw as if he were contemplating the obstacles of putting Jake out of his misery. He shook his shaggy red head, obviously not liking the odds. "Gavin still 'as use for ye, and since I try to save my kill'n for men who deserve it, I'd rather not irritate 'im by shoot'n ye without good reason. Unless ye have a good reason."

Jake grabbed the ramming pole and shoved it into the cannon to pack the ammunition, deciding he liked the Scotsman better when he didn't talk. "There should be a law against women sailing on ships."

"Yer the kind of man who believes the fairer sex should be kept home, in their place, are ye?" Connor grunted as if he agreed. "Lady Elston is surely the fairest of the fairer sex that I've seen in some time."

Imagining the huge Scotsman noticing or coming near a woman as fragile as Sarah stirred awake a primitive side Jake hadn't known he possessed. He gripped the rammer in his fist to keep from punching the other man.

He and Connor had been assigned to supervise the cannons on the starboard side of the upper deck, but now Jake wondered if he wouldn't prefer something a few levels down where it was dark and dank and he could be alone with his thoughts. He discarded the idea. The more distance he kept between Sarah and him, the better they'd both be. He was certain she needed time to recover from their latest encounter, while he . . . he needed someone to beat some sense into him.

Jake rubbed the back of his hand over his mouth, remembering the impression of Sarah's lips. Nearly an hour had passed since he'd rushed from her cabin and he still had no idea why he'd kissed her. True, during the past weeks, he'd wondered how her thick dark hair would feel in his hands, or why her skin always made him think of rain and soft woman. But he knew better than to actually touch her. Get to know her a little better, yes, frighten her into returning to England, definitely. But not terrify her with a kiss.

Jake paused with the rammer in his hands, envisioning her gripping his arms, her body tense, her mouth soft and wet beneath his. She hadn't seemed overly frightened. Resistant at first, and he couldn't say she had returned his kiss, but she hadn't fought him, either.

Had she simply endured his touch? He scowled, not liking that possibility at all. He glanced at the hatchway again, once more seeing the fierce light in her pearl gray eyes, the hot color in her cheeks. She didn't strike him as the "enduring" type. She was a fighter, stubborn, determined, willful.

Radiant.

He drew a deep breath to clear his mind, inhaled the bracing tang of the briny sea, the burning sun, and—God help him—*rain.* That soft scent that never seemed to leave Sarah's skin.

"Bloody hell." He faced the stern where four French frigates were in close pursuit. "All right, you whoresons. If you want a fight, I'm ready."

"I'm not one tae run from a skirmish, Jake-o, but are ye sure 'tis the French yer mad at?"

"I'm bloody mad at the world right now." He retrieved another wad and crammed it into the cannon to hold the ball in place. The physical exertion fueled his anger with Stuart Kilvington for lying, with the museum curator for believing the spineless marquis, with Roger for betraying him, and with Napoleon for creating a new threat. But mostly he was angry at himself for becoming distracted by a woman he had no business worrying about, or touching, or God forbid kissing. And he was furious because he had absolutely no business wanting to kiss her again.

He ran his splayed fingers through his hair and hissed another curse. No way in hell would he kiss her again; he wouldn't even think about it. Right now his entire focus had to be on evading Napoleon's ships. If they survived that, then he had to finalize his plans for finding Roger after they docked in Rosetta.

"Helmsman," Captain Dunhill shouted, "ten degrees starboard."

The helmsman confirmed the order and spun the wheel. The bow veered to the right. Jake braced his legs against the pull of the ship as it skittered over waves. He'd sailed these waters more times than he cared to count. Someday he would buy a house in Egypt and never leave. But for now, England, with its British Museum and curators and social barriers, was home.

The captain continued shouting orders aloft, changing

sails so they could capture as much wind as they could hold. The *Phoenix* sped over jewel blue water toward Egypt's coast—where the British Navy should be. But Egypt was still two days away, too far to help them now. Jake climbed the ladder to the top stern deck and maneuvered to the rear of the ship for a better look at their enemy. As fast as the *Phoenix* sailed, she had little hope of outrunning the French vessels, which were more streamlined and manned by soldiers who were trained in battle, not in shipping cargo like Captain Dunhill's crew.

The frigates cut through rolling surf, impervious to the waves that buffeted the *Phoenix's* pot-bellied hull, closing the distance, eating the space between them. Jake doubted they had half an hour before they would let loose their cannons. He clenched his fists. He couldn't lose everything this way. Two more days, two lousy days, and he would have had Queen Tiy back.

"We can't outrun them, can we?"

Jake whipped around to see Sarah standing ten feet away, her brow creased with a worried frown, her shoulders iron straight. Her hands fluttered at the waist of her frothy white gown, lightly touching her stomach, then her hips, a nervous habit he'd noticed her doing before.

"Go below, Sarah," he told her, tempted to grab her by the arm and escort her himself, but he knew better than to touch her again. Especially when she looked so small and vulnerable.

"I had to see . . . I was going crazy, Jake. Not knowing."

He cursed on a sigh.

"Can we? Outrun them?"

"Captain Dunhill is doing everything he can." *And it isn't damn near enough.* He wanted to reassure her, promise her everything would be all right, but he couldn't lie to her. *Right, I can kiss her against her will, but I can't lie to her.* Jake pressed the heel of one hand to his eyes as a vicious pounding started behind his skull. God help him, the woman was making him crazy. Gavin was right; he shouldn't have gotten involved with her. She'd made the decision to travel into a dangerous situation; it wasn't up to him to promise her anything.

"Is there something I can do to help?"

"You can stay below," he growled, moving past her. "Hidden out of the way."

Hearing the bitterness in her voice, he paused.

Her mouth forming a thin line, she looked at him with eyes as clear as cut glass, giving him a startling view of her resentment. "Since I have some experience with tucking myself away into quiet little corners, I should be a great help to everyone."

He narrowed his gaze, trying to interpret her flash of temper, but in the next instant, her emotions were hidden behind a veil of cool marble. "You'll be hurt if you stay up here, Sarah."

She nodded, broke his gaze and started to leave.

The booming sound was so unexpected, Jake didn't identify it at first. A water barrel falling, perhaps, or a sail snapping against the wind. When he saw the plume of white smoke curl off the bow of the closest frigate ship, his blood went cold.

"Sweet Mary." Jake moved in front of Sarah as if he could protect her with his body. "They can't be within range yet."

"Fire in the wind," a sailor shouted from his position high on the main mast.

The ball struck the sea barely twenty feet from the stern. Water spewed into the air and over the rail. Jake turned and caught Sarah in his arms, barely registering her shocked expression before he pulled her against him. The spray pelted his back, soaking him. He didn't need to wait for the next cannon blast to know another one would be coming and it would be even closer.

He gripped Sarah's hand and pulled her toward the

ladder. He jumped to the lower deck, turned to help her down. To his surprise, she jumped just as he had, falling into his raised hands and landing hard against his chest. He stumbled back. *Christ, she was heavier than she looked.* Another time and he would have laughed at her spirit. Now he just wanted to get her to safety so he could return to his station.

Another explosion ripped through the air. Jake ran to the hatchway, Sarah in tow. She kept up, leaping over coiled rope and a bucket of water. Passing Connor, who waited for the command to return fire with a lit fuse in his hand, Jake felt a tingling at the base of his skull. An instant later a cannonball crashed through the deck behind him. Wood splintered, flying like a thousand lethal knives. He heard screams, but he didn't stop. He had to get Sarah below, regardless that she wouldn't be much safer in her cabin than on deck.

He felt her tug on his hand, but he didn't slow. The hatchway was just ahead.

"Jake!"

"Don't stop!"

"He's hurt." She pulled his arm again, this time hard enough to make him look back. "Jake, he's been hit!"

Glancing past her, he saw Connor lying flat on his back, his arms flung out to the sides, the fuse doused in his massive hand. Blood streaked his face and turned his black shirt shiny and wet.

Jake gripped Sarah's shoulders and shoved her toward the hatchway. He lifted Connor by the shoulders and pulled him away from the cannon. "Go down without me."

"I can help him."

"Sarah—"

She fell to her knees at Connor's side. Balancing herself against the ship's chaotic rocking, she took the hem of her white muslin gown and carefully wiped away the blood on Connor's face. Jake knelt beside her, scanned the Scotsman's wounds. Most seemed superficial, cuts along his brow, a two-inch slice down his cheek.

"He'll survive," he told Sarah, whose hands were trembling, her face alarmingly pale.

She managed a jerky nod as her fingers hovered over Connor's bloody shirt. "His chest."

Jake caught her hands in his. Her tremors shot up his arm. "There isn't anything we can do for him now. When this is over . . ." Bloody hell, he thought, if he was going to lie to her now would be the time. But blast it all, the only words racing through his mind were that when all of this was over, they'd all be dead.

She looked away and tensed, gripping his shirtsleeve. "Jake, look."

He followed her gaze through the gunport. Another frigate moved forward, coming parallel to the *Phoenix*. Jake had no doubt the French cannons were within range to hit their ship, but were Jake's cannons within striking range of the French bastards?

"Men!" He shouted to the crew. "Ready your fuses!"

Jake welcomed the hum of tension racing beneath his skin. It cleared his mind, sharpened his vision. Taking the fuse from Connor's limp fingers and relighting it, he held it to his cannon. With one last look at Sarah's upturned face, he gave the order.

"Fire!"

The world exploded.

Sarah recoiled, pressing her hands over her ears to shut out the deafening roar. Vibrations pushed through her body so hard that for an instant she thought she would fly apart. White, choking smoke billowed over the deck. She could hardly see, and tried not to breathe.

"Bloody hell!" Blistering anger turned Jake's face red, his eyes violent blue.

"What happened?"

"We missed the bloody ship. Reload!"

Another explosion rent the air. She had no idea where it came from, the *Phoenix* or from the French.

Jake stood before her, fists clenched, shouting orders. Taking a rope, he strained until his tendons bulged to pull the cannon away from the gunport. He grabbed a long pole with cloth wrapped around the end, plunged it into a water bucket and pushed it down the cannon's mouth. Tossing the stick aside, he reloaded, then packed it tight with another stick. Pushing the cannon back into place, he glanced at the men to either side of him, then gave the order to fire once more.

This time, Sarah leaned over Connor to shield him, and covered her ears before the explosion, but the thunderous vibrations tore through her just the same. Jake started the reloading process again. Sarah saw the other cannons had two men manning them, but with Connor hurt, Jake was alone. She hesitated an instant, looked down at Connor and saw his eyes were open. He nodded for her to go. She picked up a cartridge and pushed it into the opening. Jake glared at her. She saw in his eyes that he wanted to order her below, but he didn't. Thank God.

She couldn't stay in her cabin if she could help save their lives.

Jake shouted for the fuses to be lit. Seconds later, the guns erupted, pitching the ship to one side as if a giant hand had slapped it. He gave another order and the process started over again, then again. Sarah did her part, lifting cannon balls and wad until her back ached and her arms were numb, and her white gown was soiled and ripped. She moved in a daze of smoke and shouts, of crashing wood and the acrid smell of blood. In some corner of her mind, she knew other men besides Connor were hurt, lying where they fell, bleeding, in pain. She wanted to help them, but Jake needed her more. If they couldn't fight back the French, none of them would survive.

"Ready!" Jake shouted. "Fire!"

The *Phoenix* heaved a massive shudder beneath the report of two dozen guns. Lifting another cannon ball, her back screaming in pain, her eyes filling with tears, she dared a glance over the rail. Her heart stopped mid-beat. A fire burned out of control on one of the frigates. Another ship had left the battle to save the sailors who had jumped to safety in the water. That left two ships, but where were they?

Jake took the cannon ball from her hands and returned it to the bucket. Pushing her toward the hatchway, he told her, "Go below, Sarah. You've done enough."

She shook her head, fear and hope pressing against her chest. "We're not finished. There are two more."

Guns on the opposite side of the ship exploded as they fired on the French. Jake glanced over her head, his eyes glazed with the fever of battle. Turning those hot blue eyes on her, he said, "Please, Sarah, I can't fight them and worry about you, too."

Taken back by the earnestness in his voice, never having heard anything so raw and sincere, she couldn't argue. Swallowing, she whispered, "Go."

Leaving his cannon, Jake ran to where Eli, Thatcher, and Gavin were operating a pair of guns positioned on the larboard side of the ship. Sarah pressed her hands to her mouth as two French vessels came into view, so close she imagined she could reach out and touch them. She flinched as the charges went off. Had the *Phoenix* hit the frigates? Would their enemy now sink in the beautiful Mediterranean Sea? Was this nightmare almost over? Or had the *Phoenix* missed? Part of her wanted to rush to the railing and see, the other part wanted to flee to her cabin and hide from the sounds of war and destruction.

Instead, she retrieved a fresh pail of water and knelt

beside Connor. He was unconscious again, his face already showing signs of bruising. Using his knife, she cut a strip of muslin off her skirt and began cleaning his wounds. As Jake had said, the cuts were superficial, but he had a huge lump on the back of his head.

She unlaced his shirt and cleaned his chest, shutting out the sounds of crying men, of screams and cheers. She closed her mind to everything except helping Connor. Then she'd find another injured man and help him. She wouldn't listen, or watch, or load the cannons. She would help those she could until there were none left to tend.

Tears welled in her eyes, blurring her vision. How had she gotten here, in the middle of a battle? She'd never seen anything so brutal, wasn't prepared for it. Jake had warned her of the dangers. Roger must have known as well, yet he'd insisted she'd be safe. Had he believed that or had he sent her into a perilous situation hoping she would save him from a curse? She didn't want to believe her own father could be so heartless. Perhaps he hadn't realized Napoleon was so close. Perhaps his illness clouded his thinking. Perhaps . . .

She pressed the back of her wrist to her brow and stopped the useless conjectures. She was here because she'd made the decision to help her father. If she died, it would be her own fault.

"Sarah."

She kept working, using another strip of her skirt to soak up more of Connor's blood. How much could a man's body hold? She was covered in his blood, had cleaned his wounds again and again, yet his cuts continued to seep. She tied a strip of her gown around his arm, praying it would be enough until she could get him below.

"Sarah."

She heard her name spoken in a deep, soft voice, but she couldn't stop her efforts. She blinked, but her eyes wouldn't clear. Tears she hadn't been aware of fell down her cheeks, hot streaks against her flushed face. And breathing—she could hardly fill her lungs with air.

"Sarah, sweetheart, stop. Look at me."

A strong hand cupped her chin, forcing her head up. Jake was there, kneeling before her, watching her with a worried frown. It was then she noticed the quiet. She glanced over the deck where men were picking up the pieces of a broken mast and throwing them over the rail. Eli and Thatcher, worn and battered, were carrying the wounded below. Her breath hitched in relief that the two men were safe. A small fire burned near the capstan, but several sailors were beating it out. Everyone's faces were streaked with smoke, their clothes torn and dirty, but several men were smiling and one man even slapped Gavin on his back and laughed.

"It's over?" she asked Jake.

"Yes." He cradled her jaw in his hand, his fingers curving around her head. "Christ, woman, you scared ten years off my life."

"*I* scared *you?*" she asked in disbelief.

"I could hardly think without worrying that you would be hurt."

He'd been concerned about her? She shook her head. Surely not. No one, not her father, and especially not Jake, *ever* worried about her well-being.

"I'm taking you to your cabin before you collapse."

He started to rise, but she gripped his arm. "It's truly over?"

"Yes, Sarah. You're safe." The corner of his mouth curved with a wolfish grin. "When we crippled the third ship, the last one broke off and ran with his tail tucked between his legs."

There would be no more fighting, no cannons or smoke or men tossed aside like discarded dolls. When a sob caught in her throat, she threw her arms around

Jake and pressed her face into his neck. She swallowed, refusing to fall apart now that the threat was over. But when Jake's arms circled her back, she thought she might lose the battle and burst into tears. He was warm and strong and whole, holding her as if he cared. The same as when he'd kissed her. Soft and gentle, making her feel protected. Wanted.

She held on tight, wanting just one more moment.

Then she remembered whom she was holding. *Jake Mitchell,* the man she had hated for most of her life. She tried to dredge up the old feelings of rage, but they only sputtered inside her chest before vanishing altogether. Perhaps, she thought, at this very moment, it didn't matter that he was her enemy. They were both alive and safe.

She could start hating him again tomorrow.

Chapter 6

Weaving a path through the crowded market sweat trickled between Sarah's breasts and down her back. The heat was a living thing, rising up from the ground, wrapping around her like a cloak. So unlike England, where clear, warm days were precious and far between. She ignored her discomfort and scanned the busy street, hardly knowing where to look first.

The singing lilt of Arabic filled the air as shopkeepers tried to lure her and other passersby to their stalls. She couldn't understand a word they said, and at the moment she didn't care. The world was full of sights and sounds she'd never imagined. And smells—all vying for a place—garlic and fried onions, the pungent scent of roasting coffee, the choking stink of camels and too many unwashed bodies. She should have been repulsed, but she wasn't. The instant she'd walked down the *Phoenix's* gangplank, stepping for the first time in her life onto foreign soil, she'd felt a connection to her father, almost understood why he kept returning to this land.

People and animals jammed the narrow streets of Rosetta. She'd learned from Captain Dunhill the name meant rosy in Latin. She could understand why the ancient Egyptians had chosen the name. Despite the unpleasant smells, the city was beautiful. Full of stone mosques and inns, mud-brick homes with lavish gardens that defied the burning sun. She'd expected to see an ocean of desert sand, not dirt so black and rich that it would cause every farmer in England to weep with envy.

Rosetta, she'd also learned was the place where a slab of black basalt had been discovered containing inscriptions in hieroglyphics, demotic, and Greek. It amazed her that without the Rosetta Stone, no one would have been able to interpret the hieroglyphics on tombs or temples. Egypt's past would still be a mystery.

"Lady Pendergrass," Eli whispered at her side.

"Shh, I told you not to call me that," she told him, tugging her bonnet down to hide her face. "I'm Lady Elston."

"I thought now that we weren't on the ship with that Mitchell fellow ye'd want me tae use your real name."

She cast an uneasy glance at the nearby stalls, half expecting to see "that Mitchell fellow" hovering nearby, as he had done since their encounter with the French. Jake had watched her with the fierceness of a hawk tracking a mouse. When they'd spoken, he'd been polite, but distant, his jaw tight, his blue eyes dark with disapproval . . . and worry. An expression she wasn't accustomed to seeing in people, and one she didn't want from Jake.

Though he hadn't repeated his arguments about her returning to England, the air had vibrated with his silent message. He'd been right about the dangers she'd face—and the trip wasn't over yet—he expected her to act like a sensible female and go home. Once he realized she intended to stay in Egypt, fury had shimmered off him like sparks off an exploding gun. But he hadn't said a word, or touched her, or tried to kiss her again.

"Thank goodness," she said fanning her face.

After surviving the battle with the French and witnessing Jake's unexpected concern for her, she'd had a hard time dredging up her anger toward him, a condition she hadn't thought possible.

She faced her helpers. "As long as Jake is within fifty miles of us, you'll continue calling me Lady Elston. He can't ever, and I mean *ever*, learn who I am." She didn't want to even think about how he would react should he learn the truth.

"Yes, ma'am," Eli said, with Thatcher echoing him.

She forced herself to walk past stalls filled with brass vases and colorful pottery, spices hanging from poles, and displays of long, flowing garments that begged her to stop for a closer look. The sweeping robes and loose dresses appeared much more comfortable, not to mention practical, than her shell blue gown with its long tight sleeves and double-ruff neckline. She wanted to stop and explore, purchase a few items to take home as souvenirs, but now wasn't the time. There was something else she had to find that was far more important.

"He should be here someplace," she said, turning in a circle, beginning to fear that she'd gone the wrong way.

"Who would that be, my lady?" Eli asked, glaring at the people bustling past him.

"Lofty Ahmed. The man Roger said I should hire to take us down the Nile. Oh, this is taking too long. I should have left one of you on the ship."

"This ain't no place for a lady," Thatcher growled protectively, a scowl flashing behind his grizzly black beard. Sarah smiled despite her building worry.

Then her heart flipped. "Look!"

She pulled her father's letter from her purse, reading his instructions once more. Smiling, certain she would succeed in the second part of her trip, she stepped over a pile of fresh dung and knocked on a door of sun-bleached wood. She didn't have time to waste. Queen Tiy was still on board the *Phoenix*.

And so was Jake Mitchell.

The crowd moved like the constant surge of an incoming wave.

Buzzards wheeled round and round high overhead, gliding on the sun-baked sky. Below, in the market bordering the rich silt banks of the Nile, too many people were pressed into too small a space, women haggling over outrageous prices and vendors incensed at being called a thief. The flowing dialect added to the cacophony of wagon wheels bumping over hard-packed earth and barking dogs chasing schools of children. Flies swarmed, irritating man and beast alike.

If not for the French soldiers scouting every street and the lack of information he'd gleaned about Roger from his sources, Jake would have been a happy man.

Standing in the shadows of a shabby townhouse of mud brick, he watched another patrol of Napoleon's soldiers march past—the third group he'd evaded so far—sending people scurrying out of their path.

Scowling, he turned to the man behind him. "He's not in the city."

"Perhaps Lord Pendergrass was attacked by the French frigates, as we were," Gavin said, his attention never leaving the busy street.

Jake followed his gaze, relaxing slightly when the armed solders disappeared around a corner. He scanned the vendors' dark shops, the stalls set up in the street, his temper rising when he didn't find what he wanted. Then with a start, he realized he wasn't looking for a thin, wiry man in his late fifties but looking for a petite woman dressed in a ridiculous blue gown and matching bonnet. Jake bit out a curse.

He'd watched Sarah leave the ship with her two companions and had had to fight every impulse to stop himself from dragging her back onboard and locking her inside her cabin. She hadn't even had the sense to dress in galabiya as he did so she'd blend in with the locals and avoid the French soldiers' notice. No, she'd marched through the dangerous streets of Rosetta as if she were taking a stroll through Hyde Park. Bloody hell, but the woman needed someone to protect her, or shake some sense into her. Or both. And it irritated the hell out of him that he wanted to be the one to do it.

"Blasted, fool woman," Jake muttered under his breath.

"Excuse me?"

"Nothing."

Gavin arched a brow as if he knew exactly what, or who, Jake had been thinking about. "Have you considered the possibility that Roger's ship sank in the Mediterranean?"

Jake had considered it, but he wasn't about to believe it. Roger was too stubborn and too shrewd to die unless it was on his agenda.

"He's not dead. I'd know it if he were. A plague of locust will undoubtedly sweep down on me on that fateful day," Jake said, disgusted. "Besides, it doesn't matter if he's been here or not. I know where he's going."

"The Valley of the Queen?"

"Where we found Queen Tiy. You return to the *Phoenix* and help Connor gather our gear. He'll probably insist he can do it on his own, but he's still injured. I'm going to hire a felucca." When Gavin raised a brow in question, he added, "A small boat that will take us down the Nile."

Gavin didn't look pleased with the idea of leaving Jake on his own, but he didn't argue. Drawing the cowl of his galabiya down to hide his face, he said, "Watch your back."

Jake grunted in acknowledgment. *Watch your back.* Something he had failed to do time and again because he had trusted the wrong people. But not any longer. He'd learned the hard way that the only person he could trust was himself.

It was a lesson he didn't plan to forget.

Moving into the crowd, he worked his way toward the cove where he knew of several boatmen for hire. It bothered him that no one had seen a trace of Roger. Had he sailed to Alexandria instead of Rosetta? It didn't make sense. Alexandria made for a longer trip down the Nile. Or was it as Gavin said, and Jake feared, that Roger's ship had been attacked by the French and was now sitting at the bottom of the Mediterranean? Lost forever.

Jake shook his head, refusing to believe that he could lose Queen Tiy, and his friend, in such a senseless way. Lost in thought, Jake stumbled, nearly knocking a woman over. He caught her by the waist to stop them both from falling. The feel of soft cloth and the scent of rain alerted him to who he held an instant before saw her.

Sarah, all flushed cheeked and dazzling gray eyes.

"Jake," she said, quickly stepping back so he was forced to release her waist. "I didn't see you."

"It was my fault," he said, annoyed that his hands tingled simply from touching her. "I didn't hurt you, did I?"

"No, I'm fine." She squared her shoulders and her hands moved nervously over her stomach. "But I'm in a hurry."

She turned to rush off, but he caught her arm, knowing he shouldn't, knowing he should just let her go wherever the hell she wanted to. Yet he heard himself ask, "Where are you going?"

"To an inn, not far from here." She smiled, but the effort failed to brighten her eyes. Instead, they turned as dark and restless as the Nile during the flood.

"So you can travel to Giza and paint the pyramids," he stated.

"Exactly."

"You're a fool, Sarah—"

He heard a warning cough and glanced behind her to see Eli and Thatcher, arms crossed over solid chests. Beside them was a donkey-driven wagon loaded with her crates. "I told myself I wouldn't say this again, but reconsider, Sarah. It's not safe here. Napoleon's soldiers are everywhere."

"I know, I've seen them, and they haven't bothered me."

"Blast it, woman, there is going to be a war." He moved closer to her, forcing her to tilt her head to keep his gaze. "If they think you're anyone of importance, they'll hold you for ransom. That is, if they don't kill you first."

She flinched, but the stubborn line of her jaw didn't change.

Unable to control the gnawing, unwanted worry he felt for her, he gripped her arms and hauled her so close her face was an inch from his. He could smell the soap from her bath on her warm skin, see the determination in the gray depths of her eyes. He didn't want to frighten her, but damn it all, as much as he wanted to stay out of her life, he couldn't.

"I won't be here to help you," he said.

"I have Eli and Thatcher," she told him, pressing her palms against his chest, igniting sparks of tension and desire that burned through his blood. Swallowing, she added, "I don't need you."

"Like hell you don't," he growled and closed his mouth over hers, surprising her as much as him. He quieted her gasp and kissed her, wanting her to take back her lie. She did need him. He kissed her hard and deep and fast, needing to shatter her control the way she shattered his. Her hands clenched his galabiya, and he felt a shudder run through her body. Her breath mixed with his, warm and moist, making him want to simultaneously damn her and claim her as his own.

An iron hand clamped down on his shoulder. He broke the kiss, not needing to know that her brute guards stood on either side of him.

He stared into Sarah's upturned face, saw the battle of desire and anger taking place in her eyes. God help him, he wanted to kiss her again, and again. And he didn't know why. Not really. How, in the name of God, had this woman worked her way beneath his skin? And why now?

"It's too dangerous to stay here, Sarah," he said, his voice rough, unrecognizable. "Return to England."

She pulled out of his hold, her chest rising as she struggled to breathe. She glanced at the people who had stopped to stare, then turned those gray eyes back to him. "The only thing I seem to be in danger of is you, Jake Mitchell."

He tensed, too incensed to say another word as she turned on her dainty little heels and rushed into the crowds. He'd tried to help her and she refused to listen. There was nothing else he could do but hope her guards would keep her safe.

Grinding his teeth and clenching his fists, Jake turned in the opposite direction and told himself for the hundredth time to forget her. Because after today, he'd never see Lady Sarah Elston and her wide gray eyes again.

Sarah studied the two feluccas, bobbing like a set of child's toys on a giant sea. After sailing on the stout, English-made *Phoenix,* these shallow, broad-beamed, single-mast boats hardly looked seaworthy. With only one deck, a tarp mid-ship provided the only protection from the grueling sun. A screen at one end offered the only source of privacy. Her stomach churned into a knot. She wasn't particularly afraid of water, having learned how to swim at a pond near her boarding school. But on the *Phoenix,* the ocean had been a dozen or more feet below her. On the felucca, all she would have to do to touch the Nile was reach out with her hand.

"I'll swear off ale, I give me word I will, if I never 'ave tae move those crates again." Breathing hard, Eli bent his round body over and rested his hands on his knees.

"We're all battened down, my lady," Thatcher said, wiping sweat from his brow with his forearm. "But there ain't much room left."

She nodded. "Which is why I hired two of Mr. Ahmed's boats."

It wasn't just the size of the crates that had motivated her decision to spend more of the money Roger had given her than she'd planned, it was the weight of Queen Tiy's gold coffin that convinced her two boats were necessary. The first boat held the box packed with the queen's canopic jars and jewelry, a trunk filled with Sarah's clothing, several others loaded with the tools, tents, and supplies Roger had told her to bring, plus the food and fresh water Thatcher had miraculously purchased that would have to last their entire trip. As the first crew boarded, the felucca's railing dipped perilously close to the waterline. Sarah was certain that if one more item were added, or if a tiny wave were to strike the hull, the boat would sink.

In the second felucca, where she planned to ride, the crate with Queen Tiy's coffin filled the center, leaving space for Sarah, Eli, Thatcher, and the steersmen with room to spare. The trip would be far from comfortable, but she wasn't about to complain.

"You are ready to sail, yes?" Lofty Ahmed asked, his coffee-brown face beaming with a smile that made the fine hairs at the base of Sarah's neck stand on end. His smile never quite reached his eyes and he never met her gaze. If it hadn't been for her father's assurance that she could trust the man, she would have hired someone else. Or at least tried to. She'd learned that Napoleon and his army of scientists and soldiers had confiscated every boat available in their war to oust the British. She considered it a miracle that Mr. Lofty had kept a few boats hidden. But even then she'd had to pay an outrageous price. She could have used her name, since Mr. Lofty supposedly knew her father, but Roger had warned her not to.

"We must leave before the sun sets, yes?" Mr. Lofty

said, bobbing his head in a manner that caused Sarah to copy him.

"Yes, we can leave." The sun hovered low on the horizon, washing the buildings and sky with a surreal, magical glow.

With Thatcher's help she climbed into the second felucca and took a seat on a side bench near the stern. She set her satchel filled with her art supplies and the iron ball grenades that Roger had given her in her lap. She wasn't sure why she kept the weapons that were supposedly powerful enough to destroy the White Tower with her, except that, like the corselet around her waist, she felt better knowing they were close. Her two guards claimed a place near the bow, folded their arms and promptly fell asleep, no doubt exhausted from hauling her secret cargo.

Her stomach clenched with excitement and fear. The next part of her adventure was about to begin. She had no idea what she would face next. Desert mountains, perhaps, valleys, the River Nile and all its life-giving mystery. Unbearable heat, she added, fanning herself with her handkerchief, moving the dry, hot air about her face. She regretted not purchasing one of the loose-robe garments she'd seen in the market.

Before boarding she'd taken the time to visit the bath house and had scrubbed her body until her skin was pink. Then she'd washed her hair with a spicy soap the woman had given her to use. For the first time since leaving London she felt completely clean, renewed and ready to tackle whatever came next.

As the boatsman in the first felucca pushed away from shore, Sarah held her breath, anticipating the moment the steersman on her craft would dig his long pole into the water and send them floating down the Nile. The Nile! She could hardly believe she had made it this far. Especially with Jake Mitchell in pursuit.

She smiled, closed her eyes and tilted her face to catch the heat of the sun. Warmth poured into her limbs, strengthening her declaration that nothing would stop her now. When Jake had bumped into her in the market, she'd thought he'd finally guessed her real identity. She'd been so certain he would demand to see inside her crates, that her mouth had gone dry and her heart had hammered against her ribs. She'd barely been able to speak.

But he hadn't demanded that she open her crates, he'd only kissed her. Senseless. Again. How could a man overwhelm every thought in her mind, numb her ability to do anything except become lost in the feel of his mouth moving over hers. And his taste, heavens, she'd always thought of Jake Mitchell as a devil, and now she knew he tasted like sin.

Sarah's mind began to spin with the memory, but when her skin began to tingle she snapped her eyes open and shook her head. Jake didn't affect her *that way*. He didn't and he couldn't because she hated him. He'd stolen her place in her father's life, and had never considered what it had cost her. He'd been selfish, flourishing beneath her father's affection, while she sat forgotten and unwanted. Yes, Jake Mitchell did affect her, but it was animosity, not desire that caused her palms to sweat and her stomach to flutter.

Sarah bent her head and briefly closed her eyes, but the images she saw were of Jake fighting fire and cannon shots to save their ship, his urgency to get her to safety, and the burning desire that had smoldered in his eyes after he'd kissed her. Sarah pressed a hand to her brow, but the images wouldn't fade. She realized she could lie to Jake about who she was, but she couldn't lie to herself about how the man she hated stirred a deep, unwanted craving inside her.

Well, fine, she thought, sighing with disgust. Perhaps she did desire him. He was sinfully handsome in an irritatingly blond, tanned, rugged sort of fashion, but that didn't mean anything. Desire was an emotion, one she could control. Just like her hatred.

She heard shouts in Arabic and her boat gave a hard lurch. She glanced up, expecting to see the steersman named Hamada maneuvering them into the river with his long reed pole. But Hamada was watching Mr. Lofty argue with a group of native men who were wearing striped, loose-fitting robes, their hoods drawn up to protect their faces from the sun. Sarah fanned herself, but only succeeded in stirring more of the hot, sticky air. She really should have purchased one of the local outfits. Perhaps she would when she reached Thebes.

"Is there a problem?" she asked Hamada, standing to get a better look. He glanced at her, his face split with a toothless grin and nodded his turban-wrapped head.

"Can you tell me what it is?"

His smile expanded and his nod increased in enthusiasm.

Sarah smiled back, realizing he didn't understand a word she said. "Well, I hope Mr. Lofty doesn't take long."

She ran her hands over her waist, pressing the warm gold of the corselet against her skin. A shiver of unease ran through her limbs. The threat of discovery wouldn't be over until the Nile stood between her and Jake Mitchell. Only then would she be able to relax. And then not for long. He would travel to the Valley of the Queens, too. She had a headstart on him, but she didn't dare go to the queen's tomb until she was sure Jake had given up his search for her father. After studying the map Roger had given her, Sarah had decided on an alternate plan. She would travel to a town on the outskirts of the Valley of the Queens named Deir el-Medineh and rent a house until Jake returned to England—empty-handed. She felt certain he was too impatient and high-strung to stay for long.

Then she would place Queen Tiy in her tomb according to Roger's instructions and seal her inside forever. Afterwards, perhaps she and Roger would start over.

Resuming her seat, Sarah clenched her hands in her lap and forced herself to stay calm. A few more minutes and she wouldn't have a thing to worry about—except cobras and scorpions and French soldiers and . . . She cut off the growing list of the dangers she still faced. Thinking about them didn't help.

Finally Mr. Lofty started for the boat, the three men he'd been talking to following in his wake. Sarah frowned. She hoped there wasn't going to be another delay.

Mr. Lofty jumped on board, spat out something in Arabic, then turned to her. "We ready now."

"Wonderful. Who are those men . . ." She trailed off as one by one the three men climbed into the felucca. "What's going on? Why are they getting on my boat?"

The last man dropped his satchel, pushed his hood back and shouted, "You!"

The blood rushed from Sarah's head as she stared into a pair of blue eyes gone wide with surprise. Eyes she'd hoped never to see again. Jake Mitchell. Dear God.

"What are you doing here? Never mind. Get off my boat!" She faced Mr. Lofty. "Get him off my boat!"

"I have room. He pay my price. Everybody happy, yes?"

"No!"

Mr. Lofty clapped his hands twice and rattled another order to Hamada. The steersman dug into the shore with his pole, sending the vessel into the Nile with a violent lurch. Sarah stumbled, catching herself against the edge of Queen Tiy's crate. Dear God.

This can't be happening.

Jake gripped her arm to steady her. She shook him off and would have stepped back, but there wasn't any place to go except into the river. "You have no right to be here. I paid for the use of this boat. I want you off right now."

"Is that so?" Jake arched a brow, his face a tight mask of annoyance. "You're supposed to be tucked away at an inn in Rosetta, preparing to paint the pyramid's at Giza."

"And I'm going to."

"Ahmed didn't mention stopping at Giza, Sarah." He turned to the boatsman. "Are we stopping at Giza, Ahmed?"

The little man held out his hands and shrugged. "If you wish, *Maulâ,* but many French soldiers are there."

"How far down the Nile are you taking Lady Elston?"

"Thebes, *Maulâ,* same as you and your friends."

"Well," Jake arched a brow, his expression bordering hostile. "Isn't that convenient."

Mr. Lofty nodded. "*Ma'lish!*"

"What did he say?" Sarah demanded.

A muscle flexed in Jake's jaw. "There isn't an English word for it. Basically, it means don't worry, things will work out fine."

"I won't stand for this," she told him. She'd had to suffer his presence on the *Phoenix,* but this was *her* boat!

"I couldn't agree more. '*Ma'lish*' doesn't apply here. Rosetta is an English garden compared to Thebes. There is no law except what the local leaders make. Skirmishes erupt between the British, French and Sâlimûn without notice."

"The Sâlimûn?"

"Evil-doers. The lawless. And, sweetheart," he added, his jaw clenching so tight she thought it might break, "once they start shooting they won't stop if a lady gets in the way."

Jake reached out as if to take hold of her arm, but he fisted his hand and lowered it to his side instead. "You can't travel there."

"I know what I'm doing." Yet the images he created made her heart hammer against her chest. Could Thebes really be as dangerous as he claimed? If so, why hadn't

Roger warned her? He'd said Napoleon wouldn't be a threat, but his fleet had nearly destroyed her ship. Who was she to believe? Her own father or the man who had taken her place in Roger's life?

No, Jake had to be exaggerating because he was irritated that she refused to obey him like a good little girl.

Jake glanced at the crate holding Queen Tiy's mummy and ran his hand over the nailed lid. Panic flooded Sarah's stomach, but she managed to fight the urge to jerk his hand away.

"You're being foolish with your life," he told her, bending close to her, sounding once more as if he cared. "What is so urgent that you have to sail to Thebes with your belongings now?"

Unnerved by the concern in his voice, she countered with, "Why are you asking so many questions that are really none of your business?"

"Yes, Jake," Gavin said from a few paces behind them. "She really isn't any of your concern."

She would have thanked the earl if not for the cool disdain in his voice.

"You lied to me," Jake said, ignoring the earl.

"I . . . I . . ." Her mind went numb.

"Why?" His voice was a low rumble, but she heard the anger he kept on tight rein.

His questions and suppressed fury provoked her own temper. He thought her to be Sarah Elston, a spoiled member of London's elite society. Perhaps there were dangers ahead, but he had no right to question her or to be angry with her.

"Where are you going?" he demanded again, the words now as lethally hard as the look in his eyes.

She tilted her chin, dredging deep inside herself to find the strength to ignore her anxiety over what lay ahead. "Where I go or why is none of your affair. Now get off my boat."

"I'm afraid it's too late for that." He nodded toward shore. She followed his gaze and her mouth dropped open. In a matter of minutes, the Nile's current had swept them far downstream. Simmering beneath the hot, dusty sun, Rosetta had dwindled into a miniature town of ancient rosy sandcastles.

"Now," he said, stepping so close he stole her ability to breathe, "why aren't you in Rosetta? And this time, try telling me the truth."

"I don't owe you an explanation, Jake." She could smell the heat of him, see the barely controlled anger that stirred in his dark blue eyes. There was no escaping him, but she had to tell him something. "But I'll tell you why I lied about staying in Rosetta. I . . . I really don't know you. You could be a thief, or worse a man who preys on helpless women. I had no intention of informing you of my real plans."

"Which are?"

"None of your business."

He grinned, making Sarah shiver. She realized that if a snake were to smile, it would look just like Jake did right now. He didn't believe her, and she didn't care. Well, she did care, because now she was trapped with him on a vessel hardly larger than a wagon.

And this time Queen Tiy was right under his nose.

Chapter 7

Jake didn't know what he wanted to do more—shake Sarah, kiss her, or throw her overboard. Perhaps he'd do all three, and in that order. Bloody hell, but he was furious.

"I should have locked you in your cabin," he ground out, his throat tight with strain.

"I appreciate your concern," Sarah said, and unlike the confident, chilly response she'd given him before in the market, she sounded unsettled. She dabbed the perspiration at the base of her throat with her handkerchief, drawing his attention to her silky white skin and her new spicy, cinnamon scent. "But I have set a course and I'm not about to change it to appease your overactive mind."

"Overactive—" Outrage shot through him so fast and hard he wanted to hit something. "You need someone to protect you."

"I have someone." She glanced toward the bow.

He rounded on her bodyguards, needing to take his frustration out on someone because Sarah's crystal gray eyes, flushed cheeks and stubborn chin were making him insane.

Eli's arms were folded over his barreled stomach and his chin drooped onto his chest. Soft snores filled the air with every breath he took. Jake was tempted to kick the man awake. How in blazes could he protect Sarah while he was asleep? He glared at Thatcher, who was at least awake and watching his mistress, his bushy black brows pulled into a frown, his large hand fingering the hilt of a short blade at his side.

"Jake, could I have a word with you." Gavin caught his arm and forced him toward a bench opposite Sarah.

Facing the lush green bank of the Nile, Jake drew a deep breath and said under his breath, "I can't believe that woman. She has no idea what she's walked into."

"Perhaps not." Gavin stared into the dark, flowing water that churned with the warning of an imminent flood, but Jake sensed that every inch of the earl's attention was focused on the woman behind them. "Or perhaps she knows exactly what she's doing. Either way, she is not, I repeat, is *not* your concern."

"Doesn't it bother you that she misled us?"

"Yes, which is why I have no problem letting her do as she pleases."

"She doesn't understand."

"She may not know who *you* are, Jake, but she knows me by reputation. I am not a thief, and I certainly haven't set out to harm a helpless woman. She has her own reasons for being here, reasons she obviously wants to keep secret."

"That's reason enough to question her."

The earl faced him. "We did not give chase across the North Atlantic to protect a woman who has intentionally put her life in danger. I, better than most, know you cannot save a woman if she doesn't wish to be saved."

"This has nothing to do with your past, Gavin."

Something dangerous and unrelenting moved behind Gavin's eyes. "We are after Lord Pendergrass and the artifacts. Nothing more."

Clenching his jaw, Jake had to admit Gavin was right. Sarah wasn't his concern, but for some infuriating reason he couldn't turn his back on her and ignore the certainty that she was in over her head. Perhaps she misled him because, traveling alone, she had sense enough not to trust strangers. But being cautious wouldn't keep her safe much longer. Egypt was a wild and unforgiving country. The people wouldn't treat a naïve, gently reared lady any different than their own kind. Here only the strong survived.

Sighing, he made a decision. He would watch out for her as far as Thebes, but once they arrived in the ancient city and went their separate ways, he had to forget her. It was the best he could do.

"Focus on Queen Tiy, Jake." Gavin picked up his satchel and claimed a seat beside Connor. "She's all that matters."

Jake nodded, but against his will, his gaze strayed to where Sarah sat on the side bench, near the stern, the warm breeze pulling the loose strands of her sable hair. One hand gripped the rail that hovered inches above the Nile's tepid water, the other clutched a satchel so tightly her knuckles shown white. She'd made it clear from the beginning that she hadn't wanted him on the *Phoenix,* and now she wanted him off the felucca. Could her dislike of him be real or was she simply being cautious around men she didn't know?

Or was her hostility a ruse to disguise some other emotion? Aside from the fact that he wasn't an earl, what about him could she object to? He'd been a perfect gentleman, showing her nothing but respect and concern. *Except when I kissed her.*

Jake frowned, remembering the sizzle of electric fire the instant his lips met hers. He'd kissed her twice, and both times the experiences had been unlike any other he'd ever known. Had she sensed the same burst of lust and was frightened by it? If so, he couldn't blame her. His response to her unnerved him. One taste of her lips had pulled him under as surely as the tidal flow of the Nile. He hadn't been able to come up for air, and in truth, he hadn't wanted to. He'd wanted to drown inside her, stay where it was rich and warm and exotically surreal.

There was something between them. It might be so minor a thing as attraction, but Jake had a sinking sensation in the pit of his gut that it was something more. *Bloody hell.* Over the years he had faced starvation and heatstroke, the threat of imprisonment and poisonous snakes, but he had never been in a situation he couldn't handle. Until now.

Despite Gavin's arguments, every instinct told Jake to protect Sarah, find the truth hidden behind her silver-gray eyes. And then what, he wondered?

Walk away from her. He'd have to walk the bloody hell away.

"What's in the crates?"

Sarah gasped and jerked around as quickly as a guilty child caught stealing a piece of candy. Jake stood on the shore, watching her crawl over her crates that crowded the first felucca. He arched one brow, and if not for the wary glint in his eyes, she might have mistaken his smirk for a lazy grin. Her heartbeat doubled its pace, as much from surprise as from the disturbing sensation of having him stand so close.

They had stopped for the night along the reed-choked bank of the Nile. While everyone was busy setting up camp, she had hurried to the boat to gather some of her things. She should have known Jake would follow her.

"The crates," he asked again when she didn't do anything more than stare at him.

"Oh, just my things. Clothes and such." And a mummy, some precious jewels, figurines. Ancient items she had not seen as yet. Might not ever see. She had hoped that before she sealed Queen Tiy inside her tomb, she would have the chance to glimpse the woman's coffin, maybe record the artifacts with her paints. But Jake had stolen that opportunity from her as well.

"It will be cold tonight. Did you think to bring blankets?" His tone implied that he doubted she'd brought anything but her silk ball gowns and cosmetics.

She bit down on her lip to stop a retort. She had blankets and tents, cookware and medicine packed inside her crates. But she hadn't risked opening the boxes for fear that their contents would cause Jake to start questioning her *again*.

Opening the nearest and safest of the trunks, she pulled out a pale green, watered silk shawl so sheer it wouldn't have kept one of the million flies swarming their camp warm, but it might keep them off of her, she thought. "This should suffice."

He shook his head in exasperation, then rested his hands on his lean hips. "Can I ask you something?"

"If I say no will you go away?"

"No." His intense blue gaze flickered from the contents of her trunk to her.

"Then why ask permission?"

"Did you learn anything about Egypt before you decided to take this trip?"

"Are you still trying to dissuade me from going to Thebes?"

"No." But the look in his eyes told her otherwise. "Usually when someone visits a foreign country they learn about the culture, the climate, *and* the dangers."

"And you assume I didn't bother."

"Considering the contents of your trunk, I'd say you're woefully unprepared for the elements."

Sarah slammed the lid closed, then wrapped the silk shawl around her shoulders. Suppressing a shiver, she climbed out of the boat, refusing Jake's help, and headed for their camp. She wanted to scream when she heard him behind her.

Gratefully sinking onto a blanket by the modest fire,

Sarah accepted a bowl from Hamada, who evidently was the cook as well as the steersman.

"*Sanyet batates,*" Mr. Lofty told her. "You like, yes?"

Sarah's mouth began to water from the delicious, spicy aroma, and even Jake's presence on the blanket beside her and the sudden tingles seeping through her skin from the corselet, couldn't ruin her appetite. Her nervous stomach had prevented her from eating very much while on the *Phoenix,* and though her stomach was still in knots, whatever the red-creamy broth was, it smelled like heaven.

"What is this?" she asked.

"Their version of potato stew." Jake took a bowl and a slice of thick, yeasty bread from the steersman. "It's simple food, unlike what you're used to."

"You shouldn't assume so much, Jake. You know nothing about me." The last words revealed far more resentment than she intended.

"Then tell me." His gaze narrowed on her. "Where do you live? Who are your friends? Have you always wanted to paint?"

"I see you're back to asking questions."

"And I see you're still trying to avoid them."

She took a bite of her stew and tried to ignore him. Flavors she couldn't identify exploded onto her tongue. She greedily emptied her bowl as she watched the Egyptian men laying colorful wool blankets around the fire, eating their meal, speaking in a language that was as ancient as the sand beneath her feet.

"Why aren't you married?" Jake asked in a voice loud enough to cause everyone to stop whatever they were doing to look at her.

"Don't you know it's rude to ask a lady such a question?"

"Ye should answer 'im, lass," Connor said, his voice a deep, rolling rumble. "Else none of us will get any peace."

Firelight darkened the Scotsman's red hair to the hue

of dried blood. The cuts on his cheek and temple were still raw. As leery as she was of Connor's size and permanent frown, she was tempted to move to his side. But she doubted that would stop Jake from hounding her. Even Eli and Thatcher gave her pitying shrugs.

Glaring at Jake, she decided she didn't need to lie overly much to satisfy his curiosity. "My family's home is outside of London, but I spent little time there. I was raised in boarding school."

"That explains it, then," Jake scoffed, soaking up the broth with the heel of his bread.

"Explains what?" she asked, not liking his arrogant tone.

"Why you are traipsing around the world without adequate protection," Gavin broke in. "I've met women like you, Sarah. Don't take offense. You had a headmistress looking after you instead of your father. It's no wonder you're somewhat . . . headstrong."

She eyed the earl, unsure if he had insulted her or complimented her.

"Why did you live at boarding school?" Jake asked, so softly that none of the other men heard him.

"My father preferred it."

"I find that hard to believe. I always thought fathers wanted their adoring little girls at home."

"Not this adoring little girl. After my mother's death, my father wanted me out of his sight." She set her bowl of stew aside, unable to eat another bite. She'd thought her stomach had been in knots before, but now it twisted so tight she wanted to double over.

"Perhaps he did what he thought best."

Sarah had to look away, hating the pitying tone of his voice. "Perhaps. Or perhaps he didn't know what to do with a daughter. It was his son he wanted."

"You have a brother?"

She wrapped her useless shawl around her shoulders, suddenly chilled to the bone. She couldn't answer Jake without revealing too much of the truth. How could she explain that having been saddled with a worthless girl, Roger Pendergrass had changed fate by taking a penniless, driven boy under his wing to mold into his own image?

"I'm sorry," Jake said as if he'd read her mind.

"You have nothing to be sorry for," she said, though it cost her dearly to voice the lie. For the hundredth time, she wondered what her world would have been like if Jake had never come into their lives. Would Roger have brought her to Egypt to share his dream of finding long-dead pharaohs? Would he have taught her about strange lands and customs, talking to her until the crisp, early hours of dawn about the new places they would explore? She wanted to believe he would have included her, but a bruised, wary part of her heart was afraid that nothing would have changed. She still would have grown up alone.

Jake drew up his legs to rest his elbows on his bent knees. She felt his gaze on her but she couldn't look away from the muscles flexing beneath the dusting of blond hair along his arms, or the rough, scarred hands that had held her twice while he'd kissed her. He seemed relaxed, confident, in control of his fate. But what would fate have given each of them if he had never met her father? Would she be burdened by a suffocating resentment? Would Jake still be a mudlark fishing out scraps of metal from the Thames, or would he have become an archaeologist despite his oppressive beginnings?

Or would he even be alive? She looked away from him and into the fire, not liking that thought.

"Sarah," Jake said, breaking another heavy silence. "I don't pretend to understand what your life was like, but I didn't intend to upset you."

"I learned to deal with my father's neglect." She pressed her lips together, surprised to hear the quiver in her voice.

If only Jake would go away and leave her alone. She didn't want to hear his apologies or heartfelt concern. She wanted him to remain an image in her mind that she could blame for the empty places in her life.

Forcing a smile, she said, "I think I'll return to the boat."

Jake caught her arm as she rose. Tendrils of heat sped over her skin, pushing her emotions dangerously close to the surface.

"You should sleep by the fire," he told her. "It's warm and—"

"Don't tell me, safe?"

"Well, it is. Hippos and desert fox roam along the banks at night."

"I'll be careful."

"It's a full moon."

"And that means what to me?"

"Cobras like to hunt during a full moon." His hold on her eased, yet she felt each of his fingers as they slid down her arm.

Sarah stared at his hand, felt his heat and a staggering sense of strength that couldn't be real. She'd spent the better part of her life hating him; she didn't want his kindness now.

If he knew who she really was, his pretense of worrying about her safety would vanish. He only cared about his quest for antiquities and glory. *The same as my father.* The reminder felt like a slap to her face, and a telltale stinging started behind her eyes. Had she been a fool to risk her life simply in the hope of gaining her father's love? Afraid she knew the real answer, she felt a crazed laugh push up her throat. Roger didn't care about her, and neither did Jake.

"Stay, Sarah," Jake said, his eyes reflecting a compassion she didn't dare believe.

"I can't." She turned to flee, not trusting her warring

emotions. Nothing in the world would force her to stay near camp. She had to be far enough way so when the tears squeezing her chest finally fell, Jake, the man she'd sworn to defeat, wouldn't be able to see them.

Chapter 8

Jake scanned the horizon, not liking what he saw. Buzzards circled on outstretched wings, silent in their search for unlucky prey. A hundred yards away pea-colored water slowly crept over empty sugarcane fields, burying them beneath a relentless tide. He glimpsed a village farther in the distance, the homes of mud brick and woven reeds momentarily safe from the inevitable flood. The Egyptians welcomed the Nile's seasonal deluge, but for a traveler, the summer months were a dangerous time to navigate the demanding river. Bloody hell, he was running out of time.

"Finally, you're scowling at something besides me."

He glanced toward the bow, where Sarah sat on a bench wearing another of her unsuitable gowns. This one had a billowing skirt of honey gold that draped what he guessed to be a hundred petticoats. Her matching caraco jacket of glazed yellow wool had half sleeves that revealed too much of her slender arms to the brutal sun. She'd wrapped another of her gossamer-thin shawls around her shoulders, covering a neckline that plunged far too low for his liking. Not that he objected to the one glimpse he'd had of her creamy breast, *full, creamy breasts* he recalled, his mouth going dry. But when he'd caught every other man on board the felucca appreciating her generous form, he'd been tempted to wrap her from head to toe in his galabiya.

A bonnet protected her exquisite face, but her cheeks

were flushed and sweat dampened her brow. Jake felt his scowl intensifying. The woman would perish from heat-stroke if he didn't do something about her attire.

"Is something wrong?" she asked, interrupting his assessment of her.

He glanced at the surging water. "The river has only begun to flood."

"What do you mean, flood?"

Looking at her, he saw the alarm in her eyes and shook his head. Did the woman know anything about Egypt? "Three, maybe four, weeks ago, the Nile was little more than a trickle of water, in danger of being engulfed by the desert. But in June, the melting snow and ice in the Sudan mountains to the south turn the river into a monstrous lake. Cities become islands."

Sarah's mouth gaped open and her eyes were bright with disbelief.

He sighed. He should have known this would be news to her. "You didn't know about the floods?"

She swallowed and looked at the churning water with unease. "Uh, yes, of course."

"The inundation happens every year," he told her, knowing she'd lied. "The Egyptians wouldn't survive without it."

A worried frown creased her brow. Jake didn't like having put it there, but her innocence, or ignorance, only proved that she had no business being in Egypt.

"What are you doing?" he asked when she started chewing on her lower lip. Startled, as if coming out of deep thought, she angled the writing tablet she held in her lap with one hand and pointed at something with a stick of charcoal she held in the other. Looking over her shoulder, he arched a brow in surprise. "I'd thought being an artist was a passing fancy of yours. I see I was wrong."

"It feels wonderful to be able to draw again." For the first time since he'd met her, she smiled at him, a tentative smile for sure, but still a smile. "And to draw things I've never seen before, well, there are no words to explain it."

His mind spun for an instant, and he hoped he didn't look as dazzled as he felt. God help him, she was beautiful. He had to clear his throat before speaking. "I understand exactly. There aren't words to describe how I feel when I see a tomb for the first time or find a clay pot that hasn't been touched by human hands for thousands of years."

"It's important to do something you love," she said, sounding distracted, though the look in her eyes was intense.

She glanced away and continued sketching the felucca and its inhabitants in amazing detail. Even in shades of black and white, she'd captured the sun glittering off the rippling water, the boyish glow in Hamada's eyes as he sang while steering the boat. The sail, half unfurled, was snapped full of wind. She'd omitted her heavy, over-sized crate that crowded the deck, but Jake saw himself standing as he had been a moment ago, staring into the distance, his face set, his eyes hard and determined. Driven. Is that how she saw him, he wondered?

After a few final strokes, she signed the bottom.

Kneeling beside her, Jake took the tablet and flipped back to the previous page. This one was of a village market, Rosetta most likely, busy with chattering women selling pottery and brass from their stalls, fresh fish from the river and home-spun garments.

He shook his head in wonder. "I could have used your talents more than once during my travels."

He handed the tablet back to her, but paused when he saw the guarded look in her eyes. "Did I say something wrong again?"

"Do you really think they're good?"

He heard the doubt in her voice and thought about the rubbing he'd made of the corselet the last time he'd seen it and wished he'd had someone of Sarah's skill draw the piece in detail. Perhaps then he wouldn't be struggling so much to decipher his blurred copy.

"They're better than good. If you weren't a woman I'd invite you on my next project."

"If I weren't a woman?" Her flushed cheeks turned a dangerous shade of red. "Do you think all women are incompetent? Or just me?"

"Neither."

"I've done quite well on my own, Jake Mitchell. Just because I'm a female doesn't make me worthless."

Recalling the pain she'd fought to hide three nights ago when she'd revealed the way her father had neglected her, he considered his answer before he spoke. "No one in their right mind would think you worthless, Sarah."

On impulse, he reached out and cupped her face in his palm. Skimming his thumb over the damp curve of her cheek, he added, "But no man in his right mind would risk your life for fear of losing you."

Her eyes brimmed with disbelief and she drew a trembling breath. Jake couldn't tear his gaze from the curve of her lower lip. His body tensed and he felt the full force of the sun burning through his skin. Desire pushed through him, making him hard and making him slightly crazed. The felucca was full of men, but damn his soul, he didn't care. At that moment he wanted to capture her lips, feel them part beneath his own. Taste the clean sweetness of her mouth.

He wanted to kiss her. Bloody hell, he'd never wanted a woman so badly in all his life. He didn't care who saw them. He'd kissed her twice before. The first time she'd been shocked, the second she had responded to his touch. The third time, he knew she would kiss him back with a passion that matched his own.

He leaned forward . . . and caught the look of horror in her eyes.

He released her as quickly as if he'd found himself holding a snake. They stared at each other, neither of them speaking. Jake didn't know what to say. "I'm sorry" didn't apply because he wasn't; he still wanted to kiss her. To his dismay, the urge was even stronger than before, building as easily as touching dry kindling to a flame. And that alarmed him. No woman had ever tempted him the way Sarah did. He hardly knew her, yet he wanted to be the knight who would protect her and the lover who would lavish her with joy.

But he wasn't the man to give her either of those things. She was a lady; he was an archaeologist who had neither reputation nor wealth. And even if he'd had those things, there would *never* be a woman like Sarah in his life. His chosen profession wouldn't allow it.

Even if he wished it otherwise.

Sarah paced the perimeter of the orderly camp that Mr. Lofty and his men had created in less time than it took her to buckle a pair of walking boots. Her heart hammered against her chest and her breathing had become an unsteady rasp. She tried to focus on her surroundings, appreciate the desert cliffs that guarded the Nile like immortal sentinels, see them through her artist's eye.

She stood on ancient ground that had been divided, literally, in half. She scooped up a handful of rich black earth, the silt damp and heavy, a result of centuries of melting snow from the mountains to the south. She had known the Nile flooded every year. Everyone knew that—only she hadn't known it would happen *now!* Jake was worried about the rising water. Should she be worried, too? Would the level of the Nile make a difference in reaching the Valley of the Queens? She prayed not, but what if this was another dangerous detail that Roger had failed to mention?

She drew a steadying breath and let the silt scatter back to the earth. If she took one step forward, she would be standing on dry, timeless sand, an oasis of shimmering tawny beige that stretched to the west, farther than her eyes could see.

The landscape was incredible, breathtaking. She wanted to sketch it but that would require sitting still and she'd been trapped on the felucca long enough. The more she paced, the more she tried to relax, the more anxious she became. She resisted the impulse to look at the reason for her distress. She knew Jake was reclined near the fire, drinking the local barley beer and studying a sheet of paper as if he hadn't a care in the world. The man had no idea that he'd tilted *her* world on its axis earlier that day.

She could still feel the imprint of his fingers. When he'd cupped her face, his touch so gentle, a warm ache had spun deep inside her body, spreading to her limbs and turning her mind to mush. No one had ever touched her that way. If her mother ever had, Sarah didn't remember it.

Jake had had every intention of kissing her. *Again.* And everything inside of her had wanted him to. She pressed her fingers to her temples to stop the sudden throbbing. How could her body want something so badly when her mind screamed "no"? Even now, after she'd reminded herself again and again that she hated Jake, she wanted to feel the strength of his fingers against her skin, look into his eyes and see the desire he didn't even try to hide, taste the rich, musky flavor of his lips. A taste she couldn't forget, no matter how hard she tried.

The man was poison, she decided, a toxin that was slowly destroying her common sense.

"You hungry, yes?" Mr. Lofty said from behind her.

Cutting off a startled yelp by slapping her hand over her mouth, Sarah whipped around.

"We eat, yes?"

Sarah nodded and preceded him toward the fire, though she didn't think she could force one bite of food down her throat.

"'Ave ye made any progress?" she heard Connor say as she took the only blanket left available—next to Jake. Connor, Gavin, Eli, and Thatcher sprawled on the other blankets with their dinner. She considered taking her food back to the boat but knew that would only draw unwanted attention. She had to act normal, in control, even if she felt like falling apart.

"Not much." A lock of sun-gold hair fell over Jake's brow as he studied a large sheet of paper. "The writing is similar to hieroglyphics, but the symbols are not exact. They don't make sense."

"Perhaps you're trying too hard," Gavin said, sipping his cup of beer.

Jake shook his head. "I'm missing something. A key, some formula that will unlock their meaning."

Unable to hide her curiosity, she asked, "What are you talking about?"

"A bloody puzzle." Jake's gaze hardened on the paper.

Gavin pulled a metal case from his coat pocket and withdrew a cigarette. "Will I offend you if I smoke, Sarah?"

"Not at all. What puzzle?"

"Jake has been trying to decipher a passage that was inscribed on the inside of one of the artifacts he found with Queen Tiy."

"A queen?" Sarah asked, feigning ignorance. "Is that what you're trying to recover?"

"Yes. She was married to Ramses the Third," Gavin said. "Though I haven't seen it, I gather the corselet she was wearing was rather impressive."

"More than impressive," Jake said. "It was one of a kind."

"And possessing some sort of secret passage," she said.

"That I still haven't been able to interpret," Jake growled, rubbing his eyes with his forefinger and thumb.

The hair at the base of her neck prickled. Were they referring to the faint symbols etched into the corselet? She briefly touched her waist and felt her skin warm and tingle in response. Without realizing her intent, she scooted close to Jake to better see his drawing, then visibly shivered when she saw what he held.

"What is this supposed to be?" she asked weakly, already knowing.

"Queen Tiy's corselet. A garment made for nobility," Jake explained, his gaze never straying from the strange symbols imbedded in the tiny squares. "This one is unusual, having hieroglyphics depicting how she plotted to have her husband, Ramses the Third, assassinated so her son could secure the throne."

A chill ran over Sarah's skin as she listened to Jake repeat the story her father had told her. The queen's lustful ambition, her guilt, her eventual capture and death.

"I don't understand," she said when he finished. "If you know how to read hieroglyphics, where is the puzzle?"

"This," Jake said, holding a second sheet of paper toward the firelight so she would see it clearly. "This was inscribed on the inside of the corselet."

Sarah took the paper from him and lightly ran her fingers over the outline of squares and the strange pictures filling them. The figures were a blurred copy, barely recognizable as what she had seen the dozen times she'd studied the corselet while locked inside her cabin.

"Is it so important that ye decipher it, Jake-o?" Connor asked, accepting a cigarette from Gavin.

"The message might be nothing," Jake said, but by his tone, she didn't think he believed that was the case. "Or it could open a new door to what we know about Egypt."

"A secret?" the Scotsman asked, blowing smoke into the air.

"Perhaps. It could be a secret of eternal life."

"Or the hiding place of Egypt's wealth?" Gavin mused.

Jake shrugged. "Without the corselet I might never know."

"But you have the drawing," she said.

Jake nodded. "The images are poorly defined. I made this copy as a precaution, not intending to use it to decipher the message. The slightest change in a symbol can change the meaning of a word. I could study this copy for years and never translate the author's words."

Suddenly feeling cold through to her bones, Sarah gave the paper to Jake. Even with her quick glimpse, she knew most of the symbols on the paper were different than the ones on the corselet. The differences were subtle, but they were there. Why hadn't Roger told her about the importance of the mysterious inscription? What if it revealed something of incredible historic value? If she buried the corselet in the tomb, would she be burying a priceless part of history, too?

If only she could say something. She recalled enough of the hieroglyphics to correct his copy. But if she did, she may as well tell him her real name and open the crates. She had to keep the information to herself, though it nearly killed her to do so.

"'E must 'ave a plan," Connor said, drawing on his cigarette.

She shook off her thoughts when she realized the men had changed the subject.

"Roger always has a plan." Jake folded the paper and slipped it into his satchel.

"Don't you think it's unusual that there hasn't been a trace of him?" Gavin stubbed out his cigarette in the sand. "Perhaps he's been detained by Napoleon."

"Let's hope not." Jake took a deep drink of his barley beer from a flask, then stared into the flickering blaze. His jaw tightened, and Sarah felt an unwanted contraction low in her body. "If the French general has Queen Tiy, I'll never be able to reclaim her."

"Anything can be . . . reclaimed." Connor uttered the word in a dangerous growl that caused Sarah to think he wasn't necessarily referring to the queen. "Ye just 'ave tae know how."

"Unless we learn differently, we'll stay with our original plan." Jake took another drink of beer, but this time his gaze found Sarah. A fire brighter than the one burning beside them blazed in his eyes. She shivered at the raw emotions she saw there, anger, determination, the need to conquer . . . desire.

She pressed her hand over the corselet, suddenly afraid that Jake would never stop until he reclaimed the queen, afraid that she might be making a mistake by following her father's wishes, and afraid the hatred she harbored for Jake was slipping away like sand.

"How long until we reach Thebes?" Gavin asked.

"Two days, at most."

Sarah tensed. Two more days and she would be free of Jake. The realization simultaneously filled her with relief and paralyzing fear. She would be on her own, in Egypt, to complete a task that never should have been thrust upon her.

"Considering the trouble we had finding a boat, do you think we'll have a problem buying the gear we'll need?"

Jake shrugged. "We'll know soon enough. The *Gurnawis's* village isn't far from the city. If we're lucky, Napoleon won't know they exist. They're the best guides and diggers in the area, but they're usually particular about who they work for. Hopefully they'll have wagons."

Sarah took mental notes. Jake wasn't the only one who needed to hire wagons, though, with Roger's map, she hoped she could do without the guides. Now that she knew whom to ask about transportation, she felt better knowing one small problem had been eliminated. She began making a list of the things she'd need to buy.

Water, for certain, and food. She had no idea how long she would have to wait before Jake gave up his quest and returned to England. She prayed it wasn't long, because even with Eli and Thatcher's protection, she knew she was ill equipped to survive for long in Egypt on her own.

"And what 'bout ye, lass?" Connor asked, rubbing a huge thumb along the new scar on his cheek. "Where might ye be stay'n once we reach Thebes?"

She blinked, surprised to find five sets of male eyes focused on her. "Me? Oh, I'm going to rent a house in a nearby village."

Eli and Thatcher ducked their heads and focused on their bowls of food.

"Is that so?" Connor smiled, the innocent deed sending a shiver of warning up Sarah's spine. The burly Scotsman rarely spoke. Hearing him now, seeing his unreadable green gaze pinned on her, she instinctively knew that something was wrong.

Jake had been the belligerent one from the beginning. Connor had been quiet and brooding, even when she'd nursed his wounds. Had they decided to change roles? Well, let them, she decided. Whether she was frightened or not, she was too close to fulfilling her promise to her father to be deterred now.

"Yes, that's so. I plan to stay in this part of the country for some time," she said, praying with all her heart that that wouldn't be the case. When the Nile crested, would Thebes become an island as Jake had claimed? If so, how long would she be trapped?

It didn't matter, she decided, she wouldn't stay in Thebes. The small village she'd seen on the map was further inland and closer to the Valley of the Queens. It had to be safe from the rising waters.

Forcing down her trepidation, she met Jake's gaze so he'd know she couldn't be swayed. "I plan to remain in Egypt until I run out of temples to paint."

* * *

Jake took another deep swallow from his flask, hardly tasting the warm, spicy-sweet drink, or feeling the slow burn building in his gut. The muscles along his shoulders were pinched and his hands ached from clenching them into fists. He'd been drinking steadily for the past three hours, but his head was still as disgustingly clear as it had been when he'd set out to get drunk. So clear, in fact, he could still feel Sarah's satiny-soft skin against his palm, smell her unique, feminine scent in the warm gusts of wind blowing off the River Nile, see himself in her wide, frightened eyes the instant before he'd almost kissed her.

"And where would this village be?" Connor asked, voicing the questions that Jake barely kept himself from asking. "Perhaps we can visit ye, make sure yer all right before we leave."

"That's not necessary." She gave all three men what Jake assumed was supposed to be a confident smile, but the corners of her very kissable mouth trembled.

"We all feel somewhat responsible for you," Gavin said, though his tone was far from convincing.

Jake glanced at his partner. He knew Gavin didn't trust women, but how could he be suspicious of someone as helpless as Sarah? Jake decided it was time to learn the details of Gavin's past. Just what the hell had happened between the earl and his wife to make him doubt a woman as vulnerable and beautiful as Sarah?

"Put our minds at ease, lass. Let us escort ye tae the place ye're stay'n."

Sarah heaved an annoyed sigh, her eyes narrowing. Even Jake stared at the two men, wondering why they were so adamant about accompanying her anywhere when they'd wanted to be rid of her from the beginning. Had Connor taken an interest in Sarah? Or Gavin? Jake glared at both men.

"I appreciate your thoughtfulness, really, I do, but it isn't necessary. The village isn't far."

"You've never been here before, Sarah," Jake heard himself say. "How would you know?"

"I have a map."

"May I see it?"

"The directions are clear."

"Once you've stepped beyond the Nile, nothing is clear."

"At least tell us the name, lass," Connor urged, "so we'll know where ye'll be. Ye took care of me on the ship. Seein' yer safe is the least I can do."

She pursed her lips, clearly reluctant, but finally she said, "If you must know, I'll be renting a house in a quaint little village called Deir el-Medineh."

A buzz that had nothing to do with the beer he was drinking erupted inside of Jake's head. "Did you say Deir el-Medineh?"

"Yes." She gave him a tight smile.

"Where you'll rent a house?"

"It's all arranged."

Jake tightened his hand around the neck of the flask and felt the thin metal give under the pressure.

"You've heard of it?" she asked.

He nodded, not trusting himself to speak.

"Then there's no reason for any of you to worry." She rose as if the subject was now closed. "I'll be fine."

"Deir el-Medineh is on our way, Sarah." Jake slowly stood, holding her gaze as his blood burned with the force of a hot, angry fire. "We'll escort you there."

"No."

"I insist," he said, the words so low and dangerous he didn't recognize his own voice.

"But—"

"There's no reason to thank me," he said, his limbs shaking. "I want to make sure you're safe."

She opened her mouth to argue, but Jake turned away, snatching up another flask, wine this time, as he headed into the desert. Whether she liked it or not, nothing was going to stop him from taking her to Deir el-Medineh.

Because he had every intention of being at her side when she arrived in a village that had been dead—and deserted—for three thousand years.

Chapter 9

The brutal Egyptian sun scorched the crowded city of Thebes, turning the air hot and dry and painful to breathe. The rancid smells of human waste and rubbish were as offensive as in Rosetta, and potent enough to overwhelm the staunchest of men. But somehow the smells and the crowds didn't matter. The worn streets that wove through sun-bleached buildings had seen the passing of four thousand years.

Everywhere Sarah looked she saw temples of every size, from box-like structures to the magnificent stone monument of Amun Re. Beyond the city, both east and west, jagged cliffs shot up to scrape an endless blue sky, nestling the ruins and valleys within a protective wall. She couldn't take it all in; her hands shook with the need to paint.

Standing on the Theban's version of a pier, she helped Eli guard her crates while the rest of the men went in search of wagons to hire. Sarah pulled at the bodice of her gown, the layers of cotton sticking to her skin. She stayed alert for a glimpse of Jake's blond head above the sea of dark-haired men. She also kept a look-out for French soldiers. Mr. Lofty had warned her that Napoleon's archaeologists and soldiers had entered the city barely a week before. While the French were searching the nearby valley for British military to fight, the archaeologists were searching the desert for artifacts. What if they found her before she returned the queen to her tomb? Her head spinning, she pressed her fingers to her temple.

Evade Napoleon, evade cobras and thieves. Evade Jake. She squeezed her eyes closed. God help her, how was she ever going to survive all of this?

It would help if she could dress like a man, she thought, envisioning Jake and envying his tan breeches and loose fitting shirts. Whether on a ship or on land, the lightweight linen moved with the breeze, revealing his well-muscled chest, the trim line of his torso, and his arms. Years of digging in the earth, searching for lost treasures had honed his body to perfection. The sun had tanned his skin a rich, honey-brown and . . . Sarah shook her head. The sun must be affecting her. Now wasn't the time to think about the wretched man's exquisite body!

She tugged on the neckline of her bodice once more, feeling as if she would melt from the building heat. If only she could wear something besides her heavy, restricting gowns. But even if it were appropriate, she couldn't don breeches now that Jake insisted on accompanying her to the village. Beneath her skirts she could disguise the corselet, but she'd have no hope of concealing the gold wrap if she wore pants.

With each passing day she'd fought down her growing panic that he would discover who she really was. And it wasn't over yet. Her stomach gave a violent quiver at the thought. How much longer would she be able to continue lying and smiling and acting as if she were on holiday? Forever, if that's what it took, she told herself.

Deir el-Medineh wasn't far. He wouldn't linger once she was settled. He'd rush to the Valley of the Queens in search of her father. She'd be rid of him, safely tucked away in her rented house until Eli and Thatcher would verify that Jake was gone.

"Tomorrow," she whispered to herself. "Tomorrow I'll be able to let down my guard."

"Did you say something?"

Sarah whirled around to find Jake standing nearly on top of her, his eyes hidden in the shadow of his hat, but she didn't need to see his expression to feel the tension radiating off his skin.

She backed up a space and cleared her throat. "Are we ready to leave?"

"As soon as we load your things."

She glanced at a pair of oxen hitched to a flatbed cart. "We need more than one wagon."

"One is all there is. Napoleon has been here."

He didn't need to say more. The French general had cleaned out Thebes of available wagons the way he had Rosetta of feluccas.

She nodded to Eli and Thatcher, willing them to pick up the crate containing Queen Tiy's coffin before Jake offered to help. Either the men didn't understand her silent message or they ignored her because Eli slapped a hand on the crate's lid and called, "Put yer backs into it, boys."

Eli, Thatcher, Jake, and Connor each claimed a corner and lifted, grunting as they struggled to slide it into the wagon.

"Stop!" she called.

Jake frowned at her. Sarah realized she was overreacting, but sweet heavens, Jake had his hands on her crate! If it fell, and broke open it would all be over. She clasped her hands at her waist and held her breath, praying they wouldn't trip or stumble or lose their hold.

She spotted Gavin standing near the oxen, watching, but Sarah felt his gaze on her more than on the men laboring with their burden. She gave him a weak smile, aware that his behavior toward her had changed. On board the *Phoenix,* he'd been polite, almost friendly, but after helping commandeer her felucca, he'd become cool, even brusque. She couldn't imagine why, and at the moment she didn't care.

Finally, after countless agonizing moments, Queen Tiy was secure in the wagon's bed. Eli and Thatcher moved away to load the remaining boxes and trunks, while Connor tied barrels of water, beer, and baskets of food to the camels. Sarah released the breath she'd been holding and tried to school her features. *I'm excited,* she reminded herself. *Not frightened out of my mind!*

"I'd like tae know what ye got in that there box, lass." Connor straightened, rubbing huge hands that showed an impression of wood.

"Just supplies I'll need."

"You have more than canvas and paints in there." Jake rotated his arm as if to loosen the muscles in his shoulder.

"Well, there are . . . are pieces of furniture. Knick-knacks and such."

"Knickknacks?"

"Things I didn't want to be without during my stay."

Jake eyed her, his jaw flexing. "I see."

His glanced at the crate, studying it too long and far too thoroughly for her liking. "Maybe we should open it to see if anything's been broken."

"Thank you but that's not necessary." Taking his arm, she drew him away from Queen Tiy, down a short alley and into the shadows of a building. "Jake, I'd like to discuss something with you."

"If you're going to try to dissuade me from escorting you to Deir el-Medineh, don't bother. I wouldn't forgive myself if something happened to you when I could have prevented it."

"I'm perfectly capable . . ."

Jake cupped her chin in his hand . . . and tilted her head back. She looked into the hard core of his blue eyes, saw the faint lines of worry that fanned out from each corner. His mouth was set in a determined line. Against her will, she felt consumed by the magnitude of his presence, the strength that flowed into her with a simple touch of his hand.

"You're not my responsibility, Sarah," he said, his voice a rough caress against her mind. "I've told myself that over and over, but the truth of the matter is that I can't turn my back on you and walk away. You're in danger here, whether you want to admit it or not."

He smiled then, a roguish, devastating, pull of his lips. "You only have to endure me for another two days. I would stay with you longer if I could, but . . ." He trailed off.

Liquid heat slid through Sarah's limbs. She couldn't decide if it was because he'd reminded her of his goal or because he was so close she could smell the intoxicating scent of his sun-warmed skin.

Struggling to clear her thoughts, she said, "But you have to find your partner and steal . . . I mean take back what he took from you."

He nodded, his hand sliding around to cradle her head. She felt each of his fingers against her neck, felt them tense as he bent toward her. Sarah sucked in a trembling breath, knowing she should stop him, but heaven help her, she couldn't. She still hated him, but if she could kiss him just once more time.

The touch of his lips was light, almost hesitant, completely unlike the two kisses they'd shared before. She was paralyzed under his caress, confused, waiting to see where he would kiss her next, how hard, and for how long. But he kept the pressure of his lips feather light, teasing her with only a hint of his taste. It amazed her how much she wanted him to take her as he had before, hard and deep, pulling emotions from her that were chaotic and wild. And dangerous.

She knew this was folly. But if she could explore a savage and perilous land, why couldn't she explore what

Jake made her feel? Two days and he would be gone. She'd never see him again. And it was only a kiss.

She leaned into him without meaning to. Her mind told her to pull away, but the pressure of his chest against hers, the sensation of clothes rubbing where they shouldn't was too new and appealing to resist. She parted her lips and felt . . . Jake pull away.

Blinking, she looked up at him and was surprised to see his expression hadn't changed. His eyes were just as hard, his jaw just as inflexible. Had the kiss not affected him at all? Had she just thrown herself at him?

Horrified, she glanced at her shoes, dusty with sand, then at her hands, which were fisted in his shirt. She released him and ran her sweaty palms down her skirt. "I . . . I must . . ."

"We're gathering a crowd," he said in a hoarse whisper.

Peering to the side, she saw a few dozen people, Eli, Thatcher, Connor, and a scowling Gavin among them, watching with great interest. "Oh, dear."

Jake took her by the arm and led her away from the onlookers. "Has anyone ever told you that you're a mystery, Sarah?"

"Never," she said, blindly following him.

"Well, you are, one that has me baffled." He stopped, but he didn't release her. Instead he slid his hand down to hers and slipped something into her hand.

She looked down to see a scarab shaped like a beetle the size of her palm and made of lapis lazuli. She turned it over and realized there were hieroglyphics engraved on both sides.

"It's beautiful," she said. "What is it for?"

"An amulet. To protect you."

"I've told you. I can protect myself."

"That's what makes you so mysterious." He brought her other hand to his lips. "I should warn you."

"About?"

"I never leave a mystery unsolved."

She tensed, but he brushed her fingers with his lips then smiled, and this time the effort touched his blue eyes.

"Do you like surprises?" he asked her.

"It depends on their nature," she managed around the pressure building inside her chest. What was this man doing to her? Why couldn't she resist the temptation to grasp his face and kiss him for real?

"Since you insist on being the adventurous sort," he told her, "mount up."

"Mount up?" He walked away, swaggered, more like, leaving her to stare after him. She was a mystery, was she? Sarah couldn't argue, because her behavior was a mystery to herself. She should be glaring at the man she hated, not smiling at him, or enjoying the warm tingles where he'd kissed the back of her hand, or loving the scarab he'd given her. And she should definitely not be having thoughts of kissing him again.

Remembering his order to mount up, she turned to climb into the wagon, and released a scream as she came face to nose with a camel.

The sun met its zenith, scoring the sky with blinding white-blue light. Jake led his small band of followers deeper into the desert. With every plodding step, the camels kicked up puffs of sand that shimmered in the scorching heat and clogged their throats. Ahead of him, the limestone cliffs concealing the Valley of the Kings and Queens quivered, as if the earth had given them a mighty shake. Jake knew that if he stared at them long and hard enough, his imagination would send the jagged peaks crumbling into a pile of rubble.

Every breath burned his lungs and his skin sizzled beneath his clothes. He glanced behind him and saw

Connor sitting erect in his saddle, a mammoth oak, un-bending, but sending his camel snarling looks. Jake grinned, recalling the shouting match between the Scotsman and the earl over riding the "mangy, heathen beast," as Connor had referred to the camel. Gavin had shed his coat sometime during the last hour, and his shirt was soaked with sweat. A flush darkened his lean face, but to Jake's surprise, the earl seemed to enjoy the harsh conditions. Eli drove the wagon; Thatcher had stretched out on the crates, a hat pulled over his face as he dozed. This was the worst, and most dangerous, time of day to travel, and normally Jake wouldn't have risked it—but Sarah had insisted they push on.

He looked at the woman who had somehow managed to consume and jumble his thoughts. The men seemed to be taking the heat in stride, but he expected Sarah to collapse in a dead faint before another hour passed. Beneath her bonnet, her cheeks were an alarming shade of red, her skin glistening with sweat. Her tidy bun had come loose of its pins and now her hair draped over her shoulders and down her back, the ends just grazing her hips. She was overdressed, again, her white muslin gown too long and possessing too many layers for even an Egyptian to withstand.

She pressed her fingers to her forehead, and Jake had to suppress the urge to call everyone to a halt. He'd done so once already, but Sarah had cheerfully announced that she would travel on without them. Jake wasn't about to let her continue on alone. But he doubted they would be pushing much farther.

He glanced at the burning sun, then back at Sarah and bit out a curse. He'd never met a more stubborn and exasperating female in his life. Or a more secretive one. There was more to Lady Sarah Elston than silky dark hair, exquisite gray eyes and a mouth that made him forget about everything except kissing her. She had lied to him from the moment they met, and she was lying to him still. A burning that had nothing to do with the brutal sun began to churn in his gut.

He should have known better to trust her; Gavin had warned him to stay away from her. Perhaps his new partner understood women far better than Jake did, because he never would have believed Sarah was anything other than the misguided lady she seemed. But if she wasn't simply misguided, what was she?

She had scant knowledge of Egypt, and none of Deir el-Medineh, or she wouldn't be planning to stay . . . he paused to correct himself . . . to *rent* a house in a ghost village that was nothing but rubble and sand. What did she plan to do once she arrived? Draw and paint the nearby temples? Hunt for lost tombs, as so many foolish tourists had begun to do? Or something else entirely? She'd claimed the arrangements had been made for her to stay in the village and she'd even brought the furniture and knickknacks she couldn't live without.

He glared at her crates and wondered what she was carrying that was so important. More inappropriate clothes? The trinkets she'd mentioned before? He didn't think so, but whatever the boxes held, they would certainly make better time if they left them behind.

Whatever her ploy, he would learn of it soon.

Sarah's head dipped and she swayed out of rhythm with her camel's plodding gait. Jake wheeled his animal around and was at her side just as she began to slide out of her saddle. He caught her arm, jolting her awake. She glanced around as if disoriented, then looked at him with glazed silver eyes.

"What happened?" she asked.

"Either you fell asleep or were about to faint."

"Faint?" She braced her hands on the horn of the saddle to steady herself. "I've never fainted in my life."

"I'm sure there are many things you've never done."

Like showing any sense. He raised his hand and called to the others, "We'll stop here to rest."

"Don't call a halt because of me. I'm fine."

He started to dismount but stopped to catch her when she swayed again. "I can see that."

"I'm just . . . a little . . . warm." This time when she swayed, her head fell back and she went limp.

Jake caught her in his arms and lifted her onto his saddle, surprised once again that she weighed more than he would have guessed. Her head rolled against his shoulder. She looked up at him, her eyes overly large in her pale face.

"I just need a moment, Jake. I'll be fine."

"People die of heatstroke in the desert, Sarah." He could feel the heat lifting off her skin and knew that beneath the layers of petticoats, skirt and Lord knew what else a lady might wear, she was burning up.

"I have to get you out of these clothes." He tried not to imagine what she would look like with her eyes drifting shut and her skin flushed, not from the heat, but from his touch. The image fixed in his mind was pure sin, but as tempting as it was, concern for her life overrode it.

"Connor, give me a hand."

"We aren't stopping," Sarah insisted, licking her dry lips. "Yes, we are."

"You aren't taking my clothes off of me, Jake Mitchell."

He had to smile at her irritated command. Even near a dead faint, the woman spoke her mind. "I've got to get you cooled down.

"Eli," he called. "Set up a tent."

Jake carefully handed her down to Connor, then dismounted. He took her back into his arms and ignored Gavin's disapproving look. Within moments the tent was up and Jake had her lying on a reed mat. It was stuffy inside the tent, but they were out of the burning rays. He quickly removed the thin shawl she'd wrapped around her neck and tucked into her bodice. He paused, his gaze fastening on the rapid rise and fall of her breast. He laid his hand over her heart, felt the quick staccato. Her skin was feather soft . . . and on fire.

Taking a flask of water, he drenched a cloth and pressed it to her brow, her cheeks, then laid it over her chest. He reached for the ties laced up the front of her bodice, but froze when he heard Gavin behind him.

"Will she be all right?"

"I'm fine," Sarah said, slurring the words. She weakly batted at Jake's hands. "Don't you dare undress me. If it needs to be done, I'll do it."

"What about the French?" Gavin asked. "We're in the open, a sitting target should they happen upon us."

"I'm aware of that," Jake said, torn between what he wanted to do, and what he had to do. Roger was somewhere ahead of him. Every minute Jake delayed reduced his chance of stopping his partner from destroying the queen. But even Roger would rest during the worst of the heat. Jake would have preferred to stop in the crevice of a sand dune or cliff, blocked from view. But there was nothing he could about that now.

He sat back on his heels, wiped sweat from his brow and wished like hell that Sarah were anywhere except here with him. She had no idea how much danger she was in, or how volatile their situation was. Or did she know Deir el-Medineh was abandoned and had another scheme planned that she wasn't sharing? He didn't like that thought, not at all, because it was all too possible.

"I'll give you two minutes to take off everything you don't absolutely need." He started out of the tent, but paused. "If I'm not satisfied, Sarah, I'll finish the job for you."

Clutching her nauseated stomach, Sarah rolled onto her side. She had never felt so ill in her life. Her head ached, her body burned with a throbbing fire. Her gritty eyes couldn't focus, and she'd swear her mouth was full of sand.

Two minutes, Jake had warned her, or he'd be back to undress her himself. She laughed dryly and blinked back hot tears. That would be a fitting end, she thought. After everything she'd endured only to fail because she couldn't withstand a little heat. Or a lot of heat, she amended. Heat that suffocated and pressed and wore her down.

And she'd only been traveling through the desert for half of one day.

Pulling up her skirt to untie the strings to her petticoat, she vowed the first thing she did once she reached Deir el-Medineh would be to buy the loose-fitting galabiyas the locals wore.

"Sarah," Jake called from outside the tent.

"It hasn't been two minutes." Taking big, gulping breaths to keep her stomach settled, she wiggled out of her petticoat. She wanted to remove her chemise, but she'd have to take off her gown in order to accomplish that. That would mean exposing herself and the corselet. She thought for a second then glanced at the tent flap. "Jake, do you have a knife I can borrow?"

"I'm coming in, Sarah."

"No! I just need your knife."

After a muttered curse, his arm shot through the opening, a vicious looking blade in his hand.

"Thank you." Turning her back to Jake in case he decided to peek, she lifted the front of her gown high around her chest and sliced the chemise's thin fabric, tearing the length from around her body and tossing it aside. She still wore the bodice, but that couldn't be helped. Shaking out her skirt, she took a deep breath, feeling cooler already. If only she could remove the corselet; the warm gold had been a comfort, until now. As the heat increased, so did the corselet's weight until it felt like an anchor pulling her under.

Finding the wet cloth Jake had used on her, she soaked it again and pressed it to her face.

"Feel better?" Jake asked from behind her, so close she felt his breath stir loose strands of her hair.

She would have started if she'd had the energy to do so. She felt his gaze on her back, accessing, questioning. No doubt he wanted to reprimand her for risking her life and everyone else's. She'd been a fool and she knew it, but Jake threw her off balance; her only goal had been to reach Deir el-Medineh as quickly as possible and get away from him.

"I'm sorry," she said, reluctant to turn around. "I should have listened to you before when you suggested we stop."

"Why are you here, Sarah?"

To prove to my father that I'm worthy of his love, she thought, wondering if she were risking her life for nothing. *To outwit you and see you hurt the way I've hurt all these years.* The last thought brought tears to her eyes.

Jake had shown her nothing but kindness and she'd done everything in her power to deceive him. Why did he have to be so likable instead of being the monster she'd envisioned? She'd spent half her life hating him, so why in heaven's name was it Jake's hands she wanted to feel and Jake's kisses she wanted to taste? Why not Connor's or Gavin's? They were handsome men. Nice enough, in their own domineering ways.

But they weren't Jake. Groaning, she pressed the damp cloth harder to her face.

"Sarah."

"Please, go away."

"I've sent Connor to find a place to set up camp. You'll be able to rest."

"Is that what you would normally do?" she asked, lowering the cloth, though she didn't turn around.

"This is hardly a normal situation."

"Then you're making allowances for me."

He didn't say anything, but she hardly noticed when a fine tingle raced over her scalp. Then she felt his fingers on her hair, lightly running over the tangled strands. Holding her breath, she looked over her shoulder at him.

His eyes were hooded, his jaw fixed. Capturing a fistful of her hair, he brought it close to his face. "I asked you before, but you didn't answer. Why are you really here?"

Though his touch was gentle, the edge in his voice left no doubt that she was being tested, and how they would proceed depended on her answer.

"I told you, I'm an artist. The tombs . . ." The lies trailed to an end as he ran the length of her hair over his rough-shaven jaw.

"You were saying?" he said, tugging her closer.

Forced to lean forward, she had to lick her lips to continue. "The tombs, I'm going to paint them."

"Is that the truth?" Jake wound his hand around the length of her hair and gently drew her within an inch of his face.

"Of . . . of course." She swallowed, almost tasting the salty-sweat tang of his skin. "Jake, what are you doing?"

"I'll be damned if I know." His mouth crushed over hers, a searing kiss that burned to her core. Stunned, she let him pull her closer, then slowly sank with him to the ground. He dragged her across his lap and into his arms. She gripped his shoulders, his muscles granite hard.

He was everything a man should be, she realized. Strong and confident, defiant and daring. *But why Jake?* A whimper escaped her throat. She shouldn't need him so much, shouldn't want to feel more of his hard body pressed against hers or yearn to understand the luscious heat coiling low in her stomach. The liquid sensations pooled in her limbs, fanning out, building until she thought Jake's scent and taste and touch would consume her.

"God, woman, you make me insane." He pressed his mouth to her throat, sending a burst of raw heat beneath her skin. Her head fell back and she felt as if she were falling, spinning and falling.

She kissed his jaw, felt his fingers tug the strings lacing her bodice. A warning blazed in her mind, but it flamed to ash as his hand slipped inside her gown and cupped her breast.

Sarah tensed, her gaze meeting Jake's, a dark flare of lust. He held her in his palm, the rough pad of his thumb grazing over her extended nipple. Again and again. Her entire body tightened, waiting, needing.

"Oh, my, Jake . . ." Her breath quivered, and she numbly shook her head, unable to say anything more.

He kissed her mouth, a harsh sweep of his tongue, before he lightly bit the line of her throat, moving lower to the curve of her neck. He kneaded her breast, rasping his callused palm over sensitive skin. He nipped and kissed his way down her chest, until finally, his lips found her.

Sarah sucked in a breath, arching against him, burrowing her hands in his hair to keep from flying apart. She never knew anything could feel so savage, so wonderful. His tongue rolled over her nipple, teasing it. Shards of lightning flashed through her body, gathered between her legs. Earlier, Jake had been afraid she would faint from the heat, but that was nothing compared to what he was doing to her now. Her thoughts spun out of control and only sensation remained. Hunger and desire and deep, soul-wrenching need.

He kissed her again, the act so breathtaking and possessive, that for an instant, Sarah thought he had pulled her inside himself. She could feel his heartbeat, the rush of his blood, the wrenching need to join with her. He broke the kiss and looked down at her, giving her a glimpse of the turmoil raging inside of him.

"If it weren't for the half dozen men outside this tent,

I'd make love to you right now." Strain deepened the creases bracketing his eyes. There was nothing tender about the rigid line of his jaw or the feel of his hands on her body. He was tense and hard and consuming, and to her amazement, if it weren't for the men outside, she just might let him make love to her.

With a resigned sigh, he pulled the edges of her bodice closed, then ran his hand over her shoulder and arm, down her side to her waist, where he paused, his brow furrowing in a frown.

"I told you to remove everything." He tightened his fingers over her hip. "Just what the hell do you have on? A chastity belt?"

The corselet. Dear God, how could she have forgotten? Pushing against his chest, she scurried off his lap.

He reached for her, but Sarah raised her hand to warn him off. "Don't . . . Jake . . . we shouldn't have done this."

She glanced around the tent for a way to escape. His gaze narrowed, the desire turning to cool blue flint. She'd seen that look often enough to know he either intended to drill her with questions again or strip off her gown to see what she had hidden underneath. Neither option appealed to her.

"I think you should leave," she said, shaking. "We can pretend this didn't happen."

"Is that so?" A rueful smile pulled his lips. "There's a reason you and I find ourselves locked in a kiss whenever we're together."

"You keep kissing me, I don't kiss you."

He arched a brow.

"Oh, very well. I kissed you back. This time."

His gaze dipped to her chest. Sarah's skin warmed as if he had bent his head and taken her again. She looked down to see her gown gaping open, her breasts in plain view. Snatching up the strings, she tied the bodice tight, nearly cutting off her own breath.

"No more kissing, Jake. I mean it. I'm sure this only happened because I'm suffering from heatstroke."

"If so, then we're both suffering."

She didn't know what to say to that, so she kept her mouth shut.

"Once Connor finds a safe place, we'll move camp and rest for a few hours." Sending one last, achingly slow glance over her body, he turned to leave, but paused halfway out the tent. "And Sarah, whatever you have on under your gown. Take it off. Or I'll do it for you."

Once alone, Sarah couldn't stop shivering, because Jake's warning had been both a promise and a threat.

Chapter 10

The world had vanished.

Night pressed against them on all sides, a moonless void that even the stars had abandoned. Standing beneath an outcropping of limestone rock, Jake kept a tight grip on his rifle, alert for any sounds. The slightest noise traveled in the desert valley. Especially at night. So far, they'd been lucky to avoid the French soldiers patrolling the area, but Jake had seen signs of their passing. Campfires that the desert had yet to reclaim, discarded baggage too heavy to carry. Jake prayed that whatever luck he had left held, because Napoleon's men were far too close for comfort.

Behind him, Sarah and Eli waited beside the entrance to a small cave, where inside Connor and Thatcher were building a fire. Gavin guarded an area to his right.

Jake didn't have to look at Sarah to know she was shivering. The instant the sun had vanished behind the distant cliffs, the temperature had plummeted from sweltering heat to near freezing. Having stayed in this cave once before, Jake had forced his small party to continue in the dark, knowing they'd be safer and warmer here than in the open desert.

Seeing a glow inside the cavern, Jake started to enter, but a bellowing curse from Connor stopped him. He shouldered his rifle, ready to shoot whatever came out of the cave. Hearing a familiar whooshing sound, he caught Sarah around the waist and threw her to the ground, covering her with his body.

"What—"

Her cry was cut off when a black swarm shot out of the cave. The bat's high-pitched squeals and beating wings were deafening, but they were nothing compared to Thatcher's and Connor's shouts as they darted into the clearing, waving their arms and pulling tiny bat bodies out of their hair.

As if someone had shut a door, the bats vanished and the only sounds remaining were the two men's roaring oaths.

"Well, if Napoleon's men didn't know we were here, they do now." Gavin picked a bat off of Connor's back and tossed it into the air.

"Bloody hell." Connor rounded on Jake. "Why didnae ye tell me 'bout those bloody things?"

Standing, Jake helped Sarah to her feet and reluctantly let go of her arm. "They weren't here the last time I stayed here."

Sarah brushed sand from her skirt with shaking hands. "Will they come back?"

"They might, but we'll be gone by then."

Everyone stood where they were, clearly reluctant to enter the cave. Jake didn't blame them. He entered the cavern to see if any other creatures were inside. In the rear of the cave, there was a faint stink of bat, proving the animals hadn't nested here for long. Once he sprinkled spices into the fire, no one would notice. Not finding anything else, he motioned for the others to join him.

While Connor and Eli brought in the gear they'd need for the night, Jake started their dinner of dried beef and *biram ruz,* a steamed creamy rice dish he favored whenever in Egypt. He glanced up to see Sarah whispering to Thatcher, who reluctantly nodded and left the cave.

"Is something wrong?" Jake asked when she came to

sit by the fire, her uneasy gaze looking everywhere but at him. He wondered if she was still unsettled by their kiss. He hoped so, because he sure as hell was.

"Thatcher doesn't like small places." She rubbed her palms over her skirt. "He's going to sleep outside."

Near her belongings, Jake guessed, wondering why a woman who could be so careless with her life could be so overprotective of some useless knickknacks. Or were they useless? She was headed to a ghost village for a reason. Was it to dig in the Valley of the Kings? Could her crates hold picks and shovels instead of china plates and teacups? Perhaps it was time to take a closer look at her cargo.

As the dark suspicions continued to churn, he handed her a bowl of rice. "Thatcher will be cold without a fire."

"He slept outside when we camped by the Nile. I'm sure he'll be fine."

"The Nile and the desert are two different places with two different kinds of danger." Jake filled another bowl and handed it to Gavin without taking his gaze from Sarah. "Even with a full moon, the desert night can be deceiving, hiding predators, creating illusions. By the river, the air is warmer, the night brighter with the moon's reflection off the water. Here, there's nothing to stop the wind. I've had to camp in the open more times than I care to remember and every time I thought the cold would cut me in half before morning."

She stared at the entrance, her spoonful of rice forgotten. After a moment, she frowned at Jake. "I think you're trying to frighten me again."

"I'm just being truthful with you," he said, then added, "the way you have been with me."

Her chin went up a notch and her eyes darkened to smoke in the firelight. After a moment, her gaze slipped to his mouth. Jake swore he could hear the unsteady rasp of her breath, see her skin warm. Then she shook herself and looked away. Jake tried to interpret her expression. Was it distress he saw? Or desire? The same relentless, unwanted desire that stirred his loins? He clenched his jaw, willing the rush of heated blood to cool. Sarah was lying to him, and until he discovered why, he had no business wanting her. Besides, they wouldn't be sleeping in separate tents tonight, but together around the fire. If he didn't keep his thoughts on something besides their last kiss, the feel of her body filling his hands, and how much he wanted to fill them with her again, he wouldn't survive.

"What is that?" she asked.

Jake blinked, afraid she'd read his mind and had noticed how his body was reacting all on its own. But she was looking at something Connor had sketched in the sand.

"'Tis nothin'." Connor started to wipe the picture away, but Sarah caught his hand and stopped him.

"It's some sort of stick?" she asked.

Jake looked over her shoulder at the drawing of a three-foot stick, the top portion curved to fit a hand. Carvings fanned down from the top, and what appeared to be a metal band circled the bottom.

The Scotsman stared at the sketch, his green eyes unfocused, obviously seeing something far different than a rough picture in the sand. "'Tis the Staff of St. Moluag."

"I've never heard of it," Sarah said. "Is it important?"

"To my family, it is. We've been the Keeper of the Bachuil, as St. Moluag's holy staff is called, since his death, over a thousand years ago."

"I would love to see it," Sarah said, smiling, but her smile faded when she glanced up and saw Connor's dark glare.

"As would I, lass. And I will, someday soon. That I vow." Connor rose and left the cave, his fists clenched, his body radiating anger.

Sarah looked at Gavin. "Did I say something wrong?"

The earl glanced after the Scotsman. "After the English defeated the Scots at the Battle of Culloden, Connor's grandfather was executed and the staff was stolen."

"Culloden." She shivered and rubbed her hands over her arms. "That battle was tragic, but it happened over fifty years ago. Why would he be upset about St. Moluag's staff now?"

"It's as he said. For a thousand years, his family guarded the staff. It was their duty." Gavin shrugged. "They have been searching for it since, without any luck. Now, Connor is the last of his line."

"So it's up to him to find it," Sarah said thoughtfully. "He's on a quest."

Gavin nodded.

"Does he expect to find the staff in Egypt?" Sarah asked.

"Perhaps," Gavin said.

Jake glanced at the cave's entrance with a new sense of understanding. "It would seem Connor and I have something in common."

Sarah traced the drawing with the tip of her fingers, then looked at him, her gaze troubled. "What do you mean?"

"We've both had something precious stolen from us."

She opened her mouth as if she intended to argue, but she snapped her jaw shut and looked away. Firelight wavered in her expressive gray eyes. She bit down on her bottom lip and her hands fisted in her skirt.

A disturbing tingle started at the base of Jake's skull. Perhaps it was the play of light, or sunstroke or his over active imagination, but he swore she looked guilty.

The embers glowed red and hot in the cave. Small flames struggling to survive emitted soft yellow light that flickered off the black ceiling and rocky walls. Sarah lay on her pallet, curled on her side, unable to sleep. The sudden snorts and bursts of snoring from several of the men were only part of the reason she was still awake.

The corselet vibrated against her skin, a faint hum that was warm and distracting. Jake was too close. She'd discounted the strange phenomenon the first few times it had happened, but she couldn't any longer. There was some connection, a bond between . . . what? Her and Jake? Jake and the corselet? Her, Jake, and the corselet? Did the guilt she was now feeling play a part? With a frustrated sigh, she turned onto her back, and almost yelped when Jake spoke.

"Can't sleep?"

His rough, low voice wound like warm honey though her limbs. She glanced across the dying fire and saw he was propped up on one elbow, watching her through lowered lids. His lips looked soft and warm, and she had the insane impulse to taste them. She looked away. "I was thinking about what you said earlier, that both you and Connor had had something precious stolen from you."

"What about it?"

"The staff Connor wants to find had been in his family for generations. I understand why he wants it back. But Queen Tiy didn't belong to you. You raided her tomb, stole her from her grave."

"Only so we can learn from her."

"By displaying her in a museum?" Sarah sat up, her sense of injustice pricked. "I don't believe the queen would appreciate what you and your partner did to her."

"She's been dead three thousand years, Sarah." Jake tossed a handful of sticks onto the fire. Golden embers curled into the air. "Do you really think she minds?"

Sarah rubbed her brow. She didn't want to have this conversation with Jake, not while she wore the corselet and had Queen Tiy snug in her crate outside the cave.

But there was a question that had been bothering her and she had to ask.

"Why is finding Queen Tiy so important? Surely there are other tombs you can raid."

Jake sat up, propped his arms on bent knees and stared into the fire. "I don't expect you to understand, Sarah, but the queen's discovery will give me back everything that was taken from me."

"How?"

"Have you ever met Stuart Kilvington? Lord Ashby as he's known in your circles." When she shook her head, he continued. "I wish I could say the same. While working with him on a dig three years ago, I found the remains of a ruined temple devoted to the gods Amon and Re-Harakhty. It wasn't grand enough for Stuart so he left, saying I could remain with the debris while he searched for something of value.

"I had sensed something about the temple. It turned out I'd been right to stay behind." Jake's eyes glazed as if he were seeing the past and was mesmerized by it all over again.

"After two weeks of digging on my own, I found a cache of silver urns and a golden crown called a uraeus. It had the head of a cobra at the brow, his hood flared and his ruby eyes as dangerous as fire."

"It sounds magnificent. But that doesn't explain why Queen Tiy is so important that you're chasing your partner across the desert to get her back."

He looked at her, his eyes full of regret and anger and resentment. "When Stuart returned and discovered what I had found, he accused me of trying to steal the artifacts. Since he had financed the trip, he felt they belonged to him. I was under the assumption they would go to the museum. When we returned to England, he went to the curator and told them that he was the one who found the uraeus and that I had tried to steal it from them."

"Surely they didn't just take his word for it."

The look in his eyes turned sharp, lethal, slicing right through her. "He's an aristocrat, I am not. Of course they believed him, and threatened to throw me in prison for theft. Stuart, being the kindhearted man he is, talked them out of it. But my reputation was ruined. I had escaped Newgate Prison, but everything I had worked for was gone. No one would risk financing me on another expedition, except for Roger Pendergrass. But now Roger has betrayed me, too."

Jake shook his head as if trying to shake himself out of the past. He lay back on his pallet, his hands behind his head and stared at the ceiling. "Now you know why reclaiming the queen is so important."

He needed her to repair the damage to his name, Sarah realized. And to prove he wasn't a thief. She fisted her hands in her lap, wishing there were something she could say that would soothe Jake's troubled gaze. But there wasn't anything she could say because Stuart Kilvington and her father weren't the only ones who had betrayed Jake.

She had too.

The Egyptian god, Auf, had protected the night from Ra's demon enemy, the giant serpent of the underground, Apep. Now Khepera, the god of the rising sun, would push away the lingering night and the blessed coolness so that sun, heat, and life could return. Or so Jake had told her.

Khepera had succeeded, Sarah thought as she dabbed sweat from her brow. Her hat kept the worst of the sun's rays off her, but fingers of heat rose from the ground, choking everything in its path. Yet despite the grueling hardship, she wanted to see more of this barren country, learn about its past. Jake had said Egyptians' lives didn't revolve around the passing of years, but the passing of seasons, beginning with the flooding of the Nile and ending with a bountiful harvest. There was a scent in the air she couldn't define, clear and clean, but old as time. The desolate landscape was hypnotic, compelling her to explore until she found the source of its magic.

When she strapped the corselet around her waist, she thought she'd understood her father's passion for antiquities, but now she knew there was more. The land called to her, just as it must have called to him, promising to reveal the secrets of ancient civilizations. Sarah knew she would return to Egypt after she sealed Queen Tiy inside her tomb, to explore the primitive cities, paint every temple she could find.

Sealing Queen Tiy's tomb. She closed her eyes when her stomach gave a rending twist. If she succeeded, Jake would lose his chance to regain the respect he had lost. But it couldn't be helped. She'd come too far to give up now. Besides, although she wished she could help Jake, she wanted the queen back inside her tomb. It was where she had rested for three thousand years, and Sarah believed that was where she belonged.

Her camel continued its rocking gait without any guidance from her; she petted his smooth neck and cleared her thoughts. She had quickly gotten over her initial fear of the animal, and had actually come to like his soft brown eyes with their long curling lashes and his mellow disposition. She wondered what her small circle of friends would say if they could see her now, hot and sweaty and covered with dust. They wouldn't recognize her; she hardly recognized herself. Never in her life would she have believed she could travel to Egypt by herself.

Well, not exactly by herself.

Her gaze strayed to the man in front of her, not wanting to appreciate his broad shoulders and trim waist, but unable to stop herself. He somehow managed to look masculine riding on the back of his gangly camel. A brown hat covered his blond head, but curls that needed to be trimmed brushed his nape. She tightened her grip on her reins, remembering the feel of his hair threaded through her fingers. Like cool silk warmed by the desert sun.

She tried to ignore that sensation, but others followed. His arms wrapped around her back, his hard chest flush against hers, the feel of his manhood pressing into her thigh. She swallowed, feeling her skin heat and blood rush to her center.

"Stop it," she whispered to herself.

"Did you say something?"

Sarah tensed, glanced to her right. Gavin rode beside her, his eyes pools of doubt beneath the shadow of his hat. "I was just wondering when we would stop."

"Soon, I imagine," Gavin said, his tone remote. "Jake said we would reach Deir el-Medineh well before noon."

"May I ask you something?"

"Of course."

"Have I done something to offend you?"

His gaze raked over her. "Why do you ask?"

"When we were aboard the *Phoenix*, you were . . ." she paused. Though he should be the one to apologize for his cool behavior, she didn't want to say something that might add to the anger that never quite left his eyes. "You were kind. Now you seem irritated that I'm here."

"Irritated? No. But I am curious."

"Curious or suspicious?"

He shrugged and a muscle flexed in his jaw. "Both."

She should stop this line of questioning. She'd heard too many rumors concerning the earl's dubious past to purposefully test his patience, but her interest was piqued. Besides, he didn't worry her nearly as much as Jake did.

"What have I done to make you suspicious?" she asked.

"I have my reasons for not trusting women, Sarah. Reasons I don't care to share with you."

He turned his mount away to rejoin his friends, leaving her to stare after him. She shook her head. Three men with too much ego, confidence, and bluster for her to handle. *Well, fine.* She couldn't wait to reach Deir el-Medineh. Another hour and she'd be rid of Connor's sullen looks, Gavin's distrustful attitude, and Jake's—her gaze traveled the length of his body—Jake's too tempting everything.

"Deir el-Medineh is just ahead."

Sarah scanned the horizon for signs of buildings or people, but didn't see a thing. Wind swept the desert, blowing sheets of choking grit straight toward them. The land wavered with heat, making distance impossible to judge.

She forced herself not to kick her camel into a run and turned to her tormentor. In as pleasant a tone as she could manage, she said, "I know you'll want to continue on to the Valley of the Queens once we reach the village, Jake, so I'd like to say good-bye now. And good luck with your venture."

"After you're settled, I'll leave," he said, watching her with an expression she couldn't interpret.

"I'll be fine." But the truth was she was worried about what would happen when they parted ways. Would the villagers welcome her? Or shun her? Did they speak English? Would Napoleon's solders capture Jake? Did she care?

"It's no inconvenience, I assure you." A muscle flexed in his jaw as he glanced at the sky. "Besides, we need to find shelter soon. The sun is nearing its zenith."

Sarah resisted the urge to repeat one of the oaths she'd heard Jake use. Would she ever be rid of him?

Once they reached the village, she would have to find a way to escape him and locate a house to rent. One had to be available, but if there weren't, she would simply tell Jake it wasn't ready yet and that she would sleep in the tents she'd brought. Considering he had urgent business elsewhere, she was certain he wouldn't stay.

With her plan set, she scanned the horizon again, but still couldn't see any dwellings or smoke from fires or the menacing buzzards that had circled over Thebes and Rosetta. The only sounds were the stir of wind, the thumping steps from the camels and the comforting jingle of the oxen's harnesses. Like the other two cities, there should be villagers leading donkeys, naked children being chased by barking dogs, tradesmen coming and going. But the surrounding sand dunes were smooth and empty. She frowned. If they were close, shouldn't she be able to see something?

"Jake—"

"When I'm finished with my business in the valley," he said, his shadowed gaze on her, "I'll return to see your paintings."

"Oh," she said, not liking the sudden, uneasy quiver in her stomach, "that would be lovely."

"Which tomb do you plan to work on first?" He raised his hand and called a halt near a small heap of crumbled rocks.

"I haven't decided." She glanced around. "Why are we stopping?"

"We're here."

"Where?"

"Deir el-Medineh."

"No we aren't."

"Yes," he said, sweeping his arm in an arc to include the sea of beige sterile land. "We are. Which house were you intending to rent?"

Not liking the malevolent look in Jake's eyes, she

glanced around and saw nothing but scattered rocks half buried beneath endless sand. "Don't be absurd, this isn't a village."

"Of course it is. Or at least it was." That muscle in his jaw flexed again. "Three thousand years ago."

A tingle sped down her spine. "What . . . what do you mean?"

In a menacingly low voice, he told her, "For five hundred years, the workmen who built the Valley of the Kings lived here."

Her heart beat hard against her chest. "No one has ever lived here. There's nothing here."

He slowly shook his head. "Look again."

She did, and saw dusty, sand-covered hills beneath a sun-bleached sky. Rocks of various sizes lay scattered across the desert floor. She looked harder and saw a pattern emerge, a maze of worn stones set in ragged squares—like that of ruined buildings.

"No." She pressed her hand to her chest. "This can't be Deir el-Medineh."

"The workers abandoned this village at the end of the New Kingdom," Jake said. "When the royal court moved north and kings were no longer buried here. Sometime around the year 1550 BC. Over three thousand years ago."

Sarah looked at him, refusing to believe he was telling the truth. "I know you never wanted me to make this trip, but it's too late to try and convince me to turn back." She glanced at Connor and Gavin, who were frowning at Jake. Clearly, they were as confused as she was. "I have a map. If you don't want to take me to Deir el-Medineh, I'll find it on my own."

"This *is* Deir el-Medineh, sweetheart." Anger and distrust radiated from Jake as he leaned toward her, his forearm resting on the horn of his saddle. "Now which house have you arranged to rent?"

Could he be telling the truth? Dear God, if so, what was she going to do now?

"Are you trying to think up another lie?" he taunted. "Perhaps there's another city nearby you plan to travel to, though I can't imagine which one. There's only desert and graves in the west."

"I won't tolerate this, Jake Mitchell," she told him, her voice shaking.

"Or perhaps you intended to visit the Valley of the Kings all along, to search for artifacts?" he continued. "Is that your real intent, Sarah?"

"Eli, Thatcher, we're leaving."

"'Fraid not, sweetheart." Jake swung down from his mount, caught Sarah by the arms, and pulled her down to him. "You're not going anywhere until you tell me the truth."

"I have."

"Don't lie to me again," he warned.

"Let go of me!"

"You can tell me the truth now, or I'll find out on my own. Why are you in Egypt?"

"Thatcher, tell him to release me."

"Mr. Mitchell, you let Lady Elston go, now." The burly man pulled a knife from his belt, the sharp blade glittering in the sun. "We've been paid tae guard Lady Elston and 'er crates, and we intend tae earn our keep."

The sound of rifles being cocked was distinctive and chilling. She turned to see Connor and Gavin holding matching guns and wearing identical expressions.

"Unless you want their deaths on your conscience," Jake tightened his hold on her arm. "Tell your men to stay calm."

"Put your knife away, Thatcher. I'm sure I can make Mr. Mitchell see reason."

"That you can. By telling me the truth."

"You're overreacting."

He shook his head and waited for her to tell him what he wanted to know.

To stall for time until she could think of another plan, she said, "If this really is Deir el-Medineh—"

"It is."

"Then you knew the village was in ruin all along. Why didn't you tell me?"

His lips curved with an unpleasant smile. "And show my hand before all the cards were dealt? You've deceived me from the beginning and I want to know why. What are you doing here?"

She opened her mouth to give an answer, anything except the truth, but the words stuck in her throat.

"Are you looking for treasures?" He shook her. "Are you meeting someone? Or are you working with Napoleon?"

"No, I—"

"There's only one way to know for sure," he said, turning away and pulling her along with him.

Sarah struggled to break free, but Jake held her tighter as he took angry, determined strides . . . straight for her crates.

Chapter 11

Jake knew he was being irrational, knew he had overstepped his bounds. Sarah wasn't his responsibility; she could travel to Mt. Sinai and brave facing the bloodthirsty Bedouin tribes for all he cared. She didn't, shouldn't, concern him. He shouldn't give a damn whether she told him the truth or lied through her pretty white teeth. His pursuit of Roger and Queen Tiy was all that mattered. Yet he continued his march toward her wagon, dragging her behind him.

He was going to end her little game and satisfy his curiosity; then he'd abandon her to her *rented* house and continue on to the Valley of the Queens. He'd already wasted too much time on Sarah. For all he knew, Roger had already sealed Queen Tiy inside her tomb. Jake's stomach plummeted with the wrenching thought.

"Let go of me." She dug her feet into the sand. "You have no right to manhandle me this way."

"Tell me what I want to know," he said without slowing.

"Connor," she cried out, "I treated your wounds. Help me."

"I'd like tae, lass," the Scotsman said, following them on his camel. "But I'm as curious as Jake-o, 'ere. Why dinnae ye make it easy on ye'self and tell 'im what 'e wants tae know."

Jake stopped to face her. Her chest heaved with anger, but the emotion in her eyes was fear. Stark, desperate fear. Was she afraid of him, or of what he might find? His instincts had warned him that she was up to something, but now he knew it for sure.

"You're in league with Napoleon, aren't you? What is he looking for?" Before she could answer, an even worse scenario occurred to him. "My God, you're working with Stuart Kilvington!"

"Release me!" She pounded her fist against his chest.

"Bloody hell," he growled, catching her wrist. "Answer me."

She wrenched free, glaring at him. "I'm not in league with Napoleon, and I've never met Stuart Kilvington."

Seeing the panic in her eyes, he was tempted to believe her, which astounded him. After enduring the suspicions and doubt from the British Museum, Stuart Kilvington's treachery and Roger's betrayal, Jake thought he'd learned how to guard his back. But staring into Sarah's righteous gray eyes, he realized he hadn't learned a damn thing. He still wanted to trust her. She made him feel more alive than he'd ever felt before. More alive and crazed and full of longing than any sane man should feel.

God help him, he couldn't trust her and he couldn't trust himself when he was near her.

He whipped out the knife he kept in his boot.

"Jake," she pleaded as he leapt into the back of the wagon. "Please, don't."

He didn't dare look at her. Wedging his blade beneath the lid of the largest crate, he worked the wood loose, moving further down until all the nails had pulled partly free. Grunting, he heaved the lid open and shoved it aside. He expected to see shovels and picks, hand axes and brushes, trowels and sieves, along with a dozen other items she'd need to search for tombs.

But what he saw sent the blood rushing from his head.

"Bloody hell," he whispered.

"Jake," Gavin called out. "What is it?"

"Dear God, Sarah." Jake took off his hat and swiped his hand through his hair, too stunned to believe his own eyes. "What have you done?"

"What I had to."

Hearing the distress in her voice, he looked at her, saw her lips quiver and her beautiful, lying, silver eyes fill with tears.

His mind spun with a strange numbing anger. He wanted to yell at her, demand an explanation, yet he couldn't move. Could hardly breathe.

"Don't keep us in suspense, Jake-o," Connor grumbled. "What's inside?"

"It seems our search has ended," Jake said despite the constriction in his throat.

"What do you mean?" Gavin moved his camel forward.

The sun beat down on Jake, but he felt cold to the bone. He thought he'd been betrayed in the worst way before, but he'd been wrong. Dead wrong.

"It seems our sweet, defenseless Sarah has made fools of us all. She's had Queen Tiy all along."

Sarah had often wondered how a person with leprosy felt; now she knew. Tainted, loathed, tarnished. No one would look at her, or speak to her, and the condemning silence made her want to scream.

Jake and Gavin were in the wagon, carefully searching every crate, scattering her clothes and art supplies in the sand, while Connor kept his rifle trained on Eli and Thatcher. She thanked what little luck she had left that they hadn't looked inside the satchel tied to her saddle. She didn't want Jake to find the iron ball grenades and realize the extent of her mission. He was furious enough with her as it was.

But he was treating her like a thief, which she resented.

In reality, she had only tried to return what Jake and her father never should have taken in the first place.

"The canopic jars are all here and intact," Jake said, wiping sweat from his brow. He held up a pale white alabaster vase. Hieroglyphics had been painted in black down the center. The lid was shaped like a man's head, his thin nose and almond-shaped eyes framed by long dark hair.

"This jar is dedicated to Taumãutef, the god of heart and lung."

"If you say so," Gavin said, sealing the smallest box. "Since you don't have a list of the queen's jewelry and figurines we'll have to assume they're all accounted for."

"I embrace with my two arms that which is in me," Jake read from the jar, his voice soft with awe. He shook his head and set the canopic jar aside. "I was afraid I'd never see these again. Now for the queen."

Sarah crept closer. This was the first time she'd seen any of the relics. The small vase was exquisite, a miracle three thousand years old. It needed to be recorded for history, and undoubtedly it would, she realized, but not by her.

Together, Jake and Gavin opened the coffin's lid, straining under the massive weight. Sarah couldn't watch, knowing Jake's gaze would narrow and his complexion would darken to a dangerous shade when he realized not quite everything was accounted for.

"She doesn't appear to be damaged," she heard him say and had to turn back. "The wrappings are still tight."

From where she stood, Sarah could see a feminine face of hammered gold, arms crossed over bare breasts. Below, detailed scenes in purple and gold, red, black and white decorated the lid. There were images of shrines, figures kneeling, as if in prayer, or perhaps asking for forgiveness.

"There doesn't seem to be any decay, thank God," Jake said with a tight smile. "And her . . ."

The instant Jake's gaze turned on her, goose bumps

skimmed over her scalp and down her back. "Where is it, Sarah?"

She clasped her hands at her waist and stared, unseeing, at the expanse of desert. She heard a thud, knew he had jumped out of the wagon. When his hands came down hard on her shoulders and spun her around, she was ready for him.

Or so she'd thought.

Anger burned like blue fire in his eyes. The muscle in his jaw pulsed with a violent beat and his tanned skin was dark with temper. His fingers bit into her skin.

"Where is it?" he repeated.

"I don't know what you mean."

He cupped her face, forcing her to meet his gaze. His scowl made her reconsider her lie, but she bit down on her bottom lip to keep from spilling the truth. "The lies are over. I want the corselet. Now!"

"I told you—"

Hauling her up so her toes dangled above the ground, he started to say something but paused, frowning at her.

"Bloody hell!" He released her and clamped his big hands on her waist. "No wonder you're heavier than you look. You're wearing it. You're bloody wearing Queen Tiy's corselet!"

"Don't be—"

"Take it off."

"No." She twisted out of his hold. "You have the queen. Now leave me alone."

"Like hell I will. If you don't remove it I—"

"Jake," Gavin said, pushing him aside. "We can deal with the corselet later. Right now I'd like to know who Lady Elston really is, how she came into possession of your queen and why she brought her here."

Sarah wrapped her arms around her waist in the futile effort to keep the corselet. Shaking, eyeing both men, she realized additional lies would be a waste of breath.

Since Eli and Thatcher were unable to come to her rescue, she was virtually helpless.

Perhaps it was time for the truth. All of it.

She tilted her chin and met Jake's furious blue gaze. "Actually, I'm surprised I made it this far without you recognizing me."

He glared at her. "Is Sarah Elston your real name or not?"

"Yes and no."

"You'd be wise not to test my patience any further," he said, his voice low enough to be a warning. "Answer the question."

Dreading the moment when she said her name and he realized just how badly he'd been duped, she said. "We've met, you know, not officially, but we've been in each other's lives for years."

His gaze raked over her. "I think I would have remembered you."

"I was a girl the last time you saw me. You were leaving with my father on another of your archaeological trips. Something about a new discovery at the Luxor temple." She could clearly see that moment in her mind, feel the two men's excitement and wanting so badly to be a part of it, only to be swamped with heartache when she was left behind.

His glare turned into a frown. "Your father? Just who is your . . . what is your name?"

"Sarah," she said, searching his eyes for some glimmer of recognition. "Lady Sarah Pendergrass."

"You're lying. Again." His jaw flexing, Jake rested his hands on his lean waist. "Roger doesn't have a daughter."

Sarah stared at Jake in disbelief, her heart plummeting to her stomach. *Did Jake forget about me, the same as my father had?* She couldn't draw a breath and her chest squeezed tight. Her eyes stung as they filled with tears.

"Roger does have a daughter," she managed.

"No, he doesn't," Jake said, pounding each word.

She gaped at him, unable to speak, remembering the hours she'd spent resenting him for taking her place in her father's life, blaming Jake for purposefully stealing her father's love.

Had she made a mistake?

She swallowed. Was it possible Jake had never known she was alive? That he hadn't intentionally pushed her aside?

Somehow that possibility hurt worse than enduring her father's neglect. She would have to admit that Roger hadn't loved her because he hadn't wanted to. Stiffening her spine and willing the tears to dry, she tried a rueful laugh, but it sounded hoarse and full of pain. "I'm afraid Roger does have a daughter, and I am she."

Jake's expression didn't soften, it became harder. "I've spent years in Roger's company, if he'd had a child, he would have mentioned it."

"I'm sure he did."

Jake gave a curt shake of his head. "Never."

Despite her willing them not to, her eyes refilled with tears. Did she mean so little to Roger that he had never spoken about her, even among his friends?

She had to turn away. "I suppose I shouldn't be surprised that he never mentioned me."

"I spent months living in his home. I've never seen you."

She stared at the blurry desert land. "After my mother's death he sent me to boarding school. I was only allowed to come home to Whitehurst Manor for two days during Christmas holiday, if Father was in town, and for one week during the summer. It was during my summer holiday when I was twelve that I first met you."

She turned back to see Jake running his hand through his hair, his face still set with anger. "I don't remember."

"You were leaving for Egypt. I wanted to go with you,

but Father wouldn't hear of it. He sent me packing back to school before my week was up."

Jake's shoulders were tense, his expression deadly. "There's no way to prove you're Roger's child until we return to London, but if by some miracle you are his daughter, what the bloody hell are you doing here, and with Queen Tiy?"

Sarah started to ask Eli and Thatcher to vouch for her, but decided Jake wouldn't believe them anymore than he did her. Then she remembered Roger's letter and knew that would be all the proof Jake would need, but before she could mention it, Gavin spoke.

"Roger asked you to bring her here."

Sarah nodded, for once grateful for the earl's cool and reasonable tone.

"Roger sent *you* to Egypt?" Jake shouted. "Alone?"

"I wasn't alone."

"Two hired hands don't count, Sarah."

"Now see 'ere," Eli said, puffing out his barreled chest.

"Don't take it personally," Jake told her guards, "but you don't know a thing about this country or the dangers involved."

Jake clenched his jaw tight and ground out a curse she'd never heard before. She saw in the steel blue of his eyes that he didn't want to believe anything she'd said. His next words proved it. "Roger wouldn't risk his daughter's life. No father would."

But that's exactly what he did, she thought, unable to admit the truth out loud. Instead, she said, "He didn't force me to come. It was my choice."

A growl of frustration rumbled from Jake's chest. "You shouldn't have been given a choice. Any man who even suggested you come here should be whipped and thrown in prison! Bloody hell, I'll beat him to a bloody pulp myself."

Jake's enraged declaration took her back. No one had

ever been concerned, let alone furious, about her welfare before. The concept was so foreign, she didn't know how to respond.

While she gaped at him, he demanded, "Now tell me the truth. How did you get the queen?"

"I've already told you—"

"How did you steal it from the viscount?"

Sarah clenched her hands into fists, letting the unfamiliar concept that he would defend her fade so that the painful blow he'd just delivered could sink in. In a matter of seconds her confused emotions sharpened into anger. "I'm not a thief. Roger is my father, in blood if not in behavior. He called me to his deathbed and pleaded for me to return Queen Tiy to her tomb so the curse could be broken. He'd asked you to do it, but you refused."

"You're bloody right I did. He was being irrational."

"So he turned to me."

"And you decided to risk your life?" Jake scoffed, pacing in front of her. "Because he believes Queen Tiy will kill him for disturbing her."

"Not entirely," she said, fighting the urge to punch the skeptical smirk off Jake's face.

"Then what could have possibly inspired you to accept such a foolish task?"

"You, Jacob Mitchell," she told him, feeling the full burst of her anger break through the walls she'd erected. "My real reason had been to ruin you!"

Re-Temu, the god of the setting sun, lured the giant orb closer and closer to the steaming earth. The last vibrant rays flooded the horizon with color: powerful blood red and bursts of white gold, splashes of dusty pink mingled with the pure, seductive shade of early night.

There was no place in the world as majestic, as timeless, or as unforgiving. And no other place in the world

Jake loved as much. This land was where he should have been born and raised, not along the filthy banks of the river Thames. Only tonight, the sight of this incredible country did little to quiet the turmoil that burned his blood like the bite of a cobra.

Jake glanced across the scattering of rocks and dust to where Connor supervised Eli and Thatcher setting up camp. Sarah was gathering her belongings, shaking them free of sand and returning them to her trunk. There was no need to continue to the Valley of the Queens. Instead they would camp in Deir el-Medineh tonight and return to Thebes in the morning.

Jake drew a deep breath, trying to calm his temper and clear his thoughts, but a storm of emotions still raged inside him. Resentment, confusion, downright anger. Because of an old man's fears, they had all endured the torturous desert and the threat of French soldiers. And it wasn't over yet. Jake turned away from camp and walked through the ruins of crumbled homes and empty streets.

As hard as he tried not to think about her, Jake couldn't stop wondering if Sarah's innocent act had been a ploy. Her wide eyes, her helpless charm. And their kisses. Had she endured them because she'd been plotting to ruin him? And why would she want to ruin him? He'd played no part in her unhappy life with her father.

Roger's daughter. Jake still couldn't believe it. He knew Roger Pendergrass better than he knew himself. If the man had had a child, he would have told Jake. They had never kept any secrets from each other. *Until now.* Could Roger really have given Queen Tiy to a naïve woman with instructions to return her to her tomb? Afraid for his life or not, Jake couldn't believe Roger would put any woman in such danger. But if Roger hadn't sent her, that meant Sarah still hadn't told him the truth. Which left the question of how she got her hands on Queen Tiy and what she'd intended to do with her.

"I warned you not to become involved with her."

Jake didn't turn around to respond to Gavin's taunt because there wasn't much he could say. The blasted man had been right.

"She still has the corselet," Gavin added.

"I'll get it from her." Had she silently laughed at him when he'd told her about pursuing Roger to reclaim the corselet, when it had been within his reach all along?

"I have no doubt you will."

Jake faced the earl, suspicious of his mocking tone. "Meaning?"

Gavin reached down to pick up one of the thousands of ostraca, the limestone chips the ancients had used to write on, littering the ground. "Meaning I'm sure that whatever is between you two isn't over yet."

"There's nothing between us," Jake insisted.

Gavin's dark, unblinking gaze held Jake's. "I lied to myself once, and it cost me everything. Take my advice, don't turn your back on that one."

He followed the earl's gaze to where Sarah was now sitting on a pile of bleached stones, bent over her drawing tablet, her pencil fast at work. Her long, sable hair hung loose down her back, shifting with the wind. Jake felt his gut tighten and his blood warm. He bit out a curse and turned away. He did *not* desire her. Only a fool would want to do anything other than strangle her after what she'd done. And he was through being made a fool. It was time to take the earl's approach to women.

Facing Gavin, he said, "It seems you were right to distrust Sarah. What made you suspect her?"

The earl laughed, a distinctly unhappy sound. "Because she's female."

"You distrust the entire female sex? Why?"

Gavin rubbed his thumb over the ostracon's smooth surface, revealing a series of hieroglyphics that could be anything from an inventory list to the names of workers, or a note to the architect. The possibilities were limitless, as was everything in Egypt.

But from the look on the earl's face, Jake could believe that Gavin had stopped believing in possibilities.

"I was married once." Gavin glanced up, his expression unreadable. "Did you know that?"

Jake nodded.

"Her name was Rachel and every man in England envied me for having her for my wife. She wasn't just beautiful, she was witty and charming, lighting up a room whenever she entered. Every day was a surprise with her. Because she was fearless."

"I know she died," Jake said, hesitant to pursue the conversation. "Did she become ill?"

Gavin laughed. "No, nothing so honorable or boring as that, not for my Rachel. After our son was born, she became restless. I wanted to raise Matthew at our home in the country, but Rachel grew bored with the quiet life and convinced me to let her take our son to the city. Fool that I was, I agreed. I had to, I couldn't deny her anything."

Gavin paused, staring into the sinking sun without seeing it, turning the piece of ostracon over and over in his hands.

"What happened?" Jake prompted when Gavin didn't say anything more.

"I joined Rachel and Matthew at our townhouse in London, a surprise, because I knew how much my wife loved surprises. I had bought her a new carriage with matching white thoroughbreds and couldn't wait to show her."

Jake started to tell Gavin to stop, not wanting to hear what would come next, but now that he had begun, the other man spoke as if he couldn't quit.

"Only the surprise was to be mine. It seemed my lovely, charming wife had taken a lover. I found them together. A cliché, I know." Gavin's mouth pulled into a tight smile. "The stately, arrogant lord cuckolded by his too beautiful, too recalcitrant wife."

"Did you divorce her?" Jake asked, knowing Gavin would have had to announce to the courts that his wife had been unfaithful. He supposed the humiliation might be enough to cause a man to distrust all women.

"Divorce? No. Once again, my wife took the dramatic way out. That night she pleaded for me to forgive her. But how could I? She destroyed everything we had. So I shut myself inside my study and drank myself into oblivion. When I awoke the next morning, it was to the news that Rachel had fled in her new carriage, taking Matthew with her. They had raced to the harbor, why there I can't say. Maybe she intended to sail away with her lover. Who knows? Whatever her destination, she never made it. A band of thieves tried to steal the carriage, overturning it, killing my wife and three-year-old son."

"Jesus," Jake said under his breath.

"Yes." Gavin looked down at the ostracon as if seeing it for the first time. He drew back his arm and flung the stone into the air. Both men watched it arch against the violet sky before it landed in a cloud of dust. "My family lay dying while I was in a drunken stupor."

"You can't blame yourself."

"Can't I?" Gavin turned to Jake, his face a hard, unforgiving mask. "I gave Rachel everything, my name, my belongings, my love. Yet it wasn't enough. She wanted more, and she took it. Do you know what she gave me in return?"

When Jake shook his head, Gavin told him, "Guilt and distrust. They are the only things I have left."

Jake wanted to tell the earl that their deaths had been an accident, that no one could have predicted what would happen. But Gavin strode away, heading away from camp. Jake let him go, suspecting the earl had heard the empty words before and didn't want to hear them again.

He glanced toward the wagons and spotted Sarah sitting on her clump of stones, her drawing tablet still in her lap, but instead of focusing on the paper, she was looking at him. A tingling heat started low in his body, but he suppressed the feelings.

Sarah may not be his wife, but she had deceived him just as Rachel had deceived Gavin. Nothing would ever make him trust her again.

Chapter 12

The three-foot-long, skinned body of a desert snake hung suspended over the fire on a skewer. Flames licked upward, browning the meat and filling the air with an aroma strangely similar to roasted chicken. Her stomach alternating between growling with hunger and rolling with queasiness, Sarah tried not to look at it. Not an hour before, Connor had returned with the writhing body of live reptile gripped in his hand. He'd grinned like a boy until Jake had informed him he held one of Egypt's most venomous snakes—cerastes, the horned viper, second only to the deadly cobra.

After scowling at the viper, Connor had laughed, then cleaved the reptile's head before Sarah knew what he had intended.

She picked up her bowl of dried fruit and hard bread, but couldn't make herself eat, afraid none of it would stay down. And not just because of the cooking snake. Her nerves were tied into knots. She wanted to pace, walk away from the camp and the suspicious looks being cast her way, but she didn't dare, not when there were poisonous creatures slithering nearby. Repeatedly, she'd been tempted to explain why she had deceived them, only to stop herself, realizing that nothing she said would change the three men's opinion of her. They thought she was either a naïve female doing her insane father's bidding or, worse, a thief who had stolen the queen and had returned to Egypt for some sinister reason.

It didn't matter what they believed, she decided, refusing to sulk. They would all return to Thebes tomorrow, then to England. Soon, she would never see Connor or Gavin again. Or Jake, she added, biting down on her lip when her heart gave a jerky beat. He sat across from her, the fire and the snake a dividing wall. He was studying something in his lap, for which she was grateful. She didn't want him to look at her, knowing she'd see the quiet rage in his storm blue eyes. Eyes that had once been warm and honest—and had burned with desire for her. Feeling her cheeks flush with the memory, she picked up a dried date and forced herself to take a bite.

"Have you made any progress?" she heard Gavin ask.

She glanced up to see Jake running his hand through his long, whiskey dark hair. "No, the images are too blurred."

His gaze clashed with hers, sending a shiver down Sarah's spine as he added, "I need the corselet."

She instinctively pressed her hands to her waist, knowing she had to relinquish the artifact. But like a spoiled child with a favorite toy, she was reluctant to do so. She'd become accustomed to its weight, it had become a shield that would protect her from the outside world. *But not from Jake.*

"Perhaps you should give it to him," the earl said. "I, for one, am curious to know what it looks like."

Sarah exchanged stares with all three men, then with Eli and Thatcher, who sat together near the shadows, watching her with pitying expressions.

Tilting her chin to put on a brave front, she replied, "You expect me to remove it now? In front of all of you?"

"It's dark enough in the wagon," Gavin said.

"Considering Connor found *that*," she said, nodding

with disgust at the snake, "not far from here, I don't think I'll be leaving the fire."

"We'll turn our backs," Connor offered.

"I'm not taking it off."

"Why not, Sarah?" Jake asked, speaking to her for the first time since he discovered Queen Tiy, hours ago.

Because once I give it to you, I'll have to admit I failed. The words were on the tip of her tongue, but she bit them back. Any chance she'd had of gaining Roger's love and respect had already vanish for good.

Unbidden, Jake's words came back to her. *Roger wouldn't risk his daughter's life. No father would.*

But Roger had put her in danger, lying to her about the threat of Napoleon's army, sending her into an environment as foreign and deadly as the moon. Would a man capable of love do that to her? After everything she'd been through, she wanted to believe there was a chance she could have the family . . . the father . . . she'd always hoped for. But she was terribly afraid that she'd deluded herself from the beginning by hoping for the impossible.

Any man who suggested you come here should be whipped and thrown in prison! Bloody hell, I'll beat him to a bloody pulp myself.

Sarah wanted to laugh at the absurdity of her situation. The man she'd wanted to ruin was the only man who had come to her defense. Perhaps he cared about her more than her father did. And now, because he believed she'd betrayed him, he hated her in turn.

Rubbing her arms to ward off a chill that had nothing to do with the cold wind blowing at her back, she made a decision. "Tomorrow. I'll give you the corselet tomorrow."

A muscle flexed in Jake's jaw and he nodded. "You'd better get some sleep, Sarah. And enjoy your time with the corselet. It will be your last time to see it."

* * *

A hush fell over the antechamber, which was crowded with the noble and curious alike. Sunlight streamed through the open doorways, shining onto faces of those she had once called friends, but who were now her foes. The stone relief of the great god Osiris towered over the room, staring down upon her with indifference, not caring whether she lived or died.

And she would die, of that there was no doubt.

She had already witnessed her beloved son Pentewere put to death, the curved blade of a dagger slicing his beautiful young body, spilling his blood onto his linen kilt, the gold embroidery stained to black.

She swayed as the room spun around her. Her only child being put to sword! Gods, no mother should endure such pain!

"You are found guilty of treason," Lord Abubakar, vizier and second in power only to Ramses III, announced from his high seat. "What have you to say?"

Wearing a plain sheath of white linen, Queen Tiy stood alone in the center of the antechamber, her wrists bound before her like a common thief. She had been stripped of all her queenly possessions, her crown of gold and garnets, all of her rings, each a thousand years old, the carnelian and jasper bracelets she'd held dear. The only item left to her was her corselet, a wrap of tiny gold squares with a waistband of lapis lazuli and emerald-cut onyx. A feast day gift from Ramses the year Pentewere had been born. A rare and precious testament of Pharaoh's love for her.

She squared her shoulders and met the gaze of each man who was her judge and jury—men who had condemned her before she'd entered the room. Three royal cupbearers, the lord of the treasury, two fan-beaters, scribes and heralds who had once bent their knee, begging to do her favor.

"You have already condemned those who were associated with me," she told the men. "The Chief of the Harem Chamber, Ramses' trusted Inspectors. My son."

"Men who testified you were behind the plot to assassinate our Pharaoh," the vizier said with scorn.

"Confessions you gained by torturing them near to death."

"Enough!" The High Priest Omair banged his staff against the stone floor. Gold rings glittered from each of his fingers, amulets wrapped both bony wrists and hung from his neck. A belt of malachite and agate in the shape of a vulture circled his waist. He glared at her from beside Ramses' empty throne, openly blaming her for the Pharaoh's death.

A death I had no part of, she wanted to scream. Willing her pounding heart to quiet, she asked, "What can I say that will convince you of my innocence?"

"We are not interested in hearing your lies," the vizier told her.

"Since you've already condemned me, sentence me now."

The vizier stood, his face flushed, his reed-thin body visibly shaking. "Who else aided you in the murder of your husband and our pharaoh? I will have their names!"

Queen Tiy held her tongue. Thirty-eight men had already been put to death, some by the executioner's knife, some by being staked to wood and left for the sun god Re to punish. She suspected a few of those men had been guilty of the charges against them, some innocent, yet each one had confessed that she had led them.

She stared at her husband's throne, empty now. She had never wanted Ramses' death, but she would have done anything to protect Pentewere. She had not plotted to seize power from Pharaoh. It was her enemies who had wanted to remove Pentewere from the line of the succession. She'd told Ramses as much, but he hadn't believed her.

So she had done what she'd had to, to keep her child alive. Yet she'd failed anyway. Her husband was gone, as was her son. She was ready to die, too. Now that Pentewere had traveled to the afterlife, she only wanted to join him.

"There are no others to name," she said, her voice as empty as her heart. "If I am to be put to death, do so now. I am finished with this world. I am ready for the next."

Lord Abubakar reclaimed his seat, a cobra smile lifting his thin lips. "You will not see the next world, Queen Tiy."

Her breath left her. "What do you mean?"

He lifted a scroll. "Your death warrant has been signed. As traitor to the laws we hold dear, for putting into motion plans that led to our Pharaoh's death—"

"I did not kill Ramses!"

"Did you not?"

"The physicians admitted they do not know the cause of his death."

"You are responsible."

"No!" she cried.

"You poisoned him."

"You lie! The physicians found no trace of poison."

"It has been whispered that you cursed him."

Trembling with fear, Queen Tiy pressed her bound hands to her waist. Her arms quivered and her legs threatened to buckle, but her voice was strong and clear as she vowed, "I put no curse on Pharaoh, but I promise you this, Lord Abubakar, if you deny my rightful place in the afterlife I will curse every man who judges me."

The men before her, from the lowliest scribe to the High Priest stared at her, their eyes wide with horror.

"Tell us how you killed him!" Vizier Abubakar demanded.

"Promise you will grant my right to enter Amentit."

"We will not subject our gods to your treachery," High Priest Omair vowed. "If we allow you to enter the next world, the gods will weigh your actions on the Day of Judgment. You will fail, and by doing so bring sin upon us all. I will not risk being thrown to the bitch-monster Amait because of your evil doings."

Silence slammed into the room, the onlookers hardly daring to breathe. Blood rushed from Queen Tiy's head, buzzing in her ears, blurring her vision. She would not see Pentewere again. They would not wander the stars that knew no rest or live among the planets that had no destination.

She would spend eternity in a bleak, endless void. Alone.

A desolate, unforgiving coldness slid into her body, winding around her limbs and up her torso, spreading throughout her mind.

Into the quiet, she whispered, "Then I curse you all."

"You will not speak unless it is to give me names!" Vizier Abubakar shouted.

"By condemning me, you condemn yourselves," she told them, rubbing her hands over the corselet without feeling it, staring at her jury without seeing them.

She lifted her gaze to the statue of Osiris, but found no comfort in the God of Eternal Life Everlasting.

She met Vizier Abubakar's frightened and furious gaze. "If I am to dwell in hell for an eternity, I shall not do so alone. By the power of our ambivalent god, Set, ruler of the Underworld, I pray to him that every one of you will join me."

"Executioner," Vizier Abubakar ordered, "you have her death warrant. See it through!"

The guard stepped forward, the same man who had ended Pentewere's life. An iron mask shielded his face, but for a pair of lifeless black eyes. Silver armor adorned his massive arms and chest. He stopped before her, his curved dagger gripped in a hand that could snap her neck. He drew his arm back and held it there for an endless second. She heard the rasp of his breath, and suddenly, felt his reluctance.

"All I want is to be with my son," she whispered.

An instant later the blade slashed for one last, fatal blow.

Sarah jerked awake, gasping, clenching her stomach. Searing hot pain shot beneath her skin. She sat up and drew one breath after another, then another until she choked on a sob.

Pressing her hands to her waist, she felt the gold squares, cold against her skin. She knew what she had to do. Only this time she wouldn't do it for her father.

She would do it for Queen Tiy.

Chapter 13

The day dawned with the temper of a dragon, fiercely hot and scorching the land. Jake had ordered everything packed into the wagons, anxious to get moving. Once the water barrels were strapped to the camels, they would be ready to leave. But even with their early start, they wouldn't be able to travel far before being forced to seek shelter from the sun. He scanned the barren horizon, ready to return to England, yet just as ready to stay. This was where he belonged, among the sand dunes and dark tombs, uncovering the past that was still so much a mystery.

Movement on a hill across the valley caught his attention. He tensed, at first expecting to see Napoleon's men bearing down on them. Shielding his eyes from the morning glare, he muttered a curse. Not French soldiers. Someone far more dangerous.

"What the bloody hell is she doing up there?" he ground out, surprised when Connor responded from behind him.

"I told the lass not tae wander off." The Scotsman shook his head. "She gave me a queer look, then said she wouldn't be long. There was something she had tae see."

"And you let her go? By herself?"

"Ye think she's going tae cause trouble?"

"She's been nothing but trouble." Snatching up a flask of water and a rifle, Jake took off after her. What was she up to? Trying to delay their trip? Looking for her allies? Or trying to get herself killed?

It took Jake less than twenty minutes to catch up with her. As he climbed the steep hill, careful to find solid footholds in the rocky slope, he watched Sarah ahead of him navigating the rocky terrain, holding her skirts up with one hand and revealing a generous amount of her slender legs. Silky white and well formed. The urge to run his hands over her pale skin to see if she was as soft as she looked had him wiping sweat from his brow. Perhaps she wasn't looking for her accomplices, perhaps she was trying to drive him insane.

Losing her footing, she started to slide down the hill. Jake sprinted the last few feet, caught her around the waist and locked her against him. Her startled yelp made him smile, but feeling the corselet beneath her gown turned it into a scowl.

"What do you think you're doing?" he demanded.

She struggled to catch her breath, then looked at him over her shoulder. The simple turn of her head gave him a clear view of the rapid rise and fall of her chest. The mounds of her breasts above her neckline were rosy from the sun and glistening with sweat. Remembering the salty-sweet taste of her skin, he fought the urge to lower his mouth to the base of her throat and work his way down. Blood rushed to his groin, the blast of desire so strong it frightened him.

He released her, but had to grip her arm when she stumbled and started her slide down the hill again.

"What are you up to now, Sarah?"

"I . . . I just . . ." She looked at him, her silver eyes glassy in her flushed face. She shook her head, as if she were lost or confused. He recalled Connor saying she'd given him a queer look, and now Jake understood what he meant. Something was wrong with her. She seemed frightened or dazed. A warning sounded in his mind. Was she using a new ploy to deceive him again?

"It's time to leave." He turned to guide her back to camp.

She pulled free and glanced up the hill. "Not yet."

"Sarah—"

"We've come so far," she said, her expression wistful and imploring at the same time. "I may never have the chance to return. I just want to see the Valley of the Kings before we leave."

"There's no time." He caught her arm, intending to drag her back to camp if need be, but she laid her hand on his chest and moved closer. He clamped his jaw tight.

"The tombs aren't far from here, are they?"

She stood so close he could smell her sun-warmed skin, see himself reflected in her eyes. "The valley is an hour's walk."

She gave him a wistful smile. "Only an hour."

"No, Sarah. We're leaving."

Her hand clenched his shirt, the simple act stopping him as soundly as if she'd chained him to the ground. How many times had he thought about having her hands on him, moving over his body, exploring him the way he wanted to explore her. The blood heating his sex made his mind spin. He stopped the dangerous thoughts, but he couldn't escape her womanly scent. And God help him, even as furious as he was with her, escaping her wasn't all that appealing. No woman had ever affected him the way Sarah did. Regardless of who she really was, or her intentions, there was a part of him that wanted her.

But want her or not, he wasn't about to fall for another one of her tricks.

"Jake," she said, wiping strands of her hair from her brow. "You have Queen Tiy. You've won. Nothing will stop you from taking her back to England."

"Napoleon is as much a threat as ever. If he or any of his

men discover us, they'll do more than take her. They'll imprison us at best, kill us at worst."

She nodded, sighing with reluctance. "I know, but I haven't seen any sign of them."

"That's only because you don't know what to look for."

She tensed. Glancing around the valley, she moved closer to him, if that were possible. "They're here?"

"Yes."

"Are they close?"

Jake couldn't stop himself from sliding his arm around her back. "Not at the moment, but that can change."

She turned her gaze back to him, bringing her lips within inches of his. Every cell and muscle in his body wanted to kiss her. Jake resisted, knowing he'd be doomed if he did.

She watched him, as if waiting for him to lower his head, press his mouth to hers, take her in a kiss as hot and devastating as any they'd shared.

"What do you think you're doing, Sarah?" he asked, his teeth clenched.

"I just want . . ." Both her hands kneaded his chest as if to silently urge him on.

"You want me to make love to you?" he asked, his voice tight with equal amounts of desire and anger. "Now, on this hillside, beneath the sun?"

She gave a feeble shake of her head. "I can't explain what I feel."

"Of course you can. You want me."

"No, I mean yes, I do want you. But . . ." She closed her eyes as if regretting her confession. Looking at him, revealing the conflicting emotions spinning inside her, she added, "But that's not what has me so confused."

"Now I'm confused."

"I know you hate me."

Jake was taken back. Hate didn't describe his feelings for her. He was furious, outraged, troubled, and vexed, torn between walking away from her forever and never leaving her side. He started to put some of his feelings into words, but she didn't give him a chance.

"I feel compelled to stay here," she said, her eyes shimmering with misery and tears. "I can't explain why because I don't understand what's happening. I only know I need to see the Valley of the Kings and Queens. Just once."

"Sarah, we can't stay," Jake said, though his voice lacked conviction.

"Just one more day." She lowered her forehead against his chest, and though he tried not to, he could feel the desperate longing inside her. "Please. Just one."

"Sarah—"

She raised her gaze to his. "You love this place, don't you."

It was a statement, not a question. Jake could only nod in answer.

"Then show it to me so I can love it, too."

Sarah almost regretted her request for Jake to show her the valley, and she was virtually certain he regretted giving in to her plea.

Sweat trickled down her temples and her damp gown clung to her like a second skin. Heat radiated off her body in suffocating waves. She resisted asking for the water skin; she'd already consumed half when Jake had barely taken a sip. He'd been more than considerate, she admitted, agreeing to remain in Deir el-Medineh for another day so she could see the ancient tombs for herself. Both Gavin and Connor had disagreed, but Jake, clearly irritated with himself for consenting to stay, had gathered two camels and led her north.

She hated deceiving him again, but after her dream the night before, having experienced the last, terrifying moments of Queen Tiy's life, feeling the woman's fear and anger and sorrow, she didn't dare tell Jake the truth. He wouldn't believe her, and if by some miracle he did, he still wouldn't return the queen to her tomb so she could live for eternity with her son.

Sarah wasn't sure she believed in everlasting life, either, but she knew the dream had been real, a message from the dead woman. Sarah touched her waist, realizing Queen Tiy had been wearing the corselet at the moment of her death.

Shivering, she tilted her face toward the sun that glared down from a bleached-white sky, baking the valley floor on which they stood. East and west, towering cliffs rose from the desert sand. A series of low hills and plateaus extended to the north. Boxing the valley in from the south was a mountainside of jutting rock that made her think of a tolerant Egyptian god, looking down upon his realm. Turning in a circle, listening to the hushed whisper of the wind, sensing the people who had walked here thousands of years before her, Sarah understood why the pharaohs had chosen this place. The isolated location was not only beautiful, it was inspiring.

"Over there," Jake said, pointing north, "is where Seti the First's mortuary temple is located."

In the distance she could discern doorways or tunnels cut into the hillsides, but no grand statues or daunting pyramids like in Giza. "Can we go inside?"

He answered her with an impatient look, then headed for the camels. "We need to head back, find some shade."

Following him, she asked, "What about Queen Tiy's tomb? We could wait out the heat there."

"We're nowhere near her tomb."

Sarah stopped in her tracks. "What?"

"She was buried in the Valley of the Queens, an hour or more to the south."

"South? But that's the direction of Deir el-Medineh."

"Exactly," he said, waiting to help her onto her camel. "Which is where we're going."

"To the Queen's Valley?" she asked hopefully.

"To the village. The valley is farther south than I intend to go. Besides, you promised to give the corselet to me today, and I'd like to study it before we start back to Thebes."

She didn't take another step. Panic shortened her breath and turned her palms clammy with sweat. How could she have made such a mistake? There were two valleys, not one? She had to find the exact location of the queen's tomb *today*. She had Roger's map, but she dreaded wandering the desert trying to find the tomb tonight—the only time she'd be able to escape Jake and the others.

He held his hand out to her. "Let's go, Sarah."

She stayed where she was, undecided.

"What is it?" he asked, his blue gaze suspicious beneath the shadowed brim of his hat.

"You'll think I'm crazy."

"I already think that."

A frantic laugh escaped her. "I feel connected to her somehow."

"Her?"

"Queen Tiy."

Dropping the camel's reins, Jake closed the distance between them. Staring down at her with an expression too indiscernible to read, he said, "You feel connected to someone who has been dead for three thousand years."

Sarah nodded. "It sounds insane, doesn't it?"

"No more than anything else you've said or done since I laid eyes on you."

She swallowed, terrified he would see through her and guess her real intention. "It's too much to ask, I know, but the valley is on the way."

"You've suffered heat exhaustion once." He crossed his tanned arms over his chest. "I won't risk it again."

She stamped down the temptation to beg. "Don't you want to see how her tomb has fared since you left it?"

She saw her answer in the brief flexing of his jaw, a clear sign that he did, but he didn't want to admit it. "If I had my pad and pencils I could make some drawings for you."

"We won't be here that long."

"We aren't going to leave until tomorrow morning." Pushing loose strands of hair from her face, she paced in a circle, then faced him. "This is my last chance, Jake. Just . . . please, take me there."

He glared at her, his face flushed from the heat, his shirt soaked and his sun-darkened skin glistening with sweat. His mouth lifted in a scowl, but she had the odd sensation that he wasn't mad at her at all.

After cursing under his breath, he admitted, "Woman, you're going to be the death of me."

No, she thought, but considering what she intended to do, he just might wish *her* dead come morning.

"Will we 'ave trouble getting back tae Rosetta?" Connor asked, raising his cup when Sarah offered to refill it with the stout barley beer. *His third,* she noted anxiously, her stomach doing a little flip.

"It's impossible to tell," Jake said, his eyes never leaving her as she topped off his cup. "When Hapi, God of the River Nile, decides to flood the river, no one can predict how generous he'll be."

"You don't really believe in a river god, do you?" Gavin asked, draining his beer, his cool gaze flicking over her when Sarah insisted on giving him more

"Who's to say they don't exist." Jake shrugged. "The Egyptians were building temples to honor their gods when the English were still prehistoric beasts living in caves."

The earl sat forward and asked, "Do you think we'll have to wait in Thebes the entire summer? I don't care for the idea of being trapped with so many of Napoleon's men scurrying about."

"I intend to return to England, even if it means we have to walk." Jake leaned against the two-foot-high remains of a mud-brick wall, his long legs stretched out before him. Firelight played over the bold arch of his cheekbones and the line of his jaw, rough with a day's growth of beard. After finishing his dinner of a salty beef stew, he had lapsed into a quiet, reflective mood—which worried her. He hadn't demanded the corselet upon their return to camp as she'd expected. Instead, he had prepared their meal, not speaking to anyone, his thoughts obviously elsewhere.

Dipping the clay jar into the barrel of beer to refill it, Sarah sat near the fire and waited for the men to empty their cups. Eli and Thatcher were scowling at their mugs, not wanting the water she'd given them, but she needed them clear-headed tonight. She gripped the jar in her hands to fight down her nervousness, and the fear spinning through her insides. Thanks to Jake for showing her the way, she knew exactly how to find Queen Tiy's tomb. All she had to do now was harness the oxen to the wagon, travel an hour to the south—in the dark—help Eli and Thatcher return the queen to her resting place, then destroy the tomb.

And all without alerting Jake, Connor, or Gavin.

She released a shuddering breath and wished she had something stronger to serve them than beer.

She thought Connor's eyes might be a little glassy, and his lids drooped as he stared into the fire. But how much would a man of his size have to drink before he passed out? She had no idea, but surely it was more than the three cups he'd consumed so far. Jake and Gavin were keeping pace with the Scotsman, but they weren't showing any signs of dozing off. Somehow she had to get them to drink more; she couldn't risk them waking up and stopping her.

Sarah inwardly cringed, hating herself for deceiving Jake again, and dreading that in the morning she would not only have to deal with his hangover, she would have to endure the full force of his hatred. Only this time, she would deserve it.

Faint wind crept through the remains of the dead city's homes, shops and storerooms, stirring the hair at Jake's nape and bringing the occasional scent of smoke to his nose. He lay on a coarse wool blanket, the cool sand shifting beneath his weight. Million upon millions of twinkling stars filled the night sky, though he didn't see them. He kept his eyes closed and his limbs relaxed, his breathing even. The day had been tiring, the heat and traipsing through the desert had taken its toll. He longed for sleep, but doubted he'd get any rest tonight. Not if what his ears were telling him was true.

He didn't need the hearing of a falcon to know someone was moving, just beyond camp if he were to guess. Instinct told him to pick up the pistol lying at his side, but common sense told him to wait. He wouldn't need a gun for this intruder.

Hearing the faint jingle of metal, then the creaking of wood, he had to force himself to continue lying still. Another minute he told himself. Just enough time to let his beautiful, cunning, foolish prowler think she had gotten away. Give her a bit of freedom before he caught up with her and wrung her neck.

After a few moments, the quiet returned. He opened his eyes and looked beyond the dying fire to the shadows where the wagon loaded with Queen Tiy's coffin should have been. He raised up on one elbow and stared at Sarah's empty pallet, a hard scowl lifting his lips.

When she'd insisted on seeing the Valley of the Kings, he'd been touched by the sincerity of her plea, but when she'd been frantic to visit Queen Tiy's tomb, he'd become suspicious. With good reason, he realized.

Retrieving his pistol, he pushed to his feet. Not bothering to saddle a camel, Jake set off on foot into the dark. It didn't require any skills in tracking to find Sarah's trail—he knew where she was going.

Chapter 14

The menacing laugh stopped Sarah dead in her tracks. She edged closer to the ox beside her. The animal snorted, his black eyes wide in the moonlight. Goose bumps raced over Sarah's skin, and her heart missed a beat before it switched to pounding mad thumps against her ribs.

"Who was that?" Eli yelped, tugging back on the reins as he stood up in the wagon.

"I . . . I don't know." Sarah clenched the four-foot stick she'd found outside of camp in one hand. She searched the shadowed sand dunes and black cliff walls for any sign of movement. The desert was magnificent during the day, hostile and beautiful in one breath, but at night, the dark contours of the land shifted on their own, looming over her one instant, only to pull away the next.

She suppressed a panicky shudder and willed her overactive imaginings to behave. There was no one here except for the three of them. If Jake were following her, he wouldn't be laughing at her in such an eerie way, he'd be shouting with rage.

"Not a who. A what," Thatcher said rather calmly. He stood at the head of the second ox, one hand on the animal's halter. "That be a hyena. I heard one once, when I was a boy."

"Are they dangerous?" she asked, thinking anything that sounded so insane couldn't be good.

"I suppose if they're hungry enough." Thatcher tugged on the ox's halter. "We'd best keep moving."

Wild animals, a French army, what else would she have to keep alert for? Recalling Jake's warning that cobras preferred to hunt at night, she searched the ground for anything black and slithering.

"It's not much farther," she told them. "We're in the Queens' valley. There's a path we need—there!" Smiling with relief, she pointed at a narrow opening between two outcroppings of limestone walls.

She led the way. "Eli, back the wagon up to the sepulchre's opening."

At the entrance, she ran her hand over the twin stone pillars framing the doorway that Jake had uncovered during his explorations months ago. She envisioned the square chamber as she'd seen it earlier that day. The air had been musty and strangely still. Faint light had revealed plastered walls, painted with colors that were as vibrant as they must have been the day they'd been made. The urge to return with her tablet and pencils and recreate the scene of daily life had been overwhelming. Moving from one wall to the next, her excitement had built until she'd seen the mural of an Egyptian god holding court. She'd immediately known it had been a portrayal of Queen Tiy's trial. The imposing God Osiris towered over a slight woman wearing a thin white sheath, the gold corselet around her waist, just as it had been in the dream. Just as Sarah wore it now.

It made her ill to think that when she sealed the doorway, she might also destroy the paintings, but the message in the dream had been clear; the queen wanted to be with her son for eternity.

Now, standing in the chamber's archway, staring into space that was pitch black and foreboding, she couldn't force herself to enter. It might have been snake and bat free that afternoon, but she wasn't about to enter the tomb without a light.

Taking a torch from the back of the wagon, she waited for Eli to light it. Then she told the two men, "I pray you can lift the coffin by yourselves."

Thatcher heaved a weary sigh. "As long as ye promise we never 'ave tae move it again, we'll manage."

She smiled at her two companions. Roger might have been an uncaring father, but he'd hired two of the most loyal and honest men she'd ever met.

But she knew a third, she admitted. Jake was loyal and honest, strong and courageous. And she was deceiving him in the worst way. She closed her eyes, her chest constricting with a sense of loss. She couldn't think about him or she'd lose courage, and change her mind and give him the queen.

If only I could.

If she turned back now, Jake never need know that she had intended to deceive him. They could start fresh and stop fighting the feelings they had for each other. She could no longer deny that she cared for him, wanted him so much that nothing else seemed to matter. Somehow, her hatred of him had become tangled, confused with feelings that frightened her. They were too intense, too everything. Desire and longing. Hope for a life she hadn't thought possible.

He made her thoughts spin and her body yearn for things she didn't fully understand. Her woman's intuition told her there would never be another man like Jake in her life.

If given the chance, she could fall in love with him. Sarah felt a pang in her heart and sucked in a breath, realizing she didn't need another chance to fall in love with Jake. She loved him already.

I love him. She stared into the pitch-dark tomb, feeling as forlorn as the empty chamber.

Once she destroyed Queen Tiy's resting place, any chance for a future with Jake would be destroyed as well. He would never hold her, except maybe to strangle her, she thought, shivering from a chill that went straight to her soul.

Suppressing the futile urge to cry, Sarah turned away from the tomb, and away from thoughts of Jake. Taking the lit torch from Eli, she entered the chamber. Light danced over the painted walls, but she refused to look at them. She kept her attention on the empty, red granite sarcophagus dominating the center of the room. The lid, carved in the likeness of Queen Tiy, lay on the floor where Jake and her father had left it months before.

Sarah knelt and tried to memorize the way the queen's arms were crossed over her chest, the life-like curve of her cheek, the way her open gaze was fixed on the ceiling. She would be the last person to ever see Queen Tiy. Because of that, she wanted to remember so she could paint every detail.

"Bugger, me back's breakin'!"

Sarah rose and hurried out of the way as her two guards struggled through the doorway, their arms trembling with strain, their faces contorted with their effort.

"Just a little further," she encouraged them. "That's it, Eli, careful now."

"My legs are about tae give," Thatcher said, wincing.

"Another few feet. Just . . . there . . . set it on the edge of the sarcophagus, then you can rest."

Breathing hard, the men did as she said. She hurried to the entrance to make sure everything was quiet. Assured that nothing would stop her now, she turned back to the exhausted pair, who were lowering the coffin into the sarcophagus.

A shiver of nerves and trepidation ran through Sarah's body. She was nearing the point of no return. Soon, it would all be over. "Now, for the lid."

Grunting, their skin glistening with sweat, Eli and Thatcher lifted the lid and slid it over the opening, sealing the queen inside, as she'd been for the last three thousand years. The men left to retrieve the crates containing her jewelry and the chest filled with the canopic jars.

Sarah stared at the queen for a moment, not wanting to leave, but knowing she couldn't waste any more time.

"Come, my lady," Thatcher said, fighting to catch his breath as he waited for her beside the door.

Swallowing hard, she nodded. Once outside, she handed her torch over to Eli and retrieved her satchel from the wagon. Opening it, she withdrew the three iron-ball grenades Roger had given her and put them in a smaller sack, along with a flint to light them. It had been a miracle that Jake hadn't found them during his search. If he had, she'd have no way to seal the tomb.

But she did have the grenades, and she *did* have to seal the tomb. There was no turning back.

"Ye better let me have those," Thatcher said.

"You're exhausted." She patted his arm and gave him a weak smile. "Besides, I have to do this."

She looked at the cliff wall that would protect the hidden chamber forever. "Eli, move the wagon if you would, please. There's only one thing left to do."

Crouched behind a pile of fallen rocks and boulders, Jake watched Sarah, his temper rising with each passing second. Every move she made and each word she spoke echoed throughout the valley. He thanked God that no one else was near; she was making enough noise to wake a sleeping mummy.

While watching her men struggle to return Queen Tiy to her tomb, he'd debated whether to stop them now or wait. He'd decided to wait and let Sarah have her moment of glory. She was obviously determined to fulfill

her promise to Roger. Now she had, but Jake intended
to let her gloat for only one brief moment. As soon as
they boarded the wagon to leave, he would order them,
at gunpoint if necessary, to retrieve Queen Tiy from her
tomb.

The two men climbed into the front seat and slapped
the oxen with the reins. The team slowly made their way
down the center of the valley floor. Jake frowned and
stepped from his hiding place. Where was Sarah? She
wasn't in the back of the wagon, and she wasn't walking. Could she still be inside the tomb? He doubted it.
Eli had extinguished their torch, and he knew Sarah
wouldn't have remained in the chamber in the dark. So
where was she?

Raising his pistol, he moved to block the wagon's path.
He couldn't see Thatcher's and Eli's expressions, but he
heard their startled oaths when they spotted him.

"That's far enough," Jake told them.

"For cripes' sake, ye scared the life out of me!"
Thatcher ran a beefy hand over his face.

"Turn the wagon around, Eli," Jake said. "You left
something in the tomb that belongs to me."

"'Fraid we can't be doin' that, Mr. Mitchell," Eli said.
"We got our orders."

"And where is Lady Pendergrass?" Keeping the gun
trained on the men, Jake skirted the wagon and
searched the surrounding area, but still couldn't see any
sign of Sarah.

"Oh, she'll be along any minute now." Thatcher
cleared his throat and looked away.

"Yeah, any minute," Eli echoed.

Jake scowled at the men, his first suspicious thought
was that they might have harmed her, knocked her unconscious and hidden her away. Or something worse. He
wanted to dismiss the idea. So far they'd shown nothing
but concern for their mistress, but the temptation to

gain more wealth than they would see in a lifetime could change a man.

"Where is she?" he demanded, raising the gun.

"There's no cause to get in a sniff," Eli said. "When she's finished blowing up—"

"Hush now," Thatcher admonished, jamming his partner in the ribs with his elbow.

A chill grazed the back of Jake's neck. "She's going to blow up the tomb?"

"That's not what I meant." Eli ran his palm over his bald head as if pushing back invisible hair. "It's like this, ye see."

"Bloody hell." Jake started for the tomb, but as Eli's slip sank in, he broke into a run. She intended to destroy Queen Tiy's tomb. "Bloody hell!"

Rounding the last curve, he skidded to a stop at the sepulchre's entrance. "Sarah?"

He tilted his head, listened for her response. A steady breeze snaked around the jagged cliff wall, creating an eerie whisper. He heard the blood rush through his head, the rasp of his breath, but nothing else.

"Sarah," he called again as he entered the tomb. He couldn't see, but he sensed it was empty. The room was still, quiet. If she wasn't inside, where could she have gone? He left the chamber to search the pathway, but still saw no sign of her. She could be hiding anywhere in the thousand crevices and gaps along the path. If she intended to blow up the tomb, she had to be nearby.

A scattering of falling rocks had him spinning around and looking up a wall of limestone rocks. Though steep, the facing was jagged and rough, an easy enough climb for a healthy man. Impossible for a pampered woman.

He scanned the sheer wall. She wouldn't be so foolish as to climb to the plateau, would she? He couldn't see her, hell he couldn't see much of anything against the deep night sky. But if he'd learned anything about his beautiful, cunning Sarah, he knew she wouldn't think about the consequences of endangering herself. Another spray of sharp limestone chips sent his heart sinking to his stomach. Then he saw her, forty feet above him, clinging to the rock face. She'd tied up her skirts and had something slung over one shoulder.

He started to call out to her again, but stopped, afraid of startling her and causing her to fall. Tucking the pistol into the waistband of his pants, he started up after her, vowing to kill her for scaring him half to death.

Sarah clung to a jagged handhold, her limbs shaking with exhaustion and fear. Her heart hammered against her chest; and every frightened breath she took hurt. *Calm down.* She had to focus, take the climb slowly. She had time. Eli and Thatcher would wait for her.

She stretched out her arm, found another jutting piece of rock and pulled herself up. She searched for a foothold, found one, but slipped. A scream caught in her throat as she slid down, scraping against the wall. She caught another ledge, jerked to a stop. The sack with the iron balls banged against her ribs. She bit back a cry of pain. Warmth flowed over her palm. Numbly, she stared at a dark trail of blood running down her wrist, soaking into the sleeve of her gown. Resting her forehead against her outstretched arm, she admitted she'd made a mistake by not letting Thatcher make the climb. She wasn't strong enough for this.

But she was here now, and she had no choice but to continue. Searching for another handhold and finding one, she pulled herself up. She could see the plateau above her. She didn't know how far she'd come, and she didn't dare look down to find out. Another few minutes, twenty at most, and Queen Tiy would be buried forever inside her tomb. She'd be safe, and Sarah could return to England knowing she'd done what the queen had wanted.

Reaching for the next perch, she froze. *Queen Tiy.* Dear God. Sarah would have gripped her waist if she'd been able, to reaffirm what she already knew.

She still wore the corselet!

How could she have forgotten to place it inside the queen's coffin? Her heart raced with a surge of panic. Now what? If she continued up and destroyed the tomb without replacing the corselet, her task still wouldn't be complete. But she didn't have the strength to climb down, return the artifact, then climb back up again. Perhaps Thatcher would do it for her. She hated giving him the task, but she saw no other way. Sarah glanced at the sky, now a bluish pink in the east. Dawn was barely an hour away. She had to hurry. Jake and the others would awaken and find her gone. A search would begin.

She paused to get her bearings, then lowered herself a few inches. She held her breath and searched with her foot for another wedge of rock to step on. Finding one, she eased down. Just as she reached for another handhold, the rock under her foot crumbled. Screaming, she caught herself against the wall and froze, afraid to move. Her heart thundered in her ears, and a panicked sob squeezed her throat.

"Bloody hell!"

The shout from below turned her panic into a cold shiver of fear. She knew who that voice belonged to. How had he found her?

Looking down, she saw his blond hair twenty feet below her, a halo shimmering in the faint light. It didn't matter how he found her. He was here, and she knew he had every intention of stopping her. She'd come too far to be caught now.

Grabbing the ledge above her, she pulled herself up, not testing her weight, just hurrying. She scaled the wall, frantic to outpace Jake. She had to reach the plateau first. *Go,* she told herself. *Just go, don't panic. Don't look down. Go!*

"Sarah!" Jake shouted. "Stay where you are, you'll fall."

His demand that she stop made her move faster. She could see the top. Another few feet.

"Blast it, Sarah, listen to me."

She pushed her tired limbs. Her fingers were scraped and raw, half frozen from the cold night wind. She didn't let the pain stop her. She kept her upward climb, pushing, blind to everything except reaching the top. She could feel Jake gaining on her. He was stronger, larger, far more suited to such a physical task. But she would beat him, *she had to,* for Queen Tiy's sake.

Finally, Sarah reached the plateau and pulled herself over the ledge. She pushed to her feet, stumbled, and went down hard on her knees. Half crawling, half walking, she moved away from the edge. Opening the bag, she removed one of the iron balls, then fumbled for the flint, but couldn't find it.

"Where is it? I know it's here."

At last, her fingers grazed the flint. Within seconds she had the fuse lit. Sparks danced in the air as the fire took hold. Standing, she started toward the plateau's edge, but stopped.

Jake. He was still on the wall. She couldn't blow it up; she'd kill him. She stared at the iron ball, knowing she had perhaps a minute before it exploded.

"Sarah," Jake called. Then she saw him, first his head, then his body as he hoisted himself over the edge. Rolling to his feet, he faced her, his eyes dark pools of anger. "Pull out the fuse."

"Move out of the way. I have to seal the tomb."

"I can't let you do that."

"I have no choice."

"Roger isn't going to die because of a superstition."

"This isn't about Roger. It's . . . there's no time to explain. Move, *please!*"

For a second he stared at her, then he raised his arms out to his sides. "Fine. Destroy it."

He moved to the right. Sarah had planned to space the three balls along the edge, causing a wide section of the wall to collapse, but now there wasn't time. One ball would have to suffice. Jake wouldn't give her the chance to light another.

She arched her arm back to throw it, but grunted as Jake plowed into her. They fell to the ground, him on top of her. The ball flew out of her hand, landing near the edge.

"Damn!" Jake pushed to his feet.

"We have to get back!" Sarah leapt up and tried to catch his arm but missed.

The cliff exploded. The ground erupted. Splinters of rock and debris shot into the air, knocking Sarah backwards.

An ominous rumble swelled, blocked out all other sounds. Sarah rolled over the rough plateau, like a rag doll being tossed aside. She lay where she landed, the air punched from her lungs, her body so battered she was afraid to move.

Dust and rubble showered down on her for endless seconds, the pattering of a bruising rain.

Finally, the quiet returned. Slowly pushing herself into a sitting position, she searched the plateau, almost afraid of what she would find.

"Jake?"

An entire section of the wall had vanished, creating a gaping hole shaped like a horseshoe. She stared at the empty space, the exact place she'd last seen Jake.

"No, please no." On her hands and knees she crawled to the ledge. "Jake," she cried, her voice a broken whisper. "Jake, please . . ."

She looked over the rim and saw a pile of boulders and fallen rocks at the base of the wall. Was he buried beneath all that rubble? A sob pushed up her throat, choking her. "No, no, please. Jake!" She blinked, but the scene was the same. She'd destroyed the tomb, and in doing so, she'd destroyed the man she loved.

Jake shook his head, clearing dirt from his eyes. He tried to draw a deep breath, but couldn't, feeling as if his chest had collapsed. He sat up slowly, then bit back a curse, wishing he hadn't moved at all. His head spun and the ringing in his ears sounded like the bells tolling at Westminster Abby. Taking a quick survey of his body, he noted a few cuts but nothing broken.

A wrenching sob caught his attention. He glanced around the plateau and stared, dumbfounded, at the gaping hole in the wall, and at Sarah, who lay at its edge, crying.

"Dear God, what have I done?" he heard her say though her sobs.

"You've destroyed Queen Tiy's tomb, for which you should be beaten."

Gasping, she spun around, her eyes wide in the predawn light. "Jake?"

He scowled at her, wishing he had the energy to carry out his threat. "How could you be so foolish—"

His tirade was cut off when she threw herself against him. Wrapping her arms around his shoulders, she buried her face against his neck, weeping loud and hard. He felt her tears against his skin, warm and wet.

"I thought I'd killed you."

"You nearly did," he growled, refusing to be affected by her outburst.

"I'm sorry. I'm so sorry. I never meant to hurt you."

"No, you just wanted to ruin me." To stop her trembling, he grudgingly wrapped his arms around her back, and ignored how good she felt against him.

"No, yes, I mean I did want to ruin you at first," she said, her voice muffled. "But not now."

Sighing, he gripped her arms and forced her back so he could glare down at her. "Then why, Sarah? Explain why you destroyed everything I've worked for? Why you . . ." he shook her, his anger building. "Why you risked your life?"

"Because of Queen Tiy, this is where she wants to be."

"Queen Tiy? Bloody hell, woman, are we back to that again?" he snapped. "She's been dead for three thousand years. Do you really think she cares where her body is?"

Tears were welled in her eyes, but her jaw firmed with conviction. "I'm positive she cares."

Before he could shake her again, or glare or yell, she caught his face between her hands and kissed him. Her lips were cold and soft, molding to his, but he held still, not returning the kiss. He couldn't forgive her. And he damn well couldn't want her, not after this.

Finally, he pulled away and had to clench his jaw when he saw the despair in her eyes. But he refused to be swayed. "You can't win my forgiveness with a kiss, Sarah."

She ran her hand down the side of his face. "You're alive. That's all that matters. If you had been hurt, or . . . worse . . . I wouldn't have been able to forgive myself."

Jake glanced toward the east, where the sun edged over the horizon. He swore under his breath. "We have to find a way off of this plateau. Do you think you can climb down?"

"Do I have a choice?"

"Considering it's a long walk back to camp from here, and we have no water, I'd say no."

"I'm sure I can do it." Though from her expression, Jake didn't think she was sure of anything.

"Let's go." He led her across the cliff wall to a place that appeared to have easy access and multiple handholds.

"I'll go first—" Hearing a noise, he scanned the horizon, and what he saw made his skin prickle with dread.

Following his gaze, she asked. "What is that?"

"A sign that our luck has run out."

"I don't understand."

"We have visitors." He pointed to the dust cloud rising at the mouth of the valley floor. Ahead of the grimy sand floating in the air, dozens of camels, horses and wagons were making their way through the Valley of the Queens.

"It seems Napoleon has found us at last."

Chapter 15

"How did they find us?" Sarah demanded, her fingers digging into Jake's arm.

"How indeed?" he said, not bothering to hold back his sarcasm. "Perhaps your blowing up the hillside drew their attention."

"So soon? Oh heavens." She pressed one hand to her brow. "Queen Tiy is sealed inside her tomb. Napoleon can't do anything to us now."

"If you believe that, be my guest and climb down to greet them." Jake pulled his pistol from his waistband, surprised he still had it after the blast. "Besides, it gets worse."

"I don't see how."

"From what I can tell, her tomb was only partially covered."

"What!" Her mouth dropped open. "Oh my God, Jake. Napoleon might find her."

Jake checked his pistol, relieved to find it undamaged. "You had better hope he doesn't."

"We have to do something. I have two more iron balls. We can ignite them."

"And seal her forever?" He shook his head. "No."

"But it would keep her safe."

Scanning the area, he started north, angling away from the cliff's edge.

"Wait." Lifting her skirt, she caught up with him. "What about Eli and Thatcher. They're down there."

"Bloody hell." Returning to the ledge, he spotted the pair still in their wagon, their attention on the valley's entrance. Jake knew the men couldn't see the oncoming army, but without a doubt they could hear their approach. He whistled to gain their attention, but it took three tries before they finally looked up.

Raising his voice as loud as he dared, Jake told them, "Napoleon's coming your way. Leave the wagon." Pointing toward a towering sand dune, he said, "There's a trail at the far side of that foothill. It will take you out of the valley. Head north and you'll find our camp."

"What about you?" Eli called.

Jake shook his head. "We'll take another route. You've got to reach Gavin and warn him. Tell him I said to return to Thebes without us."

"But—" The sounds of creaking wagons and plodding hooves increased. Then one of the men, Eli or Thatcher, he couldn't tell which, said, "Cripes, they're on top of us."

"Go!" Jake took Sarah by the arm and pulled her away from the ledge until he couldn't see the valley floor and the army wouldn't be able to see them.

Slowing to a walk, he released her arm, but couldn't help looking at her from the corner of his eye. Faint morning light washed her in pink and gold. Her dark hair was a tangled nest around her shoulders and back. Dirt smudged her pale cheeks and her eyes were red-rimmed and glassy from crying. And her gown, it had once been white, the long sleeves and prim neckline adequate for protecting her from the sun. But now the seam at her shoulder was ripped, exposing a wicked scratch that made his stomach clench. Dark stains smeared her skirt, the fabric shredded as if a wild cat had attacked her. Her small hands were bruised and . . .

He stopped and caught her wrist. Blood streaked her

arm and turned the cuff of her sleeve dark red. He turned her hand over and cursed when he saw the three-inch cut on her palm.

"It looks worse than it feels," she said, trying to tug free.

"If it gets infected, it'll feel worse than it looks." Taking his knife from his boot, he reached for her.

Sarah yelped and leaped out of his reach. "What are you doing?"

"Stand still." He caught the hem of her gown and sliced off a strip of cloth. She opened her mouth to object, but one look from him stopped her.

Wrapping the bandage around her palm, he said, "That's the best we can do for now."

"Do you think they'll make it? Eli and Thatcher?"

"They will if they find the trail." He tied off the bandage and clenched his jaw when she winced in pain. "Let's go. We have a long walk ahead of us."

"And Gavin, he'll take everyone to Thebes? Without us?"

"He'd better," Jake said, hoping the earl didn't decide to do something foolish, like try to find him and Sarah first.

"How will we . . ." She took a deep, trembling breath that sounded like she was on the verge of tears. "I mean without camels, how will we cross the desert?"

"If Napoleon hasn't already found our camp, Gavin will leave camels behind."

"And if Napoleon did find our camp?"

Jake turned away and started walking, not liking how small and helpless Sarah looked, or how much he wanted to reassure her that they would get through this alive. He was still too angry with her for destroying Queen Tiy to ease her fears.

And besides, he wasn't sure he wouldn't be lying.

* * *

Hot dusty sand slapped Sarah in the face in a relentless rhythm. They had been walking for hours, the sun slowly rising in the sky behind them, lying across the back of her neck like an iron bar. The scorching sand burned her feet through her boots, yet she continued putting one foot in front of the other, following Jake, who stopped every so often to make sure she hadn't collapsed.

They had worked their way off the plateau and were weaving their way through imposing dunes that, in her exhausted state, rose out of the ground like demonic hills of gold. She wondered if she would die in the barren desert, buried beneath the blowing sand, the dry heat mummifying her like the dead pharaohs. Then she wondered why the thought of dying didn't frighten her, as it should have.

"Sarah?"

She was so tired and thirsty. If only she'd thought to bring water.

"Sarah!"

She blinked and realized Jake was far ahead of her, then she realized she had stopped walking. "I'm coming."

But her knees buckled. She slowly crumpled, an odd sensation, as if her bones were dissolving. Collapsing onto her back, she stared at the dazzling white sky. Jake was at her side in an instant, or what seemed like an instant to her. The way her mind spun, she wasn't sure of time or if her heart was still beating.

He pressed his palm to her brow, his frown turning deadly. "Damn it, Sarah. I told you to say something when you needed to rest."

"I'm fine." She smiled at him, then traced the line of his jaw with her fingers. "You're a handsome man, Jake. Have I told you that?"

"You're hallucinating." He ground out something she didn't understand, a new curse word if she were to guess.

"I know you hate me—"

"I don't hate you."

"I don't blame you." She closed her eyes and felt as if she were sinking into the sand, millions of tiny grains slowly swallowing her up. "Sleep, if I could . . ."

"We've got to find some shade."

"We don't have time to rest. Gavin, he . . . what are you doing?" She wrapped her arms around Jake's neck when he lifted her.

"Just close your eyes, sweetheart," he said as he struggled to walk. "When you open them again, everything will be fine."

"I believe it will be," she said, wondering how he could carry her when her body felt so heavy.

"Good, you shouldn't doubt me."

"I don't." When he frowned down at her, she tried to smile but couldn't manage it. "I don't doubt you because you wouldn't lie to me, the way I've lied to you."

"We'll deal with that later. Right now I want you to rest."

She laid her head against his shoulder and closed her eyes. A moment before she fell asleep, she whispered, "I'm sorry."

Jake peered over the ridge to the valley below. The ruined buildings and wind-swept streets of Deir el-Medineh were empty. Still. Eerily quiet. Shadows from the distant hilltop stretched across the basin floor, sliding over half-buried piles of stones, stealing the heat of the day.

Jake dreaded the coming night. It would be as grueling as the day that was quickly slipping away. Without a drop of water, he and Sarah had walked for hours in one hundred and ten degree heat. He'd carried her for much of that time, letting her walk when he couldn't hold her any longer. Twice they'd stopped to rest in the shade of a hill but, not knowing what had befallen their friends, neither of them had wanted to linger.

An age-old adage crept into Jake's mind, and as hard as he tried, he couldn't ignore it.

The Egyptian desert is unforgiving; a mere man cannot carry enough water to stay alive.

He and Sarah had already gone one day without water; they wouldn't be able to survive another.

"Can you see them?" Sarah asked, her voice a rough whisper. She sat leaning against a smooth, limestone rock, her tired gaze fastened on him.

He shook his head and, trying to keep his voice hopeful, said, "They've left."

"Camels?"

"Gone."

"All of them?"

He nodded, wishing he could spare her the truth. They were trapped in the desert, and unless they went in search of Napoleon's camp, they had no hope of surviving.

She closed her eyes and didn't move, as if the news had drained the last of her strength. After a moment, she asked, "Do you think they were captured?"

Not wanting to voice his fear, he helped her stand, but kept hold of her arm as they navigated down the hill's rocky slope.

"They must have had a reason for taking all the animals," she said, and from the sound of her voice, he knew she was trying to encourage him. For that he had to smile.

"I'm sure they're fine, Sarah. I don't see any sign of a struggle. And I'm rather certain Connor wouldn't have surrendered without a fight."

"Giving up isn't the Scottish way." She started down the hillside, but stopped to stare in amazement. "Look! It's a village."

"Deir el-Medineh. The same one we were in yesterday."

"I know, but from the ground it looks like a jumbled maze of rocks. Up here I can see the outline of homes.

See, they're connected to one another, like London townhouses. And the doorways, they lead to the street."

She smiled, her expression at once delighted and sad. "Perhaps you should tell me about these people."

He frowned at her fatalistic tone, but said, "Imagine signs hanging over the doors, designating the architects from the artists, the diggers from the smiths. Children would be playing in the streets, dodging donkeys laden with the food and water that had to be brought in."

She nodded, as if seeing the village as it had been three thousand years before, dusty and hot and full of life.

"Why do you want to know about them?" he asked.

She looked at him, her cheeks drawn, her silver eyes filled with resignation. "Because I may be staying here for a while."

"I'm not leaving you on your own," he said, scowling at her.

"And I'm not going to hold you back."

He would have argued with her, but she started down the slope. He watched the sway of her hips, the way the wind caught her thick mane of hair, lifting it off her back. Part of him was still furious with her for taking away everything he'd worked for.

But even that part of him wasn't about to leave her behind.

"The ashes are cold." Sarah pushed a stick through the remains of the fire, feeling as if the last of her hope had died with the flames.

For the past few minutes, Jake had been kneeling in the sand, studying the patterns. Finally he stood and looked into the distance, toward Thebes. "Most of the hoofprints have been swept clean by the wind, which tells me they left hours ago."

"With Napoleon?"

"I don't think so." He faced her. "There aren't enough tracks for an army. Six camels, yes."

"But why would they have taken them all?"

"I don't know. But they're gone, which means we walk."

"To Thebes." She stared at him in disbelief.

"Unless you have a better idea."

"As you have pointed out time and again, I don't know this land. I have no idea what to do next. Or how to find food and water." Her voice was rising to a shrill pitch, but she couldn't seem to gain control of it. "I swear if I ever see Roger again, I'll . . . I'll . . ."

"You'll what?"

"I'm thinking." She paced in a tight circle. "What did the ancient Egyptians do to torture people?"

"Well, there was the traditional beheading." Jake arched a brow as if the idea had merit. "Or being staked to a board and left in the sun. Sometimes criminals were forced to labor in the turquoise mines in Sinai, a brutal place where the survivors are considered the unlucky ones. Then there was the quick and efficient punishment of throwing a person in with the crocodiles where they would be ripped apart and—"

"Enough!" She shuddered. "Nothing so gruesome, I think. But he deserves to be severely reprimanded for sending me here. Or maybe this is what I deserve for being so foolish."

She glanced up to see Jake grinning at her, the odd light in his eyes causing her breath to catch. "Why are you looking at me like that?"

The grin vanished and was replaced with a scowl. Turning away, he said, "We'll rest here for a few hours before we start for Thebes."

She watched him walk through the ruins, his arms loose at his sides, his long hair tawny in the fading light and wondered what he had been thinking. Before he'd lost his smile, he'd seemed amused or intrigued. What he hadn't seemed was angry.

Could he have gotten over her betrayal already? She looked away, suppressing the futile hope tightening her chest. Jake might have smiled at her, but he would never be able to forgive her.

And she didn't deserve his forgiveness, because even now she wasn't being honest with him.

She had the corselet. She could give it to him, and hope the small trinket would make up for losing everything else. But that meant ignoring the queen's plea. Sarah pressed her hands to her face and groaned. If only she hadn't had the dream. She wanted to forget the woman's anguish, but her pain was still too fresh in Sarah's mind, like a fist pressing against her heart, refusing to be ignored.

She lay down on the sand and curled into a ball, her stomach cramped with hunger and her throat burning for water. The cut on her palm a dull throb. Ignoring the pain, she focused on the choice she had to make; give the corselet to Jake, a peace token in his search for glory or find a way to return the corselet to Queen Tiy's tomb so she could be with her son for eternity.

She might not know how to survive in Egypt, but she knew she and Jake wouldn't survive much longer without water. She had no hope of making it all the way to Thebes. But the Valley of the Queens wasn't far. She could return there.

Biting down on her dry, cracked lips, Sarah realized the desert had made the choice for her.

"Sarah," Jake said, shaking her shoulder. "Wake up."

Where her gown was torn, her skin was smooth and too cold for his liking. But that would change soon enough. Dawn was only a few hours away.

She groaned and turned onto her back, her eyes silver pools in the moonlight. In a rough, drowsy voice, she said, "I'm not leaving until I have my morning tea."

"Sorry, sweetheart, no tea, but how about this?" He tilted the water skin to her lips, saw her eyes widen in surprise as she took a deep drink. "Whoa, take it easy."

She sat up, smiling, wiped a dribble of water from her chin. "Where did you get that?"

He nodded toward the far end of the small village, where the stones were piled the highest. "Over there. Two water skins, and this." He held up a wool sack. "Food."

"I might have to take back all the awful things I've been thinking about Gavin for leaving with the camels," she said, taking a piece of dried meat from him.

"Come on, we'll eat on the way."

She caught his arm, stopping him from rising. "Walk all the way to Thebes." She shook her head. "You know I can't make it."

"You're going to have to, because you're not staying here."

She sighed, and her chin tilted in a stubborn angle. "I'll only slow you down. You could go to Thebes and return for me. I'll find some shelter, conserve the water. It's the only way."

"No." He stood, hauling her up beside him. "Either we both go or we both stay."

She looked away from him to the hill that lead to the Valley of the Queens. From her yearning expression, he almost believed she wanted to return to the tomb.

Placing the water skin on her shoulder, he told her, "Trust me, Sarah, we're going to survive."

Trust me, Sarah. Trust me, Sarah. Trust me, Sarah.

Of all the things Jake could say that would tear her apart, those three words had struck hard and deep. The ache in her thighs from trudging through shifting sand was nothing compared to the anguish her conscience was suffering. She did trust him, knew that he would do anything in his power to keep her safe. And she didn't deserve it.

Just tell him, a voice screamed in her mind. *Give him the corselet. Now, and be done with it!*

She touched her bandaged hand to her waist, felt the smooth gold squares. She opened her mouth, determined to put an end to her deceit, but the words wouldn't come. She clamped her jaw shut and felt tears of frustration well in her eyes.

"Damn you, Queen Tiy," she muttered. "I'm beginning to think you've cursed me with insanity, just as you did my father."

"Did you say something?" Jake asked, pausing to let her catch up to him.

"Just . . . yes . . . will we be stopping soon?"

He glanced at the rising sun, hovering in the white sky, then he looked at her, a frown marring his lean, tanned face. "A little longer. Can you make it?"

She nodded. Unable to bear the concern in his blue eyes, she touched her head. "The hat you made for me has helped."

"It's called a turban."

"Yes, well, it used to be part of my skirt." She glanced down at her boots and her now-visible calves. She should be embarrassed, but recalling their kisses, the feel of his hands on her breasts, and how much she wished she could go back to that moment before he knew she had deceived him, she decided embarrassment would be useless.

She fell into step with him. "Will we reach the cave we camped at before nightfall?"

"No."

The water skin pulled at her shoulder, but as heavy as it was, she didn't think there was enough water in it to last more than a few days. "I've held off asking, but I need to know. How long will it take to reach Thebes?"

"A week, maybe more."

She stopped, her mouth gaping, her breath locked somewhere inside her chest. "We'll never make it."

Jake ran his palm over the golden stubble of his beard, not looking at her. "We aren't taking the same route as we did to the valley."

"Why not?"

"I don't want to risk running into Napoleon. It had been a foolish gamble before, but I'd thought I was chasing Roger."

"We made it to Deir el-Medineh without any incidents."

"Napoleon is too close. Luck is a fickle lady, I don't want to test her any more than I already have."

She plodded on beside him, the horizon shimmering in waves of heat. "We'll never make it."

Jake caught her hand and squeezed it. "Trust me, Sarah."

Her skin beneath the corselet tingled with awareness. With a weary sigh, she whispered the only response that came to mind. "Oh, bloody hell."

Chapter 16

Jake led Sarah beneath the eroded ledge of a limestone cliff. Not deep enough to be a cave, but it faced west and away from the brisk night wind.

"We'll sleep here."

Without a word, she collapsed at his feet, her half-empty water skin falling beside her. All day he had watched her struggle to keep up with him, and although he hadn't pushed as hard as he would have without her, he felt a stirring of pride that she'd kept up without complaint. Many men would have quit long ago.

"What about bats?" she asked, resting her forehead against her bent knees.

"We're all clear."

"Cobras?"

He glanced around the small shelter, but the soft white glow of the moon couldn't reach the back. He listened for movement, a telling hiss, but heard nothing. "None that I see."

"Do scorpions hunt at night, too?"

"Only if you disturb them."

"I won't disturb them if they promise not to disturb me."

Taking a slice of flat bread from the bag and a piece of dried meat, he handed Sarah her dinner. "Eat, you'll feel better."

She laughed softly, a small, quiet sound that conveyed

her exhaustion. "Roasted beef, potatoes, and hot tea would make me feel better. And a bath with bubbles and clean clothes."

"You'll have them soon enough," he said, hoping he wasn't lying. He didn't intend to let her give up, but given what lay ahead, he didn't know if she had the strength to survive. Not for the first time that day, he wondered if he'd made a mistake by bringing her with him. She could have stayed at Deir el-Medineh while he made the trip to Thebes and back. With enough food and water, and shade, she might have survived. But then he'd envisioned leaving her behind, only to return to find her dead from thirst or hunger, or poisoned from a snake bite. Or returning and not finding her at all because Napoleon had her. His decision had been made.

Leaning against the back wall, she looked at him, her expression lost in the dark. "Have you always been so optimistic?"

"When you grow up with nothing, sometimes optimism is all that stands between success and failure."

"Or life and death."

Hating that he couldn't see her face, he took the various pieces of wood he'd picked up during their trek, then looked for more inside the shelter. Using the flint Gavin had left him, he had a small fire going within minutes.

"Optimistic and resourceful." Smiling, she took a bite of her bread.

"I've spent a lot of time out here."

"And you know the dangers," she said without a trace of sarcasm or anger.

He arched a brow. "Something like that."

"I'm sorry, Jake, for the way everything has turned out." She pulled off her turban and ran her fingers through her tangled hair. "Roger used me, I know that now. If only I'd said no when he'd asked me to come here."

Resisting the urge to sit down beside her and pull her

into his arms, he said, "You told me on the plateau that you didn't seal the tomb for Roger, but for Queen Tiy. What did you mean?"

Her cheeks were red from the sun, but they flushed an even darker hue. "It doesn't matter now."

"I deserve an explanation."

"You won't believe me."

"Still, you owe me."

She watched him for a moment, and in that time, Jake could see a battle of wills taking place in her eyes. He saw fear and apprehension, doubt and what he thought might be amazement.

She blew out a breath. "After you discovered I had Queen Tiy, I realized that was it. I had tried and failed. There was nothing more I could do."

"Obviously something changed your mind. Your sense of duty to Roger?"

She looked at him as if he'd spoken in Arabic. "No. Something I can't begin to explain, and if I try you'll think I'm crazy."

"Tell me and let me decide."

"Fine, but promise you won't call me daft."

"I promise."

"Night before last I had a dream about Queen Tiy. It was so real. I could feel the heat from the sunlight streaming through the open doors, the cool stone floor beneath my bare feet. I was her, Queen Tiy, standing before the vizier. I didn't even know what a vizier was until the dream." Her eyes were smoky and troubled as they met his. "Ramses was dead. Vizier Abubakar ruled in his place, and he found me guilty of trying to murder my husband."

"You mean Queen Tiy's husband," he interrupted, the back of his neck prickling.

"I was so frightened." She winced. "I mean, *she* was so frightened. She had watched her son being put to death. And others, men who had been her protectors. She knew

there was no escaping her execution. And I was ready—"
She made a strangled sound in her throat. "*She* was ready
to die. She only wanted to be with her son for eternity. But
Vizier Abubakar denied her. She was frantic, Jake."

"Except for the vizier's name, which you could be
making up, you aren't telling me anything new. The
story is written on the corselet."

"I know, the hieroglyphics. But I dreamed it, too. I
lived it. I felt her fear and her anguish." Sarah leaned
forward, sitting on her knees. "She was only trying to
protect Pentewere. There had been a plot to kill him
and remove him from the line of the throne."

Jake stared at her, the prickling in his neck racing
down his spine. The anguish in Sarah's eyes, the urgency
in her voice, tempted him to believe her. But she'd lied
to him too many times to take her word now.

"Jake, Queen Tiy was terrified of being denied the afterlife. The thought of drifting in a void, forever, all alone,
was more frightening to her than being put to death."

"And because of this dream, you returned Queen Tiy
to her tomb."

"Yes," she said, her eyes brightening with hope that he
might believe her.

"I think you're more like your father than you know."

"What?" she said, going very still.

"I haven't called you daft, but—"

"You don't believe me."

"How can I?" he demanded, not sure which emotion
he felt more of, bewilderment or anger. "A woman,
who's been dead for three thousand years, comes to you
in a dream and tells you to put her back in her tomb so
she can spend eternity with her son. If our situations
were reversed, would you believe me?"

"I know it sounds insane," she whispered, rubbing her
brow, her movements tired, dejected. "But I was there. I
felt her."

Jake looked away, then took a bite of his flat bread, chewing, but not tasting. To hold on to his anger, he tried to think of a reason why she would fabricate such a story, but for the life of him, he couldn't come up with one. It made no sense. There was no reason to lie now. She had already destroyed the tomb; she couldn't take anything else away from him.

Besides, he thought, this was Egypt, the land of ghosts and mysteries, where the impossible became possible. Who was he to say she hadn't dreamed about Queen Tiy's last day on earth?

"Sarah," he said, clasping her hands, which were clenched in her lap. "Would you do me a favor?"

"Of course." When she looked at him, her eyes wide and liquid in the firelight, he barely resisted the impulse to kiss her. God, would he ever learn?

"Should you dream about the queen again, could you ask her what the symbols on the back of the corselet mean?"

Jake had expected Sarah to smile with relief at his jest, not burst into tears.

They circled overhead, gliding against the burning white sky. They kept pace, circling and waiting, dipping low to take a closer look, then soaring up to ride the wind. Sarah had noticed the buzzards the day they'd left Deir el-Medineh, but had dismissed them. That had been three days ago, and since then the huge, grotesque birds had increased in number, following Jake and her with eerie patience. It didn't matter if they walked all night. By morning, the buzzards found them again.

Trudging through the sand, her feet sinking up to her ankles with each step, she shook her water skin. Water sloshed inside, enough for one more day. Maybe. And they had another four days before they reached Thebes.

She continued on, the sun bearing down on her back, her mind dull and her body exhausted. One foot in front of the other. Stepping wherever Jake stepped. She followed him, kept her focus on him, because if she looked anywhere else, at the endless ocean of white sand or the unforgiving sky or the buzzards that were anticipating their death, she wouldn't be able to continue.

She had to keep going for Jake. She couldn't slow him down. If she hadn't taken Queen Tiy, he wouldn't have followed her. If she hadn't blown up the cliff, Napoleon's army wouldn't have known they were there. But she'd done all those things, and now Jake had to cross the desert with little food and water, towing a woman along who had been nothing but trouble.

She opened her flask to take a sip of the hot water, but only a trickle poured out.

"Oh, no!" she cried.

"What's wrong?"

She held out her water skin in a helpless gesture. "It's gone. My water, it's all gone."

He handed his bag to her. "I have enough."

She shook her head and forced back tears she couldn't afford to spill. "No, that's yours."

"And I'm willing to share," he insisted. "Take a drink."

Her mind spun and her stomach cramped, but the realization that none of this needed to have happened sent her to her knees. "It's my fault you're here. I won't take your water."

"I'm used to the heat, Sarah. I don't need as much." He knelt beside her. "Here, take a drink."

She pushed the skin away, and met the grim set of his eyes. "I'm not going to make it to Thebes."

"You'll make it if I have to carry you."

She shook her head and took a deep breath that somehow calmed her fear. She wouldn't make it, but Jake would.

"I've decided not to go any farther," she told him.

"Sarah—"

"There's bound to be a cave in the hills over there," she said, pointing at the rocky terrain that seemed a million miles away. "I'll wait there. I'll be fine. After you reach Thebes you can return with camels."

"I'm not leaving you."

"If you don't leave me, neither of us will make it." She laid her hand over his, gave it a reassuring squeeze. "If I'm in the shade and not exerting myself, I won't need any water."

"You're concerned about running out of water?"

"Aren't you?" she demanded.

He shrugged, the muscles beneath his dirty, cream-colored shirt flexing.

"If you're going to make it another four days, you need to conserve all the water you can."

"What about you?"

Knowing it wouldn't do any good for either of them to worry about her, she skirted the question. "Between the two of us, you have the better chance of reaching Thebes. I want you to go without me."

He studied her for a moment, his eyes as rich and blue as sapphires in the shadow of his hat. Offset by his lean face, they seemed darker, more brilliant than before, shining with passion and hunger for life. Not so long ago she had fallen asleep every night imagining his hand-some face and counting off her reasons for hating him.

Now she loved him with her entire soul. It made her wonder about fate's sense of humor.

"I can make my way to the cliffs," she said, standing and wiping sand from her skirt. A useless effort, but she didn't want to look at Jake, afraid she would start to cry.

"I appreciate your attempt to be noble, but it's not nec-essary," he said, his voice as rough as the stubble of his blond beard.

"Nobility has nothing to do with my decision." His voice was rough; hers shook with suppressed tears. "It's the sensible thing to do."

She didn't want to think about what would happen when they parted ways, how she would survive, or for how long. And her decision to stay wasn't virtuous. It was pure selfishness. She wasn't too afraid of dying; but she couldn't bear the thought of Jake suffering any more than he already had.

With a start, she realized her emotions, and her fears, were not so different than Queen Tiy's had been.

Jake glanced in the direction they had been heading, then looked at her. "All right, if you're sure."

She nodded, unable to speak. She wanted him to go without her, but the thought of him actually leaving her behind scared her to death.

"If you change your mind, you can catch up with me."

"I won't."

"Regardless, I'll be staying the night just below the dunes on the horizon. Do you see them?"

"Yes, but—"

"Do you see that small patch of green?"

"I'm not going to follow . . . Green?" She looked to where he pointed. Shading her eyes from the sun's glare, she looked, but saw nothing except more and more sand. Then she caught her breath. "Is it . . . grass?"

"It is."

"But how?" She covered her gaping mouth with her hands, afraid to believe the scrap of emerald in the distance was actually living grass.

"Is it an oasis?" she asked.

He laughed softly. "Nothing so grand. Just a watering hole."

"You knew it was here."

He lifted one shoulder in a negligent shrug.

"And you didn't tell me?" She didn't know whether she wanted to kiss him or hit him.

"I knew it *used* to be here." Sliding his hand around the curve of her neck, he drew her towards him. "I didn't want to get your hopes up. Watering holes dry out, or years of blowing sand reclaim them."

"But there's grass," she said, smiling.

"Which means there's water." He smiled in return, but the humor deepened to a tenderness that made her heart thump against her chest. "Would you really have stayed behind?"

"I've done enough to hurt you," she said, her heart pounding so loudly she thought it a miracle that he couldn't hear it.

His jaw clenched, and she thought he wanted to shout at her, but what he said surprised her just as much. "Bloody hell, Sarah, it's impossible to stay angry with you."

She started to tell him that he still had every reason to be furious with her, but just then Jake kissed her, a hard, firm kiss that was possessive and searing. His lips slanted over hers, his tongue pushing inside her mouth for a stunning moment. She held his face between her hands, loving the rasp of his beard against her palms. Loving everything about him from his mind to his heart, to the way he tasted and felt.

She loved him with all her soul, and she didn't deserve him.

Sunlight shimmered off the water's surface, blue diamonds tossed down by the gods. Jake knelt by the pond's edge to refill the skins, but his attention was solely on Sarah.

Standing barefoot in the pool with her tattered skirt hiked up to her knees, she tilted her head back to the sun and sighed, a deep, throaty sound that his body not only heard, but responded to. The first day of their trek through the desert he'd held on to his anger, nursing it with reminders that she had lied to him from the beginning. And, considering her claim to have dreamed about Queen Tiy, he suspected she wasn't being honest with him still.

But those reminders had lost some of their power when he'd also recalled how she'd blamed him for her father's neglect. He still had a difficult time associating Roger with the cold man Sarah described. He'd known Roger most of his life, thought of him as the father he should have had, knew how the old man's mind worked, what he wanted in life, what made him laugh in joy or shout in a rage. Yet in all the time they'd spent together, Roger had never mentioned having a daughter.

Sarah could be lying about her relation to Roger Pendergrass, but instinct told Jake she wasn't.

But it was more than feeling responsible for her failed relationship with her father that made it difficult to hold on to his anger. Even after years of enduring his disdain, she wanted her father's love, would endanger herself to earn it. Just by stepping foot on a ship without knowing what lay ahead proved the depth of her strength and courage. Time and again he'd seen glimpses of her compassion and her curiosity—traits difficult to find in either a man or a woman. He'd witnessed her concern for her two guards, her appreciation for Egypt's beauty. But the one selfless act he would never forget was her willingness to sacrifice herself so he might live. Had she not made that brave gesture, staying mad at her might have been possible.

But that was a lie, too, and he knew it.

He wanted her. His body wanted to possess her, his hands wanted to touch her, and his mind wanted to know that she belonged only to him.

"So what shall it be?" she asked, sending up a spray of

water with her hand, splashing him. "Stale flat bread or dried beef?"

"Neither if we're lucky," he said, standing.

Her gaze flickered down and her eyes widened for an instant when she saw his hardened state. Jake took a step toward her, suddenly determined to continue the kiss he'd given her earlier. Only this time he wouldn't stop. He'd kiss her lips and strip her ruined gown from her body, he'd learn every curve, every dip and hollow. He'd make love to her until both of them were boneless, and floating in a haze of lust.

"I'd like to bathe," she said softly.

Jake stopped within arm's reach of her, his body clamping down with desire, the feeling so close to pain he almost groaned out loud. It was too easy to imagine her naked and wet, their bodies sliding through water, joined, buried so deep nothing could pull them apart.

He dragged air into his lungs and took several steps back. Turning on his heels, he headed for the sand dunes.

"Where are you going?" she called.

Pulling the gun from his waistband, he glanced over his shoulder at her, then wished he had just kept on going. Her hair lay tangled down her back, her face was sunburned and smudged with dirt, her gown shredded to rags. He'd never seen her more beautiful, and he'd never wanted a woman so much.

"I saw some tracks earlier."

"Not large ones, I hope."

He tried to smile, but couldn't. "Have your bath, Sarah. I won't stay away for long."

Chapter 17

Sarah watched Jake leave, and kept watching until he disappeared behind a sand dune that glittered gold in the sinking sun.

He wanted to make love to her. She'd seen the need in his eyes, felt the desire radiating from his body. She pressed a hand to her chest, where her heart beat wild and reckless. His departing words had been a warning and a promise. When he returned, he would take her in his arms and kiss her, and she would let him. There wasn't anyone nearby to stop them, and she couldn't think of one reason to tell him no. She wanted him, so much she was breathless. Her body pounded with need. Her skin felt flushed and tender—and the sensations had nothing to do with the relentless Egyptian sun.

Undoing the buttons down her bodice, she let the gown drop into the water. Next she stripped off the remains of her chemise, tossing it on shore beside her boots. She looked down at her body, naked except for the corselet. She was thinner than she'd been before leaving England, but it was the corselet that drew her attention.

It had been days since she'd had a chance to see the precious artifact. Rays of sunshine struck the golden squares, splintering beams of awesome light around her. A halo of magic. She ran her palms over her hips, molded the ancient garment to her skin. As beautiful as it was, as much as she longed to paint it, she wished she'd never laid eyes on it. Because as rare and valuable as it was, she knew it would destroy any chance she had for a future with Jake.

Knowing he wouldn't be gone long, she removed the corselet and hurried over to her boots. She wrapped the artifact in the bodice of her chemise, then stepped back into the water. She removed the bandage from her hand and washed the cut on her palm. The skin was red and tender, but it was healing. Gathering her gown next, she washed it as best as she could, but her gaze continued to stray to the corselet. This was the first time she'd had it off since boarding the ship in England.

She'd grown accustomed to the way it hugged her, a warm embrace that felt as much a part of her as an arm or a leg. She had the irrational urge to put it back on, keep it with her forever. But that was impossible.

She had to replace the corselet inside the queen's tomb. *But how?* If Jake had left her at Deir el-Medineh, she could have returned to the tomb, found some way to get inside. But she was on her way back to London. There was no question that she would have to return to Egypt now. Perhaps Roger would accompany her, help her. The thought of traveling with her father didn't fill her with hope or make her stomach clench with worry. As a matter of fact, she felt nothing at all.

But with or without Roger's help, she would have to finish the task Queen Tiy had given her.

When her gown was as clean as it could get, she draped it over her boots, covering the chemise and the corselet in case Jake returned before she was through bathing.

Plunging into the water, she stayed under as long as she could, then broke through the surface, relishing the wanton feel of warm water sluicing over her bare hot skin. A laugh caught in her throat. She was a titled lady from London, bathing naked in a watering hole in the middle of Egypt. She'd come a long way from her art classes, where her greatest risk had been to paint bowls of fruit.

Kicking her legs out, she floated on her back, her arms drifting out to her sides. She stared at the clear Egyptian sky and vowed that she wouldn't limit herself to bowls of fruit any longer. She would return the corselet to Queen Tiy's tomb, but afterward she wouldn't return to England. She would stay in Egypt, travel to all the cities, learn the customs, come to know the people. Perhaps she would join an archaeological team. Perhaps Jake's. She closed her eyes when an unseen hand squeezed her chest. She would lose him. Even if he never learned she still had the corselet, she had deceived him. She'd never be able to share a life with him.

The report of a gun brought her up with a gasp. Had Napoleon found them? Oh, Lord! She searched the surrounding desert. Empty. If the shot had come from Jake, and please Lord, let it have come from Jake, then he would be returning soon.

Scrubbing her face with handfuls of sand, then attacking the rest of her body, she cleansed away the dirt and sweat from the last few days. Her skin felt vibrant, invigorated, but remorse clung stubbornly to her heart. She shook her head, forcing thoughts of the future away. They hadn't reached Thebes yet. They had now, and she intended to make the time she had with Jake count.

Spotting Jake cresting a distant sand dune, seeing his lean, muscled body, his whiskey-colored hair lifting with the wind, feeling the fierceness of his gaze pierce the space between them, she realized something new.

She didn't care if they ever reached Thebes or not.

Reaching the peak of the sand dune, Jake stopped, his heart leaping to his throat. Rays from the sun bounced off the small watering hole, washing it with light. For a terrifying instant he couldn't see anything except endless desert and calm blue water. Then he spotted a pile of clothes on the sandy shore, which meant . . .

He scanned the pool and released his breath when he finally spotted her. Submerged to her neck, she watched him, unmoving. From this distance, he couldn't see her expression, but he didn't need to. The air was charged with anticipation, as if lightning had struck nearby.

Starting down the slope, a skinned sand cat in his hand, his only thought was to reach her. But the closer he got, the more he had to force himself not to run.

As he neared the pool, she called out, "Good heavens, what is that?"

He stopped, confused, until she pointed at his right hand. He lifted it, having forgotten he'd shot the animal. "Our dinner."

She grimaced. "Dried beef would have been fine."

Jake would have replied, but just then the wind ceased for an instant, allowing the rippling pool to still. He could see the pale shape of her body beneath the blue surface, the full curve of her breasts, the faint indention of her waist.

His breath left him in a rush and he couldn't draw another. His sex filled with blood. He'd never known desire could burn, but it did, deep and fierce and so hot, he thought once he acted on it, he'd be consumed.

Sarah crossed her arms over her chest and looked away. "Jake, you're staring. If you'll turn your back, I'll get dressed."

"I rather like you where you are."

A blush darkened her cheeks to a seductive shade of red. She pushed wet strands of dark hair from her face. "Perhaps you do, but my fingers and toes have turned to prunes. Now turn around."

Jake did, but not so she could leave the pool. He gathered the wood he'd been gathering and quickly started a fire.

"Will you promise not to look?" she asked, and he heard the tinkling of water as she started to rise.

He glanced over his shoulder, caught a glimpse of pale breasts and dark nipples before she plunged back into the water. In a voice suddenly raw, he said, "That's a promise I can't make."

His hands visibly shaking, he used a stick to stake the carcass, then set their dinner over the flames to cook. He stood and faced her, and was at once struck by the conflicting qualities of the woman before him. She looked at him with large silver eyes that were both innocent and seductive. Though she held her arms crossed protectively over her breasts, she wasn't shivering with fear. He sensed her apprehension, her nervousness, and admitted he felt the same. Every cell in his body, every part of his heart and mind knew that when he made love to her, it would be like nothing he'd ever known. The thought in itself was frightening, but not enough to deny what they both wanted. Making love to Sarah would be special, unique, binding.

"Jake," she said, her gaze flickering from his face to his chest, then lower. "I know what you might be thinking, and . . ."

"Yes," he prompted her when she paused. Her gaze finally returned to his when he began to undo the laces of his shirt. "You were saying?"

She moistened her lips with the tip of her tongue. "Well, the way you kissed me earlier, it was . . . nice."

"Nice?" He frowned, thinking it was a hell of a lot better than "nice."

"And I know there's an attraction between us, but . . ."

Every muscle in Jake's body tensed when he realized what she was trying to say. She didn't want to make love to him.

He took a step back and ran his hand over his jaw, trying to clear his thoughts. Had he misread her? The look in her eyes, the feel of her hands on his body when she'd returned his kiss? Perhaps she was afraid and needed more time. Lord knows he didn't want to frighten her.

Fisting his hands, he turned away and started walking. He had no idea where he was going, but he couldn't stay near her another second without touching her.

"Where are you going?" she called after him.

"For a walk."

"Now? But why?"

He stopped, rested his hands on his hips and took a deep breath. But he didn't turn around. "So you can get dressed." *And to look for a place where I can go quietly insane from wanting you.*

He heard a splash of water, as if she were leaving the pool. Grinding out a curse, he started walking again.

"Jake, please, stop!"

He did, waited.

"You're angry."

"I'm not."

"Jake Mitchell, you've been angry with me quite often over the last month. I think I know when you're angry. And you are!"

"I'm not, Sarah. I'm just going to put some distance between us so I won't be tempted to kiss you again."

"You don't want to kiss me?"

He couldn't believe it; she sounded hurt. "Bloody hell, woman, I want to kiss every inch of you, but not if you don't want me to."

"And who said I don't want you to?"

"You did."

He heard more splashing and it took every ounce of willpower not to turn around to see if she'd left the pool. Seconds ticked. She probably had her gown on by now, he thought with regret. She'd be safely covered, her beautiful, soft pale skin hidden from his view.

"I said no such thing," she stated from directly behind him.

He could smell her wet skin, clean and cool. He ran a hand over his eyes and wondered if she was trying to kill him.

She tapped him on the shoulder. "Jake, look at me."

He turned to tell her to give him some time to cool off, but what he saw stopped the words in his throat. Water trickled over her skin, glistening pearls that danced in the sun. Wet hair clung to her shoulders and back. A thin strand curved over one bare breast, the nipple rosy and puckered, begging him to take it into his mouth.

"Jesus," he breathed.

"I had only thought to give you privacy to bathe," she told him, shifting uneasily as he continued to stare.

Hearing the worry in her voice, he pushed his hand into the hair at her nape and brought her closer. "I had thought we would bathe together."

Her eyes widened with surprise. "We can do that? I hadn't thought—"

Jake didn't let her finish. He pressed his mouth over hers, growling when she opened to him without hesitation. He was overwhelmed by her taste, sweet and wet, rich as honey. She leaned against him. Through his clothes, he could feel the fullness of her breasts, the curve of her thighs, but the sensations were teasing, erotic, and not enough.

Without breaking the kiss, he lifted her in his arms and started for the pool. He entered the water, clothes, boots, Sarah and all, and didn't stop until he was chest deep. Releasing her legs, he positioned her so she could wrap them around his waist. The feel of her pressed tight against his groin stole his ability to breathe.

"My, God, Sarah."

She threaded her fingers though his hair, held him as she kissed his mouth, his chin, the line of his jaw. He in turn ran his hands down her back to her waist, then up to fill his palms with her breasts, weighing them, molding them as he'd imagined doing so many times before. She whimpered and lightly bit the side of his neck, but when he clasped her bottom and pressed her flush against him, she went still, her breath catching in her throat.

She looked at him, her eyes glazed, her mouth gaping in surprise. "I . . ."

He moved against her and she gasped, her fingers digging into his shirt. "Jake . . ." She shivered. "Jake . . ."

He understood her inability to finish the sentence. His mind was on fire, his body ready to explode. His only thought was to plunge inside her, bury himself, find his release that would be both incredible and bittersweet.

Instead, he clasped her waist and held her away.

Breathing hard, her eyes dark with desire, she demanded. "Why did you stop?"

"We've got to slow down."

She nodded, pressing her hand to her chest, as if that would help control her breathing. "Yes, of course. You'll want to wash."

"That's not exactly what I had in mind."

"Then what?"

He pulled off one boot and threw it onto shore, the second one not far behind. Taking her hand, he placed it on his chest, where his shirt was still laced.

Wondering if she could feel the erratic beat of his heart, he told her, "I thought you could do the washing."

Sarah's mind spun with pleasure and shock. The thought of rubbing her hands over Jake's body, learning every curve and angle, and all with the pretense of scrubbing him clean, sent shivers of anticipation running beneath her skin. She had no idea what she was supposed to do, or how to proceed, and her ignorance worried her. She'd already made one blunder by making him think she didn't want him. She couldn't afford another. If he didn't touch her, do *something* to end the rush of heat spiraling through her middle, she didn't think she'd survive.

"Take my shirt off, Sarah," he said, his sensual voice sliding into her.

She undid the laces, watching her hands work and feeling as if they belonged to someone else. Surely this was all a dream. Someone else was standing naked in a pool of water, stripping Jake of his clothes. It was too unreal, too forbidden, too incredible for it to be happening to her.

He helped her pull his shirt over his head and toss it aside. She stared at the expanse of smooth tanned skin that flexed with hidden muscle. She'd thought of him as strong and gifted, even overwhelming, but now she added beautiful. The first chance she got, she intended to draw him, immortalize the masculine shape of his chest, his narrowed waist, his arms that seemed capable of protecting the world.

"Breathe, Sarah," he ordered with a soft laugh.

She drew a shuddering breath and ran the flat of her hands over his shoulders and down the slope of his chest. She bent to kiss a path down his middle, the way he'd kissed her that day in her tent.

Jake caught her arms and held her back. "Not yet."

She started to protest, but he untied his pants. Heat burned her cheeks as she watched him struggle out of his clothes. Finally, his pants joined his boots.

Sarah stood frozen, knowing what she'd like to do next, but not sure if she should. "Jake?"

"Hmm?" He lifted his hand to her breast, but stopped within an inch of touching her.

She felt her skin tighten, fill. She held her breath, waiting for the instant his fingers met her sensitive skin. Only his hand fell away, sinking into the water.

She shivered with disappointment and yearning. "Can I kiss you now?"

He shook his head, a dangerous look in his dark eyes. "No."

"Then what?"

"You still haven't washed me."

A wave of sheer pleasure swept up her spine. Smiling, she reached into the water and scooped up a handful of sand. Dividing it in half, she ran her palms up his chest, moving in circles as she covered every inch of skin she could see. Jake stood tall and tense, his nostrils flaring as he watched her progress. She cupped her hands around his neck, kneaded the taut muscles, then skimmed her fingers over his shoulders and down his arms. She wanted to close her eyes and savor the feel of his body, but she couldn't look away. His arms flexed in harmony with her touch, his stomach contracted as she grazed his waist above the waterline.

She longed to explore the parts of him she couldn't see. She understood the anatomy of a man, having seen statues and paintings in museums.

After rinsing grains of sand from his body, she said, "Now your back."

"This is hardly fair, you know," he said, his gaze fastened on her breasts.

"You insisted we do this. Are you going to complain now?"

"I should get to bathe you, as well."

"I've already bathed. While you were off killing that poor defenseless animal."

"That's the last time I'll worry about our stomachs."

"Turn," she ordered.

He presented his back, and Sarah was amazed all over again. She repeated the process, exploring and appreciating his body, knowing that hard work and sweat had created every line and contour, every honed muscle. His was not the body of an idle man who watched life move around him, but one that caused the world to spin.

She decided it was time to be more like him and take what she wanted. She grazed her hands down his back until they dipped beneath the water. Grains of sand floated away as she slid her palms lower, over the curve of his bottom, tight and firm, then around to his hips, where she paused.

"Sarah," Jake warned, his voice strained.

"Yes?" She moved closer until the tip of her breasts touched his back. Rough sand grated her nipples, the foreign sensation so incredible, she rubbed against him.

He tensed and sucked in a breath through clenched teeth. His hands fisted at his sides. "Enough, Sarah. You haven't finished yet."

"Oh, of course." She eased back until she wasn't touching him, and smiled when he shivered. Before she could stop to think, she slid her hand from his hip, down to his groin.

She wasn't sure who gasped the loudest, she or Jake. His hard, round testicles filled her palm, tightening against her fingers. She squeezed him gently, moved her hand to learn his shape.

He caught her wrist, stopping her but he didn't pull her away. "Christ, woman, are you trying to kill me?"

"I'm simply following orders." When he didn't move or respond, she said, "Could you release my hand, I'm not finished."

"I'm afraid you are."

He started to turn, but when he did, her hand closed over something else entirely.

"Sarah," he growled, and to her ears he sounded in pain.

"Oh, my," she managed in a stunned whisper. Her fingers curled around his phallus. He was hot and hard, pulsing with life. Instinctively, she ran her fingers up the length of him.

Jake's hand shot out and caught hers, forcing it away. He turned, grabbed her by the waist. Lifting her so they were eye to eye, he kissed her, plunging his tongue inside her mouth. The kiss was an act of mating, primal and hungry, nothing soft or gentle, just fierce possessiveness, untamed need.

She held on to him, her arms tight around his neck, her legs wrapped around his waist. Wherever skin touched, fire raced, shooting to her heart, searing her mind. But the place where her core pressed tight against him burned with blinding need. That was the place she wanted Jake. If he filled her there everything would be all right. She'd be whole and happy, complete. The raging fire would stop.

"Jake, please . . ." He kissed her jaw, the curve of her neck. "Now . . ."

He growled in response and carried her out of the pool, but only made it to the edge. He lowered her into the shallow water, her back and shoulder warmed by the grass, and held his body over hers. She tensed in anticipation, knowing in another moment she would be forever changed.

But Jake shifted to her side and ran his callused hand over her body, along her ribs and across her breasts, teasing her until she wanted to cry. She arched beneath his touch, clasping his shoulders, silently begging him to make love to her. He silenced her frustrated moans with his mouth and swept his palm over her stomach, slow, erotic circles, moving lower and lower, building the swell of need, until, finally, his fingers closed over her, tight and firm. She gasped in shock, her hips pushing against him.

"Jake!" She caught his wrist, but couldn't pull him away.

"Don't fight, sweetheart." He kissed her breast, laving

it with his tongue while he coaxed her with his hand. When he took her nipple into his mouth, she cried out and saw stars behind her closed lids. Seconds passed with the agonizing sensations building, churning, tightening every part of her body.

A sob caught in her throat and she tensed, only to shudder as the fire suddenly unfurled, sweeping through her in a tide of liquid heat. She gasped again and again, caught up in sensations too impossible to name.

Before her heart had a chance to settle, Jake moved between her legs. Supporting himself on his bent arms, never taking his gaze from hers, he found her opening and pushed inside.

Her climax had been breathtaking, but it had been nothing compared to what he was doing to her now. Hard and hot, she could feel the pulse of his shaft as he eased inside her. He trembled, and she knew he was trying to go slow. The first time was supposed to hurt, but she couldn't imagine anything hurting her now.

She slid her legs around his and lifted her hips to meet him.

"Don't do that," he warned her, his face dark, his jaw clamped tight.

"I want you, Jake."

"Damn it, Sarah." A pained expression flitted across his face an instant before he shoved into her. He threw his head back, a moan rumbled from deep within his throat.

Sarah couldn't breathe, couldn't move. Having Jake buried inside her was stunning, overwhelming. There hadn't been any pain. What she felt was warmth and completion and swirling pleasure. He pumped into her again and again, and she knew she'd never felt anything so right. This was where he belonged, where they both belonged.

He moved over her, inside her, his skin glistening with

droplets of water and sweat. She held on to his arms, met his fierce gaze. Instinctively, she lifted her hips and took him deeper, so deep she gasped as the world started to spin.

The spasms rocked through her, pure and stunning. She held on to them, wanting them to last, and almost whimpered when they started to fade. But just then Jake's began. He shouted her name, his head back, his body straining.

Pushing into her again and again, he held her tight and carried her off to the land of the gods.

Chapter 18

The giant sun sat low on the horizon, reluctant to give up its claim to the day. Color blazed across the sky, orange and red, yellows blending with heavenly blue.

Jake watched the kaleidoscope change and mingle. At most, they had another hour of light. Having eaten their dinner of flat bread and sand cat, Sarah grimacing with every bite, they should have started walking, found a better place to sleep. He hated leaving the watering hole, but they had to be long gone when the jackals and caracals arrived for their nightly drink.

Yet he didn't move. He couldn't, not with Sarah curled up next to him, her body warm from the sun and their last round of lovemaking. He ran his hand down her side to the indention of her waist. God, but she was small, too delicate to have endured the hardship she had. And soft, who knew a woman could be so smooth, with skin like satin?

Her breath brushed his neck as her fingers made sleepy swirls over his chest. A comforting band tightened around his heart. He wanted to stay like this forever, keep her with him.

Then he realized he wanted more than that.

He wanted to keep *her*. Forever.

Jake pressed his lips to her forehead, at once frightened and exhilarated by the thought. He'd never wanted *forever* with a woman, hadn't thought it possible. For years he'd had his life mapped out, planned in detail, and had known nothing would get in his way. He had no family left alive. Marrying had been out of the question; what kind of wife would tolerate a husband who preferred the deserts of Egypt to the safety of England? There had been nothing to stop him from pursuing his first love—archaeology.

Until now.

But could he really give up his search for Egypt's past? Did he love Sarah enough?

Jake closed his eyes and held her tight against him, tried to imagine never seeing her again, never kissing her or making love to her. He couldn't do it. God help him, he loved her.

Sighing, he let the admission sink in, take root. He loved her and knew he'd do anything within his power to protect her, stay with her. He'd heard about men who had forsaken everything for the love of a woman, but he'd never thought he'd become one of those men. Yet here he was, deciding to do just that.

But if he gave up Egypt, what would he do? Who would he be? What kind of life could he and Sarah have together? She came from comfort and wealth; he lived in the dirt.

He had no answers and, in fact, he didn't even like the questions. Then a solution occurred to him. He could give Sarah something she wanted, prove to her that he not only forgave her, but that he loved her. It wouldn't solve all their differences, but it would be a beginning.

"Sarah?" he whispered, running his fingers through her hair.

"Hmmm?" She stretched against him, a cat waking from a nap.

He rolled her onto her back. "I've made a decision."

Smiling up at him, her silver eyes glazed with seduction, she said, "You sound much too serious. I'm not ready to be serious."

As she skimmed her nails down his back, he briefly

lost his train of thought. Shaking his head, he told her, "There's something I want to do. I should have done before."

"Like kiss me?" She nibbled his jaw, then moved to the sensitive vein along his neck.

"Sarah, I'm trying—" She shifted, and suddenly she was completely beneath him, her legs cupping his, her warm body open and ready.

"You were saying?" She closed her eyes and lifted her hips, finding him.

"God save me," he growled. For the third time in as many hours, Jake pushed inside her, and let the electrifying bliss rush over him. He joined their bodies, binding them, determined to show her how much he loved her.

Later, when he could think again, he would tell her.

Sarah followed Jake like a docile pet as he led her into the pool to wash the sand and traces of their lovemaking from their bodies. She stood still while he poured handfuls of water over her, the warm liquid as enticing as the look in his eyes.

Heaven help her, she would never tire of looking at him, his sculpted mouth and strong jaw, the curve of his cheek, the possessive, smoldering emotions that darkened his gaze.

"I love you," she said, suddenly, surprising them both.

A wicked grin pulled one corner of his mouth. "Do you now?"

"I do." She swayed against him, lightly resting her hands on his arms. Jake drew her close, their bodies touching. She felt the stir of desire, but another feeling overwhelmed it. Contentment. There was no where else she wanted to be, she realized. No other man who would make her feel so incredibly alive.

"And when did you decide you loved me?" he asked, and though his voice hummed with amusement, his eyes told her how important her answer would be.

"I'm not sure. You grew on me."

"Like a wart, or something else just as pleasant?"

"Kindly give me some leeway," she said, smiling at him, wishing he'd kiss her senseless again. "I started off hating you, remember?"

"Having you rebuff me, only to take to Gavin is something I'm not likely to forget."

"Jealous?"

He shrugged, a rueful grin pulling at his kissable mouth. "I would have killed him, but he had paid my fare."

Closing her eyes, she rested her cheek against his chest, felt the steady drumming of his heart. She waited for him to tell her he loved her, too, but when he didn't say anything, just continued to hold her, she told herself not to be disappointed. She didn't want anything to spoil what they had just shared.

"It's going to be dark soon," he said, his voice vibrating against her. "We need to start walking."

She sighed, having known this moment would come, but she didn't like it. This was their watering hole, their moment, she wanted it to last.

Looking up at him, she said, "Wasn't there something you were going to tell me?"

Laughing in surprise when he lifted her in his arms and carried her out of the pool, she said, "There really isn't any hurry. We can leave after you tell me."

He set her on her feet and swatted her bottom. "I'll tell you while we dress. Unless you'd like to be here when the jackals arrive."

Her heart giving a sudden lurch, she looked around the surrounding desert. Hours before, when Jake had returned to find her still in the pool, she hadn't given their dangerous situation another thought. But reality was quick to return.

She glanced at her gown, now dry and lying across the sand, and this time both her stomach and her heart flipped end over end. The corselet. She stood frozen, unsure what to do. She couldn't put it on without Jake seeing it. And the thought of continuing her deception made her ill.

She looked at him, her heart racing so hard she was dizzy. He had put on his pants and was reaching for his shirt, which was still damp from washing. "Jake, there's something you need to know."

Slipping his shirt over his head, he said, "I think you'll want to hear what I have to say first. You know how important Queen Tiy's discovery was to me?"

"Yes," she said weakly.

"Sealing her inside the tomb again cost me everything."

"I am sorry, Jake, but—"

He held up his hand to quiet her. "You didn't seal it completely."

She drew a shuddering breath, knowing what would come next. "You intend to dig her out again."

"That was my plan. Take you home, then return after the flooding season. She's too important a discovery to leave for someone else to find."

She nodded, suddenly torn between two worlds. She wanted Jake to have his discovery, but she wanted Queen Tiy to have her peace, too. Sarah realized she had a choice to make: Jake's happiness or Queen Tiy's. Who was more important to her? She didn't have to think about the answer. She loved Jake with all her heart, he had to come first. But what if she offered him a compromise? The queen was in her tomb. Surely she could live for eternity without the corselet. If she gave the artifact to Jake he might agree to leave the queen in peace.

Her decision made, she said, "Jake, there's something I have to tell you."

His gaze skimmed over her, warmed with appreciation. "Woman, if you insist on standing there naked, we'll never reach Thebes."

Picking up her gown, he handed it to her. "Here. I think you'll be interested in hearing what I've decided."

She clenched the gown in her hands, her gaze fastened on her chemise bundled beside her boots.

"I'm not going to excavate Queen Tiy."

She stared at him, not registering what he'd said.

"I intend to return, of course. The way the tomb is now, someone will find her. I think a few more of your iron ball explosives will ensure no one will ever discover her again."

"But why?" She shook her head. "What changed your mind?"

"You did," he said, his voice low, certain.

"Me? But you didn't believe my dream."

"I don't know whether I believe Queen Tiy came to you or not, but," taking her by the shoulders, he drew her close, looked down at her with an expression Sarah thought she'd never see, "I love you," he told her. "You're far more important to me than any discovery. Repairing my reputation can wait. But what I want for us can't."

"You would sacrifice Queen Tiy for us?" Tears stung her eyes, then fell down her cheeks.

"For you."

"Oh, Jake." She threw her arms around his neck and cried into his chest. He'd made the ultimate sacrifice for her, now she had to tell him the truth. A rush of relief pushed through her. She wanted the lies over with, once and for all.

"And for Roger," he added reluctantly. "Though I intend to strangle him for sending you here. He's been my friend for too many years. I should have realized how frightened he was."

"You can really let her go?"

Jake kissed the top of her head, whispered, "I already have."

Sarah held him tight, her love for him almost hurting her chest.

His hands splayed over her back. "As tempted as I am to stay here, sweetheart, we've got to leave."

"Not yet," she said, as he pulled away. "I have to tell you what I've . . . wait!" she cried as Jake reached for her chemise.

He lifted the garment and froze, stared at the heavy weight in his hand.

"Jake, let me explain."

He turned to her, his eyes narrowed, his face drained of color. "What is this, Sarah? Or do I already know?"

"I was going to tell you."

"Were you now?"

She shivered, not liking the controlled evenness of his voice. "I couldn't stand lying to you."

He scoffed. "Since when?"

"Jake, please," she said, shaking. "Let me explain."

"I'm listening."

Clenching her gown to her to cover her nakedness, she said, "The day you discovered I had Queen Tiy, I was relieved. I had hated you for so many years, only to realize you weren't to blame for my father's neglect. I wanted you to have your discovery. I did. When I said I would give the corselet to you I'd meant it."

"But you didn't."

She swallowed, wishing he'd shout at her, scream or curse, anything besides look at her with cold contempt. "That night I had the dream."

"And you decided to return Queen Tiy to her tomb."

"Deceiving you again was the hardest thing I'd ever

done." She ignored the sardonic arch of his brow. "But the memory of her wouldn't leave me. Even now I can taste her fear, feel her tremors." Sarah tried to draw a calming breath but it shuddered through her. "I had to take her back to her tomb.

"Then you climbed the cliff."

She nodded. "When I was halfway up, I realized I still wore the corselet."

"And you couldn't go back because I was behind you."

"Yes."

"You still could have told me you had it."

"How? When?" she demanded in her own defense. "Napoleon had arrived and we had to run."

"We've been walking for days," he bit out so sharply, she flinched. "You've had plenty of opportunity."

"I couldn't tell you, because . . ." she briefly closed her eyes. "Because I had planned to somehow return the corselet to her tomb."

"Cunning to the end, eh, Sarah?" Jake laughed, a dry humorless sound.

In that instant Sarah knew any chance they'd had at a life together was lost. He would never believe her now. Never.

Damn you, Queen Tiy. Damn you.

Tremors raced through Jake's body, wild and out of control. He'd never felt such anger, such brutal betrayal. Not even the moment he'd first discovered Queen Tiy missing had he felt anything so wrenching.

He unwrapped the chemise, revealing tiny gold squares that shimmered in the fading sun. It struck him as ironic that something so incredibly beautiful had brought him so much grief. Perhaps Roger wasn't crazy, perhaps the corselet *was* cursed. "I'm curious. Just when were you going to tell me the truth?"

"It doesn't matter now. You won't believe me." She turned away, but he caught her arm and forced her to face him.

"I beg to differ."

Tears shimmered like glass in her silver eyes. He saw her distress, a silent plea for him to believe her, but he'd be damned if he'd fall for her tricks again.

Her mouth quivering, she said, "After we made love, I knew I had to give the corselet to you."

"Was that before or after you said you loved me."

"Jake, please—"

"Or was that a lie, too?" he demanded, afraid to hear the truth.

She tensed, her face going pale. "Whatever else I've done, you have to believe that I love you."

"What I believe is that you will lie to get whatever you want. Gavin was right," he said, shaking so badly he frightened himself. "Women aren't to be trusted."

She looked at him, her eyes wide and full of misery. Had it only been moments ago that he'd been the happiest man alive? He looked away from her toward the dying sun and felt a part of himself die with it.

"Get dressed," he told her. "We're leaving."

"Well, well, well. Isn't this interesting."

The strange male voice had Jake whipping around to see a group of armed men mounted on camels. He instinctively reached for his gun, but belatedly realized it was lying next to his boots, ten feet away. Sarah gasped. Jake pulled her behind him to shield her as much as he could from the two dozen pairs of eyes trying to catch a glimpse of her naked body. The men were military, and from their uniforms, they were French.

Bloody hell! Jake cursed himself. He'd allowed one of Napoleon's patrols to sneak up on him unawares. Gripping the corselet in the chemise, he held it by his side and prayed no one would notice it.

"Jake Mitchell," a man said, urging his mount to the front. "I heard you were in the area."

"Do you know him?" Sarah whispered, pressing against his back, her gown clutched to her chest.

Jake not only knew him; there wasn't a man alive that he hated more. "Stuart Kilvington, I'd say I'm glad to see you but we both know that would be a lie."

"Enemies to the end?" the Marquis of Ashby said, his thin mouth disappearing when he smiled. He glanced around the watering hole with a calculated gaze. Jake remembered those small, dark eyes, and had learned to be wary of them. "I don't see any camels. Don't tell me your luck has run out?"

His gaze briefly touched the bundle in Jake's hand before moving to Sarah. Jake knew she was desperately trying to cover herself with her gown, and knew there was nothing he could do to help her. At least not yet.

With a wicked grin, the marquis added, "Or perhaps you're as lucky as ever."

"Take your men and leave," Jake demanded.

Stuart laughed. "We came out of our way so our camels could drink. My captain had reported seeing footprints in the sand, but I'd had no idea they would lead me to you." He chuckled again. "Finding you is a boon."

"Leave."

"Or what? You're sorely at a disadvantage. But you should be accustomed to that."

"I'm sure there's a scrap of decency left in you, Stuart. Find it and leave. The lady needs to dress."

"Is she?" He arched a black brow. "A lady, I mean."

Jake took a threatening step forward, but stopped when Sarah caught his arm.

With an amused sigh, the marquis motioned to his men. "Turn your backs. The lady needs some privacy."

When everyone except Stuart had turned their mounts, Jake said, "That includes you."

"And give you the opportunity to reach for your gun?" He tsked. "That would be foolish, and we both know I'm no fool."

"No, you're just the lowest sort of scum who steals other people's discoveries."

Stuart shrugged, unruffled by the insult. "Your lady friend should hurry. I can't say how long my men will follow orders. They've been without a woman for some time, and yours seems to be quite pretty."

"Get dressed," Jake told her, trying to shield her as much as he could.

When the marquis attempted to look around him, Jake tried to distract him by saying, "When did you join with the French?"

"Who said I've joined them?"

Jake glanced at the soldiers who were sneaking covert looks over their shoulders. He clenched his free hand into a fist and stood there helpless and hating it. Hearing Sarah's frantic mutterings, he didn't bother telling her to hurry.

"Oh, you're referring to my escort." The marquis waved a hand in dismissal. "What can I say. Napoleon has become obsessed about an ancient Egyptian ruler, and is rather determined to find him. Personally I don't think he stands a chance of locating King Menes' tomb."

"The first king to unite upper and lower Egypt?" Jake frowned, immediately suspicious. Menes had been the first king to rule all of Egypt. He'd been considered a god, the ruler of the world. Napoleon was currently fighting an expensive war with England, why would he spend money to fund such an unlikely expedition?

Stuart's mouth quirked with irritation. "I should have known you would have had heard of him. Not that it matters. The king lived five thousand years ago. I doubt there's anything left of him but dust."

The marquis leaned over in his saddle just as Sarah lowered her gown.

Fighting back the urge to pound Stuart's face for looking, Jake asked, "Do you know where his tomb is?"

When the marquis smiled, Jake knew without a doubt that the man had no idea. "It's all but within my grasp."

"He was an important ruler of his time. His tomb was probably robbed in antiquity."

Pursing his lips as if disappointed that Sarah was covered, he said, "I have no doubt it was emptied a year after it was sealed."

"If you think it's a waste of time, why search for it?"

"Who said I am?" Excitement sparkled in the man's eyes once again. "Oh, I'm keeping an eye out for King Menes, but I have a plan of my own as well."

"It's good to know some things never change." Jake didn't bother to hide his sarcasm.

"Napoleon has funded the expedition with strong French francs, and has hired the best archaeologists to lead it."

"Since he hired you, I at least have the comfort of knowing he'll fail."

Stuart's eyes hardened to chips of stone. He nudged his camel closer then leaned over, extending his riding crop. Jake tensed, waiting for the sting of the slash across his face. But what Stuart did was worse. He hooked the crop beneath the corselet and lifted it from Jake's hand.

Jake caught it, intending to rip it away, but Stuart barked an order in French and suddenly, his men were behind him, their weapons drawn.

Lifting the corselet to eye level, Stuart whistled. "As with your lady, I just want to take a peek."

Futile anger burned through Jake. He could feel Sarah behind him, dressed now and trembling, her fingers digging into his sides.

After a moment of studying the hieroglyphics, the

marquis's eyes widened. "Well, I'll be damned. It seems I've found something."

"You haven't found anything," Sarah said, stepping from behind him. "That belongs to Jake. Please, give it back to him."

Stuart ignored her. "Is this what I think it is? An actual record of a murder attempt on Ramses the Third?"

Jake fisted his hands, cursing the gods and fate for bringing Stuart Kilvington back into his life. And for putting him in the position, *again,* of being helpless to stop him from taking what was rightfully his.

"Where did you find this, Mitchell?" Stuart asked, then pursed his lips. "Oh, never mind. You won't tell me. But I have an idea. We found the remains of a camp in Deir el-Medineh, and then there was an abandoned wagon in the Valley of the Queens. I'd thought it unusual, as if someone had left in quite a hurry, right after they'd set off an explosion. Could that have been you?"

Jake glanced at his gun, judged the distance, and knew if he lunged for it, the soldiers would fill him with bullets before he touched the handle. He breathed hard, clenching and unclenching his fists, every fiber of his being screaming for him to do something!

"Seems I'll have to return to the Valley of the Queens," Stuart said, enthralled with the corselet and oblivious to Jake's turmoil. Glancing at his men, he muttered a curse. "But not today, I'm afraid."

"Why," Jake said, shaking with rage. "Is there someone else's discovery you need to steal first?"

"If only that were so. No, I must return to Thebes to rendezvous with the French general. And since Napoleon holds the purse strings, so to speak, and becomes rather irritable when people make him wait, I think I'll be on my way."

With a brusque wave of his hand, he motioned for his men to move out.

"Give me the corselet." As if she were entertaining in a drawing room, wearing silks and lace instead of standing barefoot in the sand, her gown torn and filthy, Sarah held out her hand and waited. To Jake's amazement, she even tilted her chin and managed to look down her nose at the marquis.

With an amused chuckle, Stuart backed his camel away. "She's a slow one, isn't she Mitchell? She doesn't realize this artifact now belongs to me."

"You can't have it," she insisted. She rounded on Jake, her loose hair flying about her shoulders like a cape. "Tell him."

"The marquis is right," Jake said, though it nearly killed him to say it.

"But it's yours." The anxiety in her eyes echoed the rage that was choking him. But he was outmanned, and outgunned. There was nothing he could do.

To the marquis, he said, "Leave us a camel."

"Hmmm, I think not. You've always been resourceful. I'm sure you'll find a way out of your unfortunate predicament." Extending his hand, he added, "But it would be my pleasure to escort your lady friend to Thebes."

The thought of putting Sarah in Stuart's clutches nearly caused Jake to lose the last of his control, but she would be safer with the black-hearted bastard than stranded in the desert. She wouldn't have to walk, she'd have food and shelter. Once in Thebes, the authorities would help her until he caught up with her again. But she didn't give him a chance to voice any of those thoughts.

With a smile that dripped with disdain, she admitted, "Thank you, but I'd rather walk back to Thebes with a cobra wrapped around my neck."

"Go with him, Sarah," Jake said.

"I will not."

"Sarah—"

"No." Between the finality of that single word and the

determination in her eyes, he knew she wouldn't listen to reason.

"It matters not to me. Keep the woman with you." He dropped the corselet into his saddlebag, patting it. "And I'll keep this with me."

"You won't get away with this," Jake warned.

"Now, now, Mitchell, old boy." Laughing, Stuart kicked his camel into a lope, calling over his shoulder. "I got away with it once before, and I will again!"

Sarah lunged and grabbed up the gun. Jake caught her around the waist and took the weapon out of her hands before she could take aim. When she started to argue, he shook his head, but that didn't stop her.

"I won't let him take the corselet."

"Why?" he asked in a harsh voice he hardly recognized. "Because you still have to return it to Queen Tiy?"

She clamped her jaw shut and looked away, but not before he saw tears spring to her eyes.

Nearing the rise of a sand dune, Stuart reined his mount around. "No hard feelings, Jake. Just think how impressed the curator at the British Museum will be when I show him my latest find."

Stuart disappeared behind the wall of sand, leaving nothing but drifting dust and the sound of fading laughter.

He felt Sarah's tremors, but he couldn't look at her, couldn't even attempt to comfort her. He'd been willing to give up Queen Tiy for her love, but his gesture had been for nothing. Sarah didn't know how to love. She only knew how to lie.

Anger boiled up inside him. He had lost Sarah. He almost laughed at the absurd thought. He'd never really had her. Their brief time together was over, any future they might have shared had been as grand an illusion as a desert mirage.

But the corselet . . . He hoped Stuart enjoyed his time with the artifact, because he wouldn't have it for long. Whatever it took, Jake intended to get it back.

Chapter 19

The River Nile flowed northward in a constant surge of sapphire blue. Waves licked at the sandy banks, tempting Sarah to dive in and sink into its dark cool depths. A throng of people crowded the quay, unloading cargo from the newly arrived feluccas. Farther down the dock, fishermen were untangling their nets while their wives and sons sold their day's catch to passersby.

She followed Jake through the crowded, narrow streets with no idea where they were going. And to be honest, she didn't care. There were people, shops, donkeys weighed down with pottery and baskets. Smells of burning incense and cooking meat collided in the air. Her mouth watered and her stomach churned with hunger. Everywhere she looked there were people haggling over vegetables carts, priests chanting on corners, children being noisy and carefree.

She'd never seen a city more beautiful than Thebes. Every street bustled with so much life, Sarah wanted to cry.

Because everywhere she looked was proof that she and Jake had survived.

Sarah looked at him now and saw the same wide back she'd watched for the last four days, muscles tense, his long legs carving a path through the jostling streets instead of the rolling desert sand. His attention was fixed on what lay ahead of him . . . not on her. After leaving the watering hole, she had struggled to keep up with the relentless pace he'd set, afraid that if she lagged behind he might not realize it until it was too late and she was dinner for their patient escorts, the buzzards.

Unless forced to, he didn't speak to her, and he never looked at her, a fact that tore her heart. If only he would let her explain, but after her futile attempts before their encounter with Stuart Kilvington, she had given up trying to break through Jake's anger.

He was furious with her, with the marquis, with life in general, and she didn't blame him. He thought he had lost everything. But she knew otherwise. She loved him more now than ever before. She knew how betrayed he felt, how alone. The emotions rolled off him in waves of despair and frustration.

She saw in his eyes that he thought they were finished, that they would never again make love or laugh or share something new. But she knew differently. And she intended to prove how much she loved him by taking the corselet back from Stuart. She had no idea how she would go about getting it, but if she could cross a desert and live to tell about it she could procure the corselet from a miserable, disgusting little man.

Suddenly, Jake stopped at an intersection, his shadowed gaze raking over the busy streets. Sarah waited without asking the thousand questions running through her mind, knowing he wouldn't answer. She swayed and blinked to fight off her exhaustion. It amazed her that sometime in the last few days she'd become accustomed to the heat, but lack of food and miles of walking had taken its toll. Her muscles were sore and strained, searing pain shot up her feet with every step, her eyes were gritty with sand and her head pounded. And despite the scorching sun she felt a chill deep in her bones.

When he started off again without a word or a backward glance, taking a street that curved to the right, she forced herself to move, consciously lifting one aching foot up and setting it down. Up and down, up and down. The words droned in her mind like a march, compelling her to ignore the pain in her arms and legs and keep pace.

She had no idea how long they walked but, mercifully, Jake finally stopped and entered a squalid mud hut that had a sign in Arabic swinging over its door. Relieved that she might be able to rest, she reached out and caught the rough wall to steady herself. But the tremors in her limbs continued, growing stronger. In a daze, she noticed the streets were quiet and littered with trash. Naked children watched her from doorways, their eyes wide with curiosity. She and Jake had obviously walked far from the hectic marketplace, but to where or why she had no idea.

Hearing voices inside the building, Sarah started to enter, but the ground suddenly dipped beneath her feet. Her knees buckled. She caught the wall and pressed her back against it. When she started a downward slide, she had to close her eyes. A sob lodged in her throat. Heavens, she was about to faint. If she'd had the strength, she would have cursed.

Hold on, she ordered herself. If she lost consciousness, Jake would leave her. After following him across a desert, she refused to lose him now. But as hard as she tried, the blackness crept up and into her mind. The dark was cool and comforting. When it tried to take over, all she could do was sigh and let it.

"Ye bloody almost killed her!" Connor growled for the hundredth time as he paced the felucca's deck, causing the boat to rock against the current.

Soaking another strip of cloth in clean water and laying it over Sarah's forehead, Jake clenched his jaw tight and tried to ignore the Scotsman. He didn't need anyone reminding him of what he'd done. Every time he looked at her, saw her cheeks bright and slick with fever and the bruises circling her closed eyes, fear and guilt and every other damning emotion worth having bore a path through his heart.

"What were ye thinkin' mon?" Connor demanded, stopping to stare down at her, his red brows dipped in a fierce scowl.

"We've been over this already," Gavin said evenly, cupping his hand around the tip of his cigarette to light it.

"Aye, 'e wanted tae reach Thebes. Well, 'e did and he run 'er into the ground while he was at it."

No one responded or came to Jake's defense, for which he was grateful. The silence that followed Connor's latest outburst was harsh and grim and well deserved. Overhead, a flock of geese flew in a jagged skein against the vivid blue sky. Jake had the insane impulse to take Sarah by the shoulders and shake her, demand she open her eyes and look at them. He wanted her to smile with delight, gather her pencil and paper and draw them.

But he didn't touch her, and she didn't wake up.

"Perhaps we should have stayed in Thebes," Eli said, turning a date over and over in his large fingers but not eating it. "The doctor there—"

"Had done everything he could," Gavin interrupted. "It's best we return to Rosetta and catch the next ship to England. Thanks to Jake's contacts in Thebes, we know Stuart is headed for London."

"Aye, her father will be want'n tae know how she fared," Thatcher said.

"Her father?" Jake asked.

"Lord Pendergrass. 'E's the one who hired us."

Jake lowered his head to his hands. So she'd told him the truth. She was Roger's daughter.

"Who cares about the marquis or that blasted corselet, or who her father is, for that matter? 'Tis Lady Sarah we need to worry about," Eli said, pitching the date into the Nile.

"She suffered severe sun and heatstroke," Gavin said. "And the walk across the desert exhausted her. The doctor gave us medicine and told us how to care for her. He believes she'll recover."

"Might recover," Thatcher said. "'E said *might.*"

Jake ran his hand over his eyes to ease the sting from the hot dry wind, and from the sleepless nights of keeping vigil over Sarah. He wished everyone would stop talking. He knew what was wrong with her, and knew he was to blame. Sunstroke, heat exhaustion, near starvation, dehydration. When he'd found her unconscious outside the tavern in Thebes, his heart had skipped a beat. But when he'd lifted her limp body and realized how much weight she had lost, how truly fragile she was, his heart had stopped altogether.

"She never complained."

"What was that ye said?" Connor snarled.

Jake looked up, and seeing everyone's gazes fixed on him, realized he'd spoken his thoughts out loud. "She never said anything. Not to stop and rest or to slow down."

"And that excuses ye?" Connor bellowed so loud the Egyptian crew dropped whatever they were doing and scurried to the opposite end of the ship.

"I'm not making excuses." Jake stood and swiped both hands through his hair in frustration.

"She could die, Jake-o," Connor said, looking like he very much wanted to knock Jake out of the boat.

"I think we all know how seriously ill Sarah is." Gavin puffed on his cigarette, then threw it overboard with a grimace.

"And all because of a bloody corselet."

Jake reclaimed his seat beside Sarah and watched for any sign that she might wake up. A sigh, a flutter of her coal-black lashes. But there was nothing. His heart pounded hard against his chest. He had to apologize. Her life was worth far more than any tomb. She'd insisted that she still loved him and he'd tossed it back in her face. He couldn't hope that she still cared for him. Not after what he'd put her through.

Leaving the watering hole, his anger had set their grueling pace, but when she didn't complain, he hadn't slowed down; he'd never thought she'd keep quiet out of sheer stubbornness. He should have known better. Nothing stopped Sarah once she made up her mind. In that aspect, she and Jake were alike. His only stubborn thought had been to reach Thebes and find out where Stuart was meeting Napoleon.

And he'd nearly killed Sarah trying to do just that.

But none of that mattered now. The corselet, Queen Tiy, Stuart's thievery. Jake didn't care about any of it.

And he knew that if Sarah died, nothing would ever matter again.

The ground rocked in a comforting rhythm, back and forth, lulling her to sleep. Her arms felt weighted, her chest heavy, but her eyes ached as if she'd already slept too much. When a cool breeze brushed her face, she was tempted to slip back into oblivion, but the nagging dryness in her mouth and the feeling that there was something important she had to do kept her from giving in.

Time passed, her thoughts circling around her need for a drink of water and something else, something urgent that she couldn't quite recall. Gradually, she drew a full breath and forced her eyes open. She had to blink several times to focus, and even then she wasn't sure of what she saw.

Swirling white clouds moved above her, so close she could reach out and touch them. Where was she? She stared at the floating mist, trying to remember. Lifting her hand to her face, she paused when she saw tanned skin and dirty nails. She tilted her head and looked down at her gown, or what was left of it. Seeing her torn sleeve and ripped skirt brought her memory flooding back.

Egypt, the desert. She'd lost the corselet. And Jake.

She remembered arriving in Thebes, following Jake through the bustling town to a shabby mud brick hut. She closed her eyes when her head started to spin, just as it had the moment before everything went blank.

Jake, what had happened to him? She tried to say his name, but her throat was raw and wouldn't work. She struggled to sit up, moving slowly when her sore limbs rebelled. She had to find him. He was still angry with her; she needed to explain, make him understand she'd thought she'd been doing the right thing by keeping the corselet. Had he left Thebes without her? Had he found Stuart and the artifact? She had to know so she could help him.

When the ground rocked again, she lost her balance and fell back onto a bed of colorful woolen blankets, but her hand scraped across a sanded floor that was wet and weathered. A few feet away, barely visible in the fog were several boxes stacked in a neat row. She looked at them and her mouth dropped open. The boxes were hers, the ones she had packed with her clothes and art supplies!

Understanding finally settled in. She was on a felucca. But how did she get here and where was she going?

Pushing the blankets covering her legs aside, she gave her bandaged feet a brief glance before she gripped the side of the boat and tried to stand. Her legs wobbled and refused to support her. She settled for leaning against the hull, certain walking would come later. Sudden shouting at the bow made her gasp in surprise, then came scuffling and excited murmurs.

She search the fog. Were they about to be rammed by another boat? Or attacked by a dreadful hippopotamus?

When four men converged on her at once, their faces masks of worry, she could only stare in surprise.

"Ye're alive!" Eli laughed.

"Ye 'ad us worried, my lady," Thatcher said, his voice catching with relief.

"Move back, boys, you're crowding 'er." Connor knelt in front of her and ran a trembling hand through his damp red hair. "Ye shouldn't be up, lass. True enough, ye gave us a fright, but you'll be all right now. Are ye hungry? Of course yer hungry. Ye haven't eaten a bite in days."

Sarah stared at the Scotsman in amazement. She hadn't thought the burly man capable of rambling like a schoolboy.

"Connor, why don't you help Eli and Thatcher get Miss Sarah something to drink," Gavin suggested. To Sarah's surprise, the earl watched her with something like delight instead of his usual suspicious frown. "Water, perhaps."

"It don't take three of us," Thatcher said. "I'll get it."

"How are ye feeling, lass?" Connor asked, frowning.

Sarah glanced at each anxious face and tried to smile. From the startled look in their eyes, she wasn't sure she succeeded. "I'm fine," she said in a scratchy voice that sounded nothing like hers at all. She rubbed her temple. "A little headache, is all."

"I'll get yer medicine." Eli turned and disappeared into the mist.

"Where . . ." Not seeing Jake in the group, she had intended to ask where he was but a sudden knot in her throat stopped her from saying his name. "Where are we?"

"On our way to Rosetta." Gavin took the cup of water from Thatcher and passed it to her.

"But why?" She took a small sip and almost moaned as the liquid scratched her throat going down. "Is that where Stuart Kilvington is going?"

"Not that I'm aware of."

She gripped the cup in her hands, but she didn't take

another drink for fear it wouldn't stay down. If Stuart wasn't in Rosetta, but still with Napoleon in Thebes, then Jake must have stayed behind to confront the marquis. She pressed a hand to her lips to suppress the tears pushing up her throat. If she returned to England now it would be months before she saw Jake again, possibly years. Or if he decided to stay in Egypt, she might never see him again.

"I have to go back," she said suddenly, setting the cup aside so she could stand. Pain shot from her feet and up her legs. Crying out, she pitched to the side.

Gavin caught her by the arms and eased her onto the blankets. "You're not going anywhere."

"I have to. Jake is in Thebes and I'm not leaving until I see him."

The four men looked at each other, then Gavin said, "Jake isn't in Thebes."

"Did he return to the Valley of the Queens? I'll go there. I don't care where I have to go, just get me off this boat."

"He didn't—"

"Listen to me!" Frustrated that her body was too weak to stand, she balled her hands into fists and told them, "I'm not leaving Egypt without him!"

"Sarah."

She gasped, knowing that voice. She searched the fog, saw no one. Then a gust of wind swirled through the wall of mist, revealing the outline of a man. Like ghosts, the other four men moved away. Jake stepped forward, his hair damp against his head, his eyes troubled. She covered her mouth with her hands again, but this time the tears came, streaming in hot trails down her face.

"I thought you had stayed behind," she admitted, the words choked.

He knelt in front of her, but kept an arm's-length away. "There was nothing for me there."

"But Stuart, the corselet—"

"Isn't important."

"Of course it's important," she insisted. When he didn't reply she really looked at him and what she saw frightened her. His eyes were shadowed with exhaustion and something else, emotions that cut through her heart. Defeat and resignation. His face was lean and hard-edged, far different from the man she'd known even a few days before. The tendons in his forearms where they were braced on his knees were taut and his hands were curled into tight fists.

Impulsively, Sarah laid her hand over his and closed her eyes when the warmth of his skin seeped into her. She ached with the need for him to pull her into his arms and hold her, share the strength of his body. Silently tell her that he still cared. The yearning to hold him in turn nearly overpowered her.

When he didn't move, she realized his anger with her hadn't lessened. She pulled her hand away. "I'm sorry, Jake."

A muscle pulsed in his jaw and his gaze turned hot and condemning. "You have nothing to be sorry for. I'm the one who should be flogged."

She frowned. "What on earth for?"

He raked his fingers through his tousled hair, then looked at her, his blue eyes full of remorse. "For nearly killing you."

"You did no such thing. You saved my life!"

"You nearly died, Sarah."

"Not because of anything you did." Because she couldn't stop herself, she reached out and ran her palm down his face. "If anyone's to blame, then blame me. I'm the one who blew up the cliff and drew Stuart's attention."

"I could have left you at Deir el-Medineh with enough water and food," he admitted, revealing the source of his guilt. "You could have survived until I returned."

"You did what you thought was best." She straightened

and looked into the fog, which had lifted enough for her to see four brawny men prowling near the bow. "By the way, have you asked them why they didn't leave a camel for us?"

"They did. Either the animals escaped their ropes or Stuart found them before we did and took them."

Sarah held Jake's gaze for a moment longer before saying, "I'm going to get the corselet back."

When he started to object, she placed her fingers over his mouth. His eyes flared, and Sarah wished with all her heart that she could replace her fingers with her lips.

She told him, "I'm not going to let him steal what's yours."

He lowered her hand, his fingers a vise around her wrist. "You don't have a choice."

"Jake—"

"You're too ill, Sarah. I won't put you at risk again."

She heard the anger in his voice, and sensed he was directing it at himself. "I'll be fine soon. If you don't want to go after Stuart, we can return to the Valley of the Queens. Her tomb isn't covered. We can excavate it again. In a few months you can present Queen Tiy to the British Museum and prove you're the one who found her."

Jake shook his head. "Even if I wanted to, I can't. The flood season is nearing its peak. Already traveling the Nile isn't safe. In another few weeks, it'll be too hazardous."

"Then we'll stay in Rosetta until next season."

"No, Sarah. You're going home, where you'll be safe."

She stared at him, deciding he wasn't just stubborn, he was mule-headed, too. But so was she. She swore this wasn't over. Perhaps she couldn't return to Queen Tiy, and in her heart she wanted to leave the queen in her tomb, but the corselet was within reach.

And one day soon, she would give it to Jake.

Chapter 20

Four days later Jake stood at the bow of the *Spinning Star*, his hands gripping the wooden rail, his face full in the wind. The sails overhead snapped taut in the northerly breeze, sending the trading vessel slicing through jewel blue water.

Behind him, he sensed Egypt quickly fading into the distance, felt the pull of a vital bond stretching dangerously thin. He wanted to turn, take one final look, but decided against it. As much as he loved the ancient country, it would be a long time before he returned. If he ever returned. The search for buried pharaohs and forgotten temples had changed him, turned him into someone he didn't like.

As a boy, he'd discovered his path in the desert oasis, had found his strength and place in the world. It shamed him to realize that as a man he had come close to throwing away everything he valued, and all for the love of glory.

Now, he didn't know himself at all. There were too many questions he couldn't answer. Why did he want to search for artifacts? Was it really so important to uncover Egypt's past? How could he have ignored Roger's plea to return Queen Tiy when it had meant so much to him? So much that the old man had endangered his daughter's life to see it fulfilled. And when had Jake become so shallow that he would value his reputation more than Sarah's welfare?

And the last question that was the hardest to answer: What mattered to him?

He turned away from the sea and headed for the hatchway. With the setting sun, he would be expected to dine with the captain, but all he wanted was to shut himself away in his cabin.

Two decks down, he entered his small room and closed the door behind him. A short, narrow bunk with a wool blanket that smelled of the sea occupied the wall along the hull. A tiny built-in desk that could only accommodate a child filled one corner, a closet the other. With no room to walk, and only one spot to stand, he flopped onto the bed, bent his knees so he'd fit, and stared at the low ceiling.

What mattered to him?

He closed his eyes and tried to ignore the answer. *Sarah.*

As furious as he'd been with her, his fury had been nothing compared to the fear that he had hurt her, caused her to suffer. He was no better than Roger; neither of them had considered her safety. They were both driven by their own selfish needs.

How can I make it up to her? Jake rubbed his eyes to ease their sting when another question occurred to him. *What am I going to do about her? I care about her . . .* A cynical laugh rumbled deep in his chest. He didn't just care about her, he loved her. Wanted her so much she had become a constant ache in his soul. But he didn't trust her, and he didn't trust himself. So where did that leave them?

When a knock sounded at the door, he barked, "Go away. I'm asleep."

"Jake," Sarah called. "Please wake up and open the door."

He hissed a breath through his teeth. He didn't want to see her now; he had to get his emotions under control first. When she knocked again, he swung off the bed and opened the door.

"You shouldn't be up." Seeing her holding a tray loaded with food, he ground out a curse and snatched it from her hands. "What the bloody hell are you doing? You should be in bed."

Smiling brightly, she said, "Thank you, I'd love to come in."

Using the door frame as support, she limped into the room, eased past him in the tight space, and sat on the bed. Jake stared down at her, his chest tightening. Smelling of water and soap, she'd braided her hair into a rope of polished silk. Her cheeks were rosy from the sun, but shadows still circled her eyes.

"You can put the tray on the desk," she told him as she straightened her skirt of yellow saffron wool. The bodice was cinched tight, making her waist impossibly small and outlining full breasts that he could still feel in his hands. The neckline scooped low, but the pale white ruffle of her chemise covered most of her smooth skin. Skin he knew would taste sweet and rich and warm.

"You shouldn't be here, Sarah."

"I watched you standing at the bow earlier." She looked at him, her eyes smoky. "What were you thinking?"

"If you're feeling well enough to be about, then I suggest you dine with the captain and the others." Jake set the tray down on the desk, the dishes clattering, and moved aside, extending his arm as an invitation to leave.

"I'd rather stay, if you don't mind."

"I do mind," he snapped, harsher than he intended. But he couldn't look at her without wanting to touch her. And he knew touching would lead to lovemaking, which would lead to confusion and turmoil, handfuls of heartache and God knew what else.

Heaving a sigh, she stood, but she didn't leave. Instead she picked up a bowl of stew and a spoon, reclaimed her place on the bed and started eating. "You really should have some before it gets cold."

"Sarah," he warned.

"The cook on this ship has some talent, I think. We shouldn't lack for decent fare during our trip home."

Jake crossed his arms and glared down at her. "What do you think you're doing?"

She met his gaze, hers turning thoughtful. "We need to talk about what happened."

"There's nothing to discuss."

Her cheeks flushed and Jake noticed her knuckles had turned white where she gripped the bowl. "We made love. It wasn't some whimsical lark to pass the time. It meant something, to both of us."

He started to deny it, thinking it would be best for them both in the long run, but he couldn't say the words. Closing the door, he pulled the chair from the desk and sat facing her. But being so close, breathing in her feminine scent, he knew he'd just made a fatal mistake.

"We made love, Sarah, and it was . . ." *Incredible, breathtaking, life-changing.* ". . . it was good."

"Good?" she echoed as if she hadn't heard him right.

"Yes, but we can't do it again."

"Why not?" she asked, her jaw tight with annoyance. "If it was so *good.*"

He almost smiled at her disgruntled tone. "Things are confusing enough right now. I don't want to make it harder on you."

"If you don't want to make things hard for me, then stop pretending I don't exist." She gripped his hand, the soft touch forcing his gaze to hers. "I've hurt you by not being honest. I know I have, and I can't tell you how sorry I am."

"I understand why you kept the corselet."

"You finally believe Queen Tiy came to me in my dream?"

He shrugged. "It's hard to believe, but in Egypt, I've learned anything is possible."

"So you forgive me?"

He saw the hope in her eyes and had to look away from it. "It's not a matter of forgiveness."

She tapped her fingers against his hand in exasperation. "You still think you caused my injuries? Can you truly be so obtuse?"

He scowled at her but she only smiled, and to his horror her softened expression wound his stomach into knots. Blood pulsed in his loins and he knew the only thing that would stop the pounding in his ears was to touch her.

"You hurt me and I hurt you," she said, setting her bowl aside. "There's only one thing to do."

He didn't want to ask, but he did. "And that is?"

"Call a truce and start over."

"It's not that easy. There are things I must sort out first."

"Such as?"

"Such as what I'm going to do once I reach England."

She stared at him, waited for him to continue.

He told her, "I'm not going back to Egypt."

She made an unlady-like scoffing sound. "Of course you are."

She sounded so matter-of-fact that this time Jake did smile. "No."

She sobered, her eyes turning dark. "I've thought you were many things over the years, but I've never thought you were a fool."

"Damn it, Sarah," he said, standing to pace, only there wasn't anyplace to go. He sat in the chair again, ran his

hands through his loose hair. "My determination to
catch up with Stuart almost killed you!"

"Did it ever occur to you that I could have said something? I knew how exhausted I was, how thirsty and
near to collapsing, but I didn't tell you because I didn't
want us to stop." She looked away, giving him a sense
of her unease. "I knew what my deception had cost
you, and I wanted to find Stuart every bit as much as
you did."

She lifted her skirt and revealed her bandaged feet,
which were still too swollen for her to wear shoes. "I have
no one to blame for this except myself."

"Christ, Sarah," Jake said, cupping one foot in his
hands. He ran his palm over the bandage, and felt as if
he'd been pierced with a knife when she winced. "My
only thought should have been to keep you safe."

"You did. I'm here, and alive."

Aware she was trying to alleviate his guilt, he didn't
have the heart to tell her she was failing miserably.

She caught his jaw in her palm, her thumb stroking
his cheek. She watched him with eyes that should have
been hard with accusations. Instead they were warm
smoky pools, inviting him to dive in and drown in their
depths. "Give us a chance, Jake, please."

He knew if he kissed her now, the way every inch of his
soul begged him to, there would be no turning back. He
would lose himself inside her; rational thought would
become impossible. *But would that be so bad?*

Jake silenced the voice whispering in the back of his
mind. He loved Sarah, but loving her wasn't enough.
She was the daughter of a wealthy viscount; he was a penniless archaeologist who had failed himself, just as he'd
failed her. Sometime through the years, he'd become
as driven and as selfish as Roger, setting Sarah's needs
aside while he pursued his own dream.

Looking at her now, he remembered why he had

never hoped to find a woman he could share his life with.

Because it wasn't possible.

He loved Sarah, with all his heart, but archaeology was all he knew, and if he had to give that up, what kind of life could he offer her? Unfortunately he knew the answer to that question. His gift to her would be a life of poverty and hardship.

Cupping his hand over hers, he pressed a kiss to her palm. "I wish I could give you the chance you want, Sarah. But I can't. Whatever we had is over."

Sarah paced the width of the stern, one side to the other, over and over again. Though she could now wear her boots, her feet ached with each step, but she didn't stop. Her heart was racing, her nerves causing her hands to tremble. She couldn't take much more of this, she decided, pulling her shawl around her arms to protect her from the cooling wind.

For three days, she had tried to see Jake, but he'd found every excuse to avoid her. If she appeared on deck, he went below. If he went into his cabin and she knocked on the door, he would leave. He wasn't even polite about not wanting to see her, making it clear he would go wherever she wasn't.

Stopping to stare at a ripple of land that appeared far to the south, she tried to think of another way to force Jake to speak to her. She only had another week before they reached England; she had to break through his stubborn wall before then.

The sun began its downward slide into the ocean, and the wind whipped around her with a biting chill. Deciding to go below, she headed for the hatchway. At the portal, she paused, her heart leaping to her throat the way it always did whenever she spotted Jake.

He was sitting on a crate, his back against the railing, his long honey-blond hair tied back in a queue. He had one leg bent and held a sheaf of paper against his thigh. She'd seen the papers enough times to know what he was studying.

The relief of Queen Tiy's corselet.

Knowing he would only dash below deck if she approached him, she started down the ladder, only to hesitate when an idea occurred to her. Holding her shawl tight around her as if to ward off his certain rebuff, she crossed the deck and stopped in front of him.

She knew the instant he became aware of her presence. His shoulders tensed, his hand stilled, and she couldn't be certain, but she thought he had even stopped breathing.

"Have you had any luck interpreting the inscription?" she asked.

Seconds ticked by, and she had just decided he wouldn't answer when he folded the paper and shoved off his perch. "No. If you'll excuse me."

He headed for the bow, but Sarah followed him, refusing to give up. "You have no idea what it means?"

Jake stopped, rounded on her, and the pained look on his face made her catch her breath. "Bloody hell, Sarah, I need you to stay away from me."

Stunned by the fierceness in his voice, she watched him continue toward the bow. He was suffering as much as she was, the foolish, stubborn, irrational man! There wasn't any need for them to be apart, but he refused to see it.

He stopped at the bow, gripping the papers in one hand, the railing in the other. After a moment, she approached him. "Can I ask a favor of you?"

He drew a breath that expanded his wide back and lifted his shoulders. "What is it?"

"Could I see the relief?"

He turned halfway, frowning at her. "Why?"

She shrugged. "Maybe I can help."

"You read hieroglyphics?"

"Of course not. But I studied the corselet when we were sailing to Egypt."

"Yes, it was in your possession far longer than it was in mine."

She let him inflict his resentment; it was no more than she deserved. "Will you let me help?"

He looked down at the papers in his hand, then extended them to her, scowling. "I don't see what you can do, but I've done all I can."

She took the papers, wishing she had the courage to brush her fingers against his. But for now, she'd be content with this one small victory. If the gods were kind, there would be others.

"I'll work on it in my cabin," she told him.

He nodded and faced the bow. It was all she could do not to touch the sleeve of his shirt or the tips of his whiskey-blond hair where it lay against his back.

In time, she vowed. In time.

"Hit me," Connor challenged with a grunt.

Jake stared at the man, not really seeing him or any of the others gathered in the captain's cabin. His mind had drifted again, as it had for the past week. As hard as he tried he couldn't escape thoughts of Sarah, or his relentless, obsessive need for her. Never had a woman affected him so deeply, so completely that he couldn't stay focused on the matters at hand.

"Jake-o," Connor said. "The captain will be want'n his cabin back, and I'd rather have this done with first. Now, are ye goin' tae hit me, or aren't ye?"

Jake blinked and glanced at the men gathered around

the table, chips in front of them, cards in their hands. "Sorry, how many?"

Going around the table, he dealt new cards, but when he reached Gavin, the earl continued to watch Jake in that thoughtful, calculating way of his, his dark eyes piercing through a haze of cigarette smoke.

"Do you want another one?" Jake asked, impatient to have the game over with so he could leave. He knew he was lousy company and would be better off alone in his cabin.

"I'm fine," Gavin said. "It's too bad we can't say the same about you."

"What's that supposed to mean?"

"That you're a half-wit," Connor snorted.

Jake glared at the Scotsman, but that didn't stop Connor from saying, "Go to her, Jake-o. You'll be doin' us a favor."

"Aye," Thatcher said, shaking his head. "'Tis not right for a man to mope like a lovesick boy."

"'Tis embarrassing," Eli added.

"I've already said everything I need to say to Sarah." He focused on his cards, or at least tried to, but his mind wouldn't obey. "Are we going to play poker or do you four intend to irritate me all night?"

Gavin set his cards aside, his probing, unreadable gaze pinned on Jake. "You don't want to be here. And I don't blame you, really. Stop being stubborn and go to her."

Jake leaned back in his chair, crossed his arms over his chest. "I thought you of all people would applaud me for staying away from her."

"Because she lied to you?"

"Several times."

The earl nodded, an amused smile lifting one corner of his mouth. "Your Sarah is full of surprises, isn't she?"

"She isn't my Sarah."

"The point is," Gavin said, "you care about her, deeply if any of us were to guess. But you also feel guilty for leading her through the desert, and perhaps you should, but don't let that stop you from pursuing her."

"Leading her through the desert?" Jake scoffed and picked up his glass of whiskey, drained it, grimaced when the liquor burned a path down his throat. "Is that the aristocratic way of saying I nearly killed her?"

"Wallowing in self-pity doesn't suit you, Jake."

"There's more involved than my feeling guilty for harming her," he snapped.

"I'm aware of your financial situation, and the . . . difficulties you'll face when you reach England empty-handed. But Sarah isn't like other women." With a proprietary smile that Jake didn't quite like, Gavin added, "She's unique."

"How many times did you warn me to stay away from her?" Jake demanded.

"Several. And you ignored them all."

Jake took another drink, and this time he welcomed the burn. It cleared his mind. "You said never trust a woman."

"Worthy advice that I will continue to live by," the earl said, his tone just a shade harder. "But you are not me. I've spoken with Sarah."

"We all have," Connor piped in. "Don't ask me why, but the lass is in love with ye."

Jake gritted his teeth until his jaw ached, and wished everyone would just play bloody cards and shut up.

"Well, gentlemen," Gavin said, standing. "I think I'll call it a night."

The others mumbled their agreement and filed out of the room. Jake stayed where he was, scowling at the empty chairs.

At the door, the earl paused and when he spoke his voice cut through Jake like a warning. "We reach England in two days. Take advantage of that time. You may not get a second chance."

"What if I don't want one?" Jake asked, meeting the earl's haunted gaze.

"There will always be a time in a man's life when he needs a second chance. Some of us don't get it." Jake knew Gavin referred to his dead wife and son. "I suggest you not waste yours."

Chapter 21

Jake stood in the shadowed companionway. Cool air skated down the hatchway, rushing at him, over him. He heard voices on the deck above, sailors on night duty going about their business. Everyone else onboard ship was in his cabin or his hammock, sleeping while the seas were calm. He took a step away from Sarah's door, deciding he should do the same. He would speak with her in the morning, when his head was clear and his emotions were under tighter control.

But Gavin's words that he might not get a second chance stopped him and he turned back to look at the light shining from beneath her door. He had no idea what he intended to say. Maybe nothing, he thought. Maybe he would just look at her. See the expression in her silver eyes and judge if he had destroyed the feelings she'd claimed to have for him.

Irritated with himself for delaying, he knocked on the wooden door, heard rustling on the other side, and the soft sound of footsteps.

"Who is it?" she asked, her voice muffled through the panel.

"It's me." Seconds of silence ticked by, and he imagined her quietly securing the lock before she told him to go away. But the latch lifted and the door swung open.

His first glimpse of her instantly heated his blood, fueling the desire that never quite went away. God help him.

"Jake, what are you doing here?" She stood in the candle's glow, her white linen shift revealing the shadows of her legs, the curve of her hips and the indention of her tiny waist.

Without a doubt, he should have waited until morning to see her.

"I'm so glad you're here." She caught his hand and pulled him inside her room. "There's something I want to show you."

Closing the door behind her, she maneuvered around him and sat on the bed, curling her bare feet beneath her. "Look at this."

Finding it nearly impossible to tear his gaze away from the excitement dancing her eyes, he glanced at the paper she held out to him. On it, she'd drawn the corselet in incredible detail. Each gold link seemed to glimmer in the lamplight, the lapis lazuli so real, he skimmed his fingers over it, expecting to feel smooth, cool gemstones.

"You have incredible talent," he said, meaning it.

Her eyes widened in surprise, then her expression turned to genuine pleasure. He wondered if anyone had ever told her how extraordinary she truly was.

"I've studied the relief you made of the corselet," she said. "But I think some of the impressions are wrong."

He frowned at her. "Why would you think that?"

"Here, sit down, and I'll show you." She indicated the spot on the bed beside her. He took the ladder-back chair instead. They were already so close he could smell the fresh warmth of her skin. The deeply curved neckline of her shift revealed her pale throat, the line of her collarbone, and far too much of her chest for him to ignore.

God, to be able to touch her. He fisted his hands, but it didn't stop the blood from rushing to his groin, or heating his skin, or turning his desire into pain. He clenched his jaw and tried to focus on the sketch. But no amount of concentration helped. He snatched up her lace shawl from the foot of her bed and pushed it at her.

"Put this on."

A flicker of awareness crossed her face before she schooled it. "Thank you, but I'm not cold."

"Damn it, Sarah, just put the blasted thing on."

She bit down on her bottom lip, he was sure to hide a smile, and wrapped the flimsy garment around her shoulders. "Am I covered enough for you now?"

Not in the slightest, he realized. He could bundle her up in a feed sack and it still wouldn't help. He already knew what her body looked like. How she felt. How the honey-sweet taste of her skin could melt in his mouth. But he grunted his approval.

Flipping to another page, she held out the tablet. "Before I studied your relief, I drew the hieroglyphics as I remembered seeing them. Then I compared the two. There are slight variations. Enough that it might be the reason you couldn't interpret the relief. When I examined the corselet, some of the symbols were so faint I could barely see them. It's possible they were too worn to be transferred to your paper."

He stared at her, feeling a mixture of amazement and hope welling up inside him. Clearing his throat, he compared the two drawings. "You're right. They are different. Are you sure of your drawings?"

She shrugged, upsetting the neckline of her shift and her shawl so they both slipped down to reveal her rounded shoulder. "I have an eye for details."

Wondering if she was trying to torture him on purpose, Jake forced himself to look away and study her sketch. What he saw made him frown and take a closer look. "The hieroglyphic you drew is the symbol for Ramses," he explained, pointing to the first cartouche. "Mine is similar, but incomplete." He thought for a moment. "It's like half of it has been rubbed off."

"I have a theory about how that happened," she said, sitting on her knees and clasping her hands together as if to contain her excitement.

He met her gaze and felt his heart roll over with the overwhelming, painful need to touch her. "Go on."

She swallowed, and for an instant, looked unsure of herself. "During the dream, Queen Tiy thought about the corselet, and how it was all she had left. They had taken her other jewels, but the corselet was the most important to her. She was relieved to still have it."

"Do you know why?"

A sad smile pulled her lips. "It was a gift from Ramses after Pentewere's birth. She never took it off."

Jake stared at her, torn between doubt that the dream could have been real and amazement that he was beginning to believe her. "That would explain why it was worn. And why they recorded her trial on the corselet instead of a wall painting, which would have been more common."

"So you believe me?" she asked, a slow smile transforming her face from lovely to breathtaking.

A warning voice in the back of his mind told him not to encourage her. She might have unlocked the mystery of the corselet, but that didn't mean anything between them could change. He cared about her, loved her more than he'd ever loved anyone, but if he allowed her into his life, he would only hurt her again.

"What I believe is that because of you, I'll be able to unlock whatever message was written on the corselet. What good it will do me now that Stuart has it."

"We're going to get it back from him."

"*We* aren't going to do anything. I will deal with Stuart on my own."

"I want to help."

"You already have." Looking away from the yearning

in her eyes, Jake gathered the papers and stood. "It's best if I work on this in my cabin."

"You're leaving?"

Before he could stop himself, he reached out and cupped her face in his hand, rubbed his thumb over her soft cheek. She rose onto her knees, tilted her face to his for a kiss. He fought the impulses raging through his body to give her what she wanted, what he desperately needed.

Staring into her smoky eyes, he wanted with all his heart to kiss her, gather her close and let her fill the emptiness inside him. *But then what?* his conscience asked. What would he give her? Nothing but sand and hardship, poverty and danger. And that he couldn't allow.

Before he could give in, he pressed a chaste kiss to her brow, then turned away and ran.

Sarah stared at her closed door, the crashing sound of it slamming shut behind Jake still ringing in her ears. She reached up and touched her forehead where the sensation of his warm lips still lingered. A kiss on the forehead as if she were a sister or a friend.

Clenching her hands into fists, she glared at the door. The man had pushed her patience beyond reason. He wanted her, she'd seen the truth in his heated blue eyes, felt it radiate off his skin, seen the evidence that his body wanted to make love to her even if his bullheaded mind did not.

Taking off her shawl and throwing it on the bed, she jerked the door open and left her cabin. She had waited long enough. She'd given Jake time and space to come to terms with his feelings for her. Get over his ridiculous guilt that he had hurt her.

She marched barefoot down the corridor, her temper rising in parallel with her determination that he would either admit he loved her or tell her outright that he didn't care about her at all. Which would be a lie, and she swore she wouldn't allow another lie to come between them.

Reaching his cabin, she didn't bother knocking. She shoved the door open, but it only moved a few inches before banging against something solid. Through the small opening, she saw Jake sitting at the narrow desk.

"Bloody hell," he barked. "Who—"

"It's me, Jake. Let me in."

She heard more mumbled curses, then the scrape of a chair against the floor. The door shut for an instant then opened again, with Jake filling the portal like a glowering giant ready to devour an unlucky prey.

"Did you forget something?" he asked, scowling at her.

"No, you did."

He frowned, and she could tell he was tempted to shut the door in her face.

When he didn't, she told him, "You forgot to thank me properly for my help."

"Thank you. Now if you'll excuse me I'd like to continue my work."

"That's not good enough."

He signed, clearly struggling to stay angry. "What is it you want from me, Sarah?"

"Invite me in and I'll tell you."

He shook his head. "You can tell me standing where you are."

Hearing the creak of doors opening further down the hall and seeing a rather large head of tousled red hair in the dim light, she said, "Invite me in, or would you rather everyone hear you explain why you won't make love to me?"

"Bloody hell, woman," Jake snarled. He clasped her arm, jerked her into his cabin and slammed the door shut behind them. "Are you out of your mind?"

Just as stunned as Jake that she would say something so outrageous, she muttered, "I'm beginning to think I am."

"You shouldn't be here."

"I'm not leaving until we have things settled between us."

"There's nothing to settle."

She drew a breath, met his heated gaze and held it. "Make love to me, Jake."

"No."

"Yes!"

"No!"

"You want to."

"That doesn't mean I'm going to."

She was breathing hard and so was he, both of them fighting to hold their ground. She was beginning to think his stubbornness might outlast her determination to break through his walls. She needed an advantage.

One instantly came to mind. Her cheeks flushed with the thought, but she'd come too far and she loved him too much to let embarrassment stop her now. Catching the skirt of her shift, she lifted the garment over her head and dropped it to the floor.

"Sarah." Her name was a hiss from between his clenched teeth. He pointed to her shift. "Put that back on."

She shook her head and stood still, her confidence building as his burning gaze slid down her naked body. The skin over her breasts tightened, her nipples pebbled with a luscious ache that spread to her stomach, then lower, where it pulsed with a heavy, yearning beat.

He picked up her shift and thrust it at her. "Put it on."

"No." She kept her arms at her sides, battling the urge to cover herself.

"Then I'll leave." He gripped the door latch, but she moved and blocked his path.

"Make love to me, Jake. Or tell me why you won't." She held up one hand when he started to speak. "And don't you dare say its because you feel guilty that I became ill. That's not a good enough reason."

In a voice rife with anger, he asked, "If I make love to you right now, what do you think would happen afterward?"

Caught off guard by the question, she stammered, "I . . . I don't know."

"Well, I do, sweetheart," he said, towering over her. "You'll go back to Whitehurst Manor, with your cooks and your butlers."

She started to tell him she didn't live at Whitehurst Manor, rarely set foot there, but he didn't give her the chance.

"And I'll return to the shanty I live in while in London. But only until I find Stuart Kilvington, then I'll be leaving again."

"Leave? Where will you go? You said you weren't returning to Egypt."

His pupils dilated, eclipsing the blue irises and leaving nothing but fury. "I lied. Egypt is where I belong. And you belong in London. So if I make love to you, Sarah, where would that leave us? Sated? Fulfilled? You with child, perhaps? A single woman with a bastard infant to be scorned by all of England?"

She touched her stomach. She'd considered the possibility that she might be with child. But she hadn't worried over it, knowing that if she were carrying Jake's baby, there was only one thing she would do about it: celebrate.

"When you return to Egypt," she told him, shivering as much from the chill in the room as she was from the heat blazing from Jake's gaze. "I'll go with you."

He caught her by the shoulders and hauled her up to him. "You almost died there once, you aren't going back."

"Would you really leave me behind?"

Closing his eyes, he touched his forehead to hers, and released a breath through his teeth. "Damn you, Sarah. I can't do this."

"Then stop fighting me." She caught his face between her hands and forced him to look at her. "Touch me, Jake. For God's sake, please touch me."

With a growl that erupted from deep within his chest, he slammed his mouth over hers, hard and punishing. His hands circled her waist, bands of steel lifting her against the door.

The cold wood pressing into her back, Sarah clung to his shoulders, wrapped her legs around his hips, and returned his savage, hungry kiss. His mouth was hot and wet, tasting of whiskey and anger and desperate passion. She wanted more and held him tighter, pushing her hands into his silky hair.

With his fingers digging into her hips, he pushed against her core, rough wool scraping her sensitive skin. She sucked in a startled gasp, her head dropping back as her mind sizzled, burning every coherent thought to dust.

Holding her with one hand, he struggled to untie his pants with the other. She wanted to help, but she couldn't stop kissing the pulse-point at his temple, the forceful line of his jaw, the length of his tanned throat.

Heaven help her, she wanted him, all of him, and all at once.

She ran her hands over his shoulders and down his back, felt his corded muscles flex and response. She whimpered, wanting to feel his skin. She wanted his hands on her breasts, his mouth on her nipples, and she wanted to do the same to him. Tugging at his shirt, she had every intention of pulling it off, when something else stole her attention.

Jake was there, hard and pulsing, pushing his heat into her body. He held her against the door, sliding inside her core, inching deeper and deeper, filling her until her vision blurred and the room spun. Once buried skin to skin, he stopped, trembled, his breath sounding strained and painful.

She waited a moment, loving the feel of him inside her, stretching her, creating a bond she hadn't thought possible. But her body was too impatient, too desperate for her to be still for long. She tightened her legs, lifted her hips slightly, then lowered herself onto his shaft.

Jake made a low, painful sound in his throat. "Don't move."

Feeling reckless and wanton, wanting to hear that tortured sound from him again, she moved, just once, up and down. It wasn't enough.

"Sarah, I said . . ." His face dark, his eyes focused on her, Jake thrust into her hard and deep. He pushed into her again and again, setting a violent rhythm that spiraled her out of control. She felt the barriers between them collapse, the anger and distrust battered down to dust. She held on to him, unable to breathe, to think. There were only sensations, shattering, vulnerable, incredible sensations made all the sharper because she knew, *she knew,* he loved her.

She didn't intend to let him forget it.

A lulling motion pulled Sarah from a sound sleep. She didn't know what had awoken her, and knew from the heavy contentment in her body that she wasn't ready to start another day. But sensing a soft light behind her closed lids, she stretched to bring herself fully awake, or at least tried to. Her hand hit something solid. Blinking her eyes open, she saw the hull of the ship inches from her face. She tried to turn over, but couldn't do that either. Reaching behind her, she touched warm firm skin, a man's hip. Jake's, she thought with a smile as the events of the passing night came back to her.

Glancing down, she realized she was curled on her side, unable to straighten because of the short bed. Jake lay behind her, his body cupping every inch of hers. She felt the hard length of his thighs snug against her own, the slow rise and fall of his chest against her back, his hand lying protectively over her stomach.

Having never felt so incredibly, wonderfully secure, she wished time would stop. If only she could hold on to this moment forever, the small cabin and the cramped bed, the exquisite feel of Jake around her, the scent of their lovemaking still lingering in the air. Reality would intrude eventually, but until it did, she intended to savor every moment they had.

She tried to shift again, wanting to see his face. His fingers flexed against her abdomen. Tingles scurried beneath her skin. He didn't move otherwise, but she felt a change in him, a subtle tensing of his muscles, an unseen energy that started her blood pulsing slow and heavy through her limbs. She knew he was awake, and wondered if he wished they could remain like this forever, too.

Moving again, she pressed her hips to his and smiled when she felt the ridge of his groin harden against her.

"God save me, woman. Are you trying to kill me?" His voice, low and drowsy, rumbled against her back. He should be tired, she thought, and so should she. After the first time he'd made love to her—if their startling, whirlwind joining could even be called lovemaking—against the door, he'd carried her to the bed and throughout the night had shown her with his hands and body and mouth, if not his words, how much he loved her.

Nestling closer to him, she felt the answering throb of his loins against her buttocks. "You're taking up too much room."

"Am I now?" Catching her by the waist he lifted her, sliding beneath her so she lay on top of him with her back against his chest.

With a startled laugh, she demanded, "What are you doing?"

"Giving you more room."

She tried to squirm off of him, but he cupped his hands on her hips, his fingers splaying over her thighs. Then he kissed her neck, snaring her in a sensuous trap. She sucked in a breath and arched her back as fire shot through her veins. She tried to kiss him, but he ignored her.

"God help me, but you're beautiful," he whispered.

His rough palms skimmed up her body, abrading her skin. She shivered, helpless to do anything except thrust her breasts into the cold morning air, cutting off a cry when he finally captured the sensitive mounds, his thumbs playfully grazing her nipples.

She watched his hands move over her exposed body, touching, teasing, heightening her desire until she wanted to plead for mercy. She rubbed her legs against his, the friction adding to her frustration.

"Jake, please, this is no proper way to make love."

He lightly bit her neck, making her gasp, the pleasure stunning. "There's nothing proper about making love, sweetheart. But if you don't like this we can stop."

"I didn't say—" A startled laugh caught in her throat as he lifted her and turned her around so she sat straddling his waist. "Well," she managed once she caught her breath. "This is different."

"And very improper," he said with a devious grin.

Dazed by his expression, Sarah bit down on her lip. She'd seen him scowl and glower, frowning and red-faced with anger, even shaking with desire, but she'd never seen him smile like a man who was happy. This was the moment she wanted to last forever, she realized. The two of them closeted away from the world and the only thing for her to see was Jake's smiling face.

But the grin vanished, and his brow dipped with worry. "What's wrong? Did I hurt you?"

She shook her head, surprised when her eyes filled with tears.

Jake captured her hands and pressed them to his chest, over his heart where she could feel its steady beat. "What is it, Sarah?"

Freeing one of her hands, she brushed blond strands of hair from his forehead, then traced a path from his temple to his cheek, following the curve of his jaw and marveling at the complex, beautiful angles that made up his face.

"I never thought I would love anyone," she admitted. "And certainly not you."

"Fate has a sense of humor," he said, watching her, his thumbs making slow circles over the backs of her hands.

Deciding there wouldn't be a better time than now to ask the question worrying in the back of her mind, she asked, "Do you love me?"

He froze, his heart beginning a frenzied beat against her palms. "Sarah—"

"Before you answer, I'd like to say that there have been too many lies between us already." He arched a brow in a silent reprimand.

"Granted, I did all the lying, but that's in the past." And that's where she wanted it to stay. "If you don't love me then say so. But if you do, then don't be afraid to admit it."

Jake wanted to scowl, not liking the vulnerable emotion darkening Sarah's eyes. Didn't she know she'd asked a question that, regardless of his answer, would only hurt her? He was tempted to flip their positions so he could bury himself inside her body. He'd make love to her until she couldn't think, let alone ask the impossible.

Instead he tried to skirt the question. "I'm not afraid of anything. Now why don't you kiss me."

"I will after you tell me." Lifting handfuls of satin dark hair off her shoulders so it fell down her back, she revealed two perfectly round globes that were tipped with rosy nipples. While he watched, they pebbled as if he'd licked them with his tongue.

A groan tightened his throat. He started to sit up. He needed space to think—he certainly couldn't do it while she was straddling him, her soft, warm bottom snug against his groin, her breasts begging for him to taste them—but Sarah pushed against his shoulders and forced him back.

Sighing, he said, "It's not a matter of loving you or not."

"Do you or don't you?" She leaned forward until she was lying flush against his chest, her soft breasts sending arrows of desire shooting down his body.

"Woman, you're not playing fair."

"I know you desire me, Jake," she said, her tone apprehensive. "And I know what I see when you look at me. But I need you to tell me."

Feeling true regret for the first time in his life, wishing he were more like Gavin and could give her the world, he told her, "We have now, Sarah. It's all I can give you."

"Because you have no money," she said. It wasn't a question.

"I will never be able to provide you with the life you're used to."

"My life?" she said, sitting up to look out the portal. Gray morning light washed her face, yet her eyes were dark and haunted. When she spoke her voice was harsh, almost accusing. "What do you know about my life, Jake?"

"All I need to know. You come from money."

"My father has money, yes. And he gives me a modest monthly stipend that pays for my small townhouse in Cheapside. I have no cook or butler. Though I do have a young girl who serves as housekeeper and companion."

"And you've never wanted for anything," he scoffed, then wished the words back, knowing he'd said the wrong thing.

"Never . . . ?" She looked down at him with disbelief. "You don't really know me, do you."

She drew a shuddering breath, and in a blink of an eye she changed from seductress to a fragile girl who'd been abandoned. Jake realized she may not have gone without food or clothing, but she'd never been given love. And he was withholding his now. But he couldn't change his mind. He had nothing to offer her except more disappointment. It was better to face that now rather than later.

"If things were different . . ." he said. Unable to finish, he gripped her shoulders and pulled her down to him, intending to kiss her so the terrible ache in his heart would stop hurting.

"I understand. If Stuart Kilvington hadn't ruined your reputation. Or if you still had the corselet," she said, her voice sad as she traced his lips with the tip of her fingers. "If I hadn't destroyed Queen Tiy, you would be able to love me."

"I don't blame you for what you did," he said, surprised by how much he meant it. "I probably would have done the same. Hell, I should have returned Queen Tiy when Roger asked."

"I wish it had turned out differently."

He shrugged. "There are other tombs waiting to be discovered."

Something dark and unreadable flashed in her silver eyes. "And you intend to find them, all on your own?"

He knew where she was headed. "You deserve someone who can give you the world."

"You could give it to me, Jake," she whispered. "If you wanted to."

He started to argue, but she stopped him with a kiss, a slow possession that tore his heart in two. He did love her; he shook with the need to tell her. But he couldn't give her false hope. She deserved a home and family, a man who would provide for her and keep her safe. Things he was incapable of giving.

Once again, life was taking away something precious that he had found. Needing to hold on to her for a little while longer, he lifted her, then eased her warm body over his, a tight clasp that sent a shudder through his soul. Gripping her hips, he followed her rhythm and knew he would never know anything so perfect again.

This would be their last time to make love, he realized with a rending twist of his heart. She would argue, but he knew the truth. She belonged in London, he in Egypt. As much as he wanted her with him, he would never, ever risk her life again.

That would be a loss he couldn't stand.

Chapter 22

This time Sarah knew what had pulled her from a troubled sleep. Her stomach grumbling in complaint, she blinked her eyes open and tried to recall the last time she'd eaten. Pushing into a sitting position, she moaned when the tender places in her body protested. Gray light washed the dark paneled walls of Jake's cabin. One quick glance told her she was alone, which was just as well, she decided. She needed a few moments to gain control of the disappointment squeezing her chest and the tears that welled in her eyes.

Unless she could think of something drastic, Jake would return to Egypt without her. And all because he had no money.

"Stupid, foolish man," she complained as she searched for something to wear. Seeing a bowl and a pitcher of clean water on the desk, she decided on a quick bath. A few minutes later, her skin pink and covered with goose bumps, she pulled on her shift. She reached for the door latch, wanting to return to her cabin where she could think, but paused with her hand on the handle. What time was it? Given the gloomy light outside the porthole, it was safe to say it was daytime and people were up and moving about.

"Well, bloody hell," she muttered under her breath. She couldn't return to her cabin wearing only her shift. For the moment she was trapped. Seeing Jake's comb, she picked it up and attacked the tangles in her hair and tried not to think about what she would say when he returned.

She had asked him if he loved her and he'd refused to answer. She knew it was pride, and fear that he would hurt her, that had kept him from admitting his true feelings.

"Stubborn, pigheaded dolt. Why I even bother." But she knew why she bothered. She loved him. Having gone her entire life without love, she couldn't lose it now. It was too precious, too valuable to set aside or to hold at arm's length. She couldn't live afraid of what might happen. Jake was worried about providing for her and keeping her safe. He didn't understand that the only thing she needed to survive was him.

"Brainless, asinine fool—"

"Are you talking about anyone I know?"

She glanced up and wondered how she could have missed seeing him enter. She drank in the sight of him, all tall body and lean muscle. A shape and texture she was just beginning to learn. The rueful grin lifting one corner of his mouth didn't dispel the lines of worry bracketing his eyes.

She ran the comb through her hair and lowered her gaze to the tray of food he held in his hands. "No, I was referring to myself. The way I'm dressed I'm going to be trapped in here all day."

"I see where that might be a problem." He kicked the door closed behind him and set the tray on the desk. "I thought you might be hungry."

Her stomach rumbled when the smells of bacon and coffee filled the cramped room. "I suppose everyone knows I'm in here."

"I was very discreet."

She didn't need to see his grimace to know everyone from boatswain to captain knew exactly where she'd spent the night. She should be mortified, she supposed, but she wasn't.

Jake handed her a much needed cup of coffee. "The captain believes we'll reach the Thames in a few hours. By tonight, we'll be in London."

"So soon?" she said, hearing the panic in her voice. Once they docked in London, Jake would insist they go their separate ways. She had no idea where he lived or where he would go. She needed more time.

"We've had good weather." He shrugged and studied his cup as if to avoid looking at her. "I'll gather some clothes from your cabin."

"And give the crew even more to gossip about."

"You need to pack."

She knew he was trying to get rid of her, but she wasn't going to oblige him. "It won't take me long. It can wait."

"Sarah, I, uh, could use the time to work on your sketch."

She glanced at the papers folded on the desk and knew that if there were any way to convince Jake they belonged together, it would be through the drawing.

"I'd like to stay for a while longer," she said.

"Sarah—"

"To help you with the translation." When he started to object, she held up her hand. "Let me do this for you, Jake. Please. Let me have this last day."

She saw the battle in his eyes and braced herself. He wanted to say no. If he denied her, she wouldn't beg. She would return to her cabin and wait for the ship to dock in London. And pray that she could think of another way to break through his stubbornness.

But then he surprised her by nodding. He picked up her sketch, and never saw her blink back tears of relief.

"It's a bird."

"Could you be more specific?" Jake glanced at Sarah instead of keeping his attention on the drawing, and was instantly distracted by her profile. When he'd first met her, her skin had been impossibly smooth and pale. Now her cheeks were tinged pink from spending days in the sun, her face a faint honey gold. She had the straight nose of an aristocrat, but none of the coolness. No, his Sarah was exuberant, spirited and unafraid.

"Um, a hawk I think." She shook her head. "Or maybe an owl. Does it make that much of a difference?"

"One stands for the letter A, the other an M."

"Oh." She sighed. "Well, from what you've translated so far, my guess is that it's an M."

"An M it is then," he said, not wanting to tell her that guessing could lead them down the wrong path. But he didn't want to say anything that would remove the look of triumph brightening her face. "What next?"

"This is definitely an upside down fish hook."

"An S." He made a notation to the message that was slowly appearing.

"We've transcribed over half of it," she said, looking over his shoulder. "Do you have any idea what it means?"

"Not yet." Jake stretched, loosening the tense muscles in his back, then rubbed his eyes, which ached from hours of reading in the dim light.

She ran his fingers through the hair at his temple. He suppressed a shiver of pleasure and ignored the warning to pull away. "No hint of the hidden tomb you were looking for? Or a buried city?"

He caught her hand, stopping the soft caress of her fingers; he couldn't think clearly otherwise, he would only feel. And he had to keep focused on the inevitable: He and Sarah would have to go their separate ways.

"The passage isn't making sense. We must have misinterpreted some of the hieroglyphics."

"Well, let's keep working." He followed her gaze to the port window. Buildings crowding the banks of the River Thames slowly glided past. "We have another hour or so."

"Sarah." Jake held her hand in his, wishing he could stop the tremors he felt running through her.

"What will you do?" She turned her troubled gaze to his. "Return to Egypt immediately? Or stay for a while?"

"I won't leave until I get the corselet back from Stuart."

"And how do you intend to accomplish that? By stealing it?"

"If I must. He lied once before, taking credit for my discovery and ruining my reputation, all in one fell swoop. I don't intend to let him to do so again."

"So getting the corselet back is all that matters to you."

He met her guarded look and wished he could tell her the truth. He didn't give a damn about the corselet. All he cared about was her, her happiness, her safety, her life. He withdrew his hand from hers, and tried to study the relief. "We've been through this. Your place is in London."

"So you keep saying."

"You would live in Egypt?" he said, suddenly angry that she wouldn't accept their situation. "You would endure the hardships? The sand and the heat? Weeks without a decent bath or food? Would you willingly give up all the comforts you've known to stay with me?"

Her eyes widened at his sudden outburst, but she didn't back down. "I would be better prepared next time. And you would be with me. Imagine it, Jake. We could work together. I could record your discoveries while you dig."

"No."

She stared at him. "Will you at least think about it?"

"I already have."

"You won't be happy without me. You realize that, don't you?"

He didn't answer because he knew she was right. Egypt had once meant everything to him. In the desert sand, he'd found strength and comfort; in the whispering wind, he'd heard the voice of a lover promising to reveal her secrets. But all of that had changed. When he returned without Sarah, Egypt would be nothing more than a desert wasteland, a hostile country that had almost cost him the life of the woman he loved.

Feeling his resistance wearing thin, he told her, "You should go to your cabin. You haven't packed yet."

"You can't dismiss me so easily, Jacob Mitchell."

"Do you intend to leave the ship wearing that?" His gaze slid down her shift, the gauzy, nearly transparent fabric clinging to her body. Underneath the nearly useless gown he could see the color of her skin, the shape of her hip, her waist, and knew that if he touched her, she would tremble.

With her back straight and her voice curt, she picked up her drawing. "We have one more row to interpret. I'll leave when we're done."

He nodded, and wondered if he would survive that long.

But Jake schooled his emotions and was relieved when they worked together, deciphering one golden square at a time, talking only when necessary, neither of them looking at the other. The muscles in his back and neck ached as he forced all his concentration to the task, but he couldn't entirely shut out Sarah's frustrated mutterings, her warm, feminine scent, the silky gloss of her hair when she pushed it back from her shoulder, the ends grazing his arm.

As they neared the end of the verse, he caught several mistakes they'd made on earlier symbols and made the corrections. Then, as if a blindfold had been lifted from his eyes, Jake stared as a message began to unfold.

"There's only one left," Sarah said. "It looks like a snake."

Jake added the interpretation, his heart pounding, a strange buzz whirling through his mind. He sat back in his chair and frowned as he read the inscription. Then he read it again to be sure he understood it correctly.

"Jake, what is it?" She shook his arm when he didn't answer. "What does it say?"

He met her anxious gaze, and had to clear his throat to tell her, "It's a letter from Ramses."

Chapter 23

Setting the kettle of water on the stove to heat, Sarah took a cup and saucer from the sideboard in her kitchen, the porcelain rattling in her shaking hands. She muttered a curse, one of Jake's favorites she realized, and muttered a different one, this time one of Connor's. A cup of tea would settle her nerves, she thought, she hoped, she prayed, because she couldn't exist any longer with her stomach wound in knots and her heart racing against her chest.

Four days had passed since their ship had docked. Four excruciatingly long days during which she hadn't seen or heard from the irritating man she'd fallen in love with. He may have left London for all she knew. Stolen the corselet and boarded the first ship to Egypt. Alone, or at least without her.

She stared at the plate of cold meat, cheese, and fresh bread that Ellen, her housekeeper, had set out before she'd left for the market, but Sarah knew she couldn't eat it. She paced her small kitchen and reviewed her few options. She now knew waiting for Jake was futile. He had made his decision to leave her safely behind in London and he wouldn't change it. Which meant she had to go to him. Only she didn't know where he lived. His only reference had been that he stayed in a "shanty" somewhere in the city.

She knew of one man who could tell her where to find

him, but would Gavin help her? He seemed to have gotten over his distrust of her, but that didn't mean he would come to her aid.

There was another option, but Sarah didn't want to see her father yet. What if Jake didn't want her with him because he didn't love her? Roger had groomed Jake, trained him, and she knew Jake was every bit as driven as her father. Had he been speaking the truth when he'd said his only concern was to reclaim the corselet and repair his reputation? Had he dismissed his feelings for her so easily? Had she imagined that he loved her?

She had lied to Jake countless times; had she lied to herself as well? The thought made her ill.

When the water began to boil, she welcomed the distraction. Wrapping a cloth around the handle, she poured water into the teapot, sloshing the hot liquid onto the table when she heard pounding at the front door. She set the kettle down, her gaze on the hallway leading to the front of the house. She rarely had visitors, and had no idea who could be calling. She didn't dare hope it was Jake. But as she admonished herself for even thinking that he had come to see her, she ran down the hallway, her heart pounding in her throat.

Pausing only long enough to catch her breath, she opened the door . . . and felt her stomach clench as if she'd been punched.

"Roger," she said once she recovered from her shock.

They stood staring at each other, strangers with features remarkably alike. Dark hair, his threaded with gray, silver eyes that managed to shield their thoughts.

"Well," he huffed, "are you going to invite me in?"

"Of course. Come in." She stood aside and allowed him to pass.

He made it as far as the entry, then stopped, sniffing as if he'd found something unpleasant.

"I was making tea." She closed the door, but not before

she noticed Roger's driver seated in the carriage as if prepared to leave at a moment's notice. "Would you care for some?"

"I suppose." Frowning, he glanced into the tiny parlor on the right, furnished with items that were simple and well used, items she'd found in the attic at Whitehurst before she'd moved out. Roger's butler, Peels, had claimed they had once belonged to Lady Pendergrass. They were the only keepsakes Sarah had of the mother she had never really known.

She wondered if Roger remembered the woman who had used the mahogany settee with its pale blue fabric and the Chippendale desk, its top scratched and its carved legs uneven. Or if he even remembered he'd once had a wife.

"So, this is where you live." He pursed his lips with disdain. "'Tis shameful. You should be at Whitehurst."

"Why?" she asked, genuinely surprised.

"This hovel is a waste of money. You'll never find a husband living here."

She drew a deep breath and called herself a fool for hoping that he wanted her home with him. "I've been here for three years and am quite content. Since you've never visited me before, I assume you want something."

Before he could answer, she turned and headed for the kitchen, deciding he could follow her or not. She didn't care.

"Of course I want something." He hurried after her, his cane thumping eerily against the floor. "I've had my man watching the harbor and know you've been back for days. Yet you haven't given me a report. Did you succeed in the simple task I gave you, or not?"

Simple? She paused in taking down another cup and saucer. She turned to face Roger, her expression carefully blank. She refused to let him see how much his callous remark hurt. "I didn't know you were in London.

When I left, you said you would stay in the country for the summer, where you could regain your strength."

Her gaze slide over his frail body, but he was standing and glaring, so evidently he wasn't at death's door any longer. "It seems the fresh air has done wonders to heal you."

"It wasn't the damned air, girl! You returned Queen Tiy. Tell me you did."

"Yes, I completed my *simple* task."

"Ha ha!" He stomped his cane on the floor. "I knew you would."

"Everything except for the corselet."

His mouth dropped open and the color drained from his face. "Where is it?"

"Stuart Kilvington has it."

"The Marquis of Ashby? What in bloody blazes is he doing with it?"

"It's a rather long story. Would you care to hear it?"

"All I want to hear is how you intend to get it back!"

"Me?"

"Yes, you. You're the one who lost it. How could you have failed, Sarah? All you had to do was seal her inside her tomb." Punctuating each word, he added, "With her corselet!"

"I tried." Sarah clasped her hands at her waist. They were cold, icy, the same as the emotions running through her veins. Roger didn't want to hear about Napoleon's ships attacking theirs on their way to Egypt, or the lies she'd had to tell to keep Jake from discovering the truth. He didn't want to know that she'd climbed a cliff in the dead of night and had blown it up, sealing Queen Tiy's tomb. Or of her having to cross the desert on foot when Napoleon's soldiers discovered their camp and stole their camels.

And she felt certain he didn't care to hear that she'd

nearly died. No, her caring, devoted father didn't want to hear about any of that.

"You failed, Sarah," he told her, his scorn unmistakable. "I should have known you would."

A tremor of rage shot through her, but before she could unleash it, he interrupted her.

"Kilvington is in London. I heard a rumor that he had an announcement to make. It must be the corselet. You have to get it from him."

"Why?"

"Because you're the one who gave it to him."

"I didn't exactly give it to him. He was in Egypt with Nap—"

"I don't care what happened. Just get the corselet." Roger turned and limped down the hall to the front door, his gait far slower and more labored than when he'd arrived.

For a reason she couldn't explain, she followed. Anger churned inside her chest, making it difficult to breathe, but she felt something new and vastly different for the man who was incapable of loving her. She felt pity.

Opening the door he pointed at her with his cane. "You will return the corselet to Queen Tiy's tomb, Sarah. Or my death will be on your conscience."

Long after he'd slammed the door shut behind him, Sarah stood immobile. The confusion that had plagued her during the past few days vanished. Her thoughts became organized, and so clear she didn't understand why it had taken her so long to figure out what she needed to do.

She had worried Jake was just like her father, concerned with recovering the corselet so he could repair his reputation; she couldn't have been more wrong. Jake loved her, but he fought that love because he wanted to protect her.

Whereas Roger didn't have the ability to love anyone, not even his own daughter.

Turning back to the kitchen to have her tea, she came to a decision. She would do as Roger demanded and find the corselet. However, she wouldn't do it to save her father's life; she would do it to give her and Jake the life they deserved.

Jake paced the richly appointed study, mindless of the countless bookshelves filled with costly tomes, the polished walls of oak paneling, the thick Oriental rugs that cushioned his steps. He glanced at a table near the fire that held a decanter of brandy and several glasses. He considered pouring himself an unhealthy portion to quiet the unease that made it impossible for him to sit still. But since he'd already downed two since arriving at Gavin's home an hour before, he thought another might be unwise. He needed a clear mind, because if he was lucky, the earl and the Scotsman would decide it was time to act.

Nearly a week had passed since they'd returned from Egypt and he still didn't have the corselet. He knew where it was, which room it was being kept in and the exact placement of the locked box that housed it. A bribed chambermaid had gleaned that information. But, according to Connor, it wasn't yet time to make their move.

"Checkmate," he heard Gavin say. The other two men were hunched over a chessboard, absorbed in their game and oblivious to Jake's concerns.

"Not so fast there, Earl." Connor rubbed his meaty hands together as if preparing to slaughter some poor soul. He moved his knight, then sat back with a frightening smile.

Gavin shook his head. "You slipped past me this time, Connor, but you won't again."

"I'll have you know—"

"How much more time do you two intend to waste?" Jake snapped with far more impatience than he'd intended.

The two men looked at him, one with a tolerant purse of his lips, the other with a warning scowl.

Refusing to be put off any longer, Jake said, "Stuart is going to present the corselet to the museum curator tomorrow morning."

"We're well aware of his intentions." Gavin stood, an elegant, cultured move that would have intimidated most men. "We have a plan."

"A few more hours, Jake-o." Connor downed the last of his brandy and shoved up from the table. "And your precious bauble will be in your hands."

Jake knew he was being irrational, but he couldn't stand the waiting any longer. He paced to the window, but couldn't see the lush gardens beyond the glass pane. Night had fallen hours ago, and there wasn't even a sliver of moon to break the clear, black sky. From his pocket, he took out the paper he'd used to translate the corselet's mysterious verse and read it for the hundredth time, amazed by the astonishing message.

"And once ye 'ave your bauble and the respect ye deserve," Connor continued, "you'll be able tae return tae Egypt. Aye, you'll be a happy man, indeed."

Happy? Emotions as dark and foreboding as the night pressed down on Jake. He scowled, seeing a ghost of his reflection in the window. Once he left London, he didn't know if he'd ever be happy again. *But leaving her here is the right thing to do. I won't risk her life to take her with me.*

Gavin stopped behind Jake and held out a snifter of brandy. "We have an appointment to meet the curator before Stuart arrives. With your relief and the translation you made, they will have to believe us when we tell them Stuart took the corselet from you."

"We should have met him before now." Jake took a

deep sip and welcomed the burning fumes that cleared his thoughts. "Or I should have just stolen the damn thing back."

The earl clasped him by the shoulder, an act of friendship Jake hadn't expected, but desperately needed. "Trust me. If it comes down to my word over Stuart's, the curator will believe me."

A discreet knock at the door preceded the butler. The portly man who always looked as if he were attempting to hide a smile bowed, and announced. "My lord, there is someone to see Mister Mitchell."

Gavin frowned at Jake. "Who knows you're here?"

"No one. You know I haven't left your house since we returned. The last thing I want is for Stuart to learn of my whereabouts."

"Well," Connor said, heading for the door, "let's go bloody see who's payin' ye a call."

In the foyer, all three men came to a surprised halt.

Standing in the middle of a gleaming marble floor, surrounded by priceless statues and rare paintings was the last person any of them had expected to see.

Dressed in solid black pants and shirt, Eli gripped a dark hat in his hands. Dirt smudged his face and the top of his bald head. Once he saw Jake, his mouth broke into a wide smile of relief.

"Sweet Mother of Jesus!" he exclaimed. "I've been all over the city lookin' for ye, Mr. Mitchell."

"It seems you've found me, Eli." Jake crossed the foyer, noting the mud smeared over the man's hands and face. "Have you had an accident? You're covered in grime."

"That was her doin'." The stout man pushed out his bottom lip and shook his head in disapproval.

A warning tingle slipped up Jake's spine. "Her?"

"Aye, Lady Sarah."

"Why would she dirty ye up?" Connor asked as he and Gavin moved closer.

"That's why I'm 'ere. Tae tell ye what she's doin'."

The Scotsman blew out a breath. "I'm thinkin' I don't like the sound of this already."

"Well, if ye don't like it now, you sure won't like it none when I'm finished."

"Out with it," Jake demanded, already imagining the worst. Sarah on a ship, bound for Egypt, determined to complete another foolish mission. "Where is she? Is she hurt?"

"No," Eli said. "And if I know Thatcher, he won't let her get hurt either."

"What does Thatcher have to do with this?" Gavin asked.

"Lady Sarah asked Thatcher and me tae help her. We told her no, but when she said she would go by herself, we realized we had tae go with her."

"Go where?" Jake growled, barely resisting the urge to shake the information out of the man.

"Why, tae Lord Ashby's townhouse, of course."

"She went to see the marquis?" Jake's anxiety exploded into fear. She didn't know Stuart the way he did. She had no idea how ruthless the man could be.

"Not to see the marquis," Eli said, his eyes wide with panic.

"If not Stuart, then who?" Gavin asked.

"The corselet," Jake said, his heart hammering against his chest.

Eli threw his hands in the air in distress. "That's what I've been tryin' tae tell ye. She's going tae take the corselet."

"If she steals it," Gavin warned, "she'll ruin everything."

"It ain't right for a lady to be stealin," Eli said. "I'm thinkin' we shouldn't 'ave let her go tae Egypt. It was a bad influence on her."

Jake headed for the door, his boots firing like the report of a gun against the marble floor.

"Jake," Gavin said, following him.

"I'll stop her before she steals the corselet," he promised and broke into a run, heading straight for the stables. "And once I have her safe in my hands, I'm going to wring her neck."

Chapter 24

Sarah tiptoed down the dark hallway, her hands outstretched to stop herself from running into a wall or into another table full of knickknacks like the one she'd just avoided. She had no desire to alert the household staff that they had a burglar in their midst. She held her breath, listening for any sounds. Panic coated her palms with icy sweat. How had she ever thought she would get away with this? She'd never stolen anything in her life. She wasn't cut out for stealth and secrecy, and stealing went against everything she believed in.

But it's not stealing when you take back something that was stolen from you, she reasoned.

Gaining entry into Stuart Kilvington's townhouse had been amazingly simple. Within seconds Thatcher had picked the lock on the kitchen door. She didn't know why a farmer would possess such a shady skill, but she was grateful, nonetheless. Pausing, she frowned when a thought occurred to her. Were Eli and Thatcher even farmers? When she'd first met them, she had assumed they were, but what if they weren't? What if they were thieves, or worse? Would Roger have sent her to Egypt with two criminals as her only companions? She shook the disturbing thought away and continued down the hall. Eli and Thatcher had protected her, shown her more loyalty than her father ever had.

Taking note of her location, she turned right at the

end of a set of stairs and entered a side room, a study she decided, the air musty with the smell of old books. Closing the door behind her, she found a candle on the desk and lit it. She glanced around the room, sighing with relief that she'd made it this far without being discovered. But she shivered when the night wind outside blew cold and lonely.

She realized with surprise that the study was much like her father's, crammed with stone tablets carved with scenes from Egypt's past, life-size statues, pottery, mostly broken but a few were whole. Baskets of every size, shape, and state of decay were piled in the corners. She skirted the desk and began her search through the artifacts for the one she wanted. Thatcher had learned where the marquis had the corselet hidden—she hadn't asked how he'd gleaned the information, and after witnessing his skill with the lock, she wasn't sure she wanted to know.

Afraid of making any noise, she tried not to move anything. When looking beneath chairs and tables, and searching the bookcases revealed nothing, her heart began to beat at a hard, even more frightened pace. What if Stuart had the box that held the corselet with him in his bedroom? Searching his house was dangerous enough, and remembering the marquis's chilling smile when he'd left her and Jake to die in the desert, nothing would cause her to venture upstairs.

"It has to be here," she whispered, getting down on her hands and knees to look under a settee. Seeing a dark shape in the shadows, she caught her breath.

Dragging it out from beneath the couch, she gripped the box to her and almost laughed out loud. She took it to the candle, smiling as she traced the scrolled "A" engraved onto the lid with the tip of her finger. Thatcher had said the corselet would be in a box just like this one. She tried to open the lid, but it was locked. For a second, she regretted making Thatcher wait outside. She wanted to be certain she had the right one. But there was nothing to be done about it now.

She had what she came for—she hoped; now it was time to escape before anyone found her.

Blowing out the candle, she turned to leave, bumped up against something hard. A hand clamped over her mouth, another wrapped around her waist and kept her from moving.

A scream pushed up Sarah's throat, but a harsh warning stopped her from giving it life.

"Don't move."

Jake? Oh, please no, he couldn't be here! She tried to twist around, but he held her tight.

"I'm going to release you now," he whispered in her ear, his voice grating with anger. "And when I do, you're not going to say a word. You're going to follow me out of here. Do you understand?"

She nodded, and when he released her, she spun to face him. "You frightened me half to death! What are you doing here?"

"I intend to ask the same of you. Once we're out of here." He caught her by the arm and started for the door. "Now be quiet."

She pulled back. "How did you know where I was?"

"I'll explain later." Jake was standing in shadows, but she could easily imagine his scowl. "Let's go."

"Where are Thatcher and Eli?" she asked, carefully following him. "They should have stopped you from coming in here."

"I sent them home."

"You what?" she demanded in a whisper. "Oh, never mind. Jake, you can't be here. Do you realize how much trouble you'll be in if you're caught?"

"Me?" He whirled to face her. She couldn't see his

eyes, but she heard the exasperation in his voice. "What about you?"

"I know what I'm doing."

"Really?" he scoffed. "And how many homes have you broken into?"

"Jake, please, you must leave."

"We are, sweetheart. Then you're going to explain what the hell you think you're doing."

"I've got the corselet." She held out the box to him, but he didn't take it.

She heard him sigh. "Sarah, you don't know what you've done."

"I know I've stopped Stuart from taking the credit for finding Queen Tiy."

"This will only complicate matters. Leave it here."

"I will not. How can you even suggest such a thing?"

"I plan to deal with Stuart, but not like this." He opened the door a crack and looked into the corridor. He turned to her. "Put that back where you found it so we can leave."

Faint light from somewhere in the house caught the gold in his hair and as he stepped into the hall and she saw his face, she thought his furious expression might have been chipped from stone. She looked down at the box, felt the solid weight in her hands, then glanced at the settee. Put it back? How could she? He needed it to prove he was the one who discovered Queen Tiy. She looked up to see Jake's protective stance, fists clenched, shoulders straight, his feet planted as if he were prepared to fight, and she felt a surge of pride. She couldn't let Stuart ruin him again. In her hands, she held the ability to give Jake everything he'd worked to achieve. She refused to give it back now.

Clutching the box to her, she followed Jake into the foyer. He motioned for her to be quiet, then started toward the back of the house. As she had when entering, she listened for any noise, a voice or the creak of footsteps on the floor above. Having Jake with her, she wasn't nearly as nervous as when she'd first arrived.

Turning left down another hall that led to the kitchen, she touched Jake's arm, needing the simple contact. He tensed, glanced back and started to speak, but he suddenly tripped. Cursing, he lurched sideways. Sarah caught his arm, but as he fell, he jerked her off balance. Her hip bumped against something hard, a table, she realized as she fell to the floor. The knick-knacks she'd avoided earlier tumbled down around her, the crash sounding louder than an exploding cannon.

Jake knelt over her. "Are you all right?"

"I think so." Hearing voices and the pounding of running feet, she looked up at the ceiling.

"Come on." He grabbed her arm, jerked her up, then started for the kitchen.

Pain shot from her ankle, up to her thigh. She gasped. "My foot. I think it's twisted."

"I'll carry you."

"No." She shoved the box at him when he started to lift her. "It's nothing. Now go."

"Damn it, Sarah, I told you to leave the corselet."

She felt the anger rising off of him, but the sound of people rushing down the stairs frightened her even more. "Go."

"Stay close," he told her as he turned and ran down the hall.

"I intend to." She hurried after him, her heart in her throat and her teeth clenched against the pain. "Go! I know the way out."

A sudden spasm in her leg blurred her vision just as Jake escaped through the kitchen door. She was next. A few seconds and they would be out of Stuart Kilvington's reach.

And Jake would have the chance to claim the glory he deserved.

* * *

Reaching the hedgerow at the rear of Stuart's house, Jake stopped. Gripping the box with one hand, he turned and held out the other one to Sarah.

"My horse is over . . ." the rest froze in his throat.

She wasn't there!

"Dear God." He looked back at the house, his skin icy with dread. "Sarah."

He searched the shadows, saw no sign of her. The kitchen door was thirty feet away. He started for it, but paused when flickering lights appeared in the room.

He heard people speaking but was too far away to hear the words. An older man wearing a pale white robe came to the door, looked across the yard. Jake crouched behind a bush and waited until the man stepped back into the house and closed the door behind him.

Jake remained hidden, debating his options. Where was she? Still inside? In Stuart's hands? Or had she left by another route?

"Damn it, Sarah." His heart pounded against his chest, in his ears. "Where are you?"

He heard shouts and saw more lights moving from room to room throughout the house. Stuart and his servants conducting a search, no doubt, and at any moment the marquis would discover that the box containing the corselet was missing.

Jake didn't give a damn about the artifact or Stuart right now. He just wanted to see Sarah again so he could shake her for scaring ten years off his life, then he would kiss her. Hard.

Several men with lamps emerged from the back door. They divided up and began to search the yard, making their way toward Jake. He stepped further into the shadows, every impulse refusing to leave without her. But if he were discovered with Lord Ashby's box in his possession, he would lose more than his reputation. He'd be thrown into prison for the rest of his life.

Still, he hesitated, his need to protect her battling the certainty that he would be captured if he didn't leave now. She'd said she knew the way out. She'd been right behind him; if she'd intended to exit through the kitchen, she would be with him now. *Unless Stuart caught her first.*

As the servants drew closer, Jake moved deeper into the alley. He couldn't stay any longer. He had to leave.

"Sarah," he whispered, gripping the box as tightly as the fear that had its hold on him now. "You better have found another way out."

Whitehurst Manor loomed against the pressing black sky, a desolate giant that seemed to wallow in misery. Quiet and brooding, an attestation of discontent. There were no lights in any of the windows, no sound to indicate someone was awake. But with dawn still a few hours away, Jake hadn't expected to find anyone stirring.

Using the iron knocker, he banged on the front door several times before he heard movement on the other side.

Finally, a sleep-roughed voice demanded, "Who's there?"

"Jake Mitchell. Open up, Peels. I need to see the viscount."

"He's asleep, Mr. Mitchell," Peels stated through the door. "I can't wake him. However, in the morning, I will tell him you called."

"Damn it, man. Open up." Jake clenched his hand into a fist to keep from punching a hole through the door. "This is about Sarah."

"Lady Pendergrass?"

"Yes. Is she here?"

A few seconds of silence passed, then he heard the

bolt being thrown. The door swung open to reveal the butler in his night robe and cap. He held a candle that glowed over his pinched features, now drawn into a genuine frown. "Lady Pendergrass rarely comes here. And never at night."

Jake pushed his way into the foyer. "Wake Roger."

"But, sir."

"Either you get him out of bed, or I will," Jake said, not needing to raise his voice.

Peels drew himself up as if he intended to physically stop Jake from carrying out his threat. But in the end he extended his hand toward the front parlor. "Kindly wait in there. I'm sure Lord Pendergrass will be with you soon."

Jake entered the small reception room and lit several candles to push away the heavy dark. Holding Stuart's box, he paced the room, deciding to give Roger five minutes to appear or he would roust the old man himself.

To Jake's surprise, Roger hobbled into the room a few moments later with the aid of a cane. Haggard lines gouged the corners of his mouth. His eyes, the same silver as Sarah's, Jake realized, were weary and dull. But it was Roger's complexion that startled Jake the most. Roger had aged beyond his years, his skin gray and wrinkled, shrinking in on itself as if he were already dead.

"I don't appreciate having my man drag me out of bed. Especially because of you," Roger said, his tone as cutting as a knife. "What is it you want?"

Jake realized he wanted several things. He wanted to take back his refusal to return Queen Tiy when Roger had asked him. He wanted to know if his mentor was really as ill as he looked. But mostly, he wanted Roger to explain how he could have neglected a daughter as precious and wonderful as Sarah.

Focusing on what concerned him the most, he asked, "Is Sarah here?"

"Why in God's name would she be here? She has her own house. Eyesore that it is."

"Whitehurst is closer."

"Closer?" Roger gave him a measured look. "Closer to what?"

"She went to Stuart Kilvington's townhouse tonight." Jake glanced at the box in his hands. "To steal this."

A gleam flashed in the viscount's eyes, the first sign of life Jake had seen.

"Is that what I think it is?"

"The corselet," Jake admitted.

Roger barked a laugh and banged his cane against the floor. "I knew she would do it!" The viscount held out his hands. "Give it to me."

"Don't you want to know why I have this? Or where Sarah is?"

"She'll show up. She always does when I summon her."

Jake took a step back, keeping the box out of the other man's reach. "Answer a question, if you would, Roger. Did you send your daughter to Stuart's home to steal this?"

He pursed his lips, his gaze narrowing to shrewd points of steel. "I didn't tell her to steal it."

"Just what *did* you tell her?"

"The truth, that she failed. Her duty to me wasn't complete!"

Jake nodded. "She told you about sealing Queen Tiy's tomb, didn't she?"

"Yes, yes, yes." Roger waved his free hand impatiently. "But she didn't return the corselet."

"So you told her to do what? Get the artifact and return to Egypt? For God's sake, Roger, she's your daughter. How could you endanger her this way?"

"I wouldn't have had to if you had done as I'd asked."

"That doesn't excuse you."

"I'm dying, Jake. The corselet must be returned."

Jake slammed the box onto the desk and gripped the

edges so hard his hands shook. He wanted to lash out, hit something or someone. He'd never seen this side of his mentor, hadn't known it even existed.

"She almost died in the desert, Roger. And I don't know where she is right now."

"She'll turn up."

Jake glared at the older man, but before he could respond Peels interrupted them.

"Excuse me, Lord Pendergrass," the butler said from the doorway. "There is a man here to see you. I told him to leave, but he says he has an urgent message from Lord Ashby."

A shiver ran up Jake's back, lifting the tiny hairs at the nape of his neck. Not waiting for Roger to reply, he said, "Show him in, Peels."

In the next moment a man wearing Stuart's livery of red and gold entered the room. He was young, barely twenty, with brown eyes deep-set in a face like ruddy oatmeal.

With a curt nod to Roger, he said, "Lord Ashby has your daughter in his custody. He has not yet called the authorities, but will do so if you do not return the box and its contents that were stolen from his house."

"What is your name, boy?" Roger demanded.

The young man hesitated, uncertain, then he finally said, "Leon, sir."

Roger glanced at Jake, his hungry gaze slipping to the box on the desk. "Well, Leon, tell Lord Ashby to call the authorities if he wishes. He can't prove Sarah took anything."

"She was discovered in his home while trying to escape."

"Did she have whatever it is you're looking for?"

"No." Pointing at the box, Leon added, "but I'm sure Lord Ashby will be interested to know his property ended up with you."

"You don't know what you're talking about, boy. Now leave here, at once."

"Lord Ashby said to bring his box to the British Museum at seven o'clock this morning. If you fail to meet him, he will have your daughter arrested and charged with theft. You will be charged, as well, my lord." Looking at Jake, he said, "Lord Ashby also wishes you to be present, Mr. Mitchell."

"Does he plan to charge me, as well?"

"Not that I know of."

"Why the British Museum?" A warning buzz started in the back of Jake's mind.

"After the trade has been made—"

"There will be no trade!" Roger gripped his cane, and for an instant, Jake feared the man would collapse.

Leon frowned. "After the trade has been made, Lord Ashby wishes for you, Mr. Mitchell, to act as witness when he presents his current discovery to the curator. He felt certain you would not want to miss the important event."

Jake felt cold down to his bones. The floor dipped as if he'd been spun back in time and history was repeating itself. The old anger rose up in him, the betrayal and hatred, the injustice that Stuart would once again claim what was his. But as quickly as the anger flashed through him, it was just as quick to cool.

Stuart could take the credit for discovering Queen Tiy. Jake didn't care. The marquis had something of his that was far more important.

"Tell Lord Ashby I'll be there."

After Leon left, Roger limped toward Jake. "You will not give the corselet to that man."

"You would let Sarah be arrested? You risk standing trial, as well."

"If the corselet isn't returned to the tomb, I won't live long enough to stand trial!"

"What about your daughter?" Jake asked, already knowing what the man's answer would be.

"She'll survive. She always has."

Jake stared at his mentor as if seeing him for the first time. "Do you love her?"

"Love! What in God's name does love have to do with this? Sarah understands that I need the corselet."

"And you're willing to sacrifice her to get it."

"You and I are alike, Jake, that's why I took you under my wing. Taught you everything I know. You became the son I never had. We want the same things, dream about the same things, and will sacrifice family and friends to make certain those dreams come true."

Contempt spread through Jake like a disease, contempt for the older man, and for himself. Everything Roger said was true. Or at least it had been. Once he would have sacrificed anything and anyone to follow his dream. But during his last trip through the deserts of Egypt, he'd found something far more valuable than an ancient crypt.

And this time he would sacrifice everything he had to get her back.

Chapter 25

The air smelled of paper and dust and of linen-wrapped mummies, dead for countless years. Gray stone walls, as smooth as a polished sword, and just as cold, rose two stories above her. The statues of pharaohs and jackal gods she couldn't name looked on as if silently accusing those who had robbed them from their tombs.

Standing beside an empty sarcophagus, Sarah balanced her weight on one foot to ease the throbbing in her ankle. Every time she moved, the coffin's rough granite scraped her arm. She didn't mind the pain, welcomed it in fact.

Anything to distract her from the man standing at her side.

Stuart Kilvington, Marquis of Ashby, had dressed for his meeting with Jake and the curator as if he were a pharaoh expecting glorification from his subjects. He wore a double-breasted tailcoat of pearl gray, his matching pants creased with a razor sharp seam that topped the silver buckles of his shoes. He'd groomed his wavy black hair, the ends curling over his crisp white collar and the perfectly tied cravat long out of style.

In London's society, the marquis had a reputation of being handsome, well-bred. Obviously, Sarah decided, those who thought so had not seen him as he was now, with a wicked twist of his lips and a terrible glint in his eyes. A supreme air that bordered obsessiveness . . . or insanity.

He began to hum, as he had during the carriage ride to the British Museum. A tuneless melody that made Sarah want to scream.

"Not much longer now." The pleased laugh that followed made her skin crawl.

She clamped her lips together, determined not to talk to the man. She'd tried before, but soon learned she couldn't reason with the deranged.

"I trust your bindings aren't too tight." He glanced at her, smiled. "I regret having to tie you up, but you're too valuable to risk letting you slip away."

"You are no gentleman." She would have cursed, but felt certain the marquis would only laugh.

"Of course I am, just a rather unconventional gentleman."

She turned away, her vision blurring with tears of frustration. She couldn't make out the stone sphinx near the door or the cases filled with priceless rings and bracelets of pure turquoise and glittering gold. Her hands were tied, but not her feet. Yet she couldn't run. She took a step anyway and gasped as shards of fire shot up her leg.

He gave her a wry grin. "You really should see a doctor about that."

Trembling with rage, she leaned against the sarcophagus.

"Before your lover arrives, I would like for you to explain something." He forced her chin up so she couldn't escape the gleam of anticipation in his brown eyes, much like the hawk who studied its prey before breaking its back. "What is it you see in Jake Mitchell?"

Despite the pain, despite her fear, she smiled and thought her cheeks might crack from the effort. "I see everything that you are not."

"Such devotion, and so misplaced." He ran the tip of his finger along her jaw to her lips. She jerked her head away, her stomach roiling with disgust.

"He's no better than a sewer rat," Stuart continued, his tone smooth and cultured, and so cold she wondered if he was insane. "He grew up in the cesspool of London's back alleyways. If there was any justice in this world that is where he would have stayed."

Sarah clamped her teeth together, refused to voice the scathing response choking her throat. She knew Jake's worth, and it had nothing to do with his bloodline or where he'd been born. He was good and honorable, and she loved him so much she couldn't breathe.

Please Jake, don't give up the corselet for me. Take it to the curator; prove you are the one who discovered it. She would gladly take her chances with the courts.

"I believe your father would be shocked to know how . . . *intimate* the two of you are." Stuart's gaze slid over her body, a crude look that made her heart leap with a new kind of fear.

"You're detestable."

"Oh, but I forgot, Lord Pendergrass looked upon Jake as a son while the world never knew you existed. I can imagine how that made you feel."

"You don't know anything about me." She tugged on her bound wrists, the gesture more from nerves than with the hope of escape.

"Hmm. Perhaps more than you think."

Not liking his focus on her, she asked, "Why are you doing this? Are you in need of money?"

He frowned, and for an instant she thought his confusion might be genuine. "You mistake the reason for my actions. Only a fool would endure the Egyptian desert with the hope of finding their fortune. No, I have no need to earn a living. My estate provides for me quite well."

"Then what is it you want?"

"What every man who willingly endures the suffocating heat and endless sand wants. Glory. Fame and power."

"And you intend to acquire all of those by stealing Jake's discoveries?"

He shrugged. "If I must."

"You're detestable."

"I'm not an evil man, Sarah, whatever you may think of me."

"No, you're selfish and spoiled and completely without a conscience. You're no better than the bully who beats up whoever gets in the way of a toy he wants."

"Not a very flattering comparison, but accurate I suppose." He leaned close as if he were confessing a secret. "You see, I hate to lose."

She glared at him, her fear draining in the wake of renewed anger. "You will always lose to Jake, because you know in your heart that he's the better man."

"Loyalty is a very admirable quality."

"And one you've never possessed."

Sarah gasped, looking toward the door where Jake's voice had come from. When she saw him emerge from behind a statue of an Egyptian god with the mahogany box in his hand her heart raced with a crazy mixture of fear, excitement, and dread.

"You're right on time." Stuart rubbed his hands together. "And you've brought my case! How wonderful."

Jake stepped forward, the light from a nearby sconce highlighting the blond streaks in his hair, but it was the deadly emotion in his eyes that sent a shiver up Sarah's spine. It was a deadly look she'd never seen before.

He said, "I always keep my word."

"Lucky for me." Stuart turned his arrogant grin on her. "And for you, my dear. Your lover has come to your rescue."

Jake set the case on the ground and moved away. "Sarah, come here."

She shook her head. This couldn't be happening. She couldn't let him give up the corselet. "No."

Jake arched a brow and the heated anger in his eyes glowed brighter. "Stuart, take the box and leave."

"Well, this is interesting." The marquis laughed softly. "It appears she doesn't want to go with you, Jake. Perhaps she prefers the victor instead."

"Sarah." Jake's voice grated a path through her heart. "Is that what you want?"

"Of course not." She would have stomped her foot if she'd been able. "Pick up the corselet, Jake, and find the curator. You can't let Stuart take the credit."

He shook his head, the hard line of his mouth easing. "It doesn't matter."

"Yes, it does," she cried, tears spilling down her cheeks. "I won't let you lose everything."

"I haven't." Reaching down he pulled a knife from his boot.

"Stop right there." Stuart lifted his hand and aimed a small pistol at Jake. Sarah gasped, not having realized the marquis had been armed.

"No!" she screamed.

"Throw down your weapon," Stuart warned. "Or I'll shoot you."

Jake didn't spare Stuart a glance, but crossed the room to her. He didn't look at her as he sliced the ropes binding her wrists.

"Don't do this, Jake," she pleaded.

"It's done." He faced the man he had every reason to hate. Instead of lashing out as she expected him to, he said, "We both have what we came for. I believe Sarah and I will be leaving now."

"So soon?" Sliding the pistol into the waistband of his pants, the marquis retrieved his case and ran his hand over the lid in admiration. "Oh, you broke the lock. No matter. I expect the curator to arrive at any moment."

No sooner had Stuart uttered the words than the double doors to the gallery swung open and four elderly men entered. White-haired and wrinkled, they were dressed in the worn suits of their younger days. Only one walked straight, the other three were bent at the shoulders. But despite their appearance, Sarah sensed a timeless wisdom in each of them, as if they saw more than what their jaundiced eyes could reveal.

"Ah, here they are now." Stuart made a slight bow and addressed the man in the lead who possessed an air of authority the others lacked. "Mr. Davis, thank you for meeting me so early."

"You said it was important," Mr. Davis said. "We're all eager to hear about your new discovery."

"But it's not—" Sarah started, but Jake wrapped his arm around her waist and squeezed, warning her to be quiet.

She looked at him, saw the certainty in his blue eyes. "We can tell them the truth."

He shook his head. "I made a deal with the marquis. I have what I want."

In that moment, Sarah thought her heart would break. He was willingly giving up the corselet for her? No one had ever made such a sacrifice on her behalf. Sarah didn't know whether to kiss Jake for his show of love, or shake him for his stupidity.

"Mitchell?" a man with a hooked nose and a widow's peak of stiff gray hair barked in surprise. "Where in blazes have you been? You were supposed to present your mysterious discovery nearly two months ago."

"I had to leave on short notice, Mr. Jeffrey. I just returned this week."

"Did you and Lord Ashby make this discovery together, then?"

"Mitchell is here out of professional curiosity," Stuart said. "This claim is solely mine."

"Considering the past you two share, it's good to know you don't hold a grudge, Ashby." Distrust radiated off

Jeffrey's bowed body as he glared at Jake. "You could learn something from a man like the marquis."

Sarah gasped in outrage, but Jake's hold tightened even more. After a moment's hesitation, he nodded to the older man. Sarah wanted to cry, knowing what it had cost him to keep quiet. And he had done so because of her. She couldn't stand it. No matter what he felt for her, she couldn't be the reason he lost everything!

"Well, then," Davis told them, taking a monocle from his pocket. "Let's get on with it and see what you've brought."

"This is the first time anyone besides myself has seen this." Stuart set the box on a nearby display case, opened the lid, and withdrew the corselet with the flourish of a street magician. The delicate gold squares clinked softly in his hands. Light bounced off the garment, splintering into tiny iridescent stars that seemed to warm and pulse with life.

"Heavens!" the curator exclaimed.

Even Sarah felt the rush of wonder and awe as she looked on. She touched a hand to her hip, remembering and missing the corselet's comforting weight against her skin.

"What is it?" Davis asked.

"A corselet, belonging to Queen Tiy, a minor wife of Ramses the Third." Stuart laid it out on the case so the curators could get a closer look.

"Remarkable." One of the curators ran both his hands over the shadow of hair remaining on his head. Sarah didn't know his name but she thought his reaction an understatement.

Stuart pointed to the hieroglyphics. "This tells the story of how Queen Tiy led an assassination attempt on the pharaoh. She was executed in the end."

"Extraordinary." Breathless, Davis lifted his monocle and examined the piece. "Where did you find it?"

For the first time since her capture, Sarah saw the marquis's arrogance falter. "An obscure tomb in Egypt."

"Was there anything else inside? Her mummy or canopic jars?"

"No, I'm afraid the tomb was raided in antiquity." Stuart sighed, and it took all of Sarah's willpower not to slap his face. "We're fortunate the robbers overlooked this."

"A pity. But such is the way." Davis let his monocle dangle from its chain. "Well done, Ashby. I trust you'll leave this with us to study."

"Of course." The marquis rocked back on his heels in satisfaction. "I have some ideas about how it can be displayed."

"Return in a few days. We'll discuss your ideas then."

"At this rate," Jeffrey said, chuckling, "you'll have your own wing in the museum, filled with nothing but your discoveries."

"That would be a sight indeed." A sly grin lifted Stuart's thin mouth, and triumph flashed in his eyes when he glanced at Jake.

Sarah couldn't stay quiet any longer. Pulling out of Jake's hold, she limped toward the men. "Excuse me, Mr. Davis. I have a question about the markings on the back of the corselet."

"Markings?" He turned the garment over and spread it out. Clasping his monocle with thin fingers, he bent close. "Why, something has been engraved onto the back. Why didn't you mention this, Ashby?"

"It isn't important." Stuart tried to pick up the corselet, but Sarah slapped her hand down on it. He glared at her, saying, "The real discovery is Queen Tiy's story on the front."

"Perhaps, but this is very unusual," the curator said. "'Tis almost like hieroglyphics, yet it isn't."

"Haven't you interpreted it, Lord Ashby?" Sarah asked

in as sweet a voice as she could manage for the wretched man.

"Sarah," Jake warned from behind her. She ignored him, and so did the marquis.

"It's impossible. There isn't a reference to translate it. It could be a different language, or some artist's piddlings." He shrugged and held his hands out to his sides. "We may never know what it means."

"Or," Sarah said, praying her sudden idea would work, "we might learn what it means right now."

"It isn't wise to give these men false hope, my dear," Stuart said, his warning clear. "It could cause you trouble in the end."

Turning her back on the marquis, she dared a glance at Jake and saw he stood with his legs braced, his arms folded over his chests, his expression closed.

Knowing that she was doing the right thing, she told the men, "As it happens, Jake has already translated the verse."

Davis frowned. "How is that possible? Ashby said no one has seen it until now."

"Oh, Jake has seen it," Sarah assured them, trying not to gloat. "He's the one who discovered Queen Tiy."

"What?" Davis pointed his monocle at Stuart. "Is this girl's claim true?"

"Of course not. She's lying. Mitchell undoubtedly put her up to this."

The curator and his associates turned matching frowns on Jake. Sarah's heart sank as she realized her hasty plan had just gone terribly wrong. Not only was his reputation in danger of being ruined beyond repair, she had sense enough to know he might be charged with fraud.

"I am not lying," she told them.

"Sarah." Jake gripped her shoulders and pulled her back. She whirled to face him, as angry with him for keeping silent as she was with Stuart for being a reprehensible thief. But when she saw Jake's features, tight with resolve, she had to swallow her anger.

"The marquis and I have an understanding." Though he whispered, everyone had to have heard. "Regardless of what some people think, I will not go back on my word."

She bowed her head, wanting to cry, wanting to scream, wanting to go back in time and stop this from happening.

"Now that that's all settled." Stuart closed his box and tucked it under his arm. "Take good care of my discovery, gentlemen. I shall return soon to discuss the method of its display."

"You may not be able to return as soon as you'd like, you sniveling thief!" a rough voice boomed from the doorway.

Everyone started and turned to see who had made such a threat.

"As you're likely to be in prison." Roger stepped through the open door, his body thin, shrunken, a shadow of the man he'd once been. His steps were labored, his gnarled hand clutching the cane as if he would crumble without it. As he crossed the short distance, Sarah realized that although his body had betrayed him, his eyes still burned with strength and conviction.

Sarah couldn't believe it; her father was coming to their aid? Her stomach fluttered with hope.

"Lord Pendergrass." Mr. Davis made a slight bow. "'Tis been too long since we've seen you at the museum. I trust you have recovered from your illness."

"Look at me, man. Of course I haven't." Roger picked up the corselet and briefly closed his eyes, his lips moving in a silent prayer. "I had hoped to never lay eyes on this accursed relic again."

"W . . . what?" Davis stuttered. "You've seen this before?"

"Of course I have. I was with Jake when he found it."

"But this is Lord Ashby's find," the curator argued.

"It most certainly is not!" Roger barged a path through

the men. "I brought the corselet back, along with Queen Tiy's coffin and her canopic jars. And I gave them to my daughter to return to Egypt. She succeeded in everything but this." He shook the corselet in his fist. "She is going to finish the task I gave her, and none of you have a thing to say about it."

"This is your daughter?" the bald assistant asked.

"Lord Ashby," Jeffrey said, not giving her father a chance to reply. "Did you or did you not discover this corselet?"

"Of course I did," Stuart scoffed, doing his best to look down his nose with contempt. "It's not my way to disparage a fellow member of society, but we all know how eccentric Lord Pendergrass has become. His illness has made him delusional."

"Well, this just won't do." Davis snapped a handkerchief from his pocket and began scrubbing his monocle with a frenzy. "I will have the truth about who discovered this artifact before the day is out."

"And you'll have it," Stuart assured them. "Mr. Davis, perhaps you and I should return to your office where we can discuss this in private."

"Yes, leave, all of you," Roger shouted. "I have what I've come for. There is a ship for Egypt that Sarah must be on."

Sarah stood frozen in disbelief. The relief she'd felt when he'd defended Jake skittered away like dead leaves on the wind. He didn't care about helping his partner; he only wanted the corselet returned to the tomb. And thought she would do it without question!

"There is a way this can be resolved," Sarah finally said.

"And I would be glad to hear it." Finished with cleaning his monocle, Davis used his handkerchief to pat the sweat from his brow.

"Jake, tell them what these markings mean." When she turned to face him, her breath caught in her throat. He'd been quiet through the entire debate, and she'd been too caught up to worry about his reaction to it all. But now his dark eyes glittered with pride and admiration and so much love she thought her knees would turn to water. A slight smile twitched at the corner of his mouth, and she had to fight every impulse to kiss it.

Casually, as if the next few minutes didn't matter to him at all, he took a folded sheet of paper from his pocket and flattened it on the display case. The drawing was identical to the corselet, but the hieroglyphics on her sketch were far more detailed than those in the gold squares.

"Where did you get this?" Davis demanded of Jake.

"Sarah drew it a few days ago, during our return trip from Egypt," Jake said, his voice strong, confident.

"If what Lord Pendergrass says is true and she was to return the corselet to Queen Tiy's tomb, how did Lord Ashby come by it?" The curator shook his head. "This is all so confusing."

A muscle pulsed in Jake's jaw. "Sarah sealed Queen Tiy's coffin and all her possessions inside the tomb, everything except this artifact. I won't go into the details now, but she and I were stranded in the desert several days from Thebes. Stuart found us. But instead of helping us, he helped himself to the corselet."

"That's . . . that's outrageous." Davis looked from one man to the other, his pale eyes wide with incredulity.

"And a lie," Stuart said, his voice as thin as the line of his mouth.

"Sarah is an artist and made the drawing from memory," Jake continued. "I interpreted the symbols."

"I will not tolerate such slander." Stuart's face mottled with anger. "I demand that the three of you leave or I'll be forced to call the authorities."

"That might not be a bad idea, Lord Ashby," Davis said tightly.

Shaking with rage, Stuart snatched the corselet from

Roger's hand. "I have had this in my possession since I discovered it. It's obvious that Mitchell broke into my home to make his sketch. There was a burglar in my townhouse last night and I'm sure it was he."

Jake arched a brow. "If I'd broken into your home, wouldn't I have taken the corselet instead of staying to make a drawing?"

"You've obviously had this well planned. You and Roger. You're trying to set me up, make the curators doubt my word."

"Now, now." Davis waved his hand. "Settle down. Lord Ashby, no one is doubting your word."

"Tell them, Jake." Sarah took hold of his arm, felt the muscles tense beneath his shirt. "Tell them the truth."

Stuart laughed with disdain. "Or at least your version of the truth."

Jake drew a deep breath and met each of the curators' gazes. "Six months ago Roger and I were on an expedition in Egypt. We had searched a particular area for several weeks when I discovered a doorway of finely cut limestone. It led to Queen Tiy's tomb."

"Pure fabrication." Stuart rolled his eyes and shrugged in dismissal.

"Her tomb was intact, the sarcophagus and coffin, her canopic jars and jewels. The scenes on the walls of the queen and her son standing trial were undamaged and magnificent."

"Where is the tomb located?" Jeffrey asked.

"Don't you dare tell them," Roger ordered. "I won't have anyone trying to dig her up again. She's buried, and she must stay that way!"

"For what reason?" Jeffrey's asked.

"She is cursed!"

The four curators and Stuart stared in disbelief.

Sarah held her breath. She wouldn't stop Jake from revealing the queen's burial site; they had both come too far and had risked too much already. But she couldn't help feeling she was betraying the queen's last wish.

"I can't reveal the location," Jake finally admitted, placing his hand over hers as if he'd sensed her thoughts.

"You see," Stuart gloated. "He can't tell you because he doesn't know."

"This is a serious accusation, Mitchell." Davis paced in front of the group. "Unless you can prove you discovered the corselet first, I'll have to call the authorities. I don't take theft or fraud lightly."

"Neither do I." Jake met the marquis's gaze, the clash of wills so fierce, Sarah wondered why the air hadn't burst into flame.

"Read the verse to them," she urged.

"Don't listen to him, gentlemen." Stuart picked up the sheet of paper and began to wad it up.

Mr. Davis took it out of his hands.

Stuart's nostrils flared with outrage. "It's undoubtedly a verse he has invented. I have studied these markings. They are not like any hieroglyphics that we know. They *can't* be interpreted."

Jake flattened the paper, then took the corselet from Stuart. Pointing to several of the symbols on the sheaf, Jake then indicated the ones that correlated to the corselet. "These *are* hieroglyphics. If you look closely, you'll see they've been worn down."

"How?" Davis asked, bending close, securing his monocle once again.

Jake explained, "Queen Tiy wore this corselet from the day of her son, Pentewere's, birth until the day of her death."

"How could you possibly know that?" Jeffrey asked, clearly skeptical.

Jake looked at Sarah. "I know."

Her throat closed with sudden tears and she could only whisper, "Read it to them."

Chapter 26

Time began, time will end,
the lioness Tiy will live forever.
Countries tremble before His Majesty's might,
bringing gifts, bowing with fear.
Yet thine lioness gave the greatest
gift . . . divine immortality.
Set singing of light and truth,
cast all doubts behind thee.
There be only one son of my loins
there will be only one lioness to guide me.
Lo, none can take away what is in mine heart,
Lo, what love has created shall live forever.
This is the word of Ramses III,
son of Setnakhte, Great Pharaoh of
Egypt, husband to Queen Tiy

When Jake finished reading the ancient message, the silence reverberating throughout the vast room wavered with uncertainty. He studied each of the curator's faces, their furrowed brows, their thin lips pursed in doubt, the subtle shaking of their wizened heads.

Sarah stood at Jake's side, her tremors working through her hand where she touched his arm. She glanced at him, and he knew she understood their battle wasn't over. It was clear Mr. Davis and the others didn't believe the pharaoh's message was real.

"You did it, Jake." Roger grunted with satisfaction. "You translated that blasted verse!"

"Did he?" Mr. Jeffrey asked. "It sounded like gibberish to me. What did all of that mean? 'Lioness to guide me'?"

Jake ran his palm over the corselet's smooth surface. "I had hoped the message would reveal some secret. Perhaps the location of other tombs or temples. Or answer the mystery of how the pyramids were built. Something grand, magnificent. But it's none of those things. It's something better."

"It's nonsense," Stuart sneered.

"It's a testament of Ramses' love for Queen Tiy." Jake gave the drawing to Mr. Davis, who took it with trembling hands.

"If I understand this correctly, Ramses valued a minor wife and son over his firstborn," the curator said. "That wasn't done."

"No, it wasn't," Jake said. "And she was accused of plotting to kill the husband who adored her. If I were to guess, someone conspired to make her look guilty."

"So the queen and Pentewere would be removed from the pharaoh's affections and from the line of the throne!" Davis grinned, looking for all the world like a man who had solved the greatest of mysteries.

"Whoever plotted against her, succeeded." Jake scooped the corselet off the case. "I'll leave the drawing with you, Mr. Davis. But I have to take this with me."

Holding the corselet in one hand and Sarah with the other, he headed for the door.

"Stop!" Stuart shouted.

"Don't listen to him," Roger ordered. "Sarah must be on that ship. I have it all arranged. Eli and Thatcher will be waiting for her!"

Jake kept walking, supporting Sarah when she began to limp. Fury and relief, anger and validation rolled through him like a wave. He needed time to sort out what had just happened, but he'd do it elsewhere. Nothing would cause him to stay in the museum another minute.

Until he heard the collective gasp behind him.

The fine hairs at his nape lifted in warning. Jake turned to see the marquis, his body trembling, his bleached face dripping with sweat, his extended hand holding a pistol that shook.

"Give the corselet to me," the marquis demanded.

"It's over, Stuart." Jake pushed Sarah behind him, out of harm's way. "You managed to ruin my name once. But you've failed this time."

Mr. Davis's mouth dropped open. "Are you talking about the crown Stuart found at Abu Simbel? The one he accused you of stealing?"

"I discovered that crown, Mr. Davis," Jake said, and knew in that instant that the curator believed him. "Just as I discovered Queen Tiy."

"No one will believe a street rat." Stuart tightened his grip on the gun. "Give the corselet to me!"

"There are more tombs in Egypt." Turning his back on the marquis, Jake added over his shoulder, "Perhaps you'll find one some day."

The small parlor smelled of lemon and passing time and some flower Jake couldn't name. The settee with delicately carved feet had once been fine, but the upholstered arms were thinning, the stuffing showing through in some spots. The oval rug beneath his dusty boots wouldn't have been fit for Roger's kitchens, yet the faded colors and intricate pattern suited Sarah's quaint home. He saw traces of her in the paintings on the wall—hers undoubtedly—the charcoal pencils carelessly lying on a table, and the books stacked haphazardly next to them. The mix-matched room radiated comfort and filled him with the overwhelming sense to stay.

But however quaint, he didn't like the idea of her living here alone. Roger should have forbidden it. Since her father hadn't, Jake decided it was up to him to see that she moved.

"I don't have anything stronger than tea." Sarah limped into the room in a rustle of wrinkled petticoats and crinoline. She still wore the gown she'd had on when he'd found her burglarizing Stuart's home, and her hair had come loose of its bun. Dirt smudged her cheek, and exhaustion shadowed her eyes.

He'd never seen her look lovelier.

"I told you not to go to any trouble," he said as she set the serving tray on a table. "You shouldn't even be standing."

"I'll be fine. And after everything that has happened I could use something to calm my nerves." Smiling tentatively, she handed him a cup.

Standing because he was too agitated to sit, Jake frowned down at her, not liking her behavior. Ever since they'd left the museum she'd been polite, a perfect lady, as if she were trying to distance herself from him. He wished he knew why. What she was thinking? Did she want him to leave? Stay? If only he knew. It would make what he had to tell her so much easier.

After taking a drink of his tea, he asked the question foremost on his mind. "The ship for Egypt will sail in a few hours. Will you be on it?"

She paused with the cup an inch from her lips, looked at him over the rim. Her eyes darkened, gathering like storm clouds over a restless sea. He knew that look, knew she had set her mind to something. "There's no reason for me to return."

"What about your promise to Roger?"

Emotions skittered across her face, but she quickly schooled them, giving him a glimpse of the controlled woman he'd first met. "I don't owe him anything. Besides, we both know he isn't cursed. And he isn't dying." She grimaced. "At least I hope he isn't."

"And Queen Tiy?" he asked, wishing for the closeness they'd shared while on the ship, and so afraid he had destroyed it by turning her away.

She glanced at the table near the front door where he'd dropped the corselet. "She's sealed inside her tomb, that will have to be enough for her. Besides, she was a woman of remarkable courage. I think the world should know about her."

Jake set his cup aside. Wanting to close the narrow distance between them, but knowing it was too soon, he stood there with his arms crossed over his chest. "What will you do with the corselet? Give it to the museum?"

Her startled gaze flew to his. "I'm not going to do anything with it. It belongs to you."

"I don't want it."

"But your reputation. You need it, you deserve to take credit for the discovery."

"My reputation isn't important." He retrieved the corselet from the hall table.

"Jake Mitchell," she said, her jaw clamped tight. "Are you trying to make me crazy?" Pointing to the golden belt in his hands, she added, "Recovering that is all that has mattered to you."

Something cold and uncomfortable clenched his chest. "You're right. Since the first time I set foot in Egypt, I've been driven to find the discovery of a lifetime. And I have."

He forced the corselet into her hands. She tried to shove it back. "I don't want this."

He took a step away from her, holding his empty hands out to his sides. "I'm leaving on that ship to Egypt."

A flare of panic shot through her eyes. Swallowing, she finally nodded. "I understand. You belong there. Well," she looked at the gold squares glinting like dull stars in her hands, "I won't keep you."

"You'd better hurry and pack your things if you're coming with me."

She tensed, her features going still. "Come with you?"

"Yes."

"Why?" she demanded, and to his surprise, she clenched her fists in anger. "You've made it perfectly clear. I don't belong in Egypt."

"There's no doubting that you have a lot to learn." Taking a step toward her, he caught the womanly scent that was only Sarah, and knew he couldn't leave England without her, couldn't *live* without her.

As quickly as her temper flared, her shoulders slumped. The anger drained out of her, leaving hope and fear battling in her gaze. "Why do you want me to go with you, Jake?"

"Because like some men," he said, wanting to kiss the confusion from her eyes. "I don't intend to leave my wife behind."

"Your . . ." Tears brimmed, slipped down her cheeks.

He clasped her hands, the corselet caught between them. "Egypt will be empty without you, Sarah. *I* will be empty with you."

She shook her head. "But you said—"

"I said a lot of things. What I failed to mention is how much I love you."

"And how long have you loved me?" she asked, trying to sound indignant but failing. "From the moment you were redeemed by the curator, perhaps?"

"Far longer than that." He wrapped his arms around her waist, drawing her flush against him.

"When?"

"I believe it was the moment you first touched my hand, right after I saved Queen Tiy from falling into the Thames."

With a watery smile, she said, "Liar."

He cupped one side of her face, traced the curve of her cheek, the delicate line of her jaw, her trembling rosy lips. "I want you with me."

"I want that, too," she admitted. "So much it frightens me."

"It will be dangerous."

"I don't care."

"I love you, Sarah."

With a mischievous smile, she asked, "Enough to help me pack?"

Jake lifted her in his arms, laughing when she squealed in surprise. He had never believed in love, had never dared believe he would be lucky enough to share his life with a woman, any woman. Especially one he couldn't live without.

Taking the stairs to her bedroom two at a time, he thanked the gods that he had been wrong.

Epilogue

The limestone cliff bore the scars of drought and sun, of endless, blinding wind. Brutal crevices cut a path through towering rock walls like creases on the face of a withering man. Dust blew in sudden gusts. Buzzards circled overhead, patient sentinels against an unforgiving sky.

Sarah drank in the harsh landscape, loving it almost as much as she loved the man stalking across it to reach her. She fingered the tablet of paper on her lap, but her attention was fixed on the way Jake's body moved as he navigated the rocky terrain, the way tension radiated off of him and how his fists clenched the closer he came.

She knew why he was in a temper. The sun had long ago reached its zenith. Heat burned through her gown, baking her insides. She should have quit working hours ago, but the valley had demanded she continue. The snaking valley floor, the jutting cliffs had to be recorded for the explorers who would follow. Soon the land, the sheer mountain walls, would change. The wind and the river would see to that.

When Jake came to a halt before her, wearing dusty clothes and his favorite scowl, she gave him her brightest smile and asked, "Do you really think someone framed Queen Tiy?"

"What I think," Jake said after he caught his breath, "is that you don't know how to follow orders."

His eyes were turbulent pools of blue, his mouth a

firm line. He was definitely a man who needed to be kissed. "I'll stop soon."

"You said that the last time I came to check on you. Over an hour ago." He snatched the pencil from her hand and tossed it and her paper onto a nearby rock. "You'll either walk to our tent now, Mrs. Mitchell, or I'll carry you there."

A small shiver passed through her as she stood. Mrs. Mitchell. Jake's wife. Her husband. They were words she would never tire of hearing. Thank heaven the captain of their ship had been able to marry them. Propping her hands on her hips, she looked from her husband to the site where he'd spent the past three weeks digging. His two helpers stood waist-deep in shell and dust. "You three haven't quit."

"Only because time has grown short. Gavin has to leave soon." Jake took her by the arm, and though she was prepared she still gasped when a fine shiver ran through her where the corselet hugged her waist.

Sarah pressed her hand to her hip, letting Jake lead her to their camp a few yards away. She had told him she wanted to wear the corselet to keep it safe from thieves while Queen Tiy's tomb was being cleared. In reality she wanted it close to her for as long as possible, secretly hoping she would have another dream, perhaps learn more about the woman it belonged to.

"Gavin still hasn't told you why he must leave?" she asked.

Jake sighed, his eyes hooded with concern for his friends. "Just that it has something to do with Napoleon. Nothing more."

"I wish he and Connor could stay." She slid her arm through Jake's. "It won't seem right without them. But I'm glad they offered to help."

At their tent, Jake caught her by the shoulders and planted a kiss on her forehead. "Rest."

"What kind of kiss is that for your new wife?" She laced her arms around his neck, not intimidated at all by his scowl.

"If I kiss you now, I'll never get back to work."

"Jake," she said, running her fingers through the curling ends of his hair. She didn't have to say another word. His mouth found hers, a deep, breath-stealing kiss that caused her knees to tremble and her heart to race. She would never get used to the magical feel of him, the way he tasted or his unique scent.

A shrill whistle broke through the luscious haze in her mind. Jake pulled away and glanced toward the dig site. He looked at her, smiled. "They've broken through to the sarcophagus."

"So soon?" She pressed her hands to her waist, the gold warming against her skin. She would have to give it up, but she didn't know if she was ready.

"Are you sure you want to do this?" he asked, as if reading her mind.

She nodded, hesitantly at first, then with conviction. "I'm sure."

Jake cupped her face in his rough hands. "Roger isn't cursed."

"I know," she said.

"He's fine, happily digging outside of Luxor instead of helping us here."

"I'm not doing this for my father." She lifted her skirt and unhooked the corselet from her waist. The gold squares danced in her hands as she held it out beneath the hot Egyptian sun. "This is for Queen Tiy."

Jake grazed his fingers over the golden belt. "She means a lot to you, doesn't she, Sarah?"

She met her husband's gaze, felt an incredible thrill to know he belonged to her. "You didn't answer my question. Do you think she was framed for Ramses' death?"

"We'll never know for certain."

"I kept hoping for another dream," she finally admitted, feeling a strange kind of panic in her chest, as if she were leaving something unfinished. "I want to know who turned against Queen Tiy and Pentewere."

"They've been dead for three thousand years. It doesn't matter now. But if you'd rather keep it, just say so."

She shook her head and gave the belt to Jake. "You gave some excellent advice once. There are other tombs in Egypt. Perhaps we'll find one some day."

Slipping her hand into his, she followed him up the trail toward Queen Tiy's tomb. She didn't regret giving up the corselet; it belonged in the past.

While she and Jake, their life and their love, belonged to the future.

Author's Note

Occasionally, during the course of a story, it becomes necessary to alter certain facts. This was the case when I wrote SHADOW OF THE SUN. While Jake Mitchell was able to read the hieroglyphics on Queen Tiy's corselet in 1798, in actuality, this would not have been possible.

It wasn't until July, 1799, that a basalt slab containing a single text—a decree of the priests of Memphis in honor of Ptolemaios V, 196 BC—was discovered in the small village of Rosetta, Egypt. Written in three different languages, Demotic, hieroglyphics, and Greek, the discovery of the Rosetta Stone promised to open the doors to Egypt's past. But it wasn't until 1824, when Jean Francois Champollion completed his translations, that we were able to read and understand the ancient words.

Today, the Rosetta Stone resides at the British Museum in London.

However, other facts in this story are quite true. Queen Tiy, a minor wife of Ramses III, was found guilty of plotting her husband's murder. And it's true that Ramses died unexpectedly, though not violently as his mummy can testify, before her trial concluded.

Was Queen Tiy forced to commit suicide before the entire court? Historians can't be certain. The Judicial Papyrus in Turin, which documents the assassination attempt and the resulting trial, is not complete. The fate of the queen has been lost, but it is almost certain she would not have escaped the same punishment as her son and accomplices.

We'll never know if Queen Tiy actually cursed those who sat in judgment of her. But the papyrus mentions the use of magical spells and wax images. Whether the queen used magic or not, it is true that several of those who convicted her were later brought to trial and punished, losing their noses and ears. Certainly they thought they had been cursed.

And finally, if Queen Tiy's mummy has been discovered, it has not been documented. It is believed there are tombs in the Valley of the Queens still waiting to be unearthed.

Wouldn't it be wonderful if Queen Tiy and her secrets were among them?

I hope you enjoyed SHADOW OF THE SUN.

Tammy Hilz

Put a Little Romance in Your Life with
Georgina Gentry